ROGER LANGRIDGE'S

SNARKED!

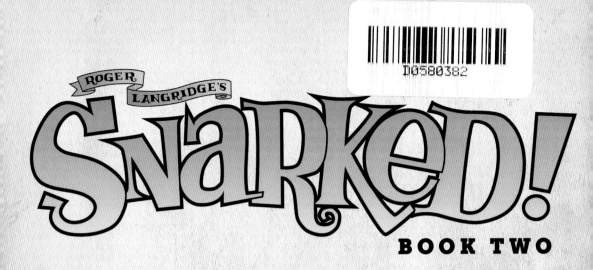

BOOK TWO

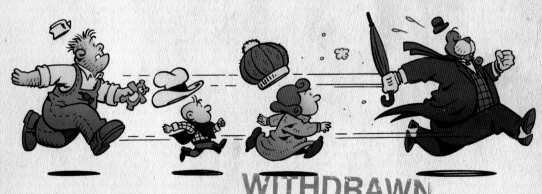

SHIPS AND SEALING WAX

ROSS RICHIE Chief Executive Officer • **MATT GAGNON** Editor-in-Chief • **WES HARRIS** VP-Publishing • **LANCE KREITER** VP-Licensing & Merchandising • **PHIL BARBARO** Director of Finance
BRYCE CARLSON Managing Editor • **DAFNA PLEBAN** Editor • **SHANNON WATTERS** Editor • **ERIC HARBURN** Assistant Editor • **ADAM STAFFARONI** Assistant Editor • **CHRIS ROSA** Assistant Editor
STEPHANIE GONZAGA Graphic Designer • **CAROL THOMPSON** Production Designer • **JASMINE AMIRI** Operations Coordinator • **DEVIN FUNCHES** Marketing & Sales Assistant

kaboom!

SNARKED Volume Two — September 2012. Published by KaBOOM!, a division of Boom Entertainment, Inc., 6310 San Vicente Boulevard, Suite 107, Los Angeles, CA 90048-5457. Snarked is Copyright © 2012 Boom Entertainment, Inc. and Roger Langridge. Originally published in single magazine form as SNARKED 5-8. Copyright © 2012 Boom Entertainment, Inc. and Roger Langridge. All rights reserved. KaBOOM!™ and the KaBOOM! logo are trademarks of Boom Entertainment, Inc., registered in various countries and categories. All characters, events, and institutions depicted herein are fictional. Any similarity between any of the names, characters, persons, events, and/or institutions in this publication to actual names, characters, and persons, whether living or dead, events, and/or institutions is unintended and purely coincidental. KaBOOM! does not read or accept unsolicited submissions of ideas, stories, or artwork.

A catalog record of this book is available from OCLC and from the KaBOOM! website, www.kaboom-studios.com, on the Librarians Page.

BOOM! Studios, 6310 San Vicente Boulevard, Suite 107, Los Angeles, CA 90048-5457. Printed in China. First Printing.
ISBN: 978-1-60886-276-4

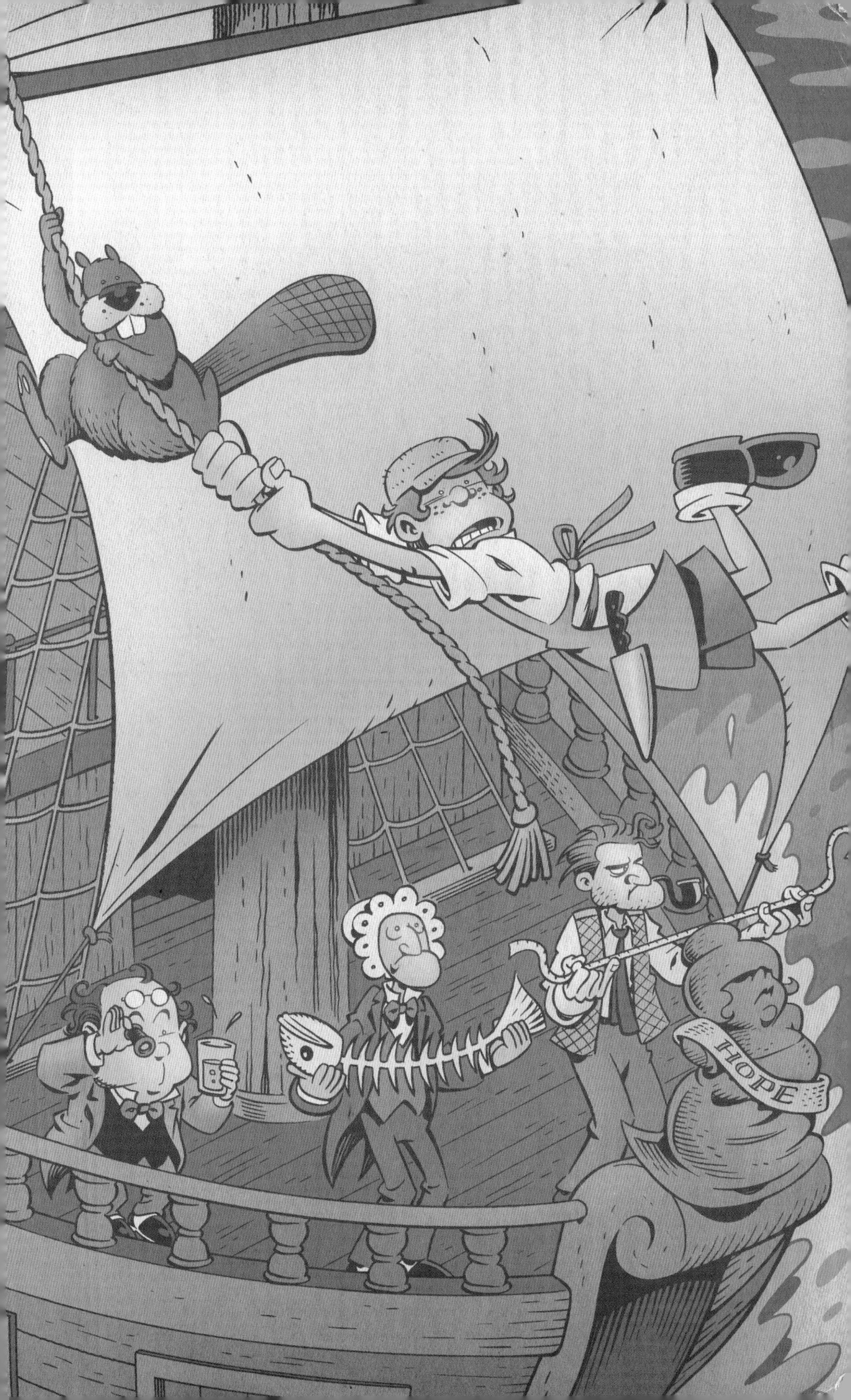
HOPE

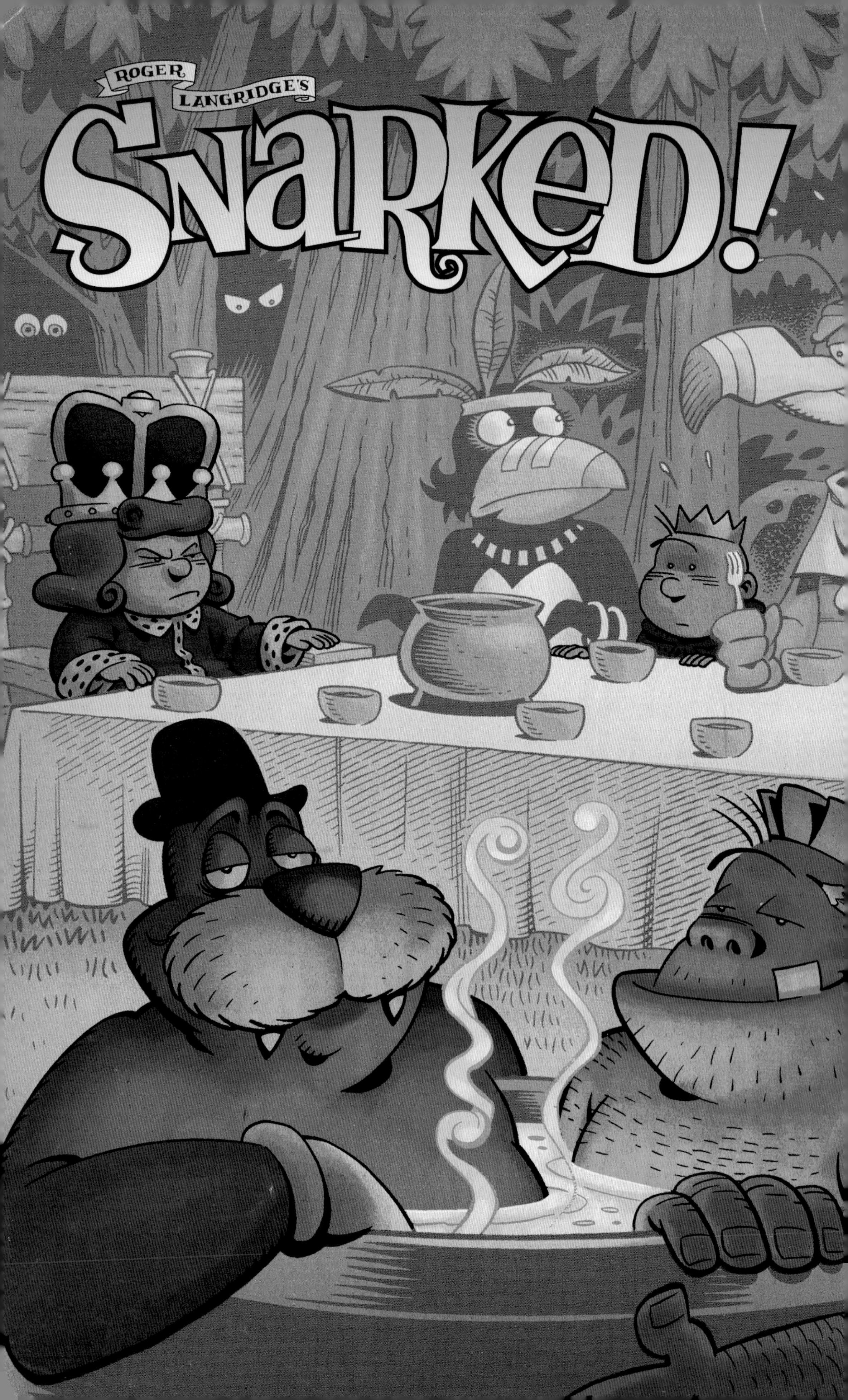
ROGER LANGRIDGE'S
SNARKED!

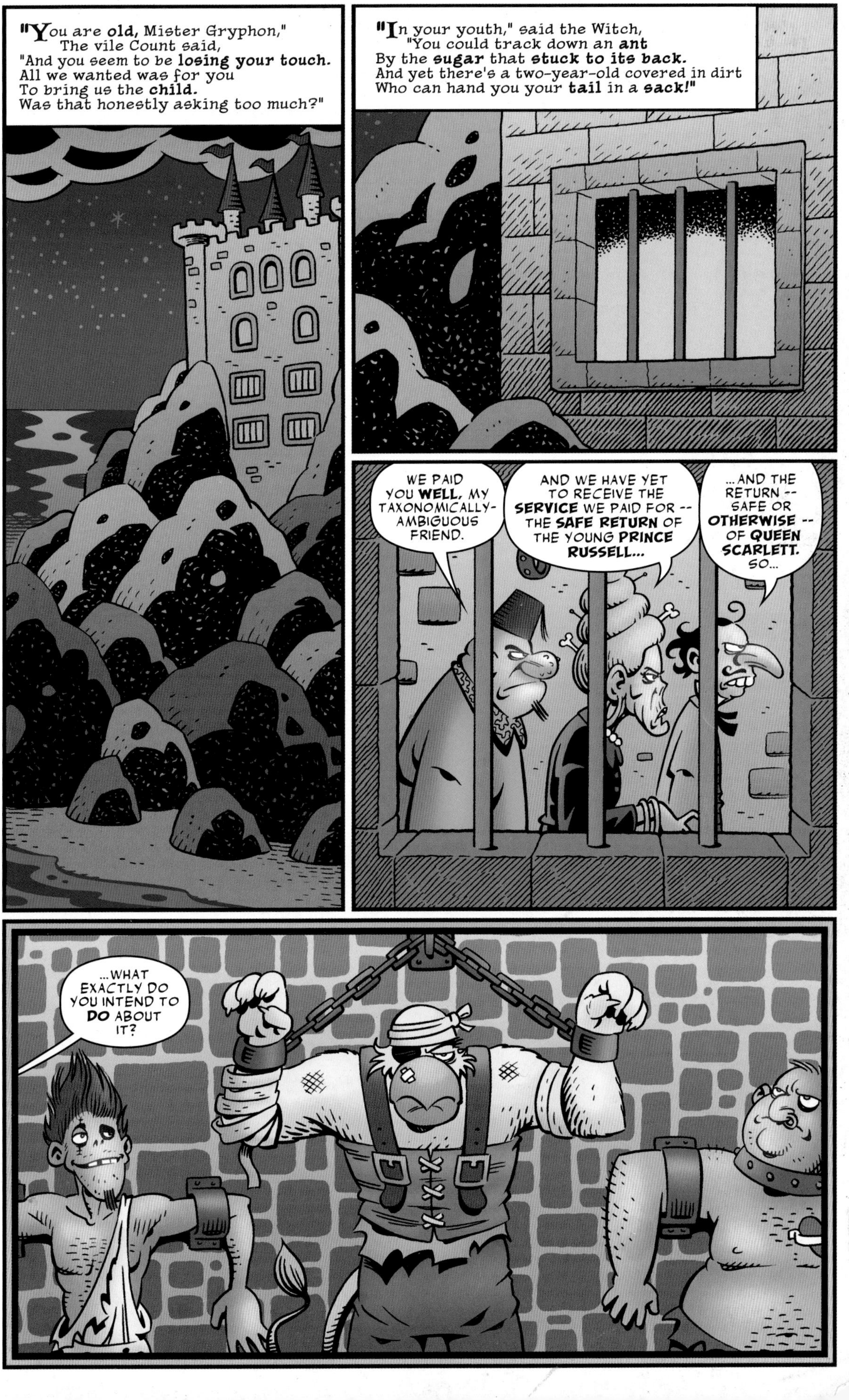
"You are old, Mister Gryphon," The vile Count said, "And you seem to be losing your touch. All we wanted was for you To bring us the child. Was that honestly asking too much?"
"In your youth," said the Witch, "You could track down an ant By the sugar that stuck to its back. And yet there's a two-year-old covered in dirt Who can hand you your tail in a sack!"
WE PAID YOU WELL, MY TAXONOMICALLY-AMBIGUOUS FRIEND.
AND WE HAVE YET TO RECEIVE THE SERVICE WE PAID FOR -- THE SAFE RETURN OF THE YOUNG PRINCE RUSSELL...
...AND THE RETURN -- SAFE OR OTHERWISE -- OF QUEEN SCARLETT. SO...
...WHAT EXACTLY DO YOU INTEND TO DO ABOUT IT?

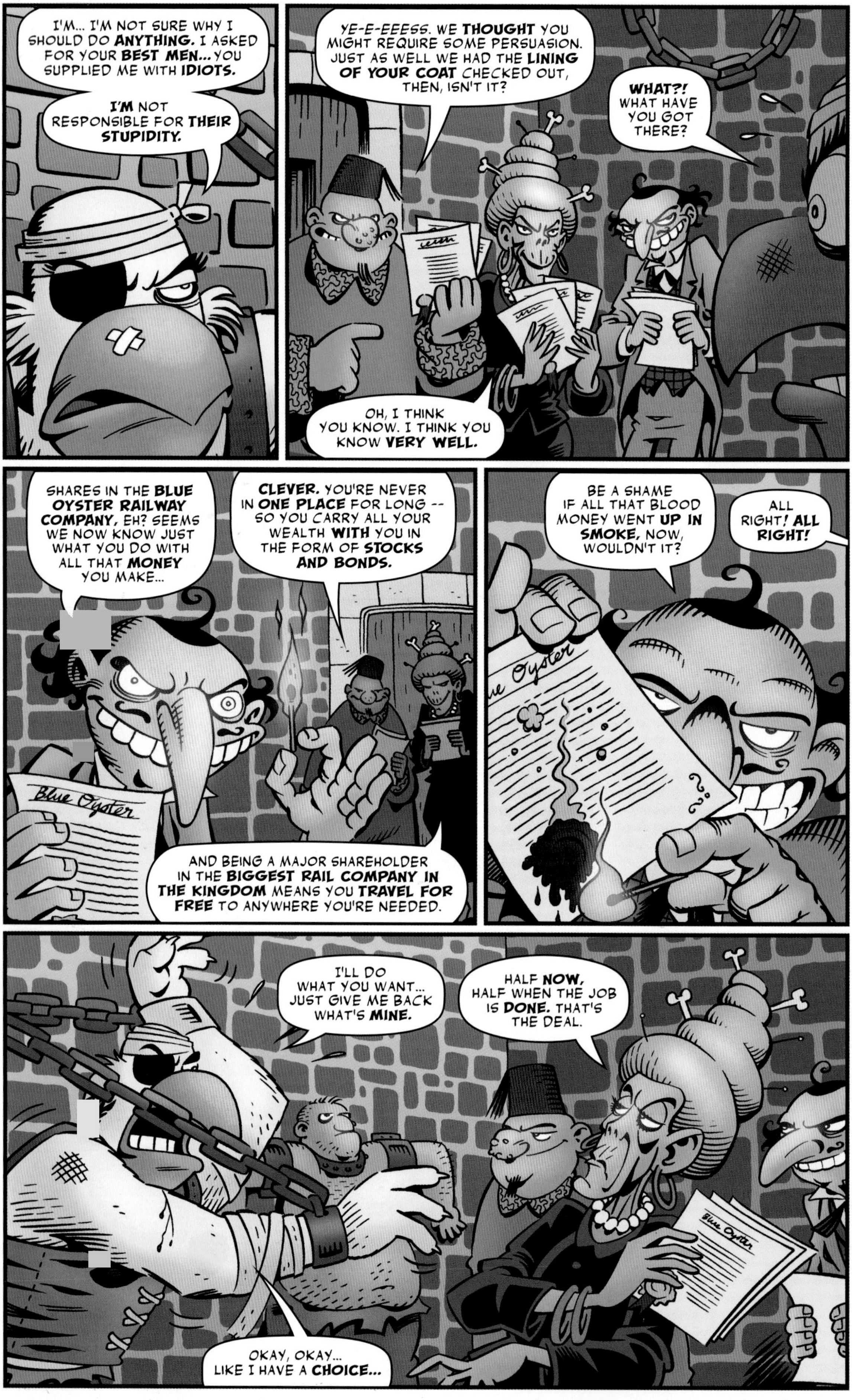
I'M... I'M NOT SURE WHY I SHOULD DO ANYTHING. I ASKED FOR YOUR BEST MEN... YOU SUPPLIED ME WITH IDIOTS.
I'M NOT RESPONSIBLE FOR THEIR STUPIDITY.
YE-E-EEESS. WE THOUGHT YOU MIGHT REQUIRE SOME PERSUASION. JUST AS WELL WE HAD THE LINING OF YOUR COAT CHECKED OUT, THEN, ISN'T IT?
WHAT?! WHAT HAVE YOU GOT THERE?
OH, I THINK YOU KNOW. I THINK YOU KNOW VERY WELL.
SHARES IN THE BLUE OYSTER RAILWAY COMPANY, EH? SEEMS WE NOW KNOW JUST WHAT YOU DO WITH ALL THAT MONEY YOU MAKE...
CLEVER. YOU'RE NEVER IN ONE PLACE FOR LONG -- SO YOU CARRY ALL YOUR WEALTH WITH YOU IN THE FORM OF STOCKS AND BONDS.
Blue Oyster
AND BEING A MAJOR SHAREHOLDER IN THE BIGGEST RAIL COMPANY IN THE KINGDOM MEANS YOU TRAVEL FOR FREE TO ANYWHERE YOU'RE NEEDED.
BE A SHAME IF ALL THAT BLOOD MONEY WENT UP IN SMOKE, NOW, WOULDN'T IT?
ALL RIGHT! ALL RIGHT!
ue Oyster
I'LL DO WHAT YOU WANT... JUST GIVE ME BACK WHAT'S MINE.
HALF NOW, HALF WHEN THE JOB IS DONE. THAT'S THE DEAL.
Blue Oyster
OKAY, OKAY... LIKE I HAVE A CHOICE...

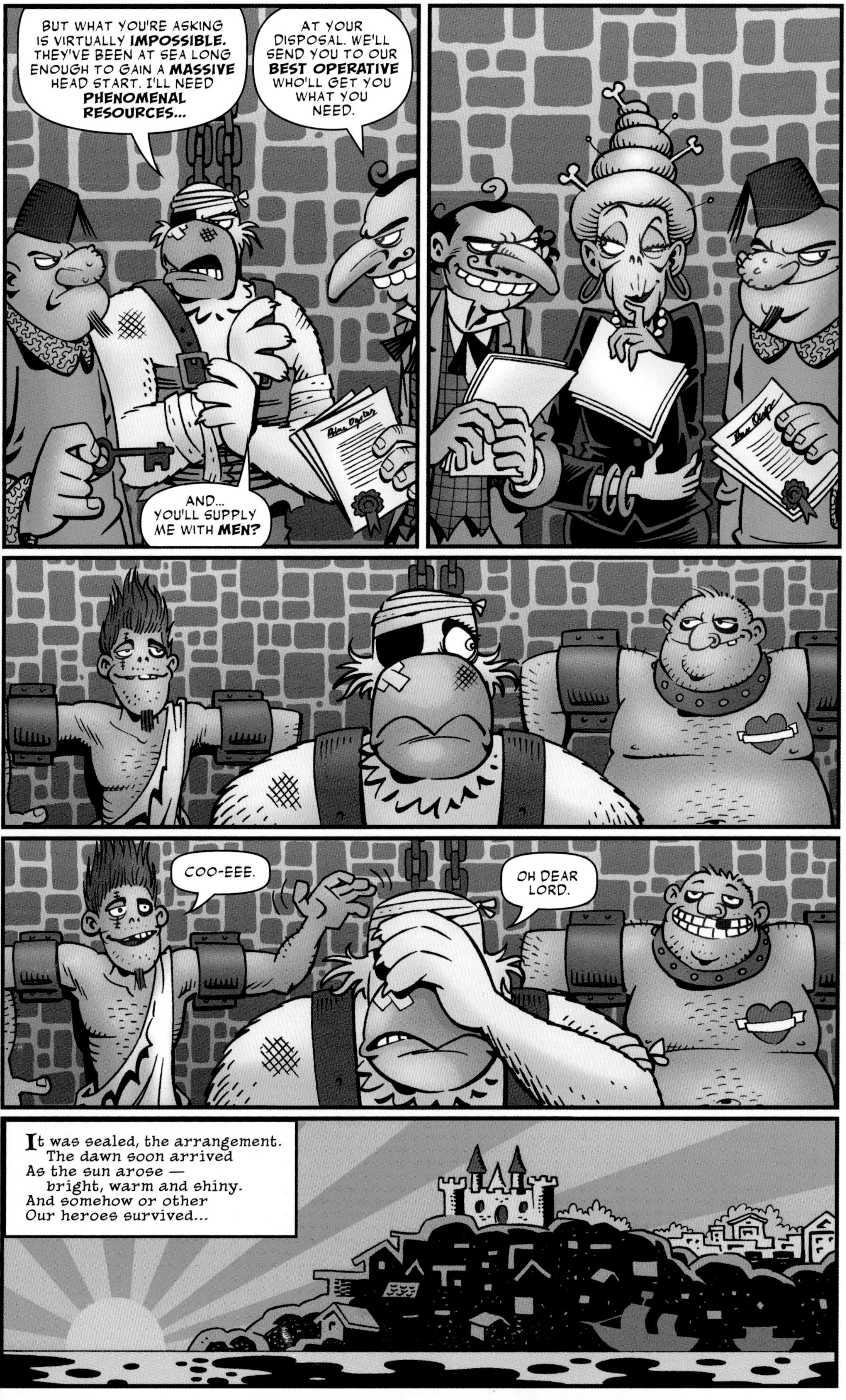
BUT WHAT YOU'RE ASKING IS VIRTUALLY **IMPOSSIBLE.** THEY'VE BEEN AT SEA LONG ENOUGH TO GAIN A **MASSIVE** HEAD START. I'LL NEED **PHENOMENAL RESOURCES...**
AND... YOU'LL SUPPLY ME WITH **MEN?**
AT YOUR DISPOSAL. WE'LL SEND YOU TO OUR **BEST OPERATIVE** WHO'LL GET YOU WHAT YOU NEED.
COO-EEE.
OH DEAR LORD.
It was sealed, the arrangement.
The dawn soon arrived
As the sun arose —
bright, warm and shiny.
And somehow or other
Our heroes survived...

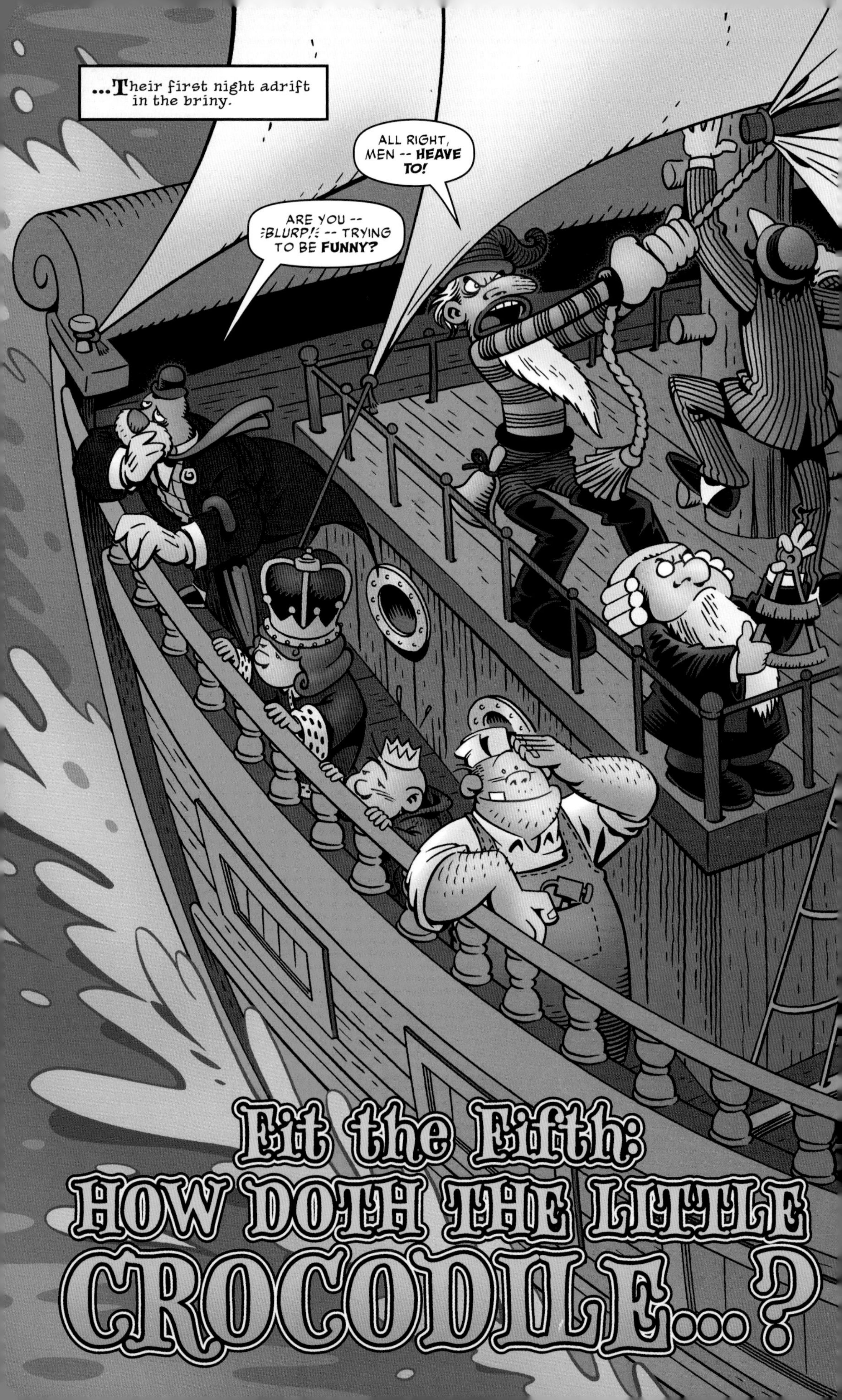
...Their first night adrift in the briny.
ALL RIGHT, MEN -- HEAVE TO!
ARE YOU -- BLURP! -- TRYING TO BE FUNNY?
Fit the Fifth:
HOW DOTH THE LITTLE CROCODILE...?

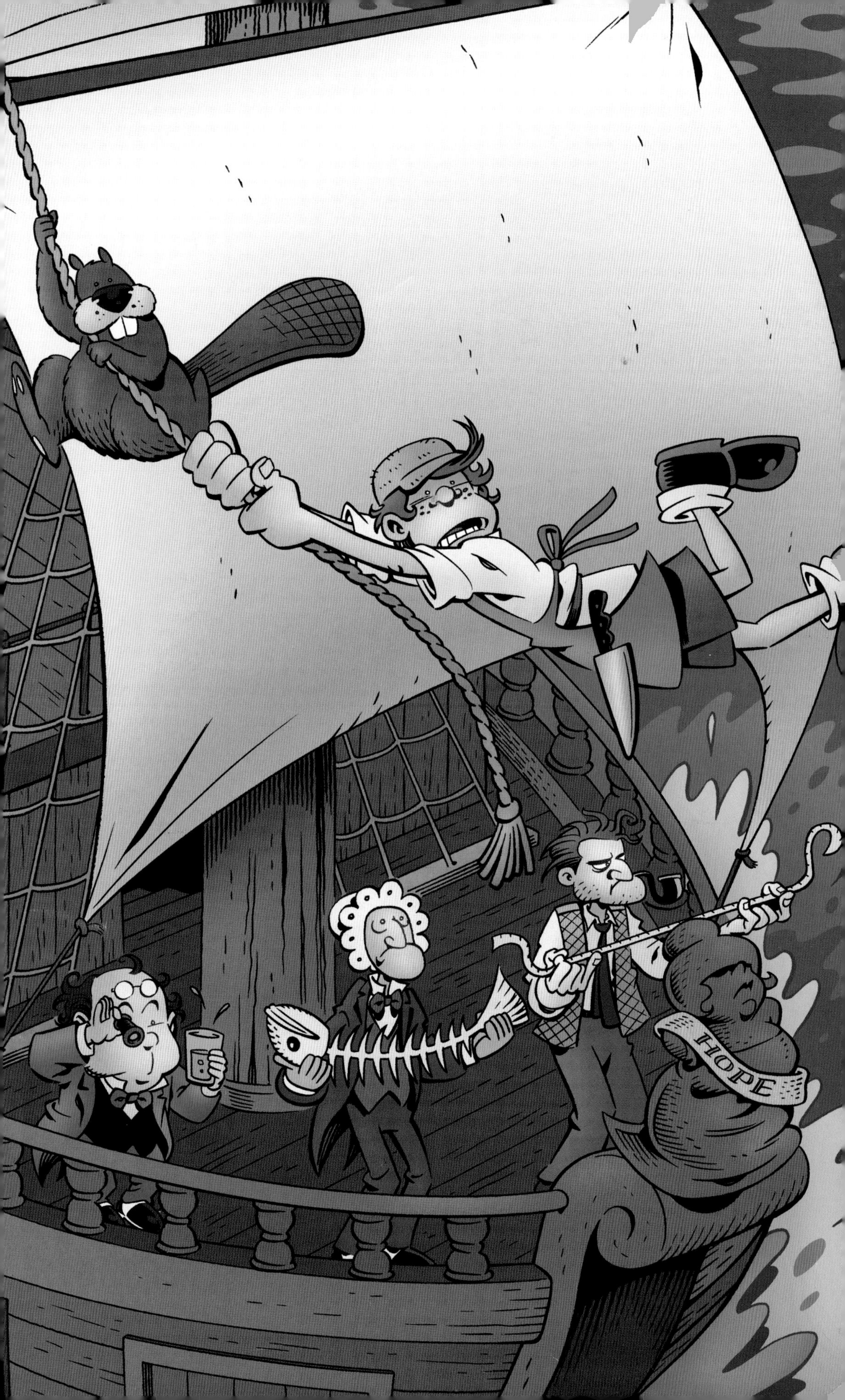
HOPE

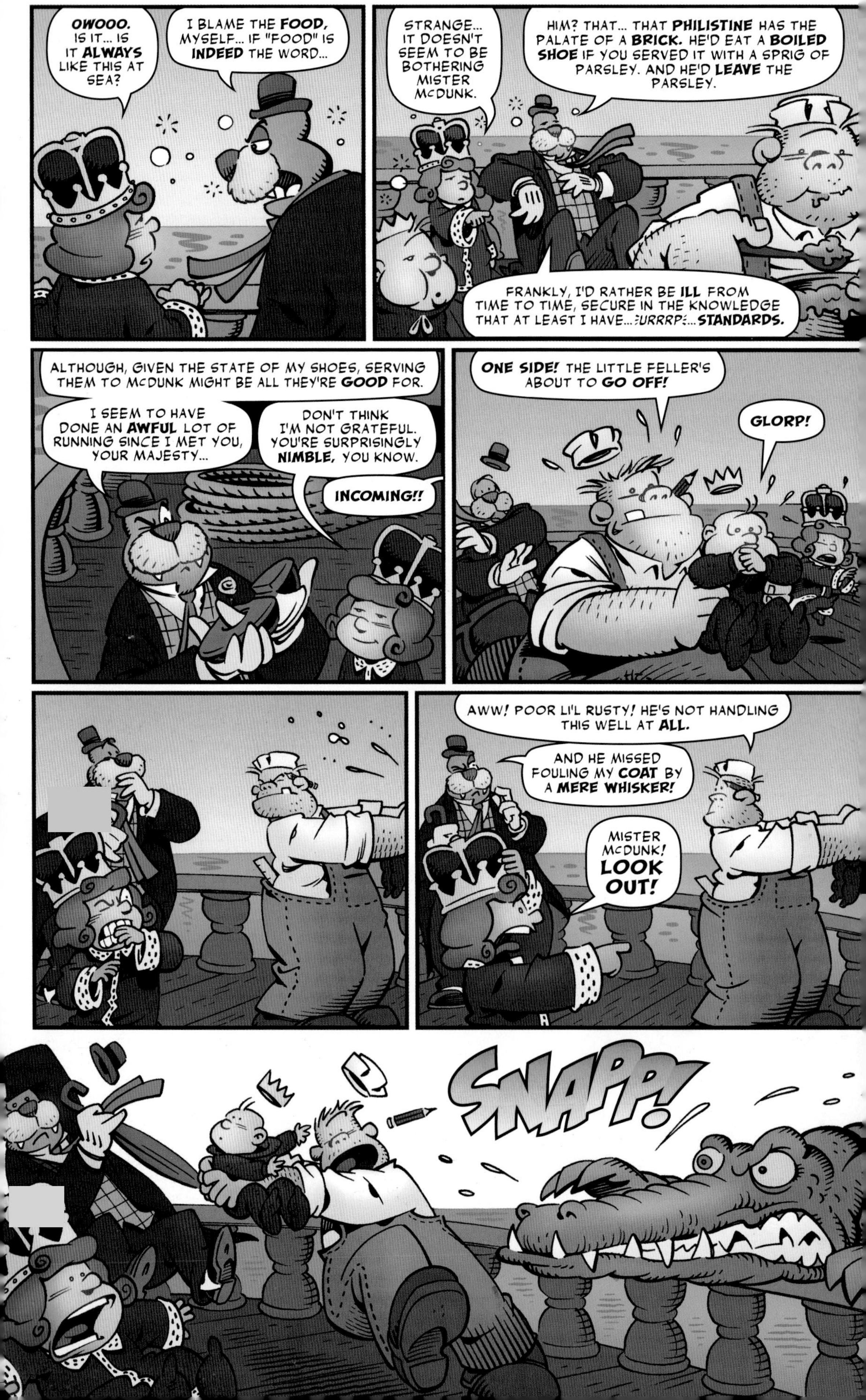
OWOOO. IS IT... IS IT ALWAYS LIKE THIS AT SEA?
I BLAME THE FOOD, MYSELF... IF "FOOD" IS INDEED THE WORD...
STRANGE... IT DOESN'T SEEM TO BE BOTHERING MISTER McDUNK.
HIM? THAT... THAT PHILISTINE HAS THE PALATE OF A BRICK. HE'D EAT A BOILED SHOE IF YOU SERVED IT WITH A SPRIG OF PARSLEY. AND HE'D LEAVE THE PARSLEY.
FRANKLY, I'D RATHER BE ILL FROM TIME TO TIME, SECURE IN THE KNOWLEDGE THAT AT LEAST I HAVE... URRRP... STANDARDS.
ALTHOUGH, GIVEN THE STATE OF MY SHOES, SERVING THEM TO McDUNK MIGHT BE ALL THEY'RE GOOD FOR.
I SEEM TO HAVE DONE AN AWFUL LOT OF RUNNING SINCE I MET YOU, YOUR MAJESTY...
DON'T THINK I'M NOT GRATEFUL. YOU'RE SURPRISINGLY NIMBLE, YOU KNOW.
INCOMING!!
ONE SIDE! THE LITTLE FELLER'S ABOUT TO GO OFF!
GLORP!
AWW! POOR LI'L RUSTY! HE'S NOT HANDLING THIS WELL AT ALL.
AND HE MISSED FOULING MY COAT BY A MERE WHISKER!
MISTER McDUNK! LOOK OUT!
SNAPP!

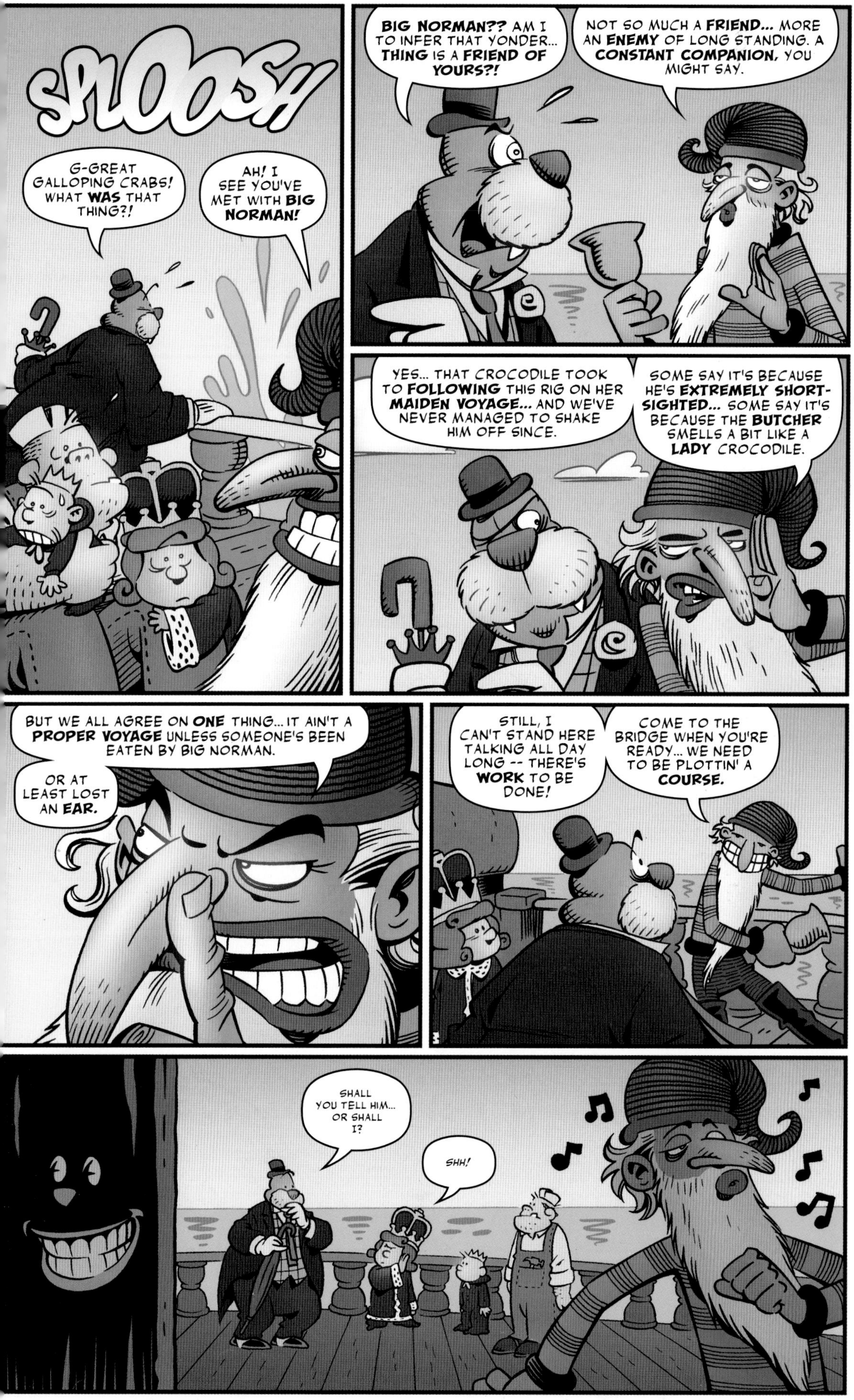
SPLOOSH
G-GREAT GALLOPING CRABS! WHAT WAS THAT THING?!
AH! I SEE YOU'VE MET WITH BIG NORMAN!
BIG NORMAN?? AM I TO INFER THAT YONDER... THING IS A FRIEND OF YOURS?!
NOT SO MUCH A FRIEND... MORE AN ENEMY OF LONG STANDING. A CONSTANT COMPANION, YOU MIGHT SAY.
YES... THAT CROCODILE TOOK TO FOLLOWING THIS RIG ON HER MAIDEN VOYAGE... AND WE'VE NEVER MANAGED TO SHAKE HIM OFF SINCE.
SOME SAY IT'S BECAUSE HE'S EXTREMELY SHORT-SIGHTED... SOME SAY IT'S BECAUSE THE BUTCHER SMELLS A BIT LIKE A LADY CROCODILE.
BUT WE ALL AGREE ON ONE THING... IT AIN'T A PROPER VOYAGE UNLESS SOMEONE'S BEEN EATEN BY BIG NORMAN.
OR AT LEAST LOST AN EAR.
STILL, I CAN'T STAND HERE TALKING ALL DAY LONG -- THERE'S WORK TO BE DONE!
COME TO THE BRIDGE WHEN YOU'RE READY... WE NEED TO BE PLOTTIN' A COURSE.
SHALL YOU TELL HIM... OR SHALL I?
SHH!

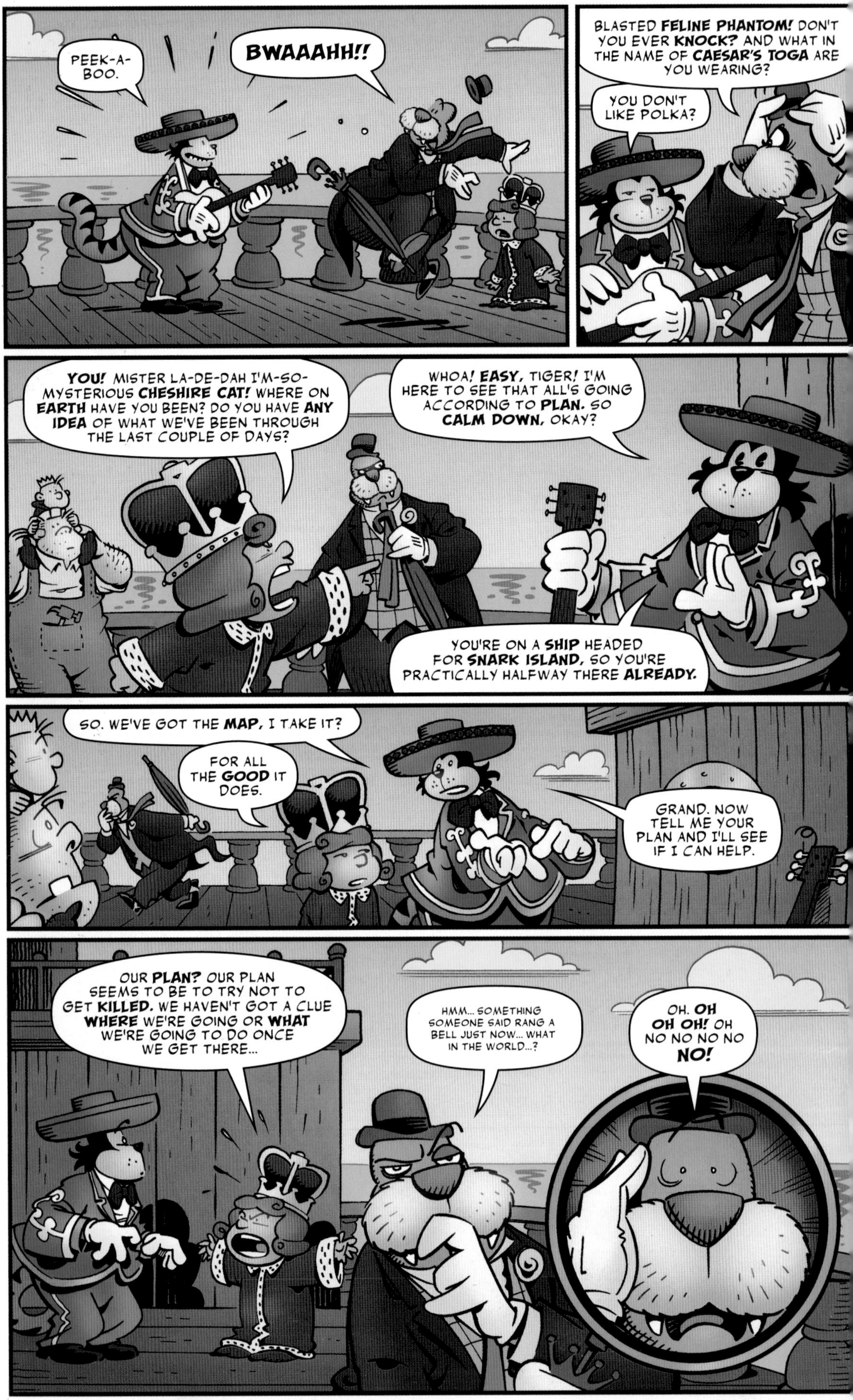
PEEK-A-BOO.
BWAAAHH!!
BLASTED FELINE PHANTOM! DON'T YOU EVER KNOCK? AND WHAT IN THE NAME OF CAESAR'S TOGA ARE YOU WEARING?
YOU DON'T LIKE POLKA?
YOU! MISTER LA-DE-DAH I'M-SO-MYSTERIOUS CHESHIRE CAT! WHERE ON EARTH HAVE YOU BEEN? DO YOU HAVE ANY IDEA OF WHAT WE'VE BEEN THROUGH THE LAST COUPLE OF DAYS?
WHOA! EASY, TIGER! I'M HERE TO SEE THAT ALL'S GOING ACCORDING TO PLAN. SO CALM DOWN, OKAY?
YOU'RE ON A SHIP HEADED FOR SNARK ISLAND, SO YOU'RE PRACTICALLY HALFWAY THERE ALREADY.
SO. WE'VE GOT THE MAP, I TAKE IT?
FOR ALL THE GOOD IT DOES.
GRAND. NOW TELL ME YOUR PLAN AND I'LL SEE IF I CAN HELP.
OUR PLAN? OUR PLAN SEEMS TO BE TO TRY NOT TO GET KILLED. WE HAVEN'T GOT A CLUE WHERE WE'RE GOING OR WHAT WE'RE GOING TO DO ONCE WE GET THERE...
HMM... SOMETHING SOMEONE SAID RANG A BELL JUST NOW... WHAT IN THE WORLD...?
OH. OH OH OH! OH NO NO NO NO NO!

SNARK ISLAND! YOU SAID **SNARK ISLAND!!**

YES, I, UH, I HEARD THE **ROYAL ADVISORS** TALKING ABOUT IT WHEN I STOLE THE **MAP**... I-I'M SURE I MENTIONED THAT ALREADY...

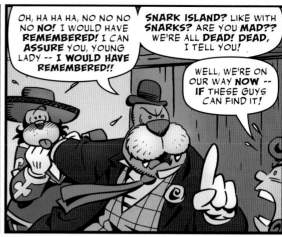

OH, HA HA HA, NO NO NO NO NO! I WOULD HAVE **REMEMBERED!** I CAN **ASSURE** YOU, YOUNG LADY -- **I WOULD HAVE REMEMBERED!!**

SNARK ISLAND? LIKE WITH **SNARKS?** ARE YOU **MAD??** WE'RE ALL **DEAD! DEAD,** I TELL YOU!

WELL, WE'RE ON OUR WAY **NOW** -- IF THESE GUYS CAN FIND IT!

WAIT, WAIT, WAIT. HE DIDN'T KNOW YOU'RE GOING TO **SNARK ISLAND?** YOU DIDN'T **TELL** HIM?

WHO, THIS **COWARDLY TUB OF GUTS?** SURE I TOLD HIM! DO YOU THINK WE'D HAVE MADE IT THIS FAR IF I **HAD?**

HMM... OKAY. I SEE YOUR POINT. BUT YOU'RE ON YOUR WAY **NOW**, RIGHT? YOU CAN TELL THEM EVERYTHING NOW THAT IT'S **TOO LATE TO TURN BACK**, RIGHT?

ON OUR WAY **WHERE?** THE MAP WAS **BLANK!**

SNAP

NO, NO, NO. YOU'RE JUST **LOOKING** AT IT WRONG. YOU NEED TO --

YOU! YOU MISERABLE **FURBALL!** YOU REALIZE THAT THE CREW ARE GOING TO **HEAD FOR HOME** THE VERY **INSTANT** I TELL THEM OUR DESTINATION, DON'T YOU? AND THERE'S A WELCOMING COMMITTEE FOR ME **THERE,** TOO -- A **GRYPHON** WITH A LENGTH OF **HEMP** THE **SAME** SIZE AS MY COLLAR!

EITHER I DIE ON **SNARK ISLAND**... OR I'M **LYNCHED** IN MY **OWN BACK YARD!!**

OH, DEAR. THEN I SUPPOSE YOU'LL JUST HAVE TO SNEAK OFF THE SHIP AT DEAD OF NIGHT AND **RUN** FOR IT. SUCH A SHAME YOU'LL NEVER GET TO SEE THE **TREASURE,** BUT I UNDERSTAND...

YOU'RE **DARN RIGHT** I'LL SNEAK OFF! I'LL SNEAK LIKE NOBODY'S EVER SNEAK... SNUKT...

SNUH...

TREASURE?

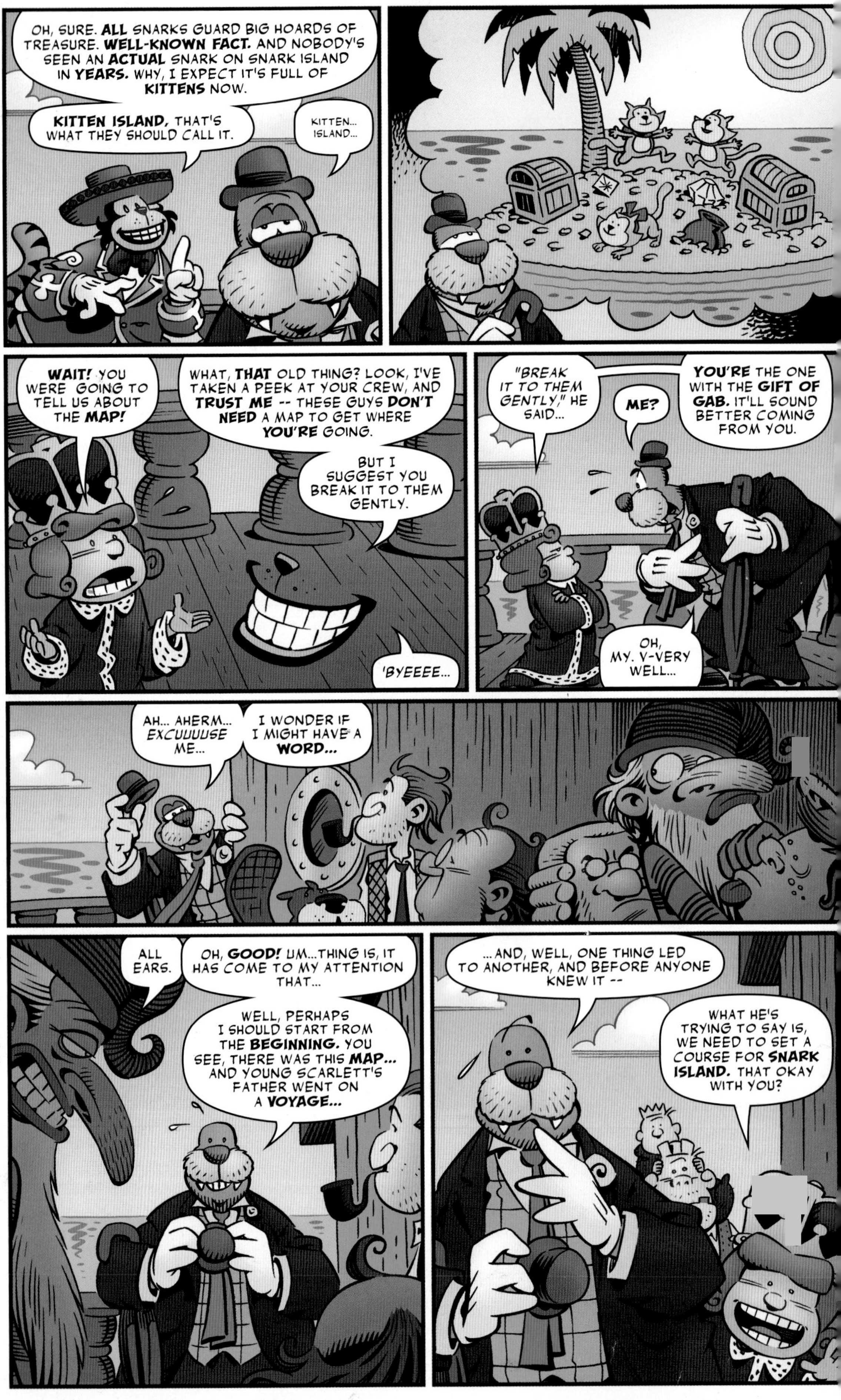
OH, SURE. ALL SNARKS GUARD BIG HOARDS OF TREASURE. WELL-KNOWN FACT. AND NOBODY'S SEEN AN ACTUAL SNARK ON SNARK ISLAND IN YEARS. WHY, I EXPECT IT'S FULL OF KITTENS NOW.
KITTEN ISLAND, THAT'S WHAT THEY SHOULD CALL IT.
KITTEN... ISLAND...
WAIT! YOU WERE GOING TO TELL US ABOUT THE MAP!
WHAT, THAT OLD THING? LOOK, I'VE TAKEN A PEEK AT YOUR CREW, AND TRUST ME -- THESE GUYS DON'T NEED A MAP TO GET WHERE YOU'RE GOING.
BUT I SUGGEST YOU BREAK IT TO THEM GENTLY.
'BYEEEE...
"BREAK IT TO THEM GENTLY," HE SAID...
ME?
YOU'RE THE ONE WITH THE GIFT OF GAB. IT'LL SOUND BETTER COMING FROM YOU.
OH, MY. V-VERY WELL...
AH... AHERM... EXCUUUUSE ME...
I WONDER IF I MIGHT HAVE A WORD...
ALL EARS.
OH, GOOD! UM...THING IS, IT HAS COME TO MY ATTENTION THAT...
WELL, PERHAPS I SHOULD START FROM THE BEGINNING. YOU SEE, THERE WAS THIS MAP... AND YOUNG SCARLETT'S FATHER WENT ON A VOYAGE...
...AND, WELL, ONE THING LED TO ANOTHER, AND BEFORE ANYONE KNEW IT --
WHAT HE'S TRYING TO SAY IS, WE NEED TO SET A COURSE FOR SNARK ISLAND. THAT OKAY WITH YOU?

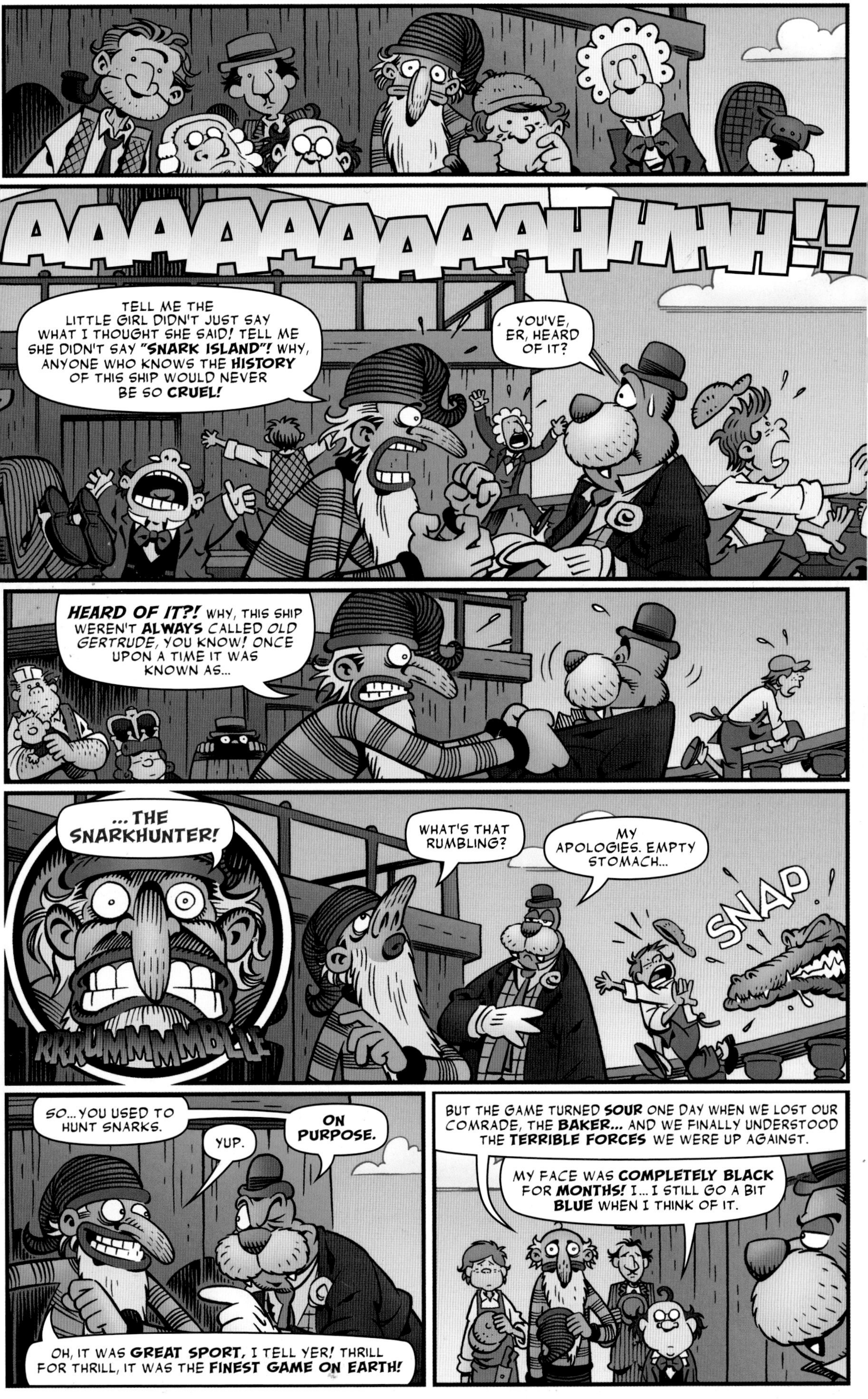
AAAAAAAAAHHHHH!!
TELL ME THE LITTLE GIRL DIDN'T JUST SAY WHAT I THOUGHT SHE SAID! TELL ME SHE DIDN'T SAY "SNARK ISLAND"! WHY, ANYONE WHO KNOWS THE HISTORY OF THIS SHIP WOULD NEVER BE SO CRUEL!
YOU'VE, ER, HEARD OF IT?
HEARD OF IT?! WHY, THIS SHIP WEREN'T ALWAYS CALLED OLD GERTRUDE, YOU KNOW! ONCE UPON A TIME IT WAS KNOWN AS...
... THE SNARKHUNTER!
RRRUMMMMBLE
WHAT'S THAT RUMBLING?
MY APOLOGIES. EMPTY STOMACH...
SNAP
SO... YOU USED TO HUNT SNARKS.
YUP.
ON PURPOSE.
OH, IT WAS GREAT SPORT, I TELL YER! THRILL FOR THRILL, IT WAS THE FINEST GAME ON EARTH!
BUT THE GAME TURNED SOUR ONE DAY WHEN WE LOST OUR COMRADE, THE BAKER... AND WE FINALLY UNDERSTOOD THE TERRIBLE FORCES WE WERE UP AGAINST.
MY FACE WAS COMPLETELY BLACK FOR MONTHS! I... I STILL GO A BIT BLUE WHEN I THINK OF IT.

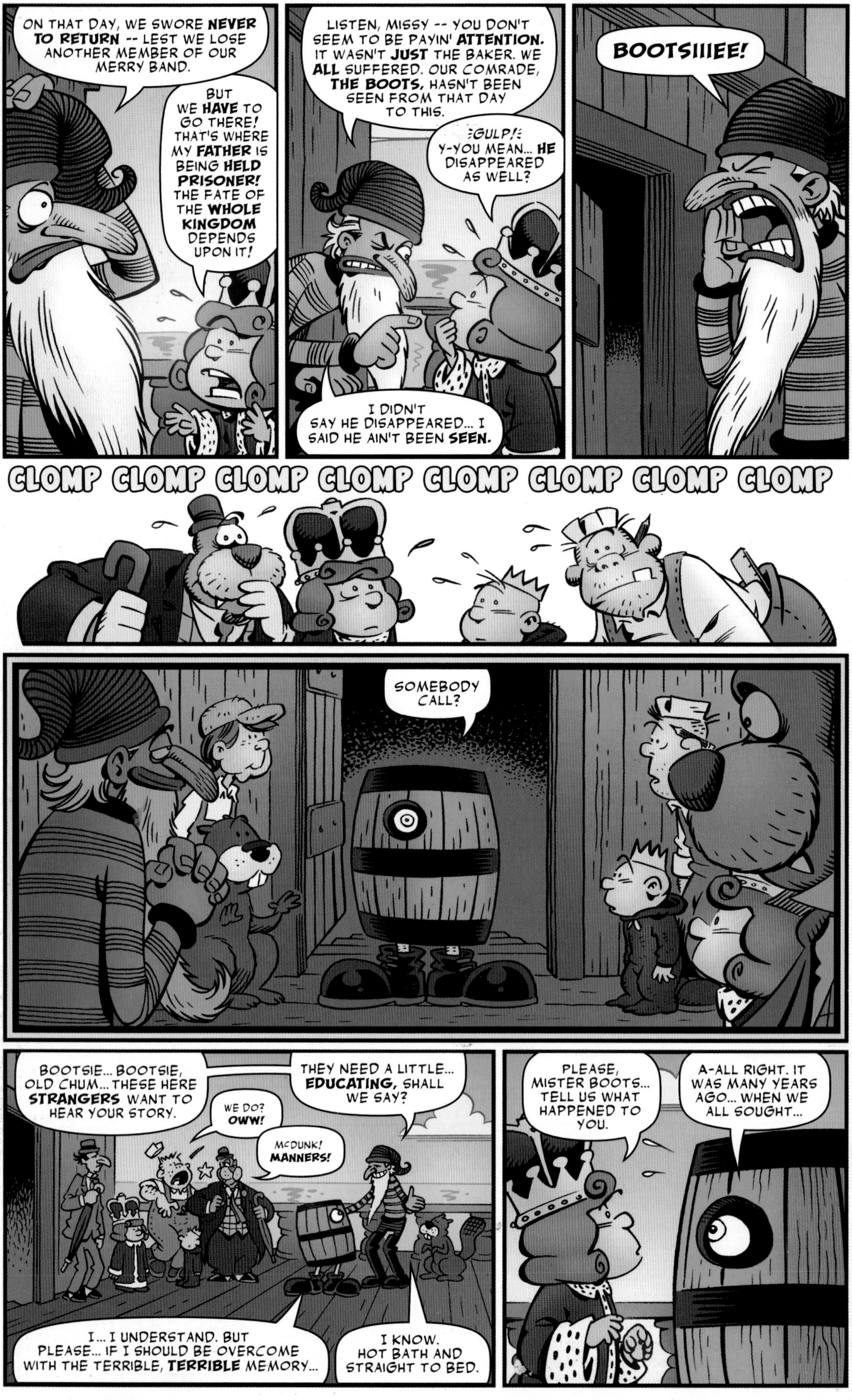
ON THAT DAY, WE SWORE NEVER TO RETURN -- LEST WE LOSE ANOTHER MEMBER OF OUR MERRY BAND.
BUT WE HAVE TO GO THERE! THAT'S WHERE MY FATHER IS BEING HELD PRISONER! THE FATE OF THE WHOLE KINGDOM DEPENDS UPON IT!
LISTEN, MISSY -- YOU DON'T SEEM TO BE PAYIN' ATTENTION. IT WASN'T JUST THE BAKER. WE ALL SUFFERED. OUR COMRADE, THE BOOTS, HASN'T BEEN SEEN FROM THAT DAY TO THIS.
GULP!
Y-YOU MEAN... HE DISAPPEARED AS WELL?
I DIDN'T SAY HE DISAPPEARED... I SAID HE AIN'T BEEN SEEN.
BOOTSIIIEE!
CLOMP CLOMP CLOMP CLOMP CLOMP CLOMP CLOMP CLOMP
SOMEBODY CALL?
BOOTSIE... BOOTSIE, OLD CHUM... THESE HERE STRANGERS WANT TO HEAR YOUR STORY.
THEY NEED A LITTLE... EDUCATING, SHALL WE SAY?
WE DO? OWW!
McDUNK! MANNERS!
I... I UNDERSTAND. BUT PLEASE... IF I SHOULD BE OVERCOME WITH THE TERRIBLE, TERRIBLE MEMORY...
I KNOW. HOT BATH AND STRAIGHT TO BED.
PLEASE, MISTER BOOTS... TELL US WHAT HAPPENED TO YOU.
A-ALL RIGHT. IT WAS MANY YEARS AGO... WHEN WE ALL SOUGHT...

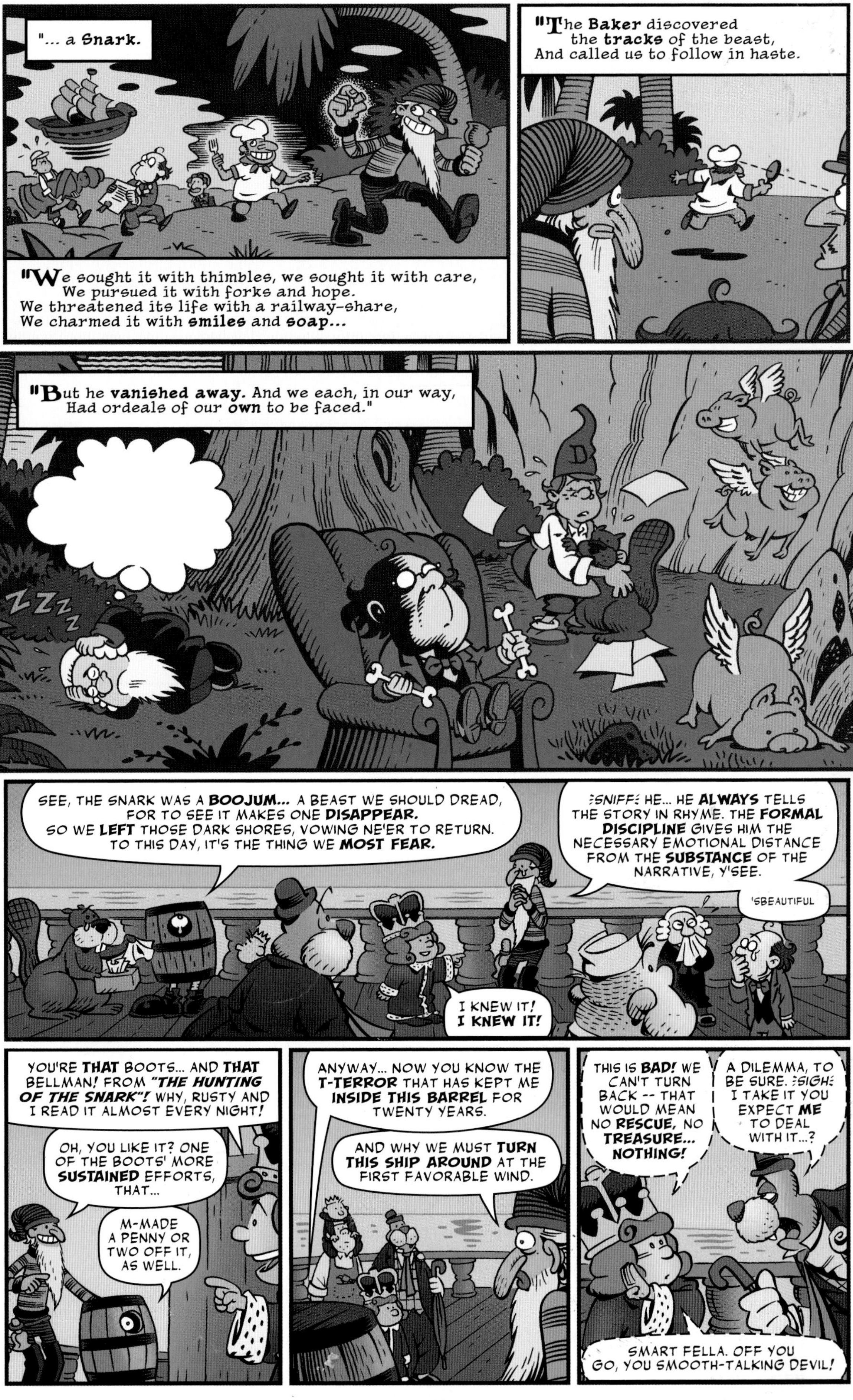
"... a Snark.
"The Baker discovered the tracks of the beast, And called us to follow in haste.
"We sought it with thimbles, we sought it with care, We pursued it with forks and hope. We threatened its life with a railway-share, We charmed it with smiles and soap...
"But he vanished away. And we each, in our way, Had ordeals of our own to be faced."
ZZZZ
SEE, THE SNARK WAS A BOOJUM... A BEAST WE SHOULD DREAD, FOR TO SEE IT MAKES ONE DISAPPEAR. SO WE LEFT THOSE DARK SHORES, VOWING NE'ER TO RETURN. TO THIS DAY, IT'S THE THING WE MOST FEAR.
:SNIFF: HE... HE ALWAYS TELLS THE STORY IN RHYME. THE FORMAL DISCIPLINE GIVES HIM THE NECESSARY EMOTIONAL DISTANCE FROM THE SUBSTANCE OF THE NARRATIVE, Y'SEE.
'SBEAUTIFUL
I KNEW IT! I KNEW IT!
YOU'RE THAT BOOTS... AND THAT BELLMAN! FROM "THE HUNTING OF THE SNARK"! WHY, RUSTY AND I READ IT ALMOST EVERY NIGHT!
OH, YOU LIKE IT? ONE OF THE BOOTS' MORE SUSTAINED EFFORTS, THAT...
M-MADE A PENNY OR TWO OFF IT, AS WELL.
ANYWAY... NOW YOU KNOW THE T-TERROR THAT HAS KEPT ME INSIDE THIS BARREL FOR TWENTY YEARS.
AND WHY WE MUST TURN THIS SHIP AROUND AT THE FIRST FAVORABLE WIND.
THIS IS BAD! WE CAN'T TURN BACK -- THAT WOULD MEAN NO RESCUE, NO TREASURE... NOTHING!
A DILEMMA, TO BE SURE. :SIGH: I TAKE IT YOU EXPECT ME TO DEAL WITH IT...?
SMART FELLA. OFF YOU GO, YOU SMOOTH-TALKING DEVIL!

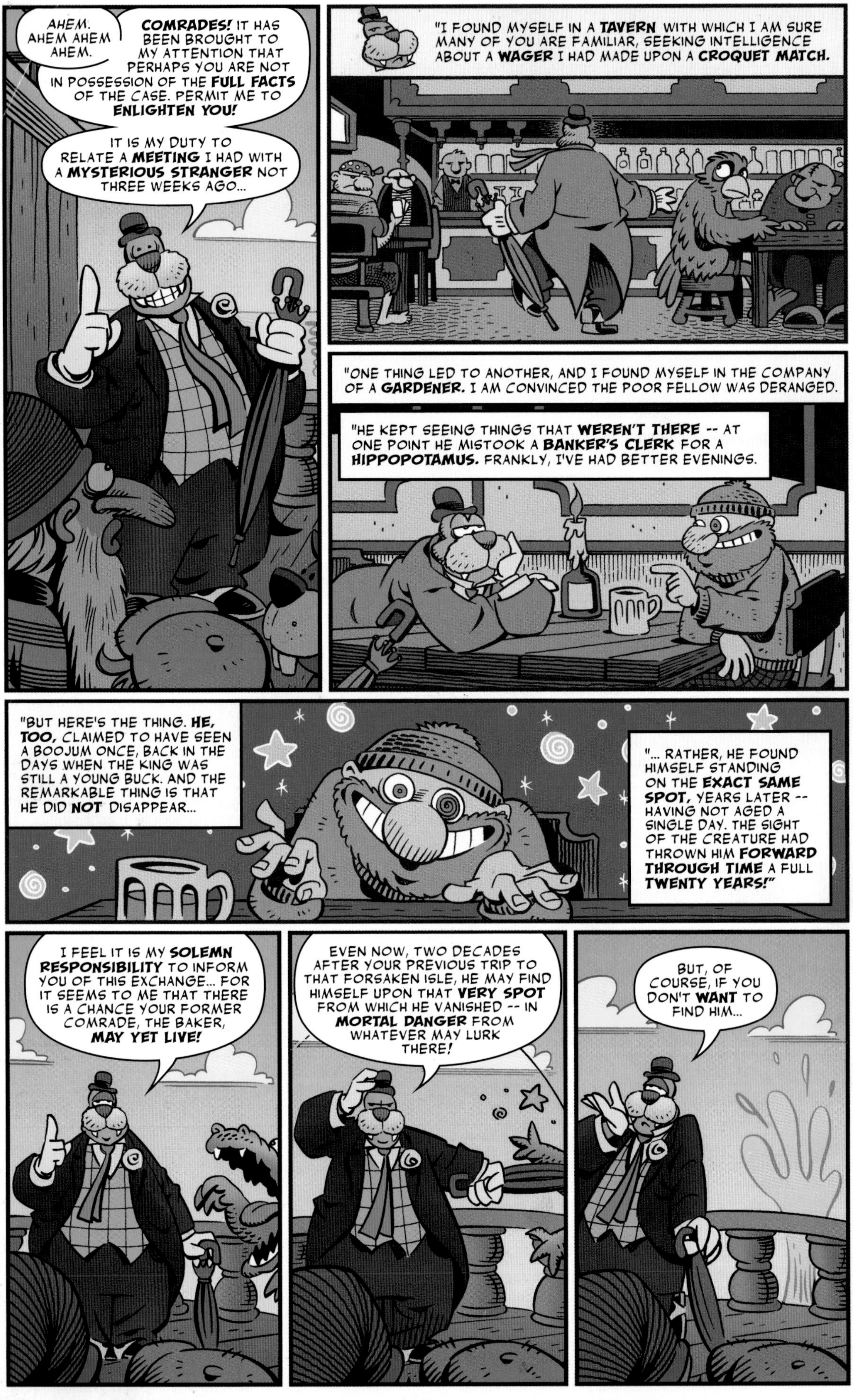
AHEM. AHEM AHEM AHEM.
COMRADES! IT HAS BEEN BROUGHT TO MY ATTENTION THAT PERHAPS YOU ARE NOT IN POSSESSION OF THE FULL FACTS OF THE CASE. PERMIT ME TO ENLIGHTEN YOU!
IT IS MY DUTY TO RELATE A MEETING I HAD WITH A MYSTERIOUS STRANGER NOT THREE WEEKS AGO...
"I FOUND MYSELF IN A TAVERN WITH WHICH I AM SURE MANY OF YOU ARE FAMILIAR, SEEKING INTELLIGENCE ABOUT A WAGER I HAD MADE UPON A CROQUET MATCH.
"ONE THING LED TO ANOTHER, AND I FOUND MYSELF IN THE COMPANY OF A GARDENER. I AM CONVINCED THE POOR FELLOW WAS DERANGED.
"HE KEPT SEEING THINGS THAT WEREN'T THERE -- AT ONE POINT HE MISTOOK A BANKER'S CLERK FOR A HIPPOPOTAMUS. FRANKLY, I'VE HAD BETTER EVENINGS.
"BUT HERE'S THE THING. HE, TOO, CLAIMED TO HAVE SEEN A BOOJUM ONCE, BACK IN THE DAYS WHEN THE KING WAS STILL A YOUNG BUCK. AND THE REMARKABLE THING IS THAT HE DID NOT DISAPPEAR...
"... RATHER, HE FOUND HIMSELF STANDING ON THE EXACT SAME SPOT, YEARS LATER -- HAVING NOT AGED A SINGLE DAY. THE SIGHT OF THE CREATURE HAD THROWN HIM FORWARD THROUGH TIME A FULL TWENTY YEARS!"
I FEEL IT IS MY SOLEMN RESPONSIBILITY TO INFORM YOU OF THIS EXCHANGE... FOR IT SEEMS TO ME THAT THERE IS A CHANCE YOUR FORMER COMRADE, THE BAKER, MAY YET LIVE!
EVEN NOW, TWO DECADES AFTER YOUR PREVIOUS TRIP TO THAT FORSAKEN ISLE, HE MAY FIND HIMSELF UPON THAT VERY SPOT FROM WHICH HE VANISHED -- IN MORTAL DANGER FROM WHATEVER MAY LURK THERE!
BUT, OF COURSE, IF YOU DON'T WANT TO FIND HIM...

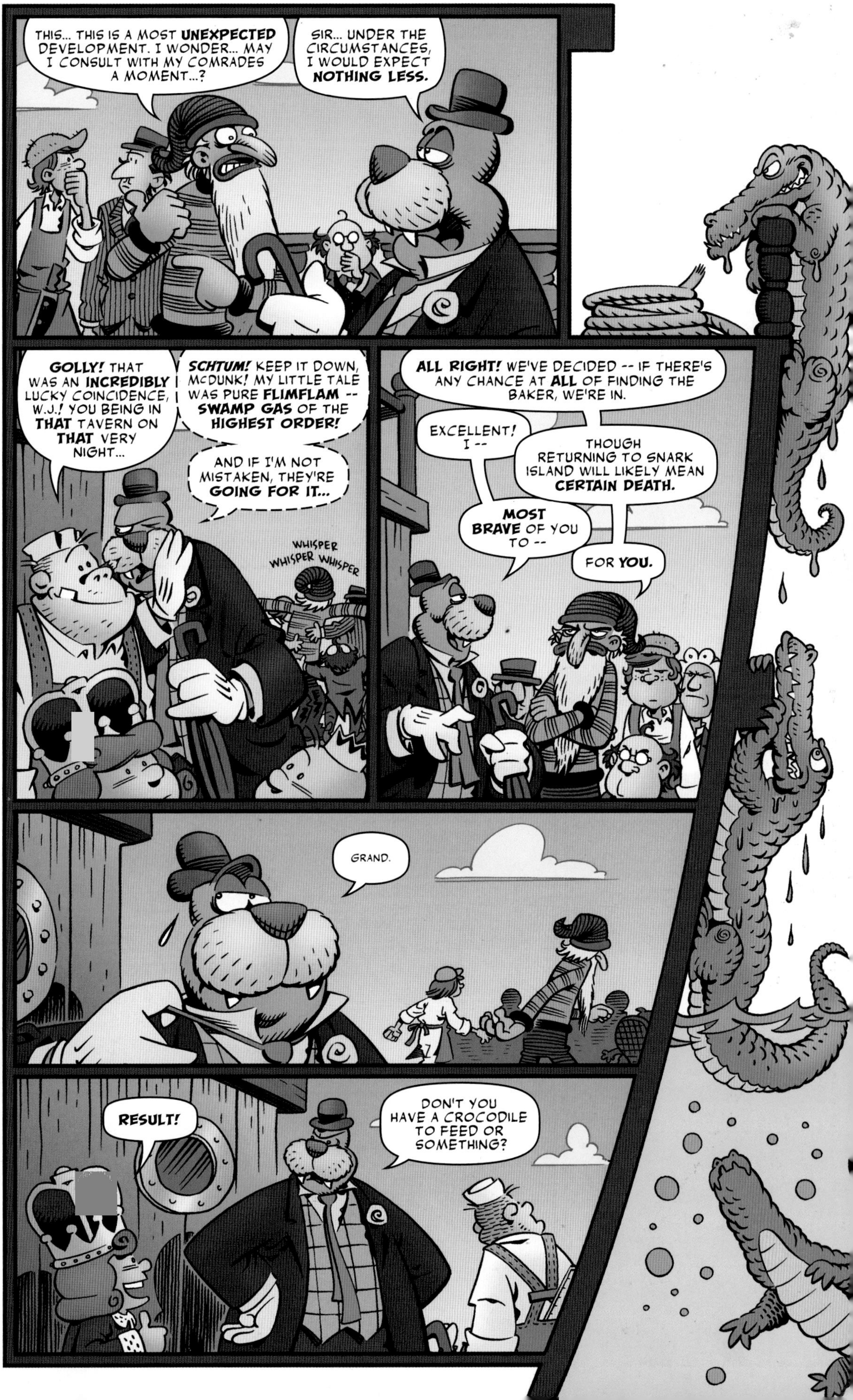
THIS... THIS IS A MOST UNEXPECTED DEVELOPMENT. I WONDER... MAY I CONSULT WITH MY COMRADES A MOMENT...?
SIR... UNDER THE CIRCUMSTANCES, I WOULD EXPECT NOTHING LESS.
GOLLY! THAT WAS AN INCREDIBLY LUCKY COINCIDENCE, W.J.! YOU BEING IN THAT TAVERN ON THAT VERY NIGHT...
SCHTUM! KEEP IT DOWN, McDUNK! MY LITTLE TALE WAS PURE FLIMFLAM -- SWAMP GAS OF THE HIGHEST ORDER!
AND IF I'M NOT MISTAKEN, THEY'RE GOING FOR IT...
WHISPER WHISPER WHISPER
ALL RIGHT! WE'VE DECIDED -- IF THERE'S ANY CHANCE AT ALL OF FINDING THE BAKER, WE'RE IN.
EXCELLENT! I --
THOUGH RETURNING TO SNARK ISLAND WILL LIKELY MEAN CERTAIN DEATH.
MOST BRAVE OF YOU TO --
FOR YOU.
GRAND.
RESULT!
DON'T YOU HAVE A CROCODILE TO FEED OR SOMETHING?

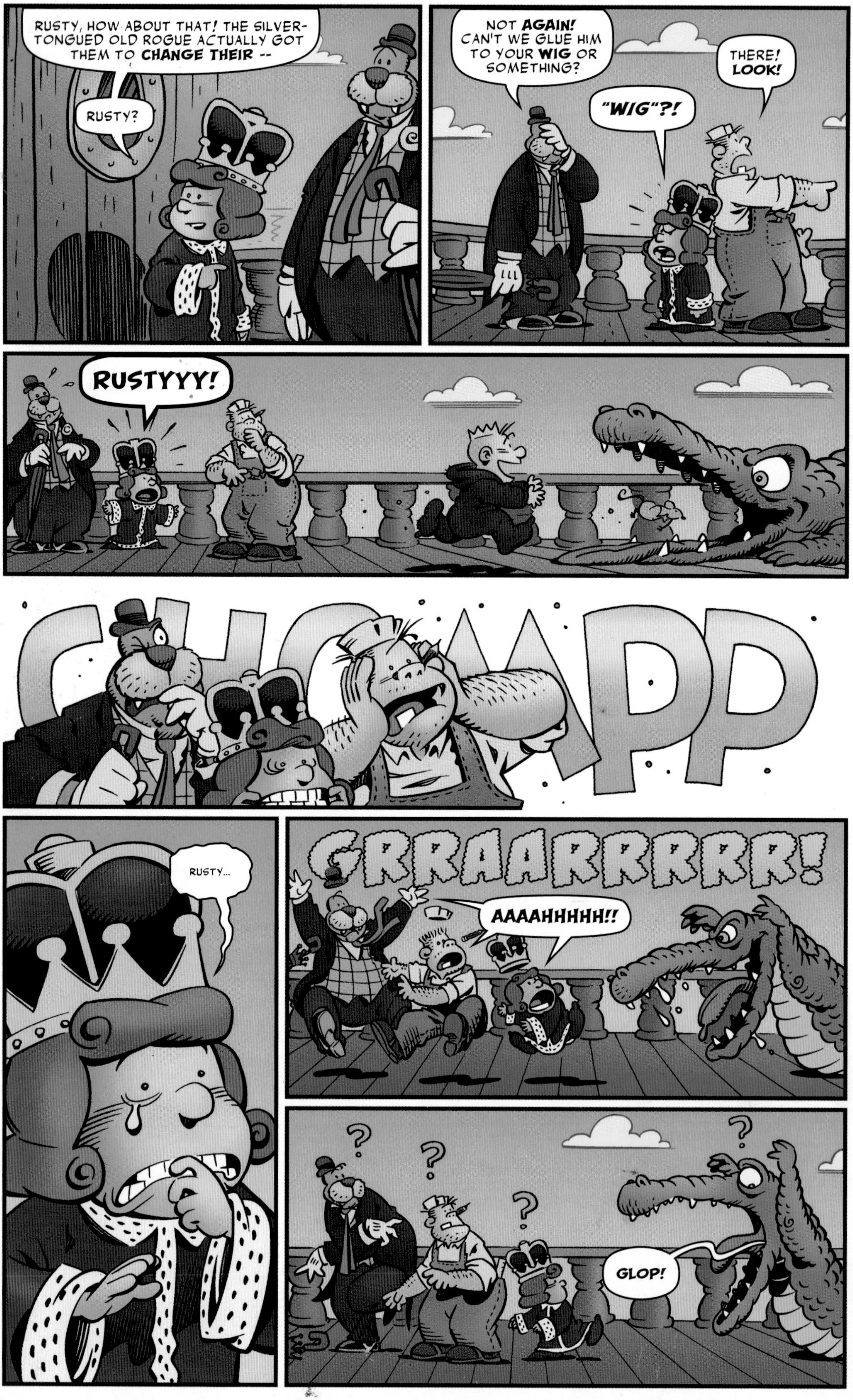

RUSTY, HOW ABOUT THAT! THE SILVER-TONGUED OLD ROGUE ACTUALLY GOT THEM TO CHANGE THEIR --
RUSTY?
NOT AGAIN! CAN'T WE GLUE HIM TO YOUR WIG OR SOMETHING?
"WIG"?!
THERE! LOOK!
RUSTYYY!
CHOMPP
RUSTY...
GRRAARRRRRR!
AAAAHHHHH!!
?
?
?
?
GLOP!

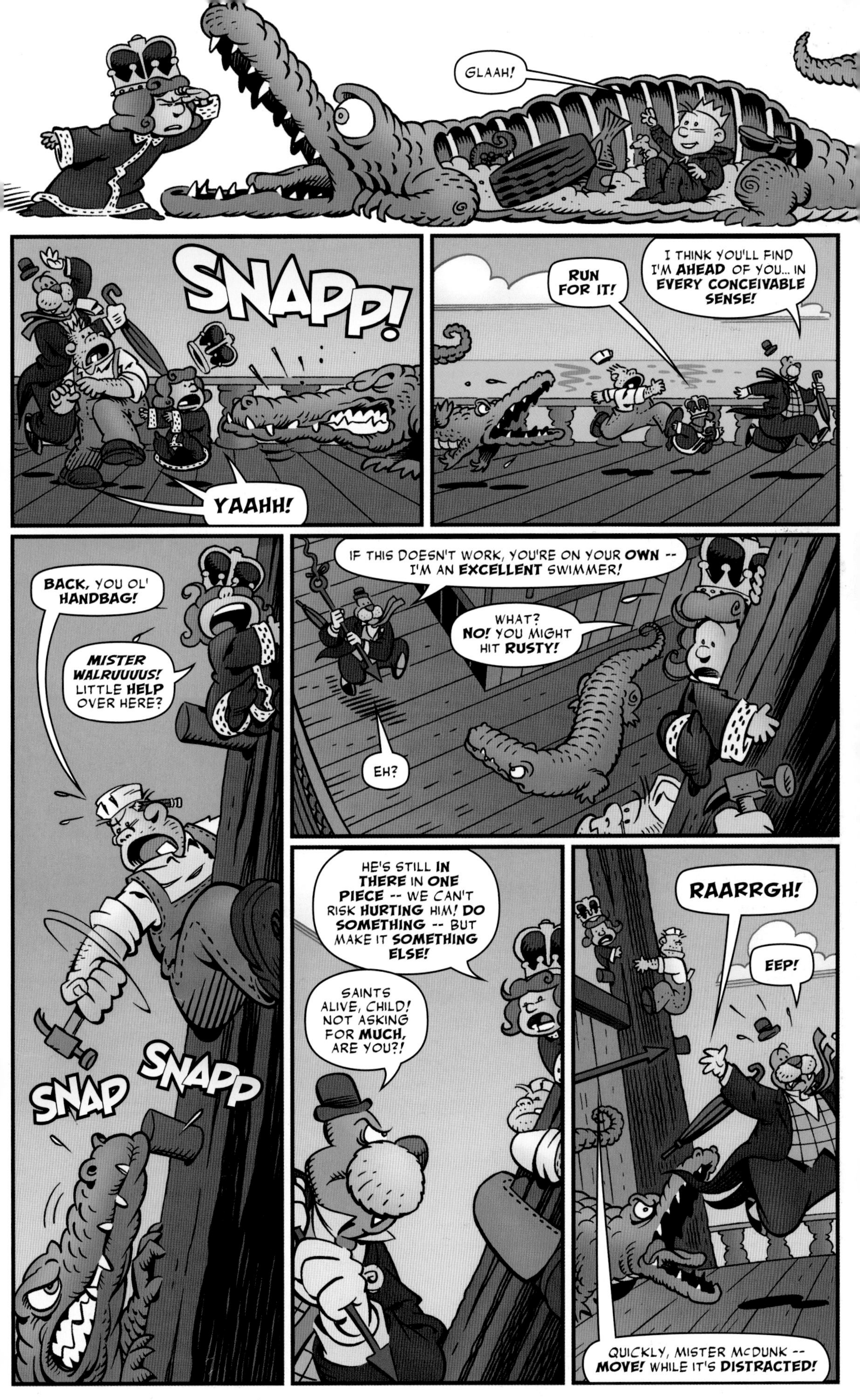
GLAAH!
SNAPP!
YAAHH!
RUN FOR IT!
I THINK YOU'LL FIND I'M AHEAD OF YOU... IN EVERY CONCEIVABLE SENSE!
BACK, YOU OL' HANDBAG!
MISTER WALRUUUUS! LITTLE HELP OVER HERE?
SNAP
SNAPP
IF THIS DOESN'T WORK, YOU'RE ON YOUR OWN -- I'M AN EXCELLENT SWIMMER!
WHAT? NO! YOU MIGHT HIT RUSTY!
EH?
HE'S STILL IN THERE IN ONE PIECE -- WE CAN'T RISK HURTING HIM! DO SOMETHING -- BUT MAKE IT SOMETHING ELSE!
SAINTS ALIVE, CHILD! NOT ASKING FOR MUCH, ARE YOU?!
RAARRGH!
EEP!
QUICKLY, MISTER McDUNK -- MOVE! WHILE IT'S DISTRACTED!

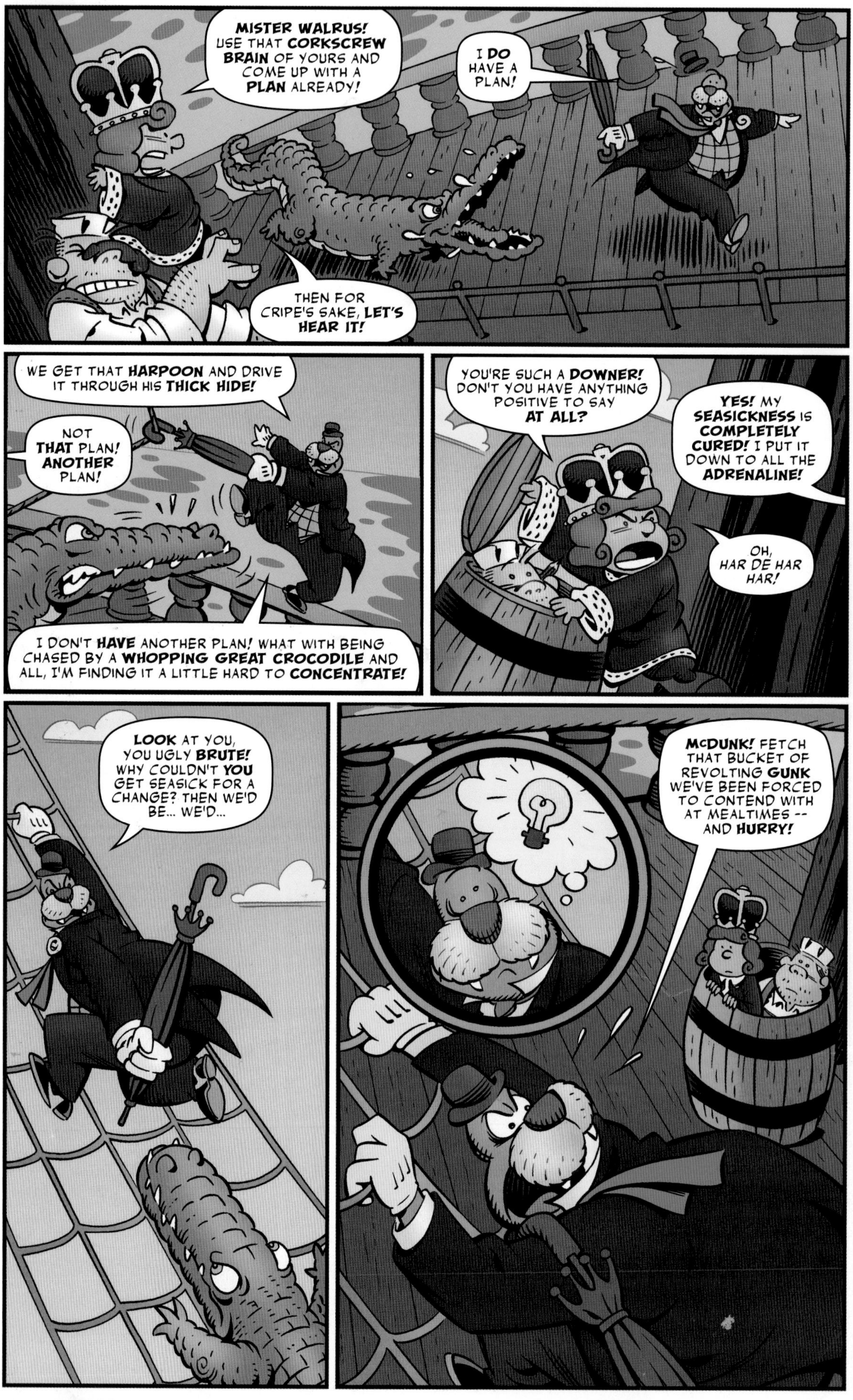
MISTER WALRUS! USE THAT CORKSCREW BRAIN OF YOURS AND COME UP WITH A PLAN ALREADY!
I DO HAVE A PLAN!
THEN FOR CRIPE'S SAKE, LET'S HEAR IT!
WE GET THAT HARPOON AND DRIVE IT THROUGH HIS THICK HIDE!
NOT THAT PLAN! ANOTHER PLAN!
I DON'T HAVE ANOTHER PLAN! WHAT WITH BEING CHASED BY A WHOPPING GREAT CROCODILE AND ALL, I'M FINDING IT A LITTLE HARD TO CONCENTRATE!
YOU'RE SUCH A DOWNER! DON'T YOU HAVE ANYTHING POSITIVE TO SAY AT ALL?
YES! MY SEASICKNESS IS COMPLETELY CURED! I PUT IT DOWN TO ALL THE ADRENALINE!
OH, HAR DE HAR HAR!
LOOK AT YOU, YOU UGLY BRUTE! WHY COULDN'T YOU GET SEASICK FOR A CHANGE? THEN WE'D BE... WE'D...
McDUNK! FETCH THAT BUCKET OF REVOLTING GUNK WE'VE BEEN FORCED TO CONTEND WITH AT MEALTIMES -- AND HURRY!

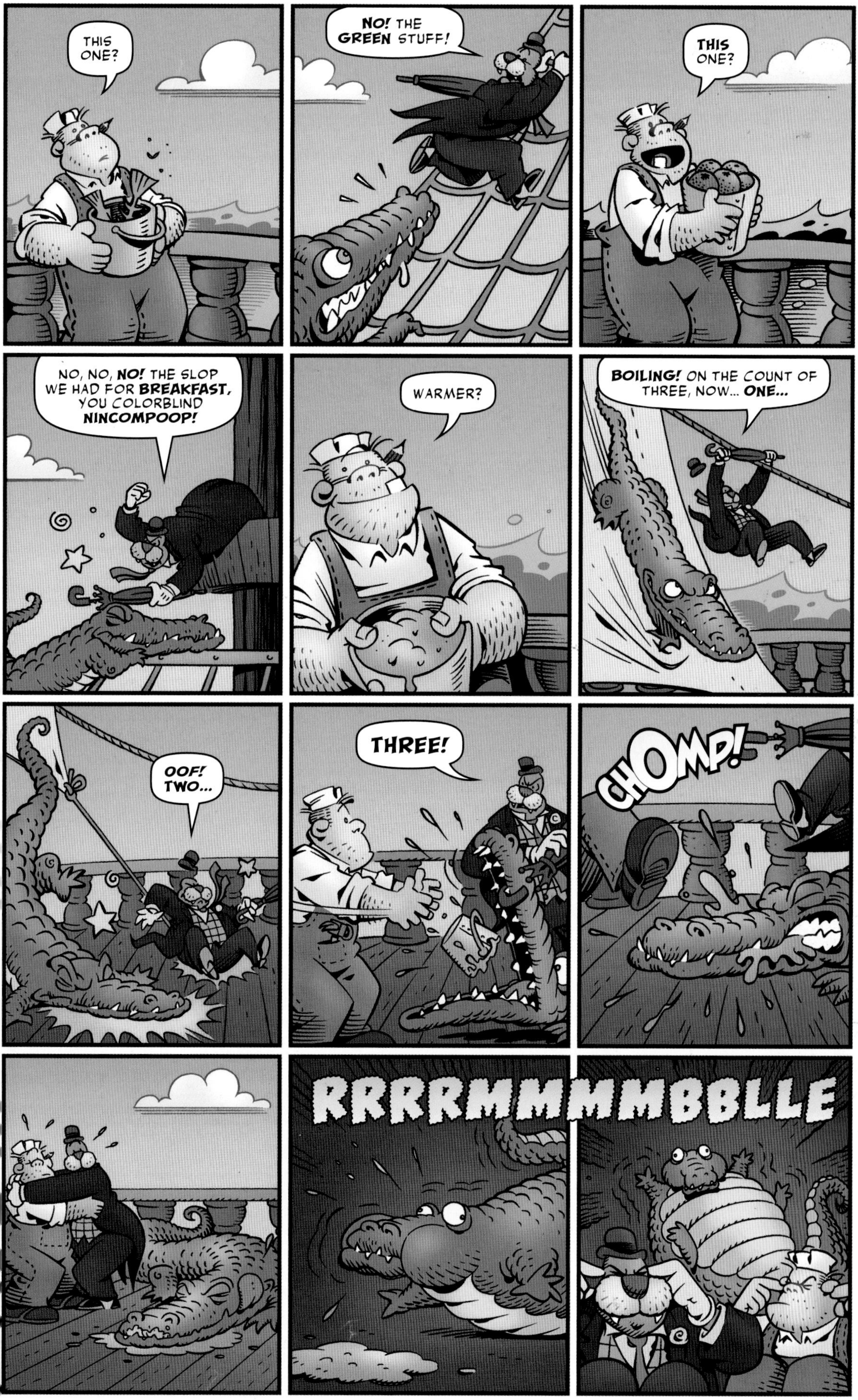
THIS ONE?
NO! THE GREEN STUFF!
THIS ONE?
NO, NO, NO! THE SLOP WE HAD FOR BREAKFAST, YOU COLORBLIND NINCOMPOOP!
WARMER?
BOILING! ON THE COUNT OF THREE, NOW... ONE...
OOF! TWO...
THREE!
CHOMP!
RRRRMMMMMBBLLE

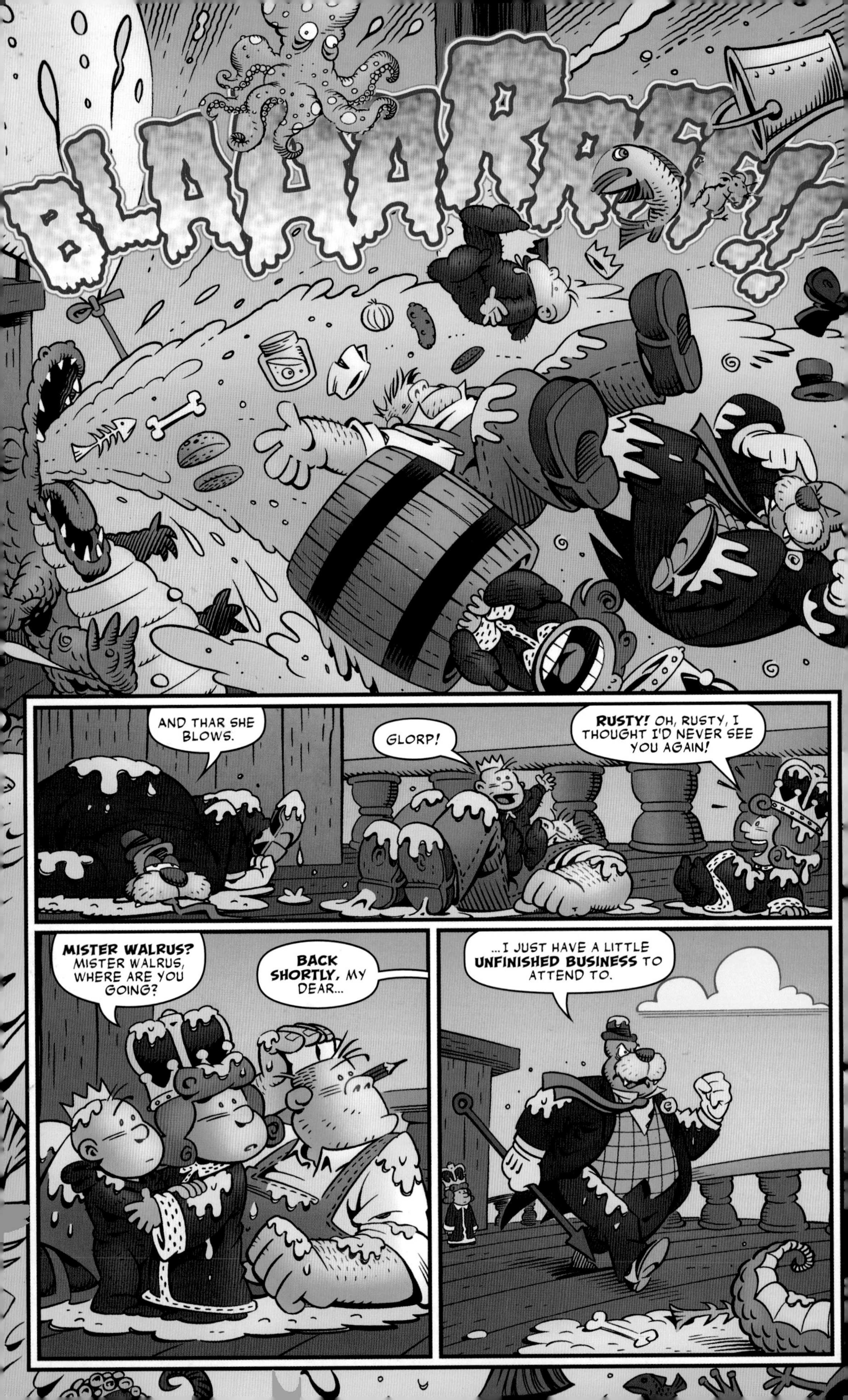
BLAARRGH!!
AND THAR SHE BLOWS.
GLORP!
RUSTY! OH, RUSTY, I THOUGHT I'D NEVER SEE YOU AGAIN!
MISTER WALRUS? MISTER WALRUS, WHERE ARE YOU GOING?
BACK SHORTLY, MY DEAR...
...I JUST HAVE A LITTLE UNFINISHED BUSINESS TO ATTEND TO.

It was odd, on Old Gertrude,
How vastly improved
The **menu** immediately became.
It seemed that some **meat**
Had arrived on the scene
That the **Butcher** found
tricky to name...

ANOTHER SLICE, ANYONE?

THANKS, FRIEND, BUT I'M ABSOLUTELY **STUFFED.** WE SHOULD **DRY AND SALT** THE REST OF THE MEAT -- WITH A BIT OF LUCK IT'LL LAST US THE **REST OF THE JOURNEY!** WE **OWE** YOU ONE!

MY DEAR BELLMAN -- IF MY HUMBLE EFFORTS HAVE AT LEAST ENABLED US TO ENJOY THE **CULINARY ARTS** DURING OUR PRESENT TRAVAILS, I FEEL **AMPLY REWARDED.**

FRIENDS -- **TO THE WALRUS!** HIP, HIP...

HOORAAAY!

OH! WELL, I... HARRUMPH! DEAR ME! HOW VERY... WELL, WELL...

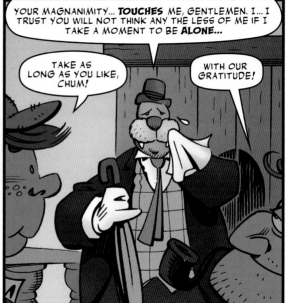

YOUR MAGNANIMITY... **TOUCHES** ME, GENTLEMEN. I... I TRUST YOU WILL NOT THINK ANY THE LESS OF ME IF I TAKE A MOMENT TO BE **ALONE...**

TAKE AS LONG AS YOU LIKE, CHUM!

WITH OUR GRATITUDE!

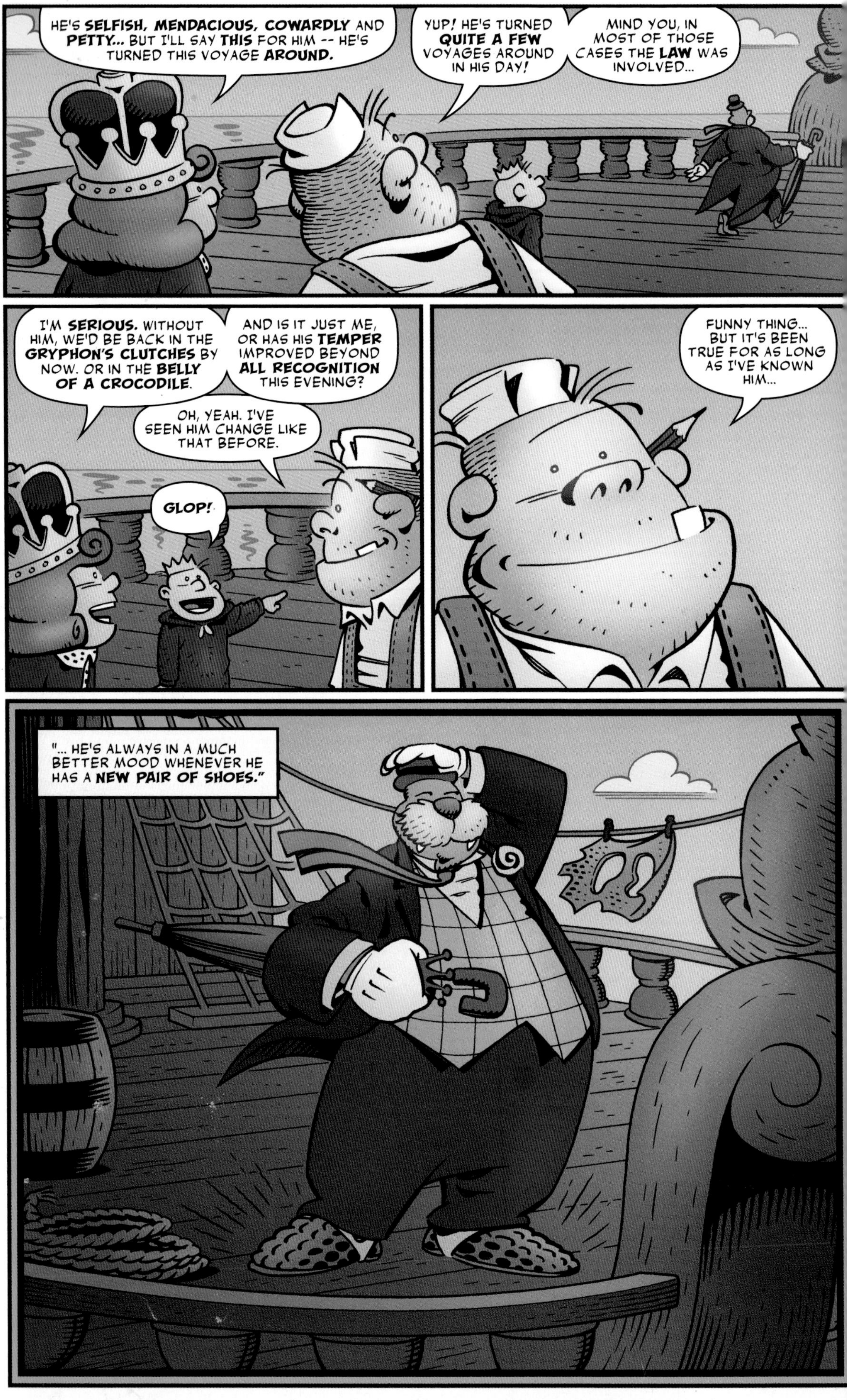
HE'S SELFISH, MENDACIOUS, COWARDLY AND PETTY... BUT I'LL SAY THIS FOR HIM -- HE'S TURNED THIS VOYAGE AROUND.
YUP! HE'S TURNED QUITE A FEW VOYAGES AROUND IN HIS DAY!
MIND YOU, IN MOST OF THOSE CASES THE LAW WAS INVOLVED...
I'M SERIOUS. WITHOUT HIM, WE'D BE BACK IN THE GRYPHON'S CLUTCHES BY NOW. OR IN THE BELLY OF A CROCODILE.
AND IS IT JUST ME, OR HAS HIS TEMPER IMPROVED BEYOND ALL RECOGNITION THIS EVENING?
OH, YEAH. I'VE SEEN HIM CHANGE LIKE THAT BEFORE.
GLOP!
FUNNY THING... BUT IT'S BEEN TRUE FOR AS LONG AS I'VE KNOWN HIM...
"... HE'S ALWAYS IN A MUCH BETTER MOOD WHENEVER HE HAS A NEW PAIR OF SHOES."

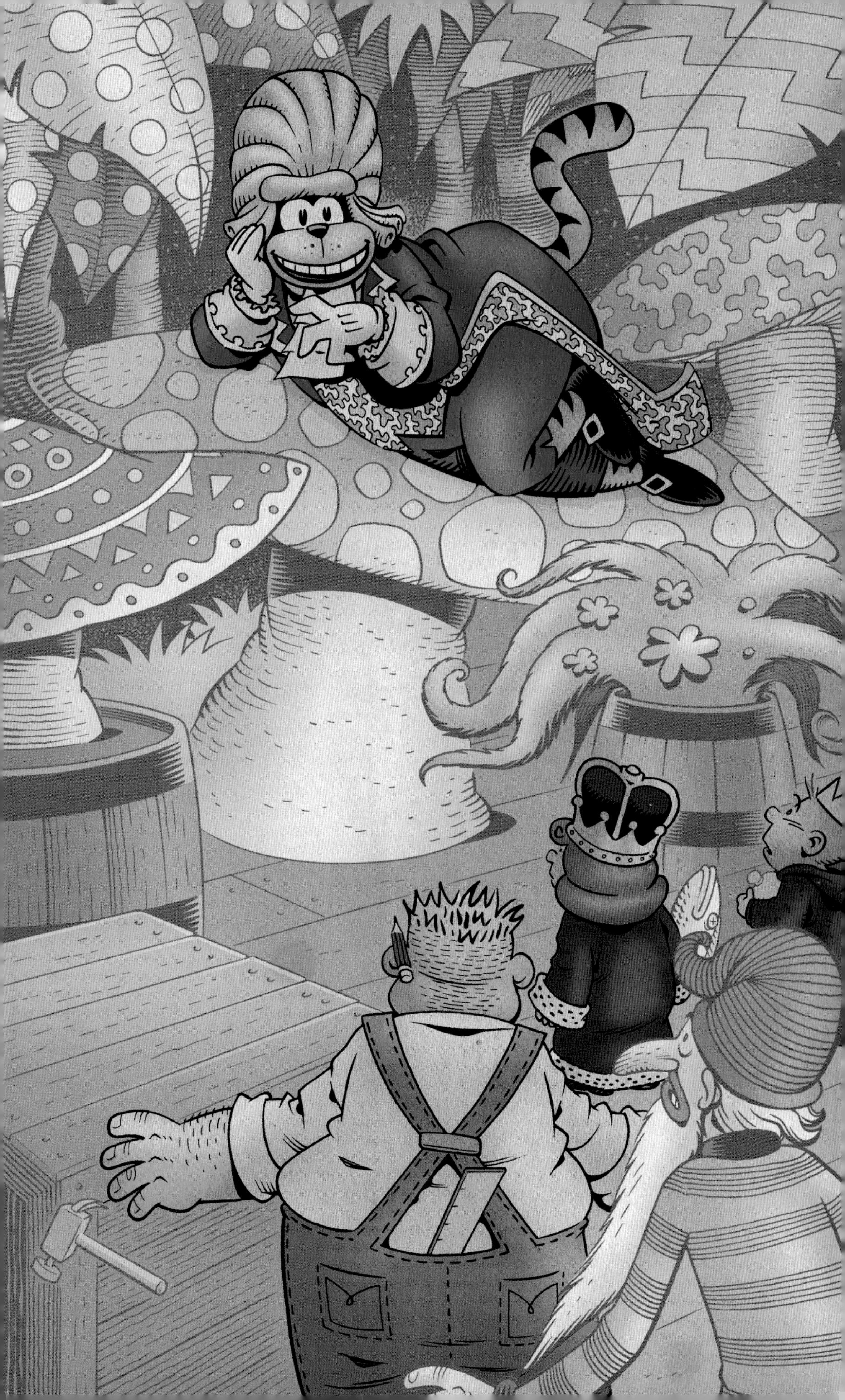

FIT THE SIXTH

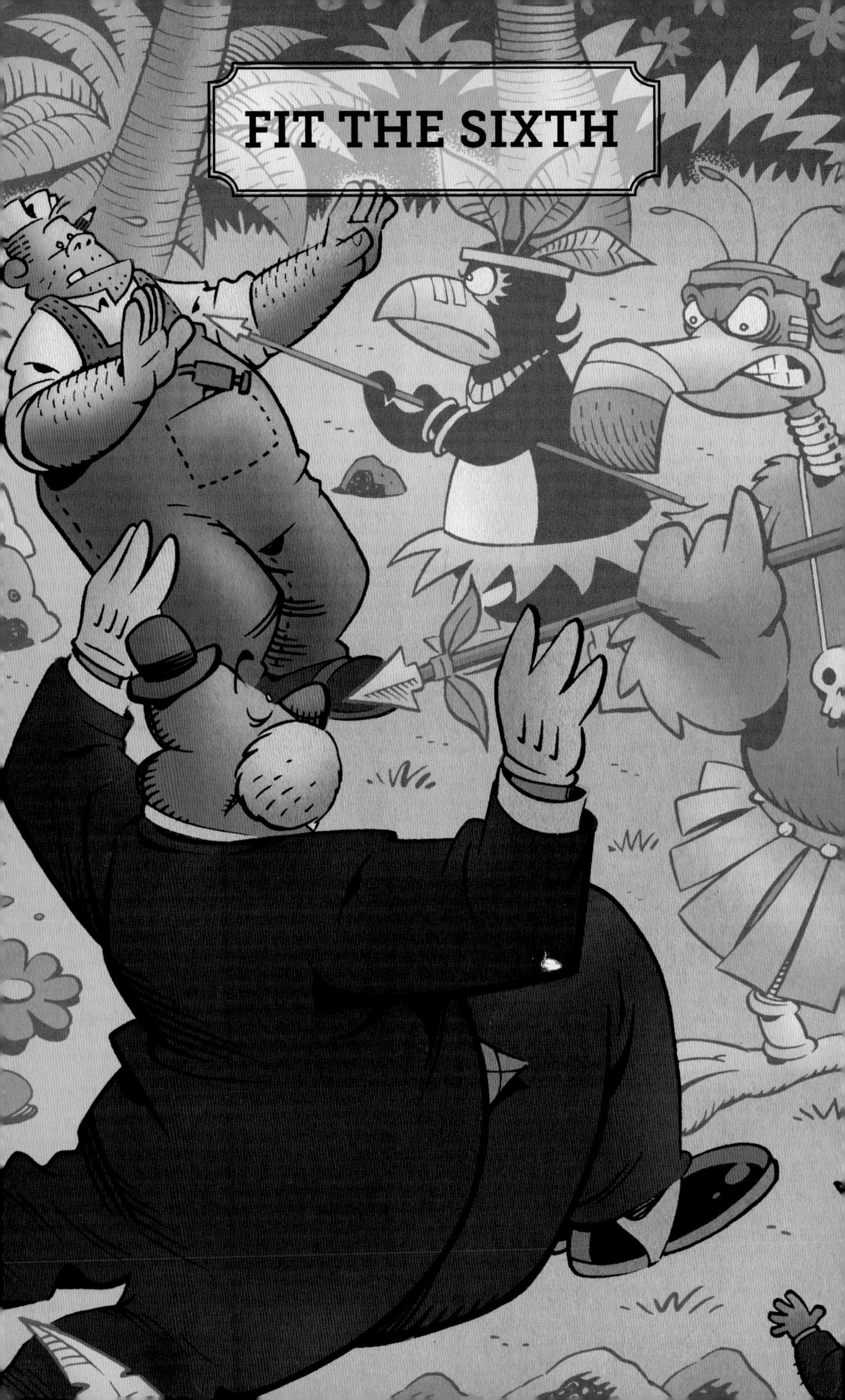

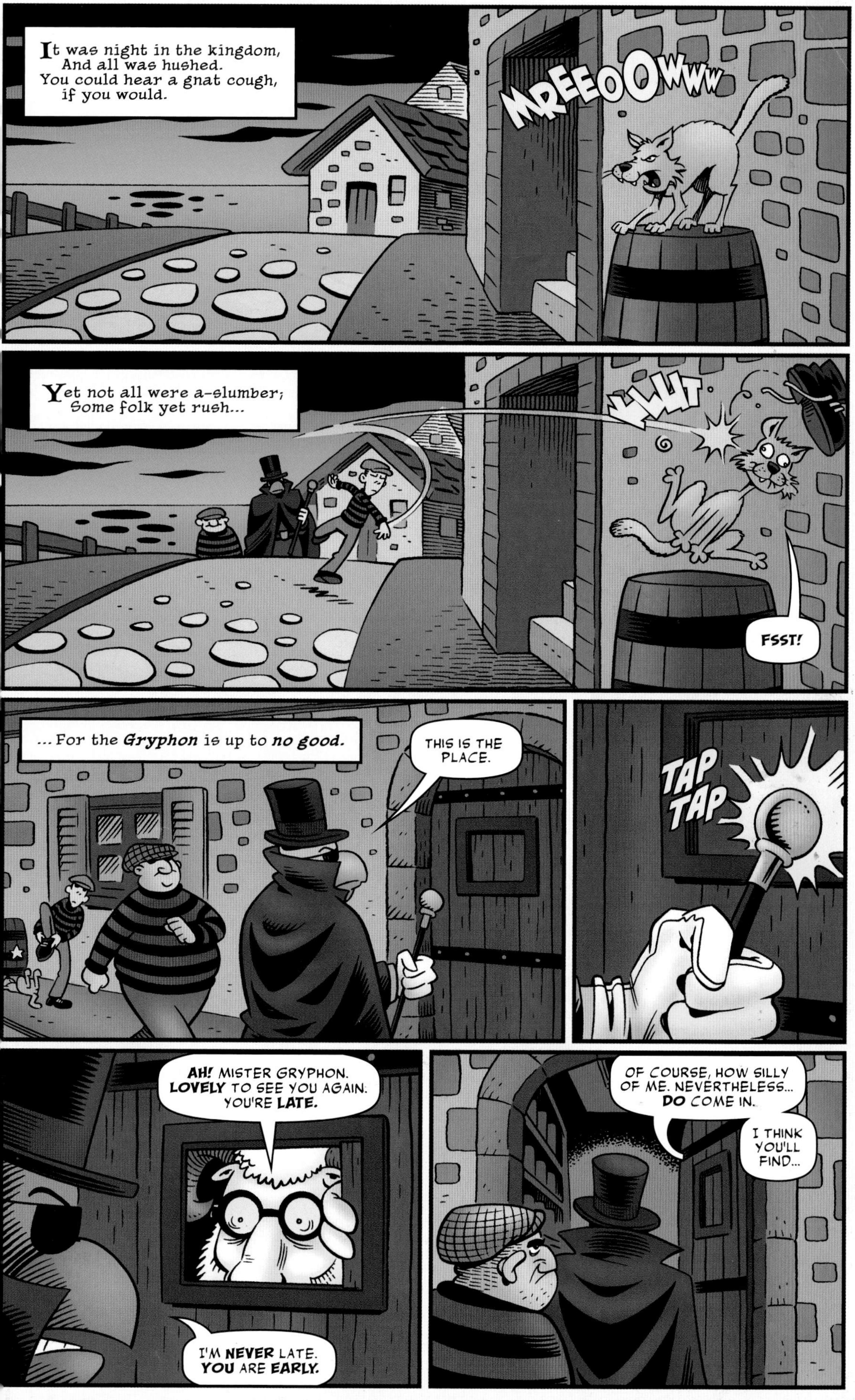
It was night in the kingdom, And all was hushed. You could hear a gnat cough, if you would.
MREEOOWWW
Yet not all were a-slumber; Some folk yet rush...
KLUT
FSST!
...For the Gryphon is up to no good.
THIS IS THE PLACE.
TAP TAP
AH! MISTER GRYPHON. LOVELY TO SEE YOU AGAIN. YOU'RE LATE.
I'M NEVER LATE. YOU ARE EARLY.
OF COURSE, HOW SILLY OF ME. NEVERTHELESS... DO COME IN.
I THINK YOU'LL FIND...

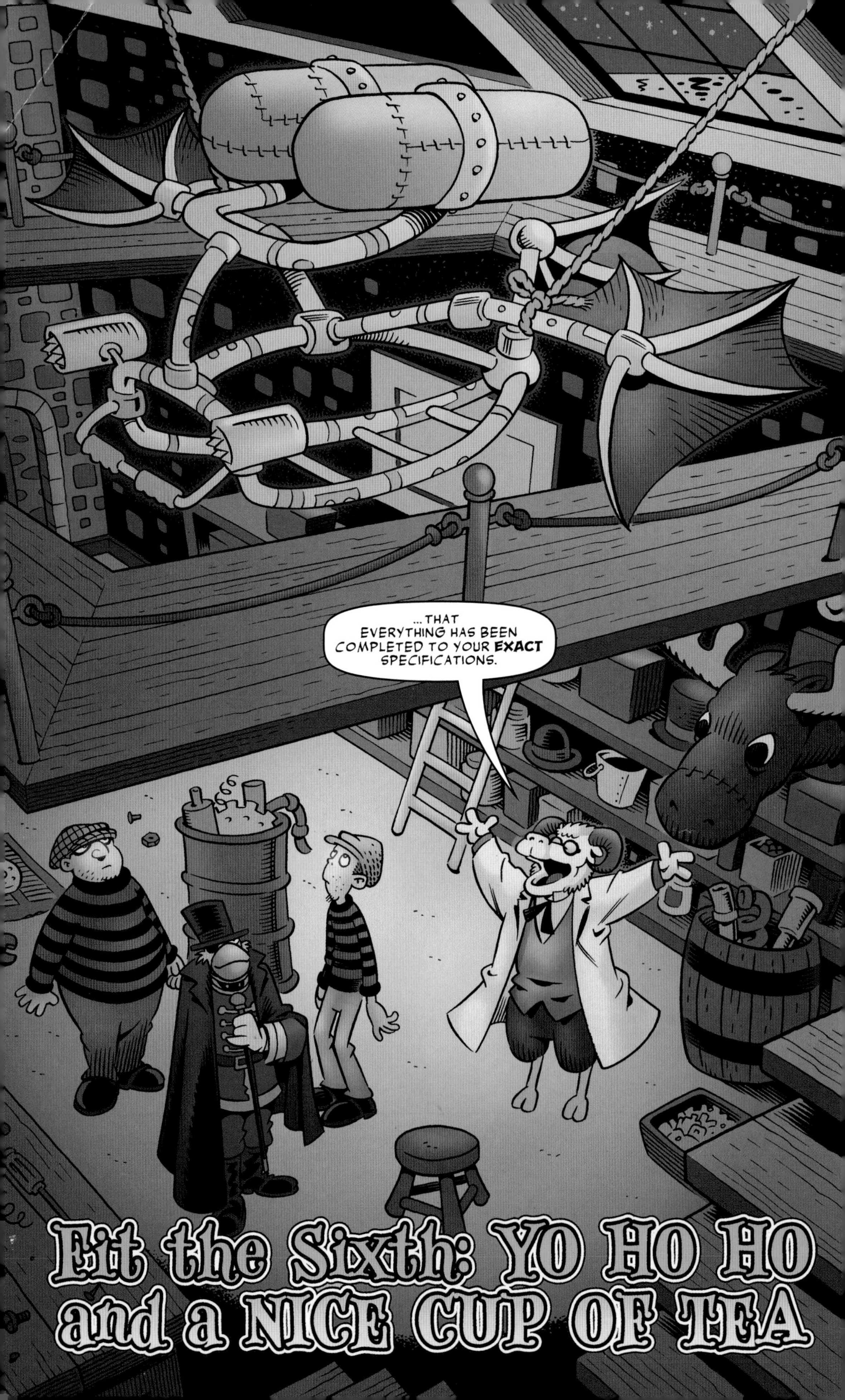
...THAT EVERYTHING HAS BEEN COMPLETED TO YOUR EXACT SPECIFICATIONS.

Fit the Sixth: YO HO HO and a NICE CUP OF TEA

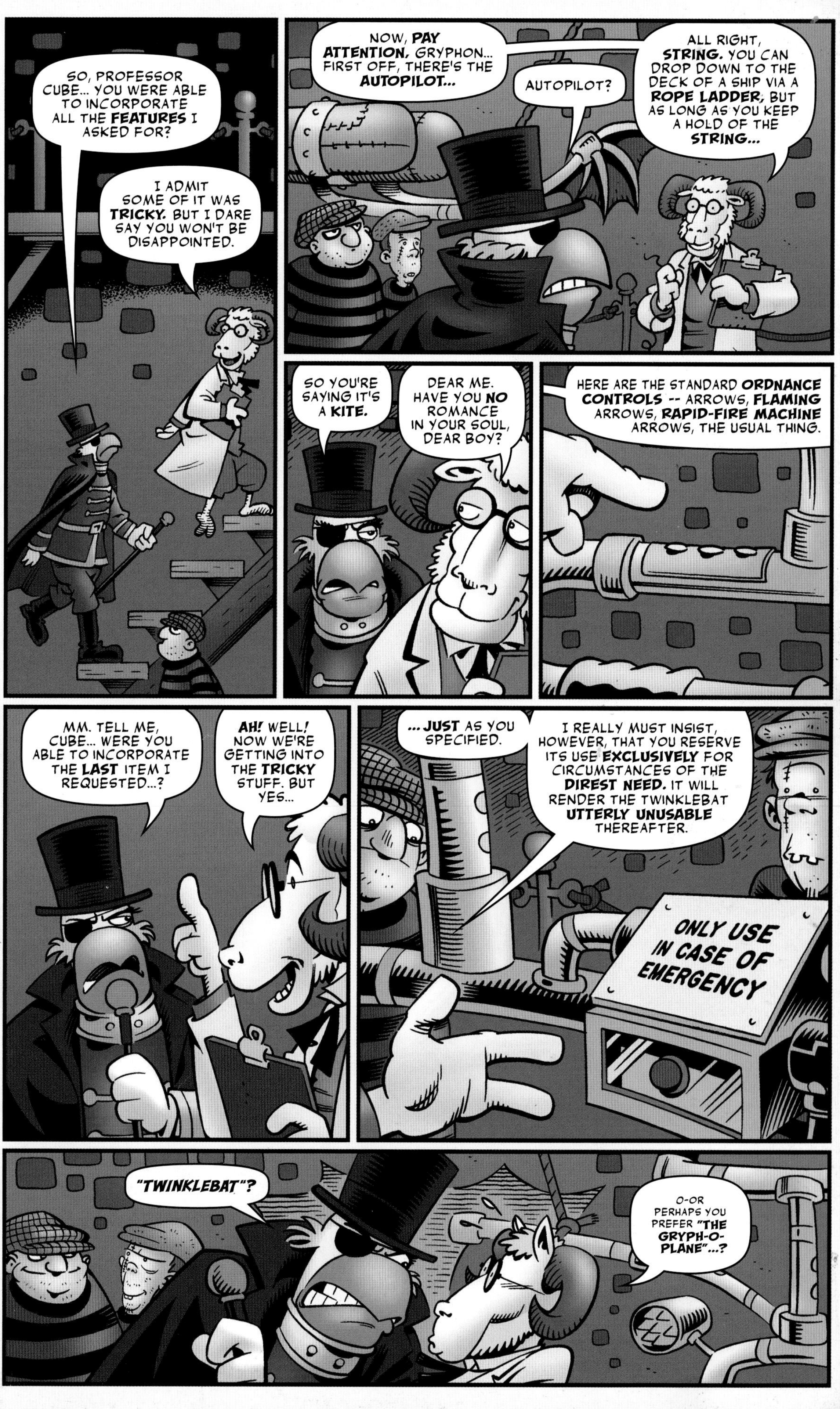
SO, PROFESSOR CUBE... YOU WERE ABLE TO INCORPORATE ALL THE FEATURES I ASKED FOR?
I ADMIT SOME OF IT WAS TRICKY. BUT I DARE SAY YOU WON'T BE DISAPPOINTED.
NOW, PAY ATTENTION, GRYPHON... FIRST OFF, THERE'S THE AUTOPILOT...
AUTOPILOT?
ALL RIGHT, STRING. YOU CAN DROP DOWN TO THE DECK OF A SHIP VIA A ROPE LADDER, BUT AS LONG AS YOU KEEP A HOLD OF THE STRING...
SO YOU'RE SAYING IT'S A KITE.
DEAR ME. HAVE YOU NO ROMANCE IN YOUR SOUL, DEAR BOY?
HERE ARE THE STANDARD ORDNANCE CONTROLS -- ARROWS, FLAMING ARROWS, RAPID-FIRE MACHINE ARROWS, THE USUAL THING.
MM. TELL ME, CUBE... WERE YOU ABLE TO INCORPORATE THE LAST ITEM I REQUESTED...?
AH! WELL! NOW WE'RE GETTING INTO THE TRICKY STUFF. BUT YES...
...JUST AS YOU SPECIFIED.
I REALLY MUST INSIST, HOWEVER, THAT YOU RESERVE ITS USE EXCLUSIVELY FOR CIRCUMSTANCES OF THE DIREST NEED. IT WILL RENDER THE TWINKLEBAT UTTERLY UNUSABLE THEREAFTER.
ONLY USE IN CASE OF EMERGENCY
"TWINKLEBAT"?
O-OR PERHAPS YOU PREFER "THE GRYPH-O-PLANE"...?

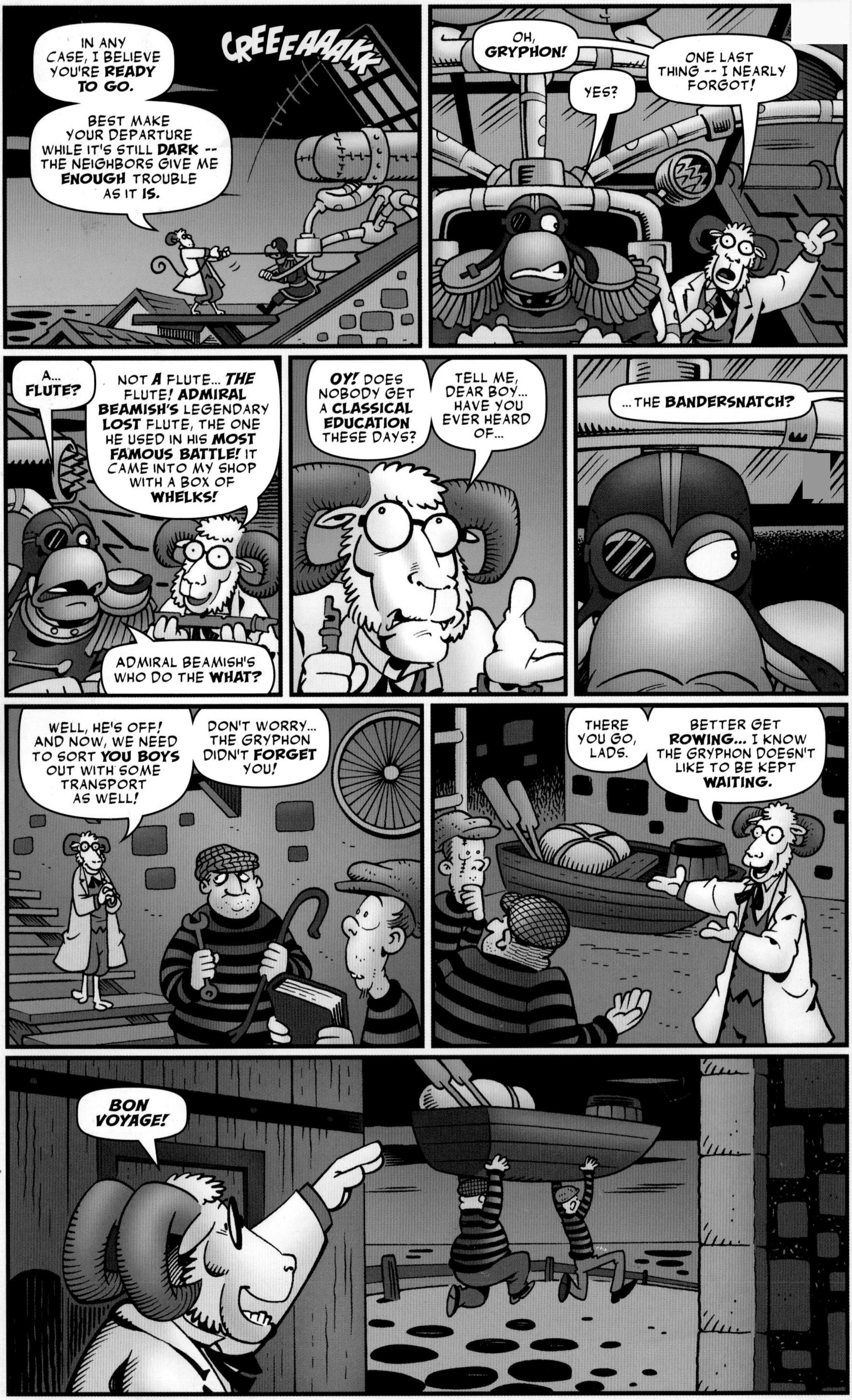
IN ANY CASE, I BELIEVE YOU'RE **READY TO GO.**
BEST MAKE YOUR DEPARTURE WHILE IT'S STILL **DARK** -- THE NEIGHBORS GIVE ME **ENOUGH** TROUBLE AS IT **IS.**
CREEEAAAKK
OH, **GRYPHON!**
YES?
ONE LAST THING -- I NEARLY FORGOT!
A... **FLUTE?**
NOT ***A*** FLUTE... ***THE*** FLUTE! **ADMIRAL BEAMISH'S** LEGENDARY **LOST** FLUTE, THE ONE HE USED IN HIS **MOST FAMOUS BATTLE!** IT CAME INTO MY SHOP WITH A BOX OF **WHELKS!**
ADMIRAL BEAMISH'S WHO DO THE **WHAT?**
OY! DOES NOBODY GET A **CLASSICAL EDUCATION** THESE DAYS?
TELL ME, DEAR BOY... HAVE YOU EVER HEARD OF...
...THE **BANDERSNATCH?**
WELL, HE'S OFF! AND NOW, WE NEED TO SORT **YOU BOYS** OUT WITH SOME TRANSPORT AS WELL!
DON'T WORRY... THE GRYPHON DIDN'T **FORGET** YOU!
THERE YOU GO, LADS.
BETTER GET **ROWING...** I KNOW THE GRYPHON DOESN'T LIKE TO BE KEPT **WAITING.**
BON VOYAGE!

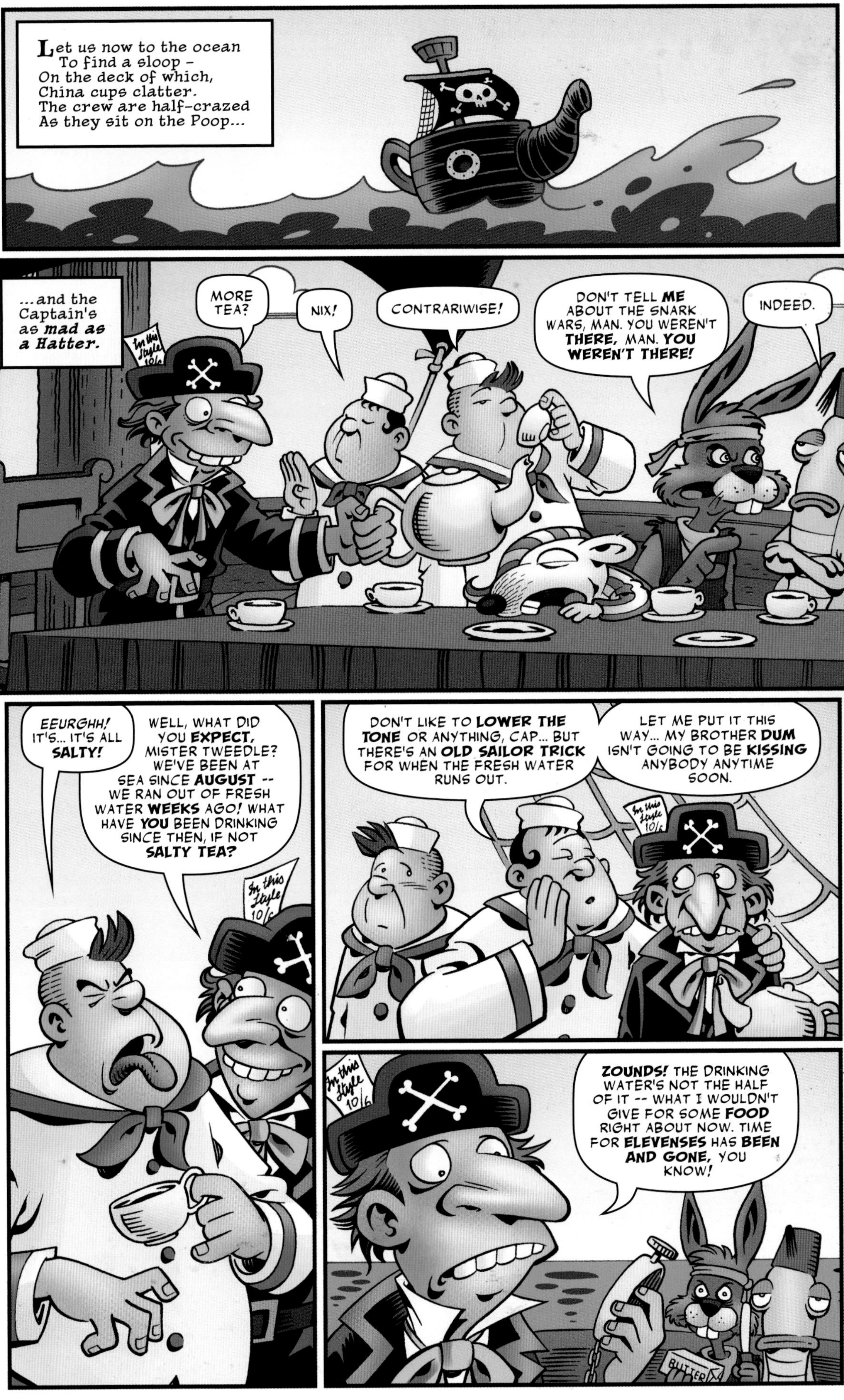

Let us now to the ocean
To find a sloop –
On the deck of which,
China cups clatter.
The crew are half-crazed
As they sit on the Poop...
...and the Captain's as mad as a Hatter.
MORE TEA?
NIX!
CONTRARIWISE!
DON'T TELL ME ABOUT THE SNARK WARS, MAN. YOU WEREN'T THERE, MAN. YOU WEREN'T THERE!
INDEED.
In this Style 10/6
EEURGHH! IT'S... IT'S ALL SALTY!
WELL, WHAT DID YOU EXPECT, MISTER TWEEDLE? WE'VE BEEN AT SEA SINCE AUGUST -- WE RAN OUT OF FRESH WATER WEEKS AGO! WHAT HAVE YOU BEEN DRINKING SINCE THEN, IF NOT SALTY TEA?
DON'T LIKE TO LOWER THE TONE OR ANYTHING, CAP... BUT THERE'S AN OLD SAILOR TRICK FOR WHEN THE FRESH WATER RUNS OUT.
LET ME PUT IT THIS WAY... MY BROTHER DUM ISN'T GOING TO BE KISSING ANYBODY ANYTIME SOON.
ZOUNDS! THE DRINKING WATER'S NOT THE HALF OF IT -- WHAT I WOULDN'T GIVE FOR SOME FOOD RIGHT ABOUT NOW. TIME FOR ELEVENSES HAS BEEN AND GONE, YOU KNOW!
BUTTER

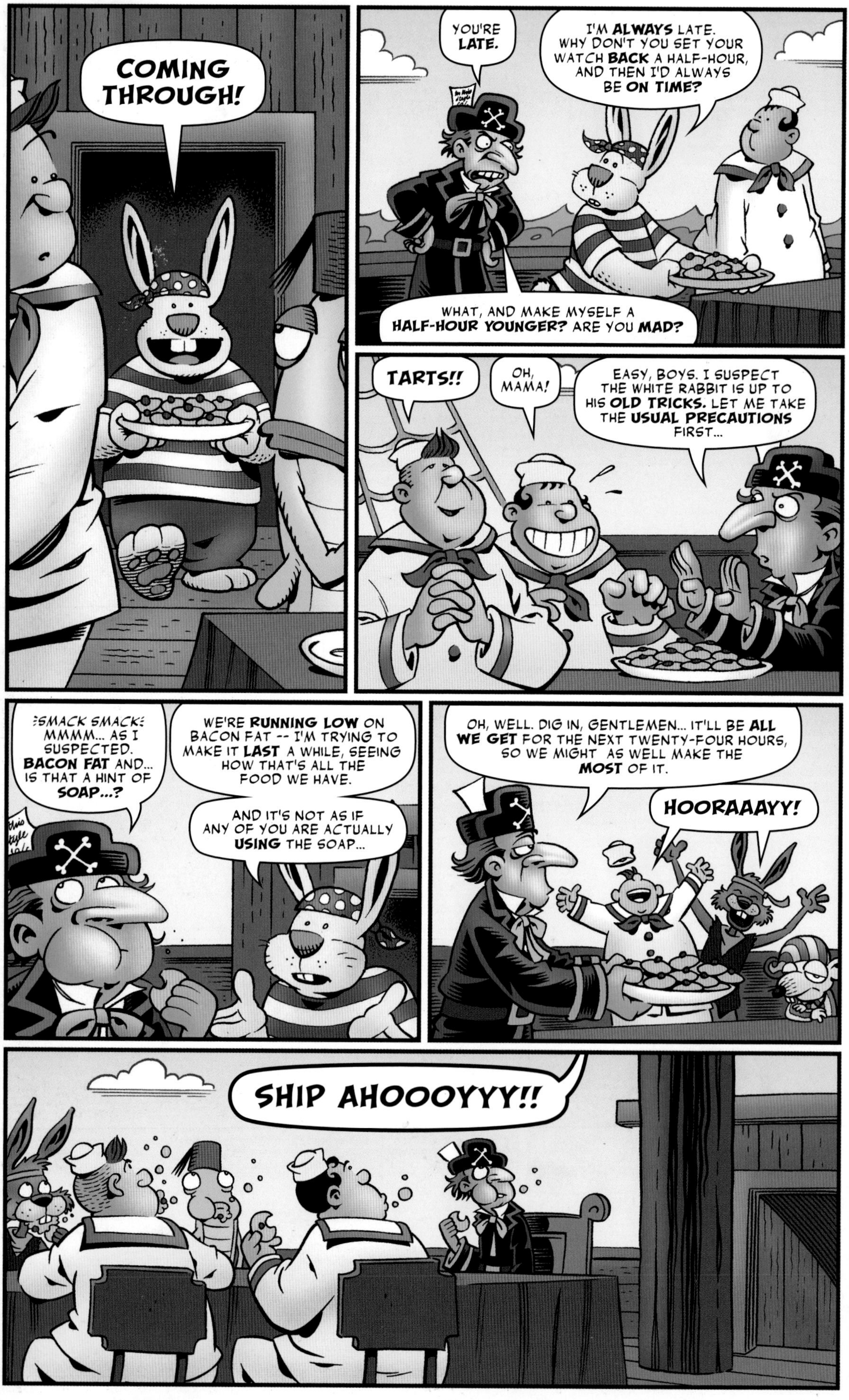
COMING THROUGH!
YOU'RE LATE.
I'M ALWAYS LATE. WHY DON'T YOU SET YOUR WATCH BACK A HALF-HOUR, AND THEN I'D ALWAYS BE ON TIME?
WHAT, AND MAKE MYSELF A HALF-HOUR YOUNGER? ARE YOU MAD?
TARTS!!
OH, MAMA!
EASY, BOYS. I SUSPECT THE WHITE RABBIT IS UP TO HIS OLD TRICKS. LET ME TAKE THE USUAL PRECAUTIONS FIRST...
SMACK SMACK MMMM... AS I SUSPECTED. BACON FAT AND... IS THAT A HINT OF SOAP...?
WE'RE RUNNING LOW ON BACON FAT -- I'M TRYING TO MAKE IT LAST A WHILE, SEEING HOW THAT'S ALL THE FOOD WE HAVE.
AND IT'S NOT AS IF ANY OF YOU ARE ACTUALLY USING THE SOAP...
OH, WELL. DIG IN, GENTLEMEN... IT'LL BE ALL WE GET FOR THE NEXT TWENTY-FOUR HOURS, SO WE MIGHT AS WELL MAKE THE MOST OF IT.
HOORAAAYY!
SHIP AHOOOYYY!!

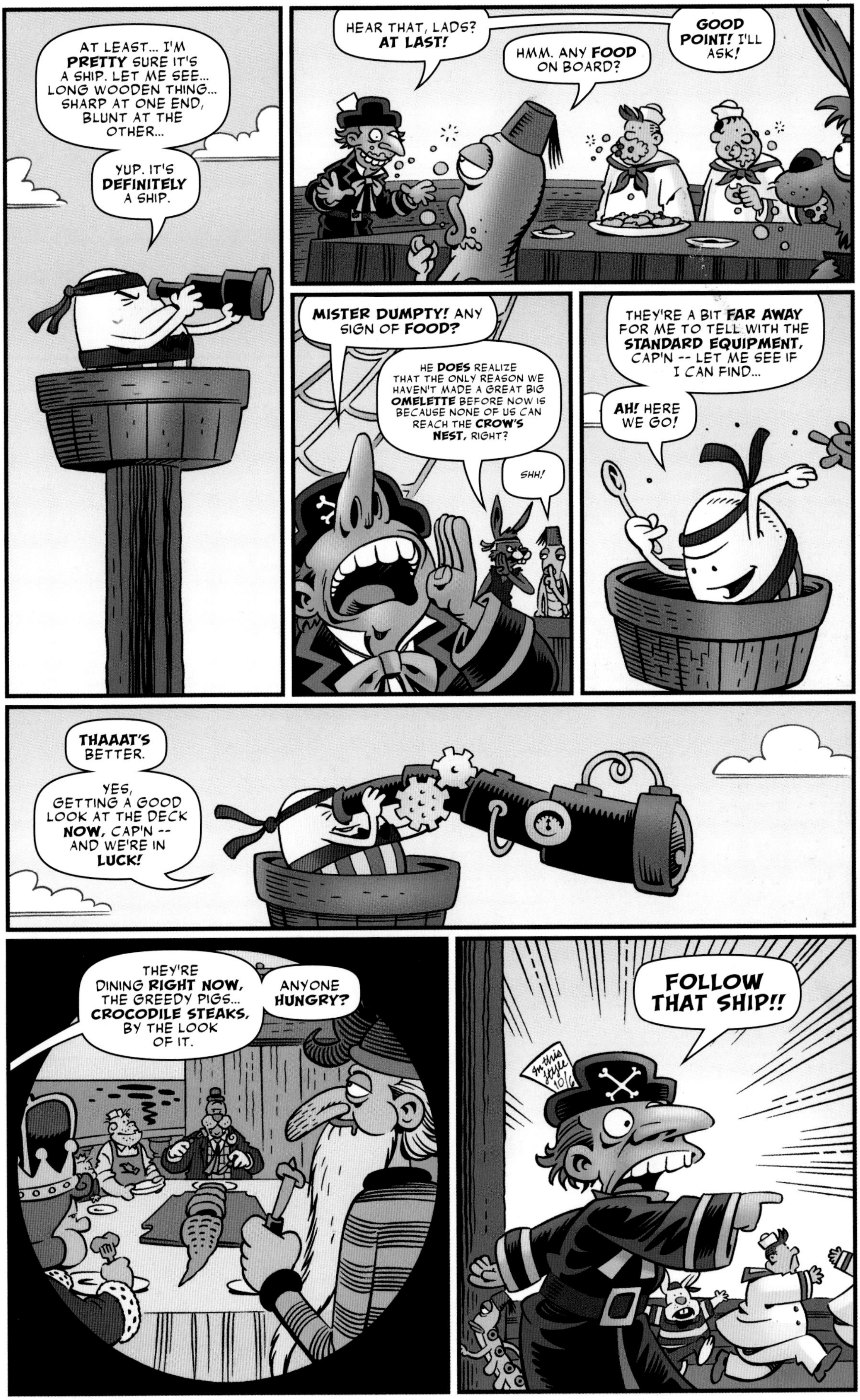
AT LEAST... I'M PRETTY SURE IT'S A SHIP. LET ME SEE... LONG WOODEN THING... SHARP AT ONE END, BLUNT AT THE OTHER...
YUP. IT'S DEFINITELY A SHIP.
HEAR THAT, LADS? AT LAST!
HMM. ANY FOOD ON BOARD?
GOOD POINT! I'LL ASK!
MISTER DUMPTY! ANY SIGN OF FOOD?
HE DOES REALIZE THAT THE ONLY REASON WE HAVEN'T MADE A GREAT BIG OMELETTE BEFORE NOW IS BECAUSE NONE OF US CAN REACH THE CROW'S NEST, RIGHT?
SHH!
THEY'RE A BIT FAR AWAY FOR ME TO TELL WITH THE STANDARD EQUIPMENT, CAP'N -- LET ME SEE IF I CAN FIND...
AH! HERE WE GO!
THAAAT'S BETTER.
YES, GETTING A GOOD LOOK AT THE DECK NOW, CAP'N -- AND WE'RE IN LUCK!
THEY'RE DINING RIGHT NOW, THE GREEDY PIGS... CROCODILE STEAKS, BY THE LOOK OF IT.
ANYONE HUNGRY?
FOLLOW THAT SHIP!!

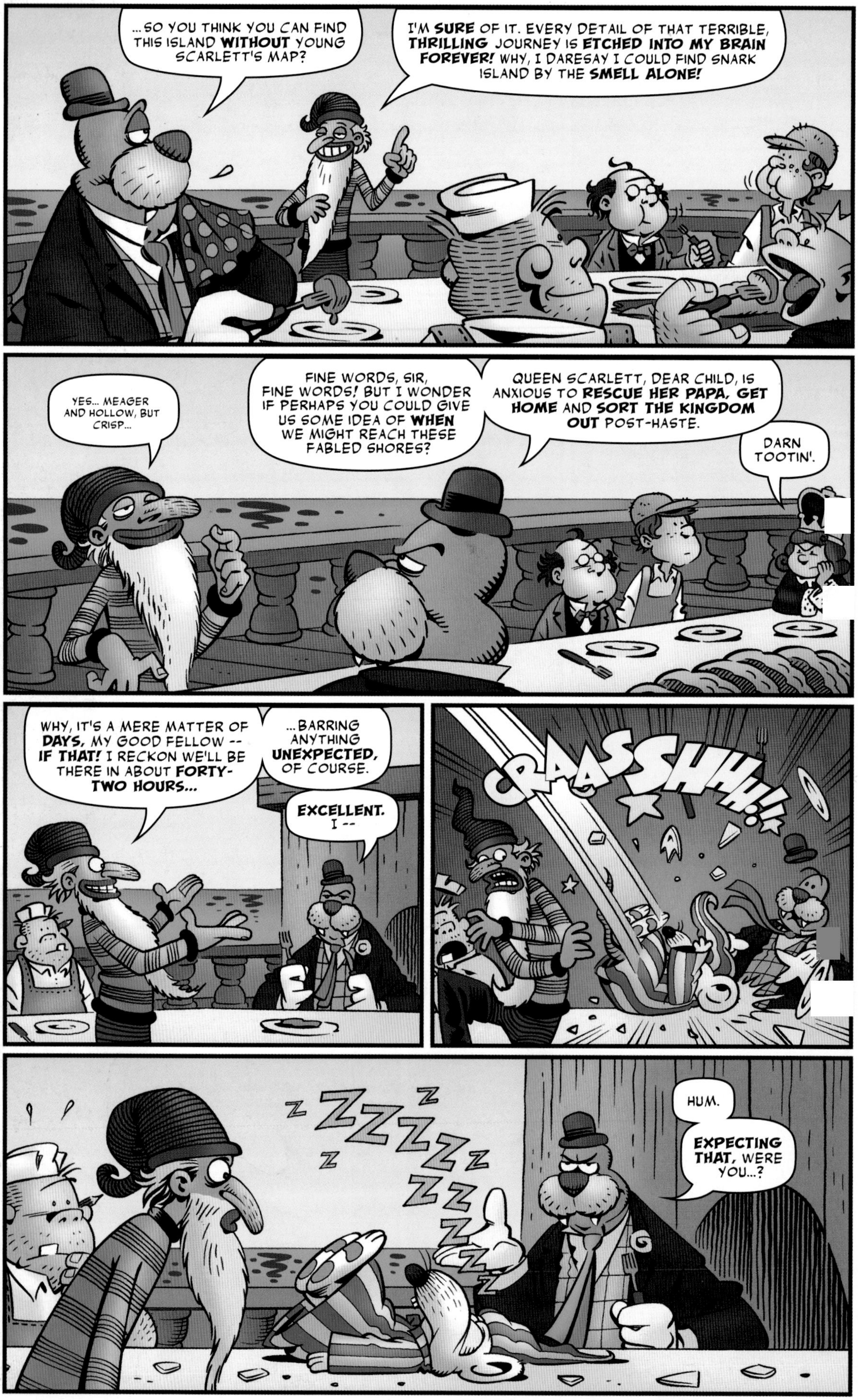

...SO YOU THINK YOU CAN FIND THIS ISLAND WITHOUT YOUNG SCARLETT'S MAP?
I'M SURE OF IT. EVERY DETAIL OF THAT TERRIBLE, THRILLING JOURNEY IS ETCHED INTO MY BRAIN FOREVER! WHY, I DARESAY I COULD FIND SNARK ISLAND BY THE SMELL ALONE!
YES... MEAGER AND HOLLOW, BUT CRISP...
FINE WORDS, SIR, FINE WORDS! BUT I WONDER IF PERHAPS YOU COULD GIVE US SOME IDEA OF WHEN WE MIGHT REACH THESE FABLED SHORES?
QUEEN SCARLETT, DEAR CHILD, IS ANXIOUS TO RESCUE HER PAPA, GET HOME AND SORT THE KINGDOM OUT POST-HASTE.
DARN TOOTIN'.
WHY, IT'S A MERE MATTER OF DAYS, MY GOOD FELLOW -- IF THAT! I RECKON WE'LL BE THERE IN ABOUT FORTY-TWO HOURS...
...BARRING ANYTHING UNEXPECTED, OF COURSE.
EXCELLENT. I --
CRAASSHHH!!!
HUM.
EXPECTING THAT, WERE YOU...?

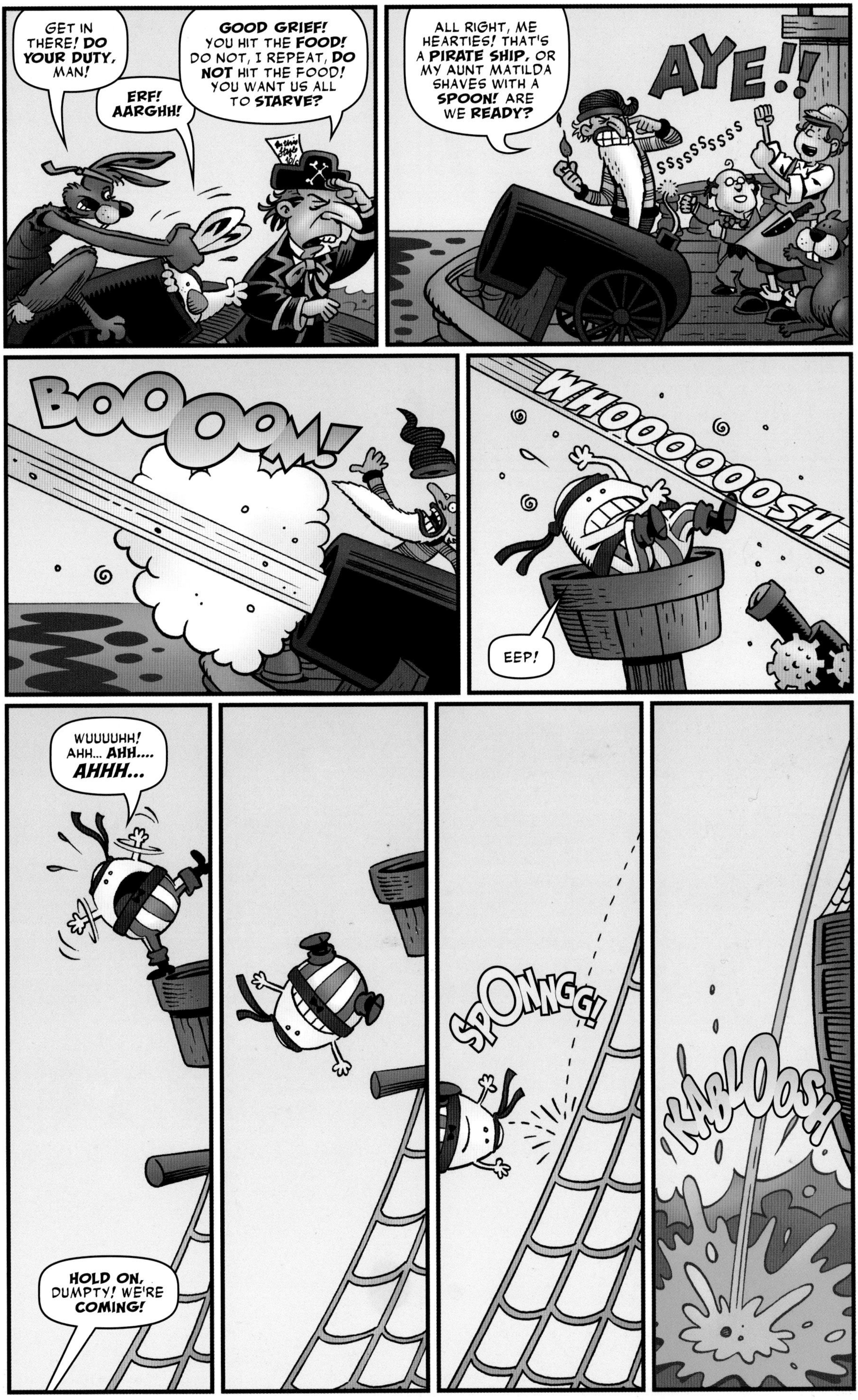
GET IN THERE! DO YOUR DUTY, MAN!
ERF! AARGHH!
GOOD GRIEF! YOU HIT THE FOOD! DO NOT, I REPEAT, DO NOT HIT THE FOOD! YOU WANT US ALL TO STARVE?
ALL RIGHT, ME HEARTIES! THAT'S A PIRATE SHIP, OR MY AUNT MATILDA SHAVES WITH A SPOON! ARE WE READY?
AYE!!
SSSSSSSSSS
BOOOOM!
WHOOOOOOOSH
EEP!
WUUUUHH! AHH... AHH.... AHHH...
HOLD ON, DUMPTY! WE'RE COMING!
SPONNGG!
KABLOOSH

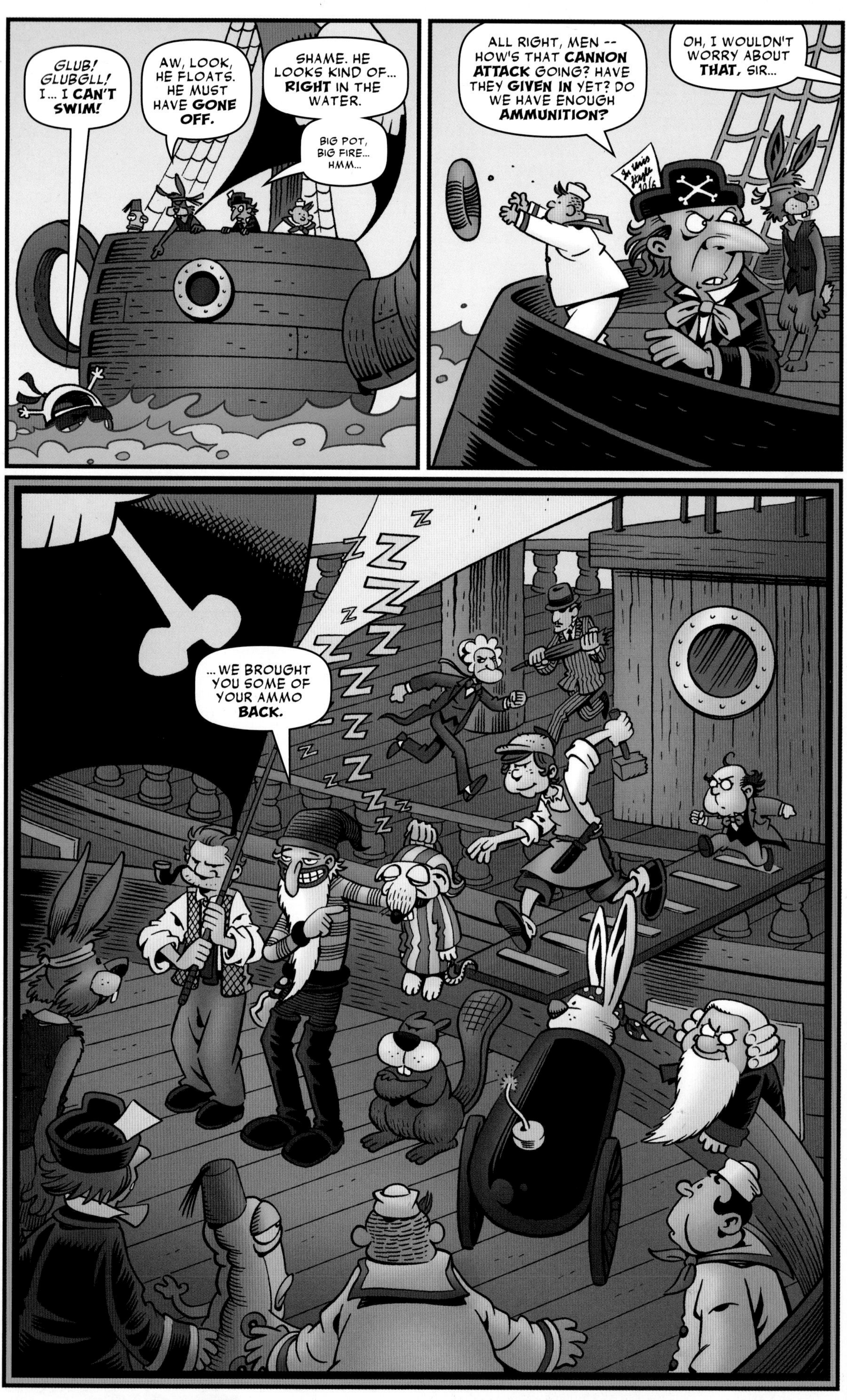
GLUB! GLUBGLL! I... I CAN'T SWIM!
AW, LOOK, HE FLOATS. HE MUST HAVE GONE OFF.
SHAME. HE LOOKS KIND OF... RIGHT IN THE WATER.
BIG POT, BIG FIRE... HMM...
ALL RIGHT, MEN -- HOW'S THAT CANNON ATTACK GOING? HAVE THEY GIVEN IN YET? DO WE HAVE ENOUGH AMMUNITION?
In this style 10/6
OH, I WOULDN'T WORRY ABOUT THAT, SIR...
...WE BROUGHT YOU SOME OF YOUR AMMO BACK.
Z Z Z Z Z

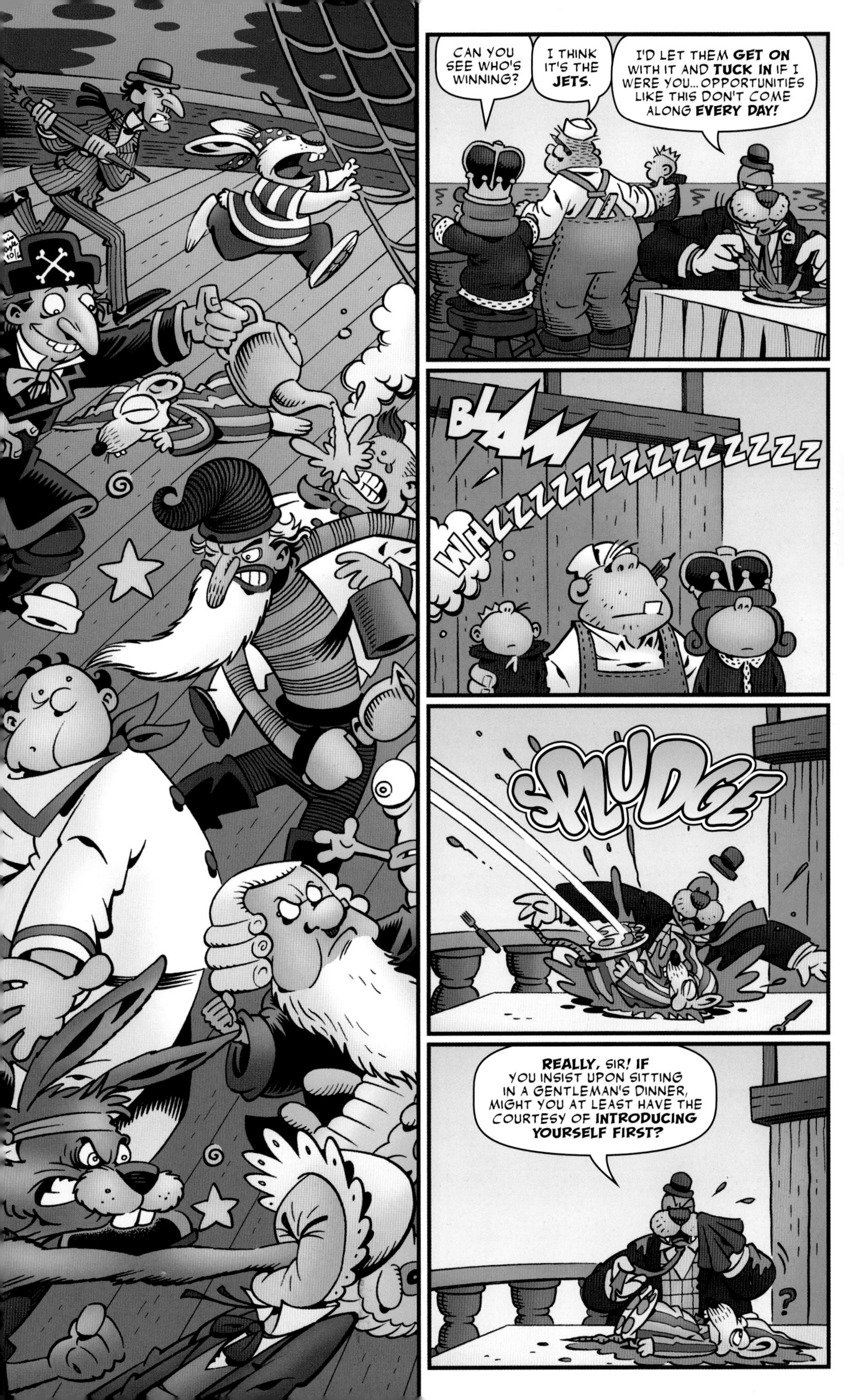
CAN YOU SEE WHO'S WINNING?
I THINK IT'S THE **JETS**.
I'D LET THEM **GET ON** WITH IT AND **TUCK IN** IF I WERE YOU... OPPORTUNITIES LIKE THIS DON'T COME ALONG **EVERY DAY!**
BLAM
WHZZZZZZZZZZZZZZZZ
SPLUDGE
REALLY, SIR! **IF** YOU INSIST UPON SITTING IN A GENTLEMAN'S DINNER, MIGHT YOU AT LEAST HAVE THE COURTESY OF **INTRODUCING YOURSELF FIRST?**
?

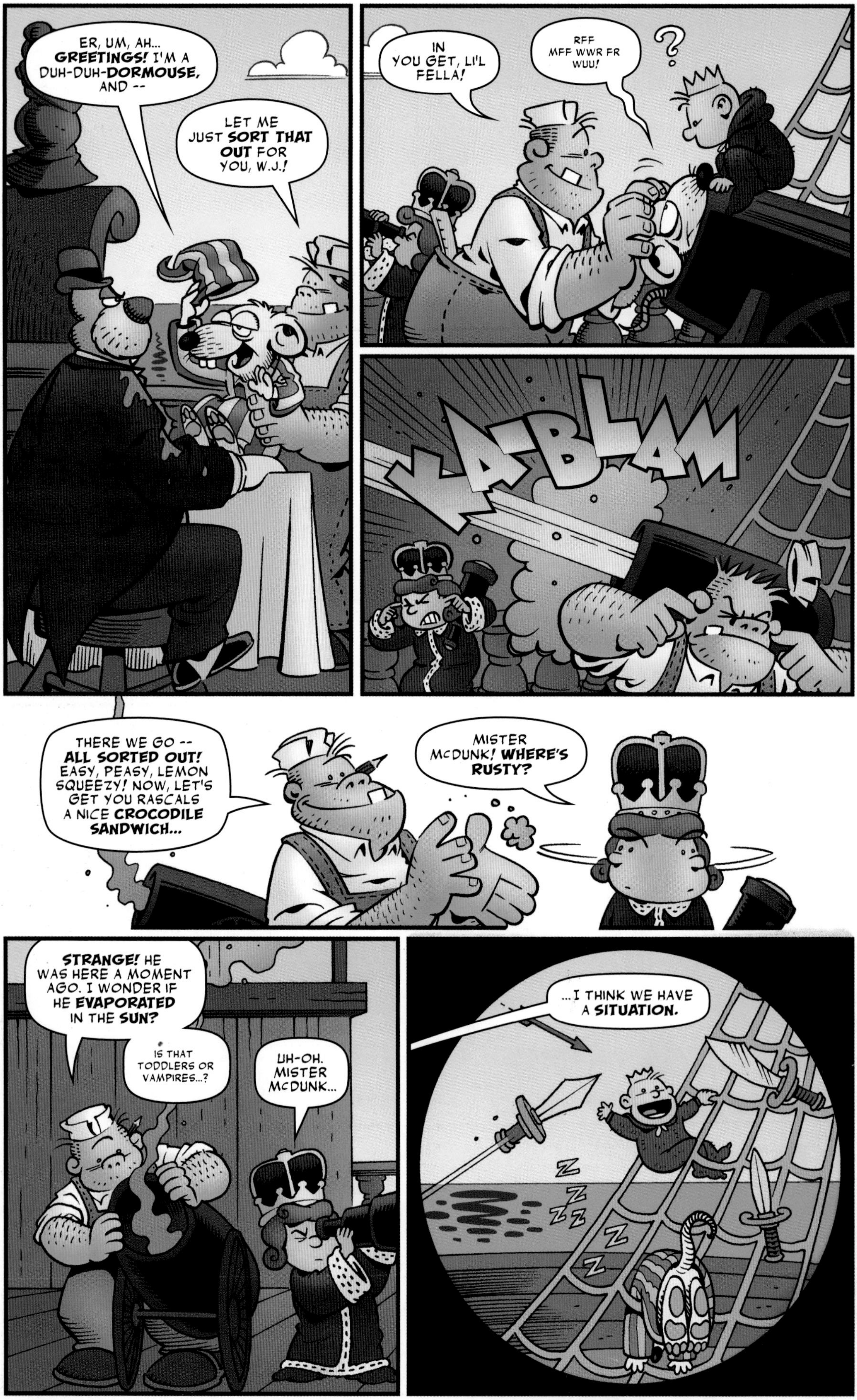
ER, UM, AH... GREETINGS! I'M A DUH-DUH-DORMOUSE, AND --
LET ME JUST SORT THAT OUT FOR YOU, W.J.!
IN YOU GET, LI'L FELLA!
RFF MFF WWR FR WUU!
?
KA-BLAM
THERE WE GO -- ALL SORTED OUT! EASY, PEASY, LEMON SQUEEZY! NOW, LET'S GET YOU RASCALS A NICE CROCODILE SANDWICH...
MISTER McDUNK! WHERE'S RUSTY?
STRANGE! HE WAS HERE A MOMENT AGO. I WONDER IF HE EVAPORATED IN THE SUN?
IS THAT TODDLERS OR VAMPIRES...?
UH-OH. MISTER McDUNK...
...I THINK WE HAVE A SITUATION.
Z Z Z Z Z Z

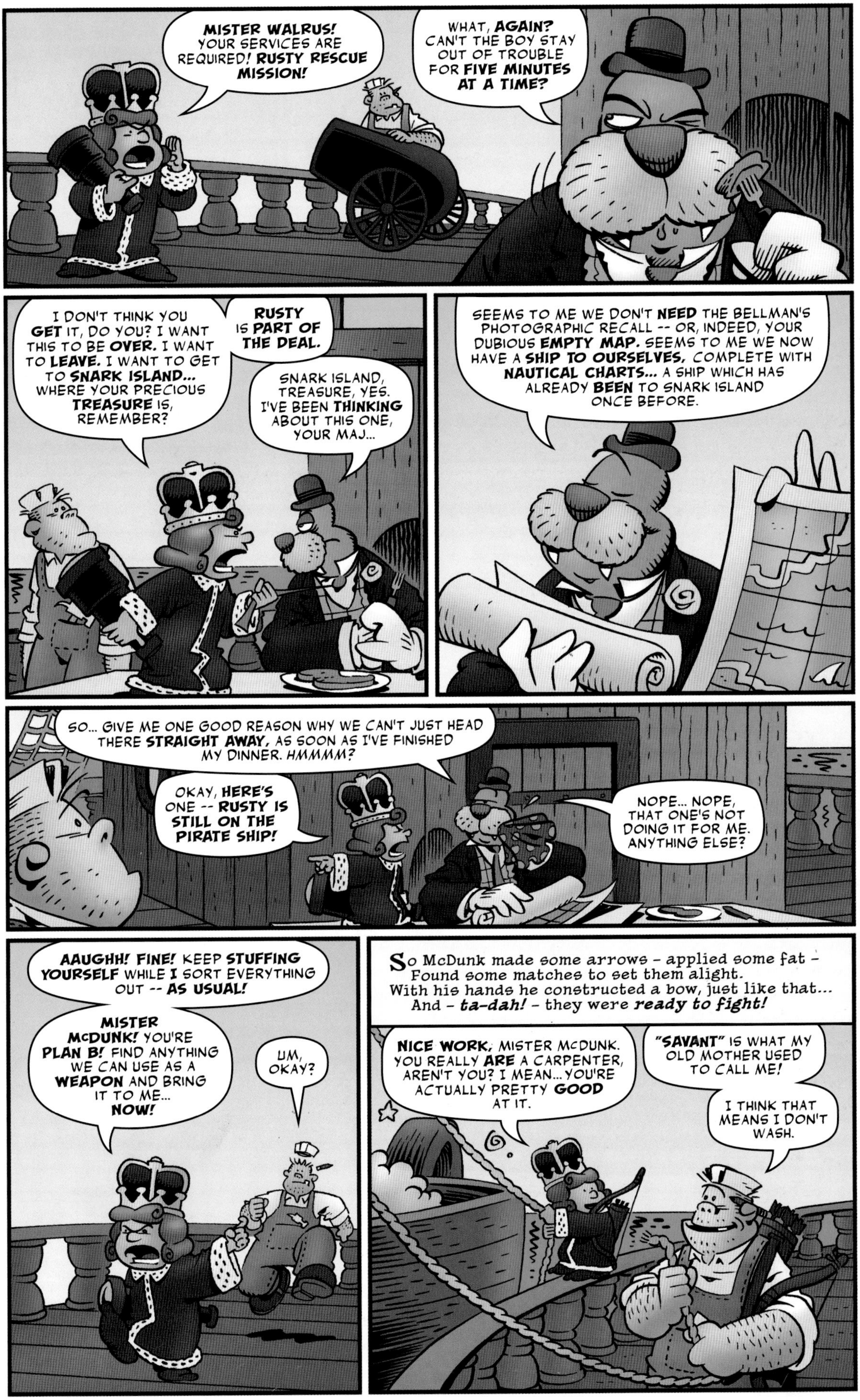
MISTER WALRUS! YOUR SERVICES ARE REQUIRED! RUSTY RESCUE MISSION!
WHAT, AGAIN? CAN'T THE BOY STAY OUT OF TROUBLE FOR FIVE MINUTES AT A TIME?
I DON'T THINK YOU GET IT, DO YOU? I WANT THIS TO BE OVER. I WANT TO LEAVE. I WANT TO GET TO SNARK ISLAND... WHERE YOUR PRECIOUS TREASURE IS, REMEMBER?
RUSTY IS PART OF THE DEAL.
SNARK ISLAND, TREASURE, YES. I'VE BEEN THINKING ABOUT THIS ONE, YOUR MAJ...
SEEMS TO ME WE DON'T NEED THE BELLMAN'S PHOTOGRAPHIC RECALL -- OR, INDEED, YOUR DUBIOUS EMPTY MAP. SEEMS TO ME WE NOW HAVE A SHIP TO OURSELVES, COMPLETE WITH NAUTICAL CHARTS... A SHIP WHICH HAS ALREADY BEEN TO SNARK ISLAND ONCE BEFORE.
SO... GIVE ME ONE GOOD REASON WHY WE CAN'T JUST HEAD THERE STRAIGHT AWAY, AS SOON AS I'VE FINISHED MY DINNER. HMMMM?
OKAY, HERE'S ONE -- RUSTY IS STILL ON THE PIRATE SHIP!
NOPE... NOPE, THAT ONE'S NOT DOING IT FOR ME. ANYTHING ELSE?
AAUGHH! FINE! KEEP STUFFING YOURSELF WHILE I SORT EVERYTHING OUT -- AS USUAL!
MISTER McDUNK! YOU'RE PLAN B! FIND ANYTHING WE CAN USE AS A WEAPON AND BRING IT TO ME... NOW!
UM, OKAY?
So McDunk made some arrows - applied some fat -
Found some matches to set them alight.
With his hands he constructed a bow, just like that...
And - ta-dah! - they were ready to fight!
NICE WORK, MISTER McDUNK. YOU REALLY ARE A CARPENTER, AREN'T YOU? I MEAN... YOU'RE ACTUALLY PRETTY GOOD AT IT.
"SAVANT" IS WHAT MY OLD MOTHER USED TO CALL ME!
I THINK THAT MEANS I DON'T WASH.

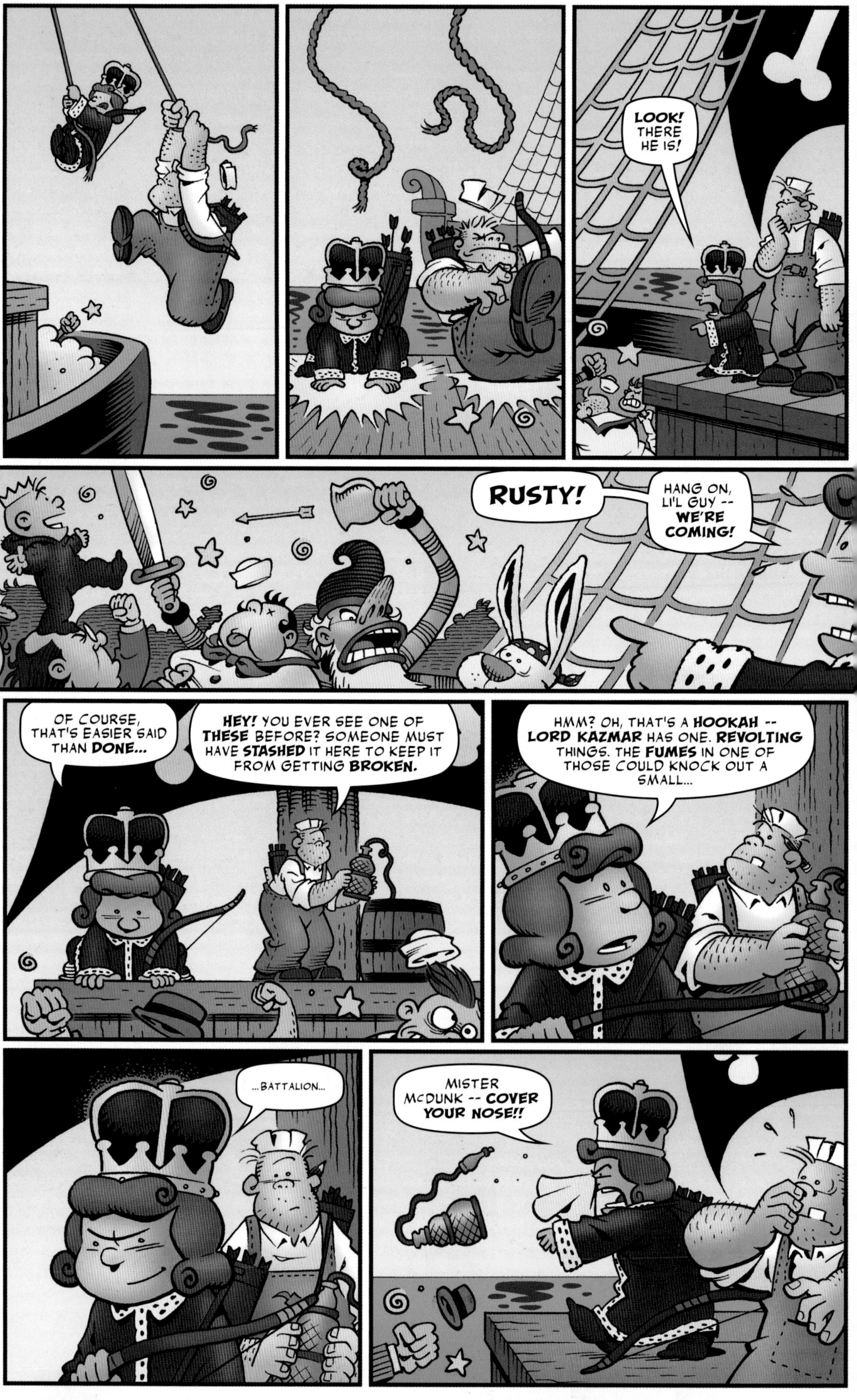
LOOK! THERE HE IS!
RUSTY!
HANG ON, LI'L GUY -- WE'RE COMING!
OF COURSE, THAT'S EASIER SAID THAN DONE...
HEY! YOU EVER SEE ONE OF THESE BEFORE? SOMEONE MUST HAVE STASHED IT HERE TO KEEP IT FROM GETTING BROKEN.
HMM? OH, THAT'S A HOOKAH -- LORD KAZMAR HAS ONE. REVOLTING THINGS. THE FUMES IN ONE OF THOSE COULD KNOCK OUT A SMALL...
...BATTALION...
MISTER McDUNK -- COVER YOUR NOSE!!

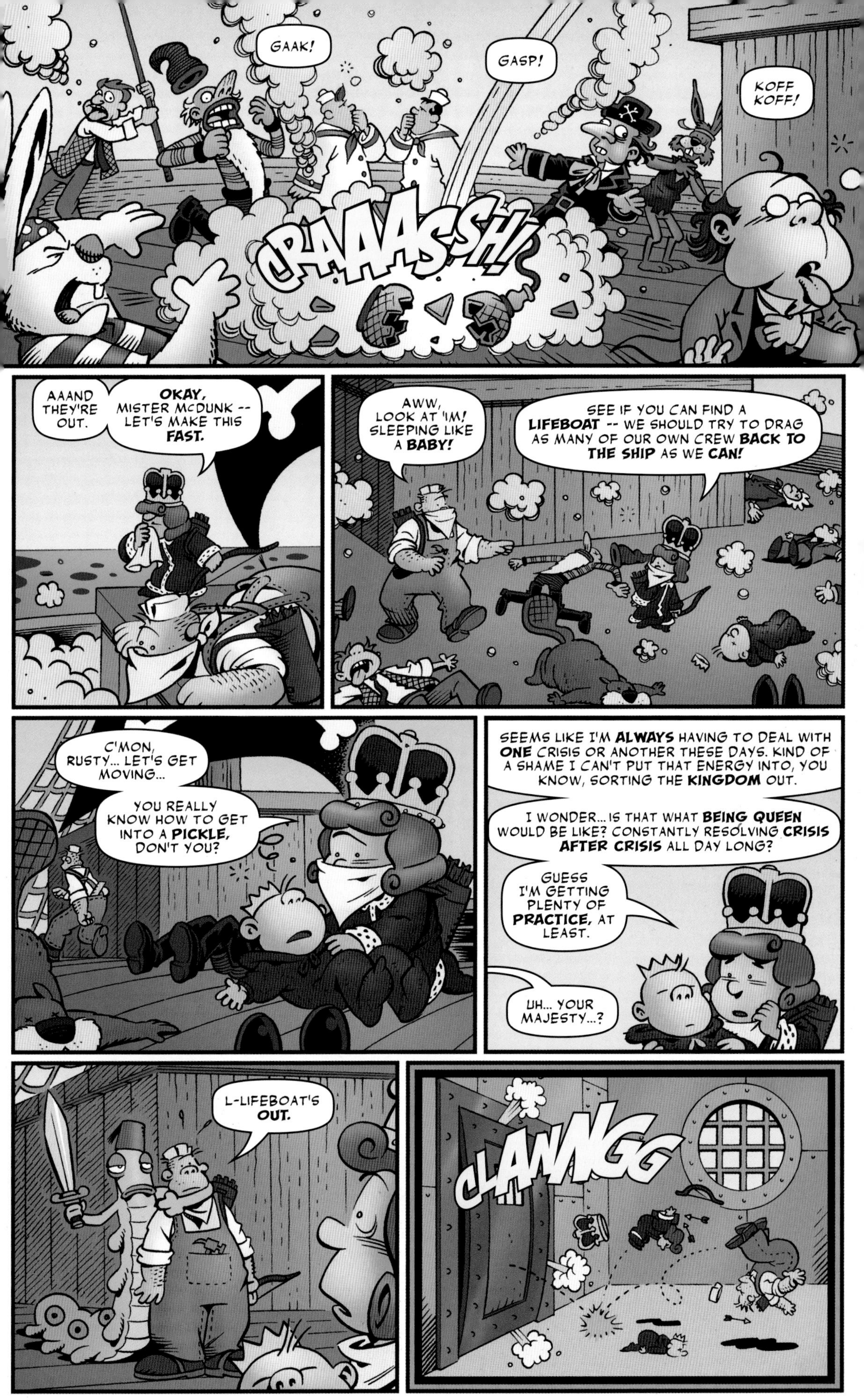
GAAK!
GASP!
KOFF KOFF!
CRAAASSH!
AAAND THEY'RE OUT.
OKAY, MISTER McDUNK -- LET'S MAKE THIS FAST.
AWW, LOOK AT 'IM! SLEEPING LIKE A BABY!
SEE IF YOU CAN FIND A LIFEBOAT -- WE SHOULD TRY TO DRAG AS MANY OF OUR OWN CREW BACK TO THE SHIP AS WE CAN!
C'MON, RUSTY... LET'S GET MOVING...
YOU REALLY KNOW HOW TO GET INTO A PICKLE, DON'T YOU?
SEEMS LIKE I'M ALWAYS HAVING TO DEAL WITH ONE CRISIS OR ANOTHER THESE DAYS. KIND OF A SHAME I CAN'T PUT THAT ENERGY INTO, YOU KNOW, SORTING THE KINGDOM OUT.
I WONDER... IS THAT WHAT BEING QUEEN WOULD BE LIKE? CONSTANTLY RESOLVING CRISIS AFTER CRISIS ALL DAY LONG?
GUESS I'M GETTING PLENTY OF PRACTICE, AT LEAST.
UH... YOUR MAJESTY...?
L-LIFEBOAT'S OUT.
CLANNGG

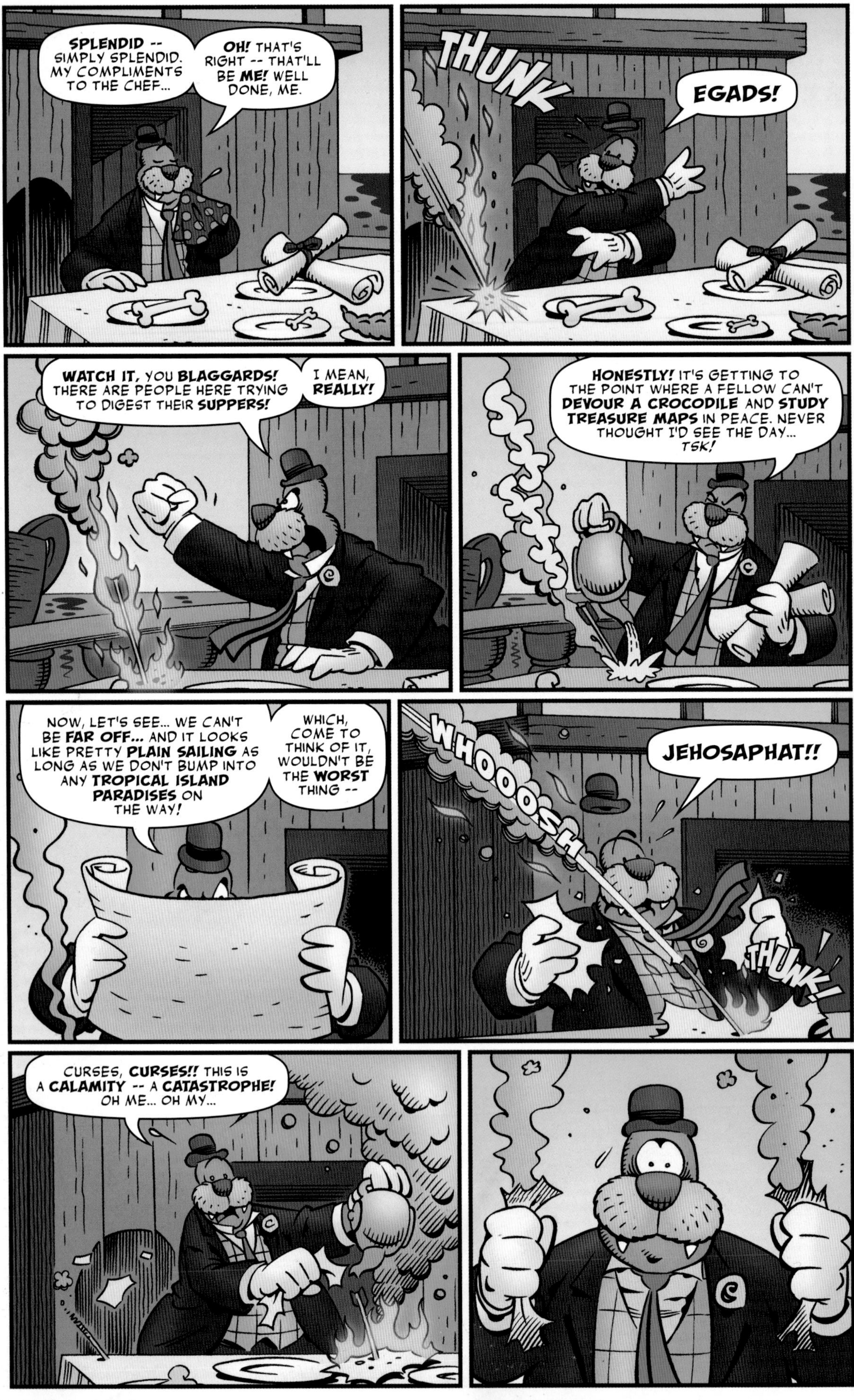

SPLENDID -- SIMPLY SPLENDID. MY COMPLIMENTS TO THE CHEF...
OH! THAT'S RIGHT -- THAT'LL BE ME! WELL DONE, ME.
THUNK
EGADS!
WATCH IT, YOU BLAGGARDS! THERE ARE PEOPLE HERE TRYING TO DIGEST THEIR SUPPERS!
I MEAN, REALLY!
SSSSSSH
HONESTLY! IT'S GETTING TO THE POINT WHERE A FELLOW CAN'T DEVOUR A CROCODILE AND STUDY TREASURE MAPS IN PEACE. NEVER THOUGHT I'D SEE THE DAY... TSK!
NOW, LET'S SEE... WE CAN'T BE FAR OFF... AND IT LOOKS LIKE PRETTY PLAIN SAILING AS LONG AS WE DON'T BUMP INTO ANY TROPICAL ISLAND PARADISES ON THE WAY!
WHICH, COME TO THINK OF IT, WOULDN'T BE THE WORST THING --
WHOOOOSH
JEHOSAPHAT!!
THUNK!!
CURSES, CURSES!! THIS IS A CALAMITY -- A CATASTROPHE! OH ME... OH MY...

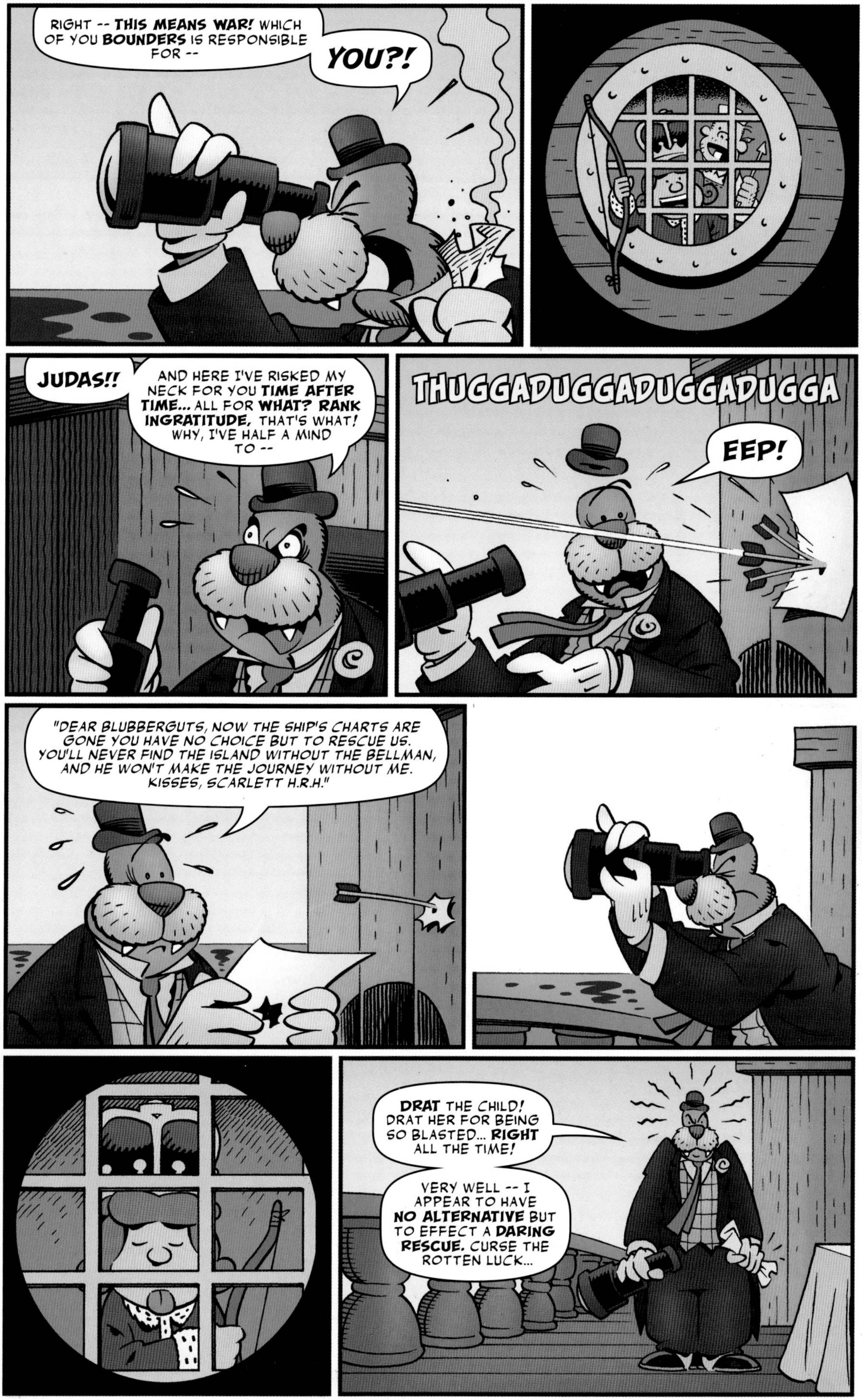
RIGHT -- THIS MEANS WAR! WHICH OF YOU BOUNDERS IS RESPONSIBLE FOR --
YOU?!
JUDAS!!
AND HERE I'VE RISKED MY NECK FOR YOU TIME AFTER TIME... ALL FOR WHAT? RANK INGRATITUDE, THAT'S WHAT! WHY, I'VE HALF A MIND TO --
THUGGADUGGADUGGADUGGA
EEP!
"DEAR BLUBBERGUTS, NOW THE SHIP'S CHARTS ARE GONE YOU HAVE NO CHOICE BUT TO RESCUE US. YOU'LL NEVER FIND THE ISLAND WITHOUT THE BELLMAN, AND HE WON'T MAKE THE JOURNEY WITHOUT ME. KISSES, SCARLETT H.R.H."
DRAT THE CHILD! DRAT HER FOR BEING SO BLASTED... RIGHT ALL THE TIME!
VERY WELL -- I APPEAR TO HAVE NO ALTERNATIVE BUT TO EFFECT A DARING RESCUE. CURSE THE ROTTEN LUCK...

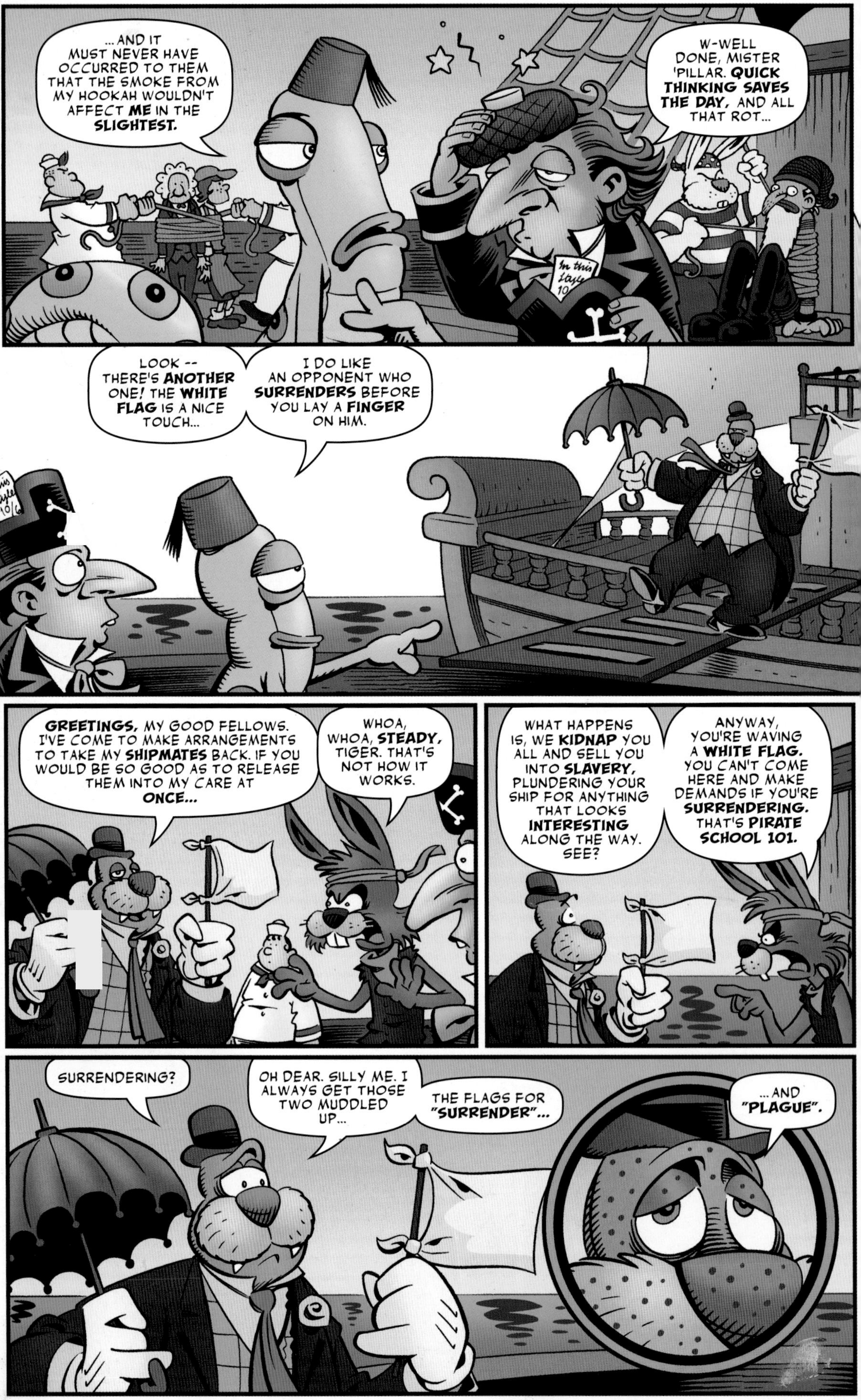
...AND IT MUST NEVER HAVE OCCURRED TO THEM THAT THE SMOKE FROM MY HOOKAH WOULDN'T AFFECT **ME** IN THE **SLIGHTEST.**
W-WELL DONE, MISTER 'PILLAR. **QUICK THINKING SAVES THE DAY,** AND ALL THAT ROT...
LOOK -- THERE'S **ANOTHER** ONE! THE **WHITE FLAG** IS A NICE TOUCH...
I DO LIKE AN OPPONENT WHO **SURRENDERS** BEFORE YOU LAY A **FINGER** ON HIM.
GREETINGS, MY GOOD FELLOWS. I'VE COME TO MAKE ARRANGEMENTS TO TAKE MY **SHIPMATES** BACK. IF YOU WOULD BE SO GOOD AS TO RELEASE THEM INTO MY CARE AT **ONCE...**
WHOA, WHOA, **STEADY,** TIGER. THAT'S NOT HOW IT WORKS.
WHAT HAPPENS IS, WE **KIDNAP** YOU ALL AND SELL YOU INTO **SLAVERY,** PLUNDERING YOUR SHIP FOR ANYTHING THAT LOOKS **INTERESTING** ALONG THE WAY. SEE?
ANYWAY, YOU'RE WAVING A **WHITE FLAG.** YOU CAN'T COME HERE AND MAKE DEMANDS IF YOU'RE **SURRENDERING.** THAT'S **PIRATE SCHOOL 101.**
SURRENDERING?
OH DEAR. SILLY ME. I ALWAYS GET THOSE TWO MUDDLED UP...
THE FLAGS FOR **"SURRENDER"...**
...AND **"PLAGUE".**

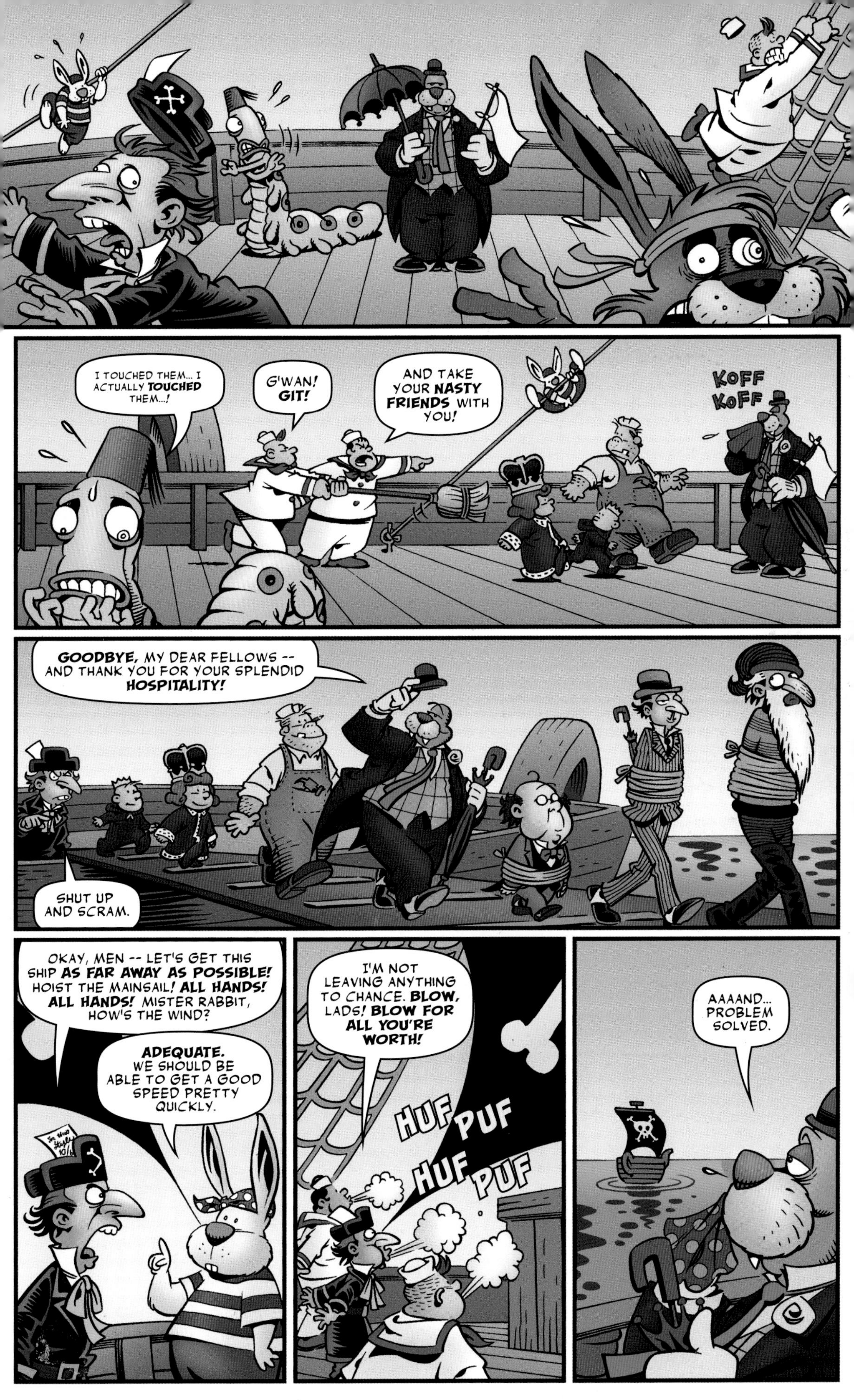
I TOUCHED THEM... I ACTUALLY TOUCHED THEM...!
G'WAN! GIT!
AND TAKE YOUR NASTY FRIENDS WITH YOU!
KOFF KOFF
GOODBYE, MY DEAR FELLOWS -- AND THANK YOU FOR YOUR SPLENDID HOSPITALITY!
SHUT UP AND SCRAM.
OKAY, MEN -- LET'S GET THIS SHIP AS FAR AWAY AS POSSIBLE! HOIST THE MAINSAIL! ALL HANDS! ALL HANDS! MISTER RABBIT, HOW'S THE WIND?
ADEQUATE. WE SHOULD BE ABLE TO GET A GOOD SPEED PRETTY QUICKLY.
I'M NOT LEAVING ANYTHING TO CHANCE. BLOW, LADS! BLOW FOR ALL YOU'RE WORTH!
HUF PUF
HUF PUF
AAAAND... PROBLEM SOLVED.

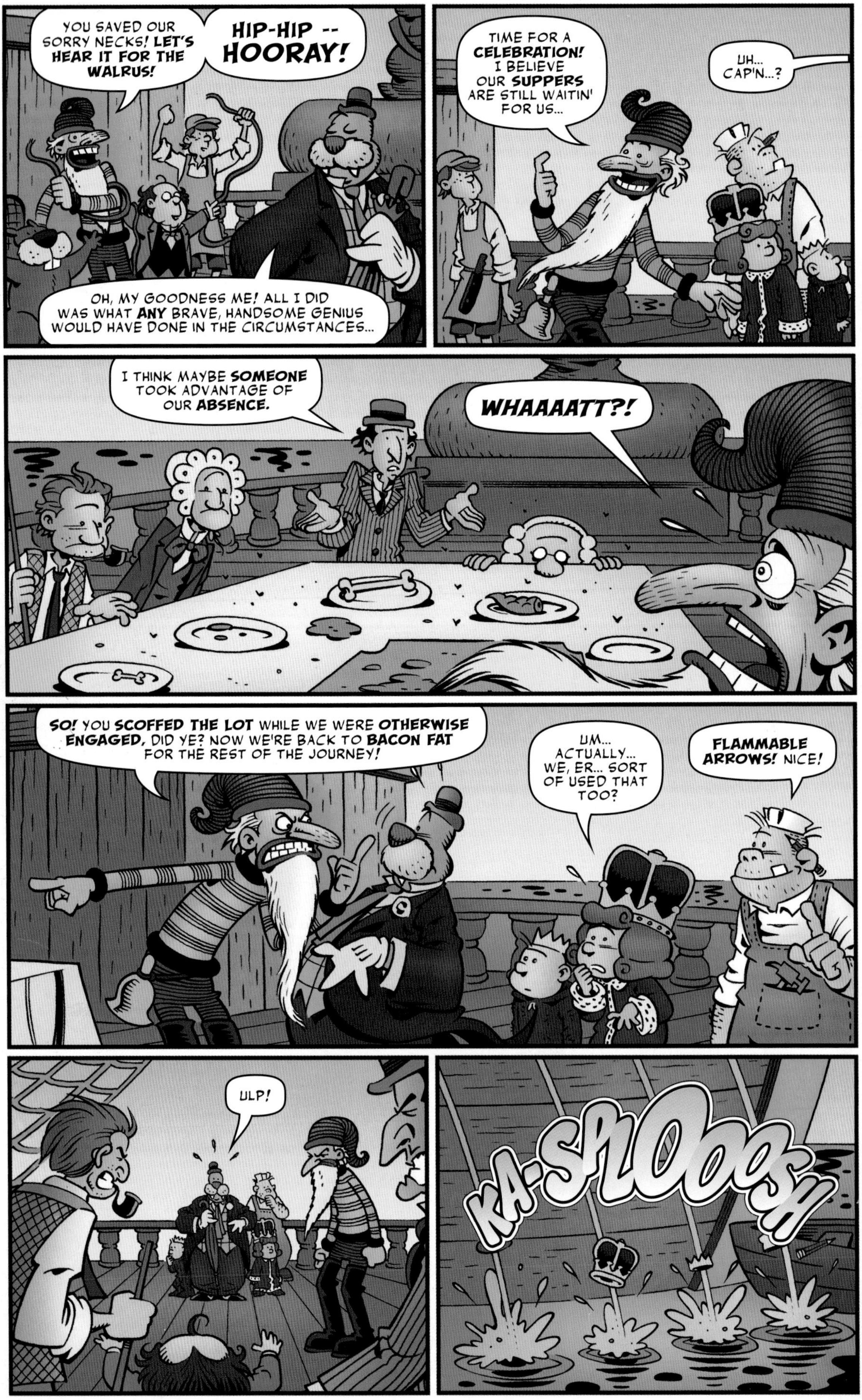

YOU SAVED OUR SORRY NECKS! LET'S HEAR IT FOR THE WALRUS!
HIP-HIP -- HOORAY!
OH, MY GOODNESS ME! ALL I DID WAS WHAT ANY BRAVE, HANDSOME GENIUS WOULD HAVE DONE IN THE CIRCUMSTANCES...
TIME FOR A CELEBRATION! I BELIEVE OUR SUPPERS ARE STILL WAITIN' FOR US...
UH... CAP'N...?
I THINK MAYBE SOMEONE TOOK ADVANTAGE OF OUR ABSENCE.
WHAAAATT?!
SO! YOU SCOFFED THE LOT WHILE WE WERE OTHERWISE ENGAGED, DID YE? NOW WE'RE BACK TO BACON FAT FOR THE REST OF THE JOURNEY!
UM... ACTUALLY... WE, ER... SORT OF USED THAT TOO?
FLAMMABLE ARROWS! NICE!
ULP!
KA-SPLOOOSH

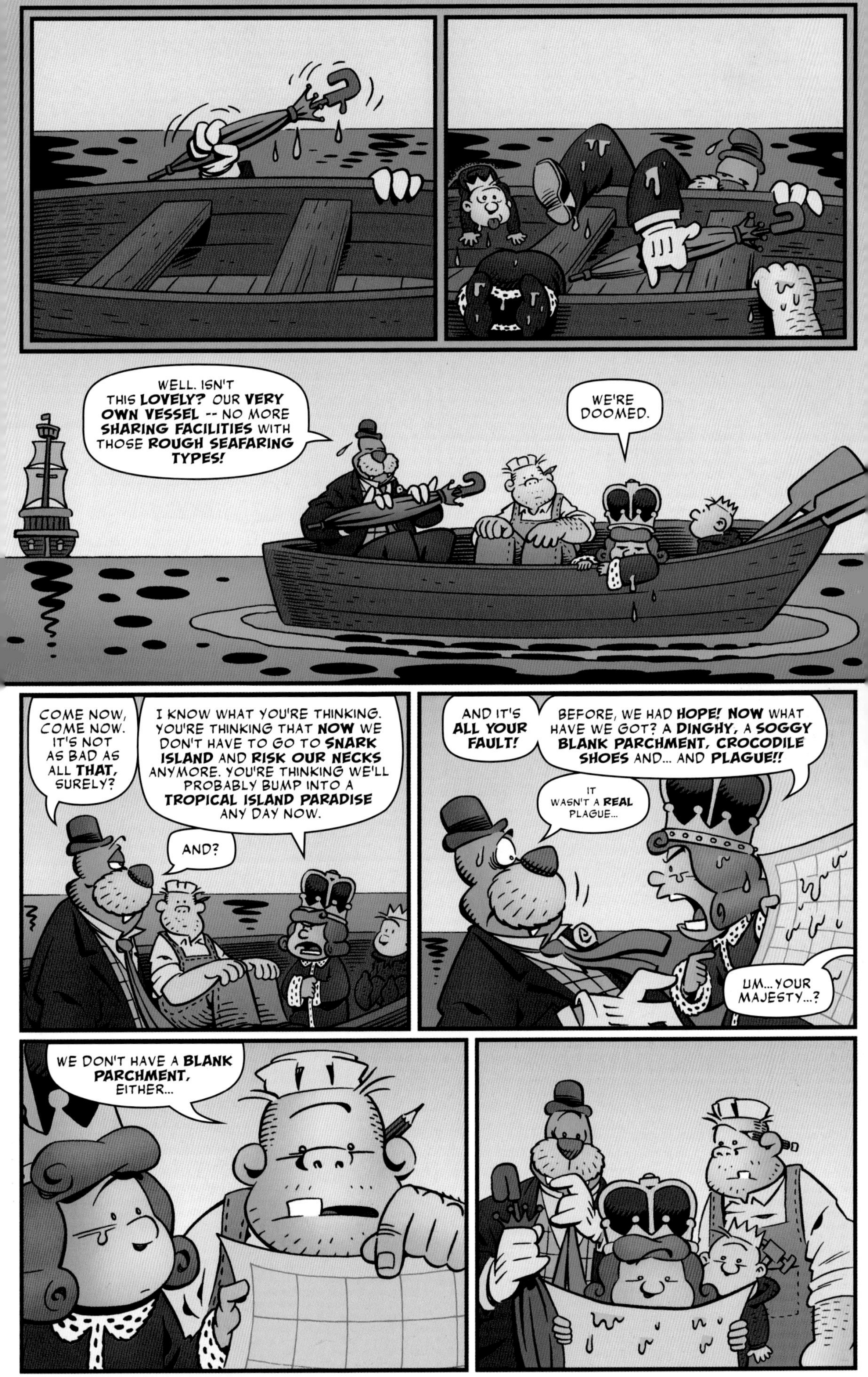
WELL. ISN'T THIS LOVELY? OUR VERY OWN VESSEL -- NO MORE SHARING FACILITIES WITH THOSE ROUGH SEAFARING TYPES!
WE'RE DOOMED.
COME NOW, COME NOW. IT'S NOT AS BAD AS ALL THAT, SURELY?
I KNOW WHAT YOU'RE THINKING. YOU'RE THINKING THAT NOW WE DON'T HAVE TO GO TO SNARK ISLAND AND RISK OUR NECKS ANYMORE. YOU'RE THINKING WE'LL PROBABLY BUMP INTO A TROPICAL ISLAND PARADISE ANY DAY NOW.
AND?
AND IT'S ALL YOUR FAULT!
BEFORE, WE HAD HOPE! NOW WHAT HAVE WE GOT? A DINGHY, A SOGGY BLANK PARCHMENT, CROCODILE SHOES AND... AND PLAGUE!!
IT WASN'T A REAL PLAGUE...
UM...YOUR MAJESTY...?
WE DON'T HAVE A BLANK PARCHMENT, EITHER...

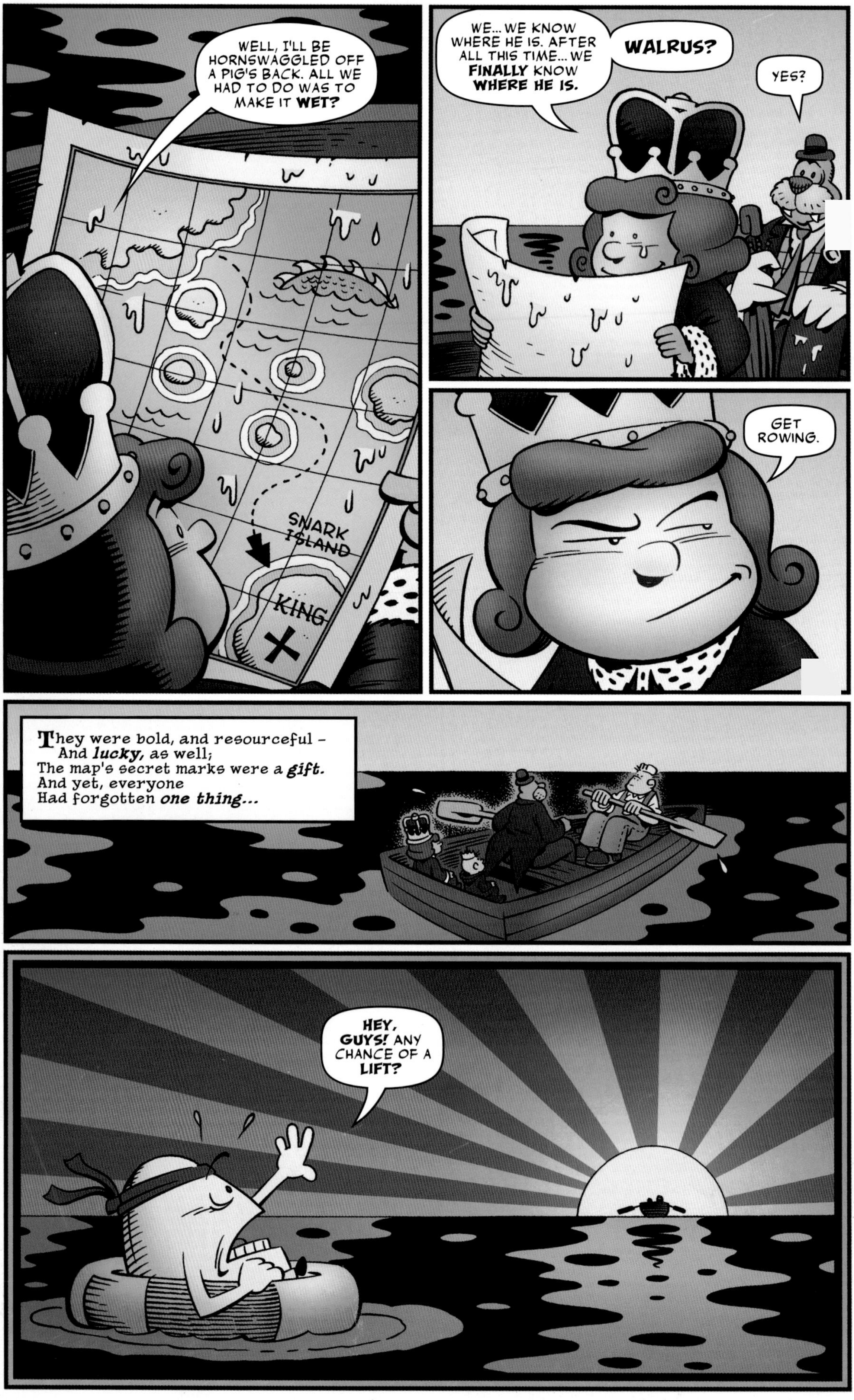
WELL, I'LL BE HORNSWAGGLED OFF A PIG'S BACK. ALL WE HAD TO DO WAS TO MAKE IT WET?
SNARK ISLAND
KING
WE... WE KNOW WHERE HE IS. AFTER ALL THIS TIME... WE FINALLY KNOW WHERE HE IS.
WALRUS?
YES?
GET ROWING.
They were bold, and resourceful –
And lucky, as well;
The map's secret marks were a gift.
And yet, everyone
Had forgotten one thing...
HEY, GUYS! ANY CHANCE OF A LIFT?

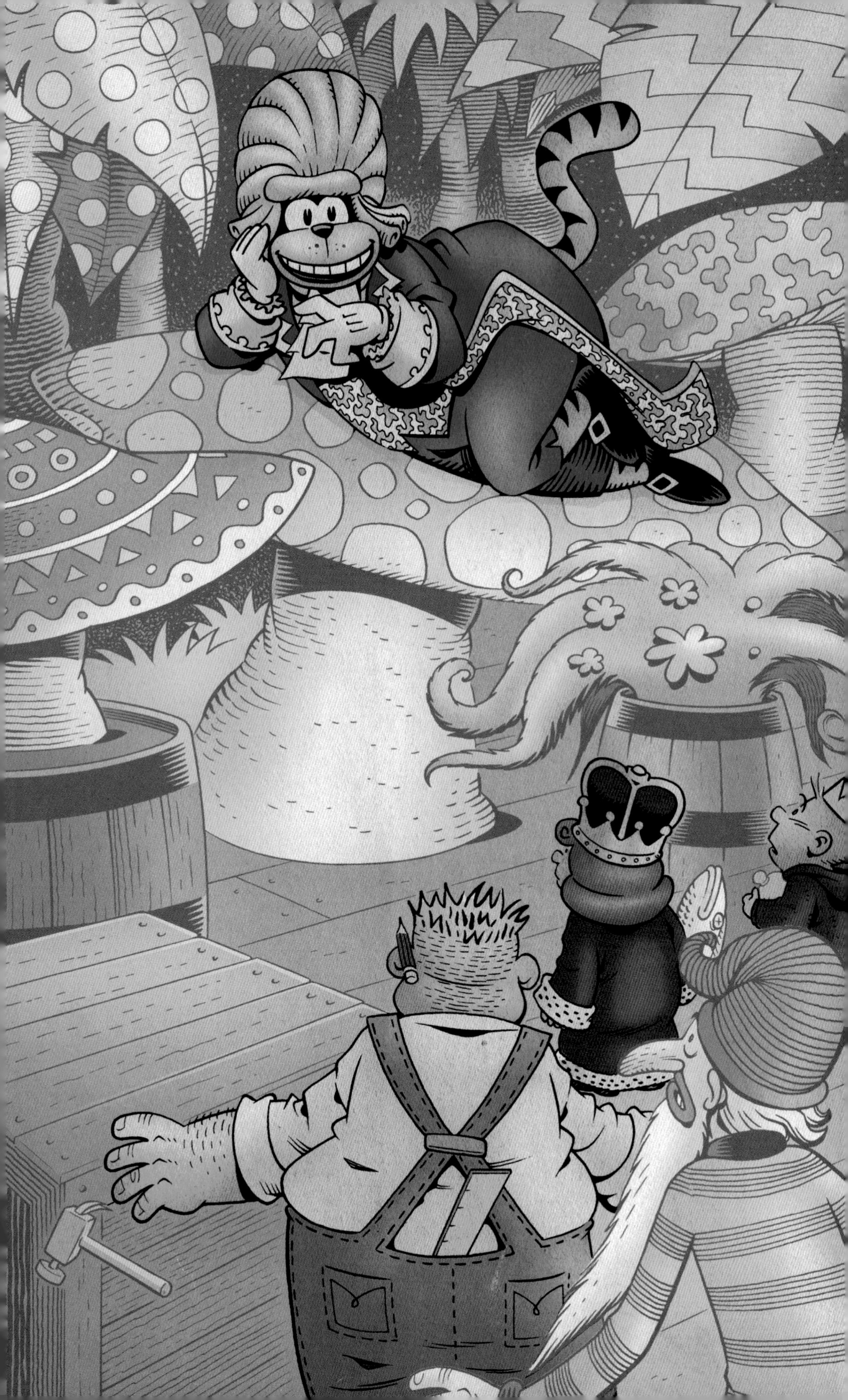

FIT THE SEVENTH

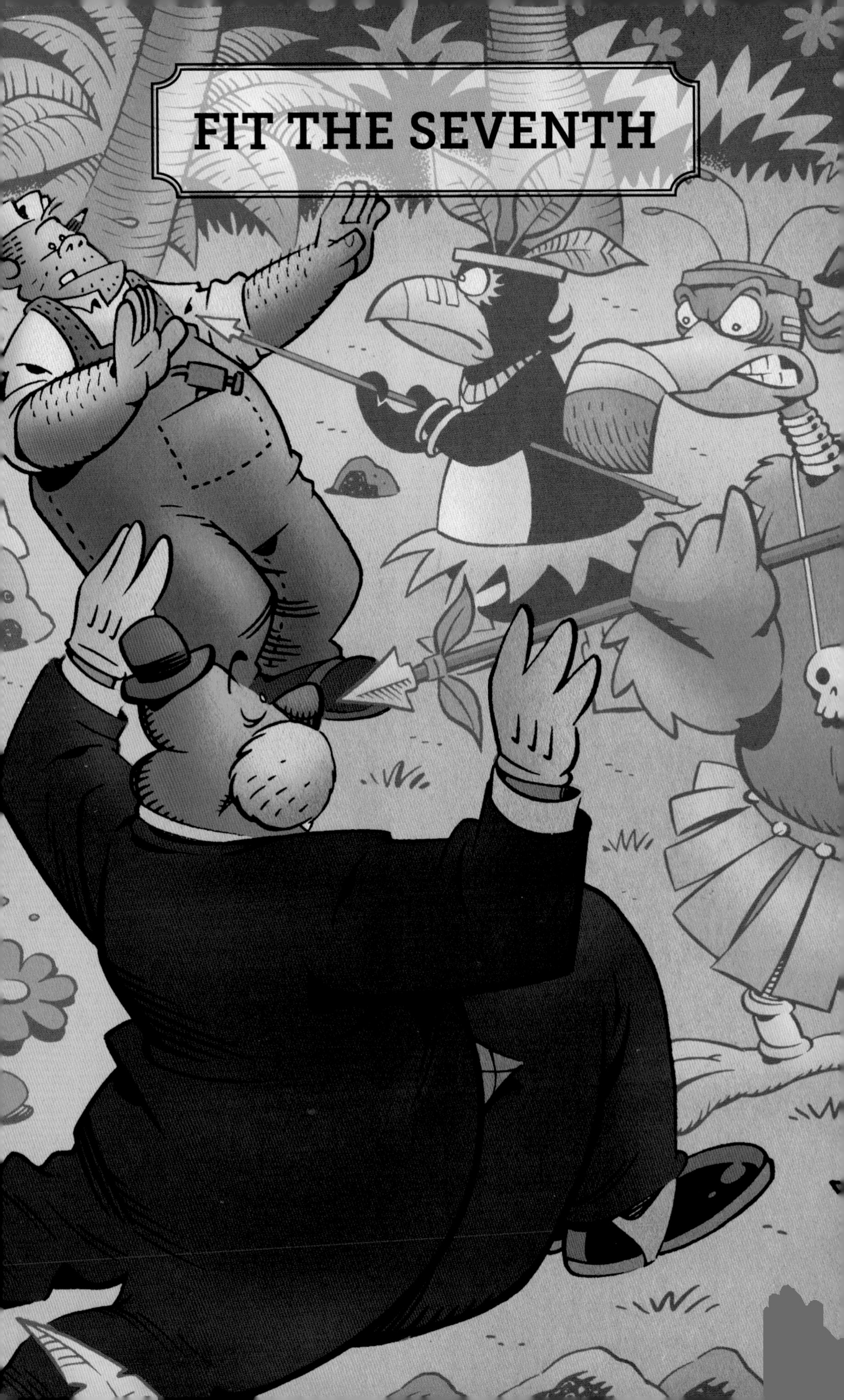

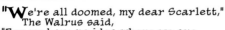 "**W**e're all doomed, my dear Scarlett,"
The Walrus said,
"For we have no idea where we are.
Yet you constantly want us to row to Snark Isle;
Don't you think it will be rather far?"

THIS IS **RIDICULOUS.**

COME ON, WALRUS -- YOU'RE JUST **NOT TRYING!** WE HAVE A **MAP**, DON'T WE? WE HAVE A **BOAT, OARS** AND **EIGHT STRONG ARMS** BETWEEN US!

AND **NO NAVIGATIONAL INSTRUMENTS WHATSOEVER!** CAN **YOU** TELL WHERE WE ARE BY LOOKING AT THE STARS? BECAUSE I MOST CERTAINLY CAN **NOT!**

WOW. YOU REALLY ARE A **CUP-HALF-EMPTY** KIND OF GUY, AREN'T YOU?

NO, I'M SIMPLY NOT LIVING IN A **FANTASY WORLD** HELD TOGETHER BY GIRLISH DREAMS AND **SHEER WILLPOWER**, UNLIKE **SOME** PEOPLE!

OUR BEST HOPE -- OUR **ONLY** HOPE -- IS TO BE **RESCUED** BY SOME **PASSING VESSEL.** UNLESS THAT HAPPENS, WE'RE ALL DEAD. **DEAD**, I SAY!

OH, **POOH!** LOOK... WE'VE GOT A **BOAT**, WE CAUGHT THAT **SARDINE** TWO DAYS AGO, AND THE SEA HAS BEEN **LOVELY AND CALM** THE WHOLE TIME.

THINK HOW MUCH **WORSE OFF** WE COULD BE! THE **WEATHER** HAS BEEN **WONDERFUL...** RIGHT?

RRRRMMMBLLLLE

So it rained. And our heroes
Clung on for dear life,
As the storm filled the blackening sky.
Yet Scarlett steadfastly
Refused to lose heart...

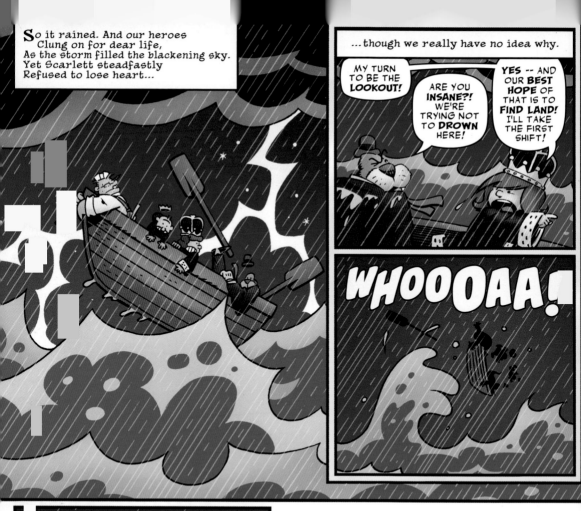

...though we really have no idea why.

MY TURN TO BE THE LOOKOUT!

ARE YOU INSANE?! WE'RE TRYING NOT TO DROWN HERE!

YES -- AND OUR BEST HOPE OF THAT IS TO FIND LAND! I'LL TAKE THE FIRST SHIFT!

WHOOOAA!

GLORP!

GOT YOU, YOU LITTLE RASCAL! YOU'RE NOT RUNNING OFF THIS TIME!

GEE, W.J. -- YOU STOPPED ME FALLING OVERBOARD! YOU REALLY ARE A TRUE FRIEND!

WHY, THINK NOTHING OF IT, MY DEAR MCDUNK... CAN'T HAVE YOU FEEDING THE ANCHOVIES, NOW, CAN WE?

THAT WOULD BE... A TERRIBLE WASTE.

YOUR MOVE, McDUNK...

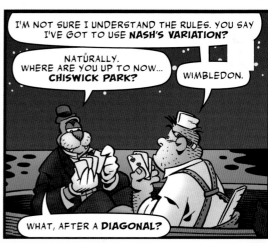

I'M NOT SURE I UNDERSTAND THE RULES. YOU SAY I'VE GOT TO USE **NASH'S VARIATION?**

NATURALLY. WHERE ARE YOU UP TO NOW... **CHISWICK PARK?**

WIMBLEDON.

WHAT, AFTER A **DIAGONAL?**

ALL RIGHT... QUEENSTOWN ROAD.

HAH! MORNINGTON CRESCENT!

AWW!

RULES OF THE GAME, OLD BOY... **RULES OF THE GAME!** KINDLY ROLL UP YOUR **TROUSER LEG,** IF YOU PLEASE...

ALL RIGHT... I GUESS YOU WON FAIR AND SQUARE.

QUITE SO, QUITE SO. YOU KNOW **I'D** DO THE SAME FOR **YOU.**

TRY... TRY TO BE GENTLE, WON'T YOU?

SIR! YOU CUT ME TO THE QUICK! AS IF I COULD EVER BE **ANYTHING ELSE!** I --

LAND AHOOOYYY!

EGAD! THE CHILD IS **RIGHT!** WE'RE SAVED! **SAVED!!**

DOES THIS MEAN YOU'RE NOT GOING TO EAT ME NOW?

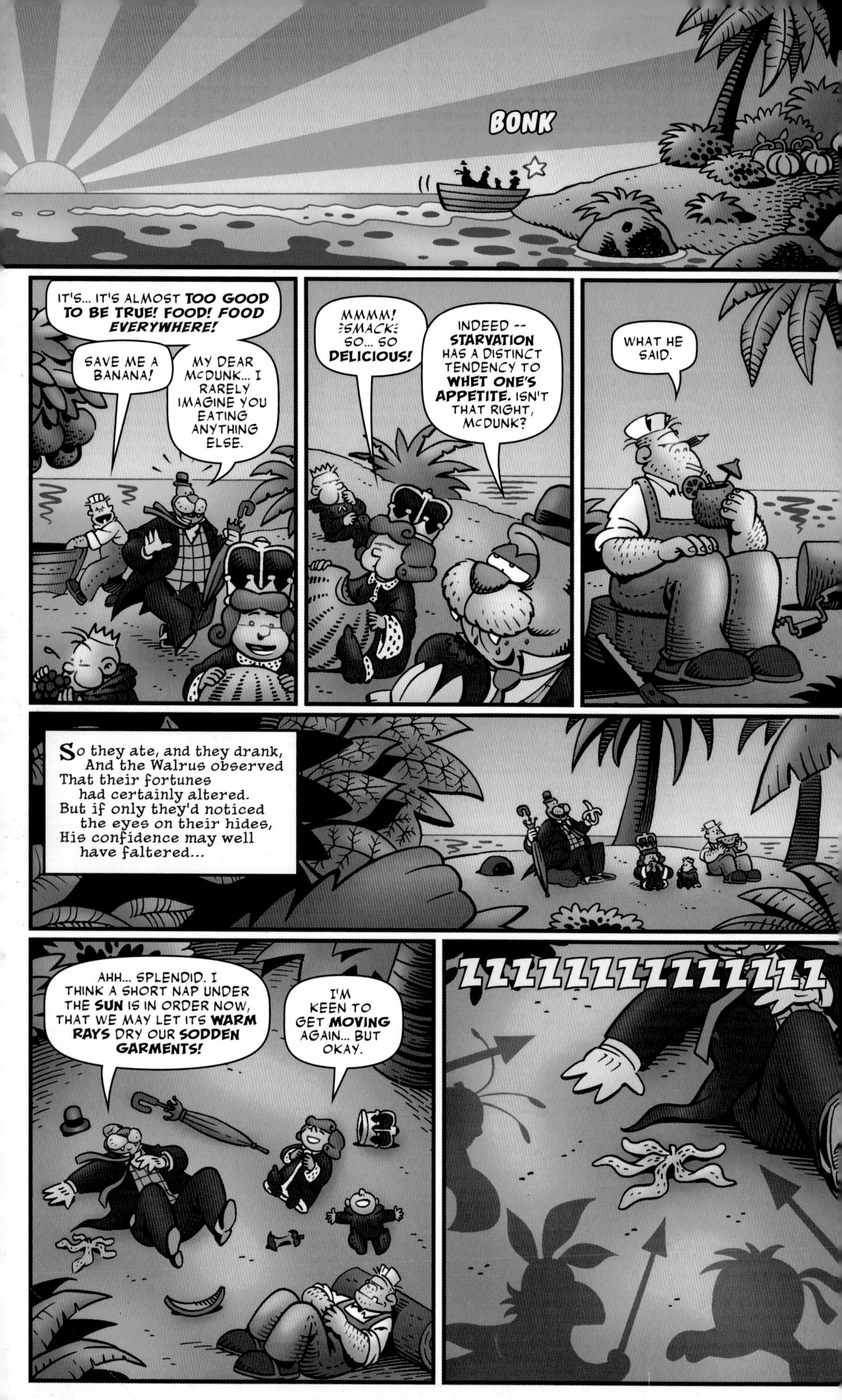

BONK
IT'S... IT'S ALMOST TOO GOOD TO BE TRUE! FOOD! FOOD EVERYWHERE!
SAVE ME A BANANA!
MY DEAR McDUNK... I RARELY IMAGINE YOU EATING ANYTHING ELSE.
MMMM! SMACK SO... SO DELICIOUS!
INDEED -- STARVATION HAS A DISTINCT TENDENCY TO WHET ONE'S APPETITE. ISN'T THAT RIGHT, McDUNK?
WHAT HE SAID.
So they ate, and they drank, And the Walrus observed That their fortunes had certainly altered. But if only they'd noticed the eyes on their hides, His confidence may well have faltered...
AHH... SPLENDID. I THINK A SHORT NAP UNDER THE SUN IS IN ORDER NOW, THAT WE MAY LET ITS WARM RAYS DRY OUR SODDEN GARMENTS!
I'M KEEN TO GET MOVING AGAIN... BUT OKAY.
ZZZZZZZZZZZZZZZZ

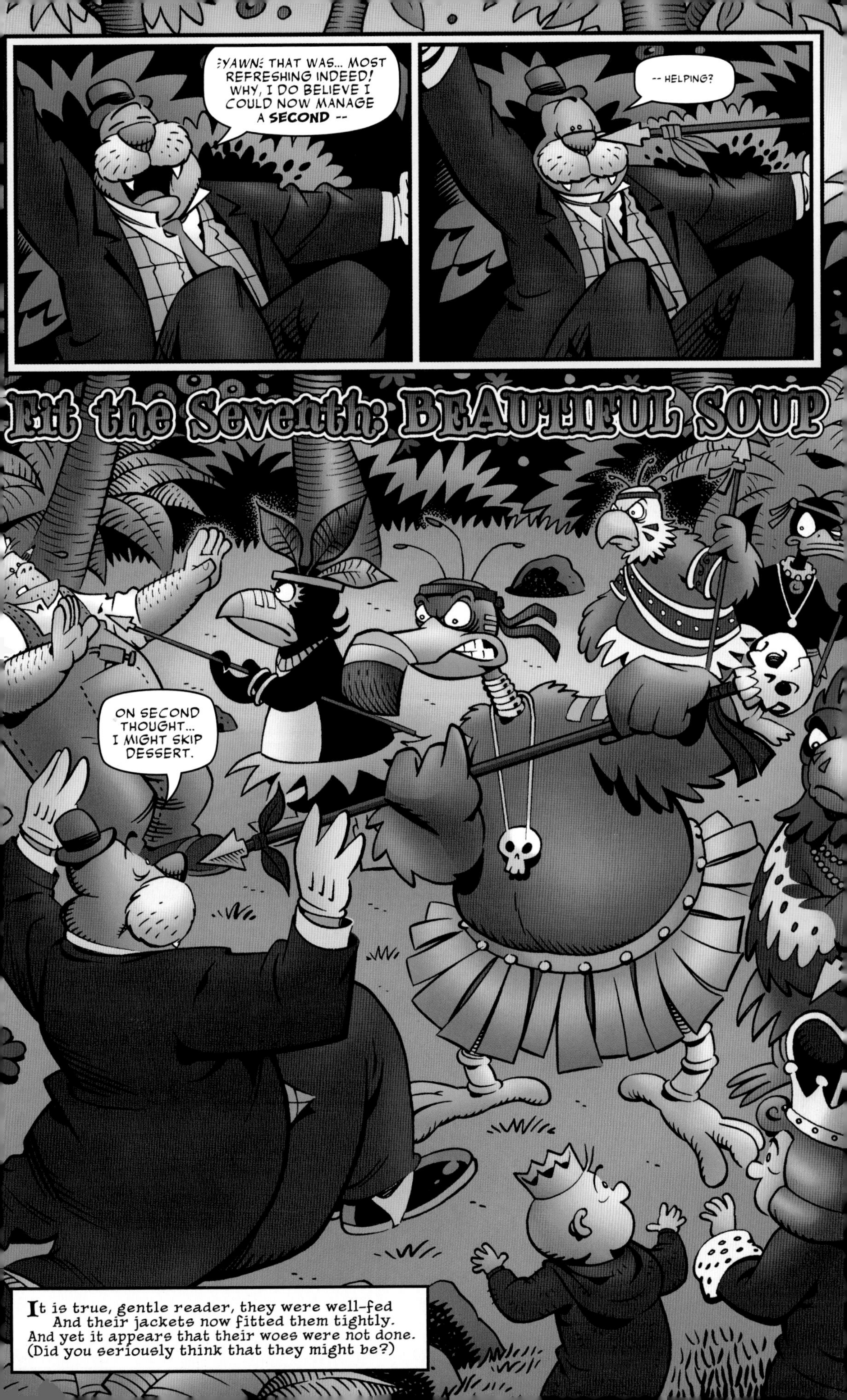
YAWN THAT WAS... MOST REFRESHING INDEED! WHY, I DO BELIEVE I COULD NOW MANAGE A SECOND --
-- HELPING?
Fit the Seventh: BEAUTIFUL SOUP
ON SECOND THOUGHT... I MIGHT SKIP DESSERT.
It is true, gentle reader, they were well-fed
And their jackets now fitted them tightly.
And yet it appears that their woes were not done.
(Did you seriously think that they might be?)

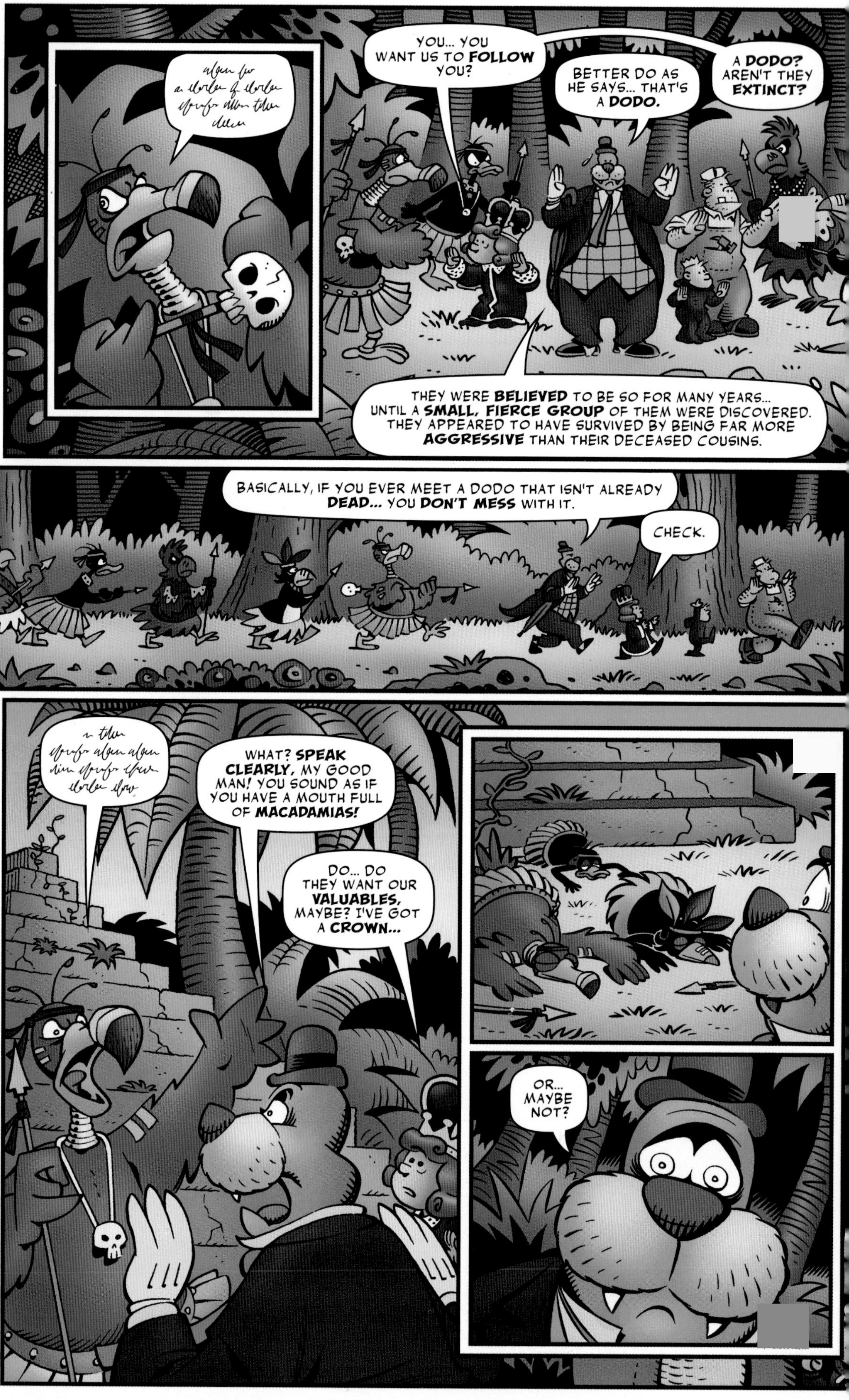
YOU... YOU WANT US TO FOLLOW YOU?
BETTER DO AS HE SAYS... THAT'S A DODO.
A DODO? AREN'T THEY EXTINCT?
THEY WERE BELIEVED TO BE SO FOR MANY YEARS... UNTIL A SMALL, FIERCE GROUP OF THEM WERE DISCOVERED. THEY APPEARED TO HAVE SURVIVED BY BEING FAR MORE AGGRESSIVE THAN THEIR DECEASED COUSINS.
BASICALLY, IF YOU EVER MEET A DODO THAT ISN'T ALREADY DEAD... YOU DON'T MESS WITH IT.
CHECK.
WHAT? SPEAK CLEARLY, MY GOOD MAN! YOU SOUND AS IF YOU HAVE A MOUTH FULL OF MACADAMIAS!
DO... DO THEY WANT OUR VALUABLES, MAYBE? I'VE GOT A CROWN...
OR... MAYBE NOT?

nfnfn nfnfn thn nbn nnbnn bnnn bnn fn fn nfnnfn bnnn nfnn!!

WHAT'S THAT...? **FOUR MONTHS**, YOU SAY? AND THEN THE **RAIN**...?

DON'T TELL ME YOU CAN ACTUALLY **UNDERSTAND** THAT GOBBLEDYGOOK HE'S SPOUTING?!

WELL, IT'S... YOU REMEMBER OUR OLD LANDLADY, **MRS. GROLLICKS**, IN THAT BOARDING HOUSE IN SPLOTVIA?

YE-E-ESS...

IT'S A LOT LIKE HOW SHE USED TO TALK WHEN SHE FORGOT TO PUT HER **TEETH** IN.

nbn bnnn bnnn nfnn fn bnnn bnnff n dnn nfnn fn bnnn

BASICALLY, HE SAYS THEY'VE BEEN SUFFERING A TERRIBLE **DROUGHT**... BUT THEN **WE** ARRIVED, BRINGING **RAIN** WITH US!

THEY THINK WE'RE **RESPONSIBLE**. THEY THINK WE'RE **RAIN GODS** -- AND THEY WANT TO **KEEP** US HERE ON THEIR ISLAND AND GIVE US **WHATEVER OUR HEARTS DESIRE!**

I... SEE.

WELL... I'LL ADMIT THE ARRANGEMENT HAS **POSSIBILITIES**...

...AND PERHAPS IT WOULD BE SOMEWHAT **RUDE** OF US TO JUST SUDDENLY **DISAPPEAR** WITHOUT SO MUCH AS A **BY-YOUR-LEAVE**...?

THIS IS **RIDICULOUS!** WE'RE ALL **FED AND WATERED** NOW -- WE SHOULD PUT AS MUCH FOOD IN THE BOAT AS WE CAN AND **GET MOVING!**

COME NOW, YOUR MAJESTY -- A LITTLE **REST AND RECUPERATION** CAN SURELY DO US NO HARM? WE'LL GET RIGHT BACK ON THE TRAIL OF YOUR DEAR DADDY ONCE WE'RE **PROPERLY REFRESHED!**

OOOOH... ALL RIGHT, YOU RAT! **ONE DAY'S REST!** BUT WE'RE TAKING THIS A **DAY AT A TIME!** THE LOCALS HAVE **WEAPONS** -- OR HADN'T YOU NOTICED?

WEAPONS? **PSHAW!** MERELY A **SENSIBLE DEFENSE** AGAINST THE **LOCAL WILDLIFE**.

I'M CERTAIN NOTHING CAN **POSSIBLY** GO WRONG...

...NOTHING AT ALL...

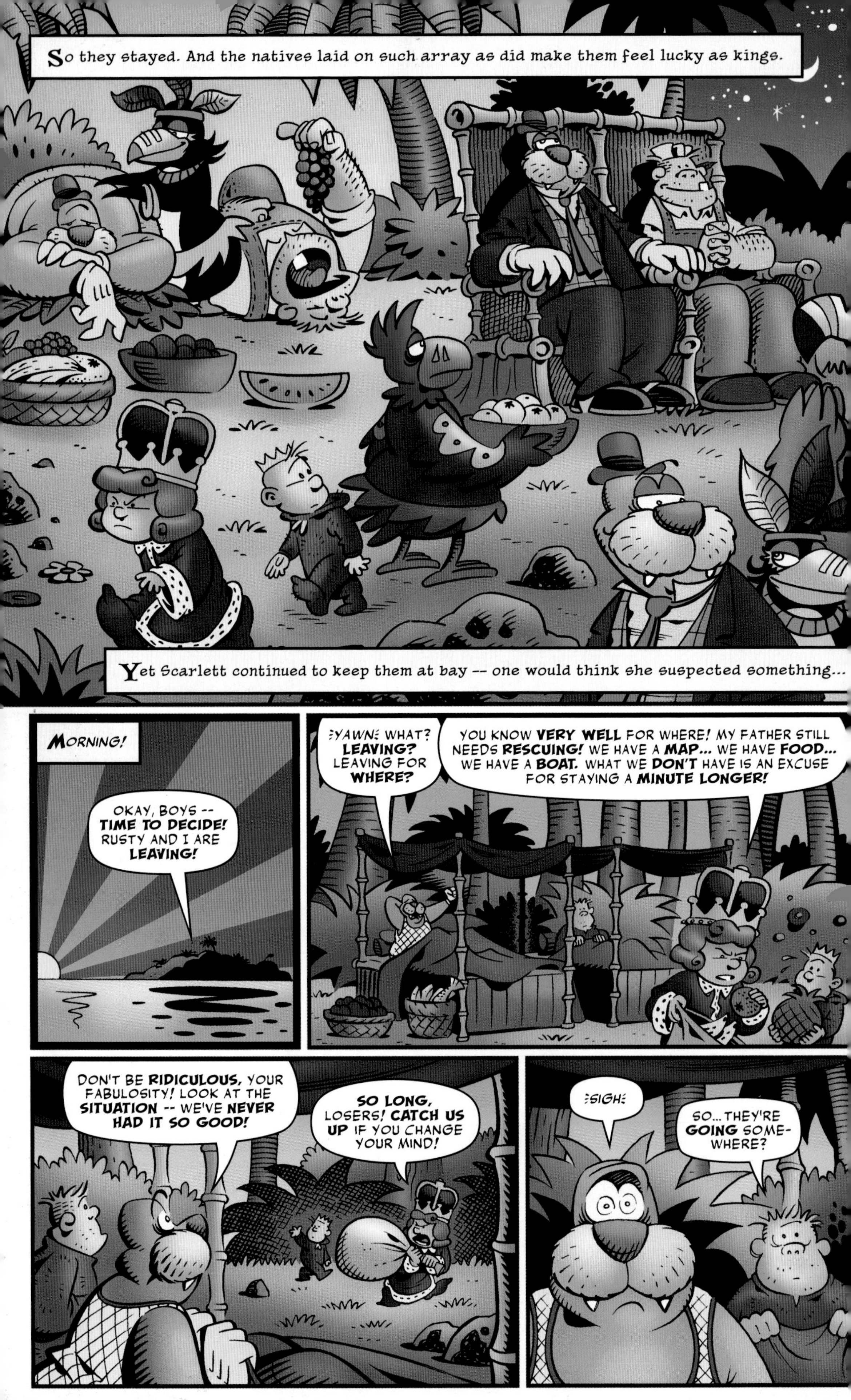
So they stayed. And the natives laid on such array as did make them feel lucky as kings.
Yet Scarlett continued to keep them at bay -- one would think she suspected something...
MORNING!
OKAY, BOYS -- TIME TO DECIDE! RUSTY AND I ARE LEAVING!
:YAWN: WHAT? LEAVING? LEAVING FOR WHERE?
YOU KNOW VERY WELL FOR WHERE! MY FATHER STILL NEEDS RESCUING! WE HAVE A MAP... WE HAVE FOOD... WE HAVE A BOAT. WHAT WE DON'T HAVE IS AN EXCUSE FOR STAYING A MINUTE LONGER!
DON'T BE RIDICULOUS, YOUR FABULOSITY! LOOK AT THE SITUATION -- WE'VE NEVER HAD IT SO GOOD!
SO LONG, LOSERS! CATCH US UP IF YOU CHANGE YOUR MIND!
:SIGH:
SO... THEY'RE GOING SOME-WHERE?

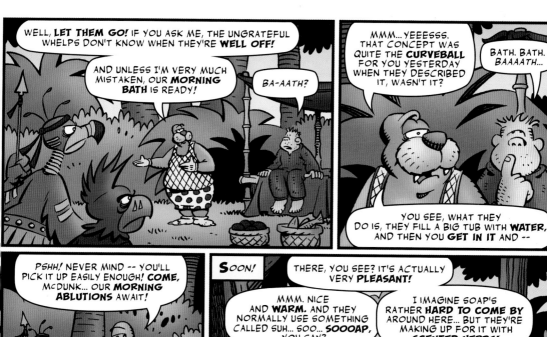

WELL, **LET THEM GO!** IF YOU ASK ME, THE UNGRATEFUL WHELPS DON'T KNOW WHEN THEY'RE **WELL OFF!**

AND UNLESS I'M VERY MUCH MISTAKEN, OUR **MORNING BATH** IS READY!

BA-AATH?

MMM...YEEESSS. THAT CONCEPT WAS QUITE THE **CURVEBALL** FOR YOU YESTERDAY WHEN THEY DESCRIBED IT, WASN'T IT?

BATH. BATH. BAAAATH...

YOU SEE, WHAT THEY DO IS, THEY FILL A BIG TUB WITH **WATER**, AND THEN YOU **GET IN IT** AND --

PSHH! NEVER MIND -- YOU'LL PICK IT UP EASILY ENOUGH! **COME, MCDUNK... OUR MORNING ABLUTIONS** AWAIT!

SOON!

THERE, YOU SEE? IT'S ACTUALLY VERY **PLEASANT!**

MMM. NICE AND **WARM.** AND THEY NORMALLY USE SOMETHING CALLED SUH... SOO... **SOOOAP,** YOU SAY?

I IMAGINE SOAP'S RATHER **HARD TO COME BY** AROUND HERE... BUT THEY'RE MAKING UP FOR IT WITH **SCENTED HERBS!**

YES... AND **VEGETABLES. CARROTS** AND **CELERY** AND... OH, LOOK! THEY'RE PUTTING ON **NAPKINS!**

YES, I --

NAPKINS?

AH.

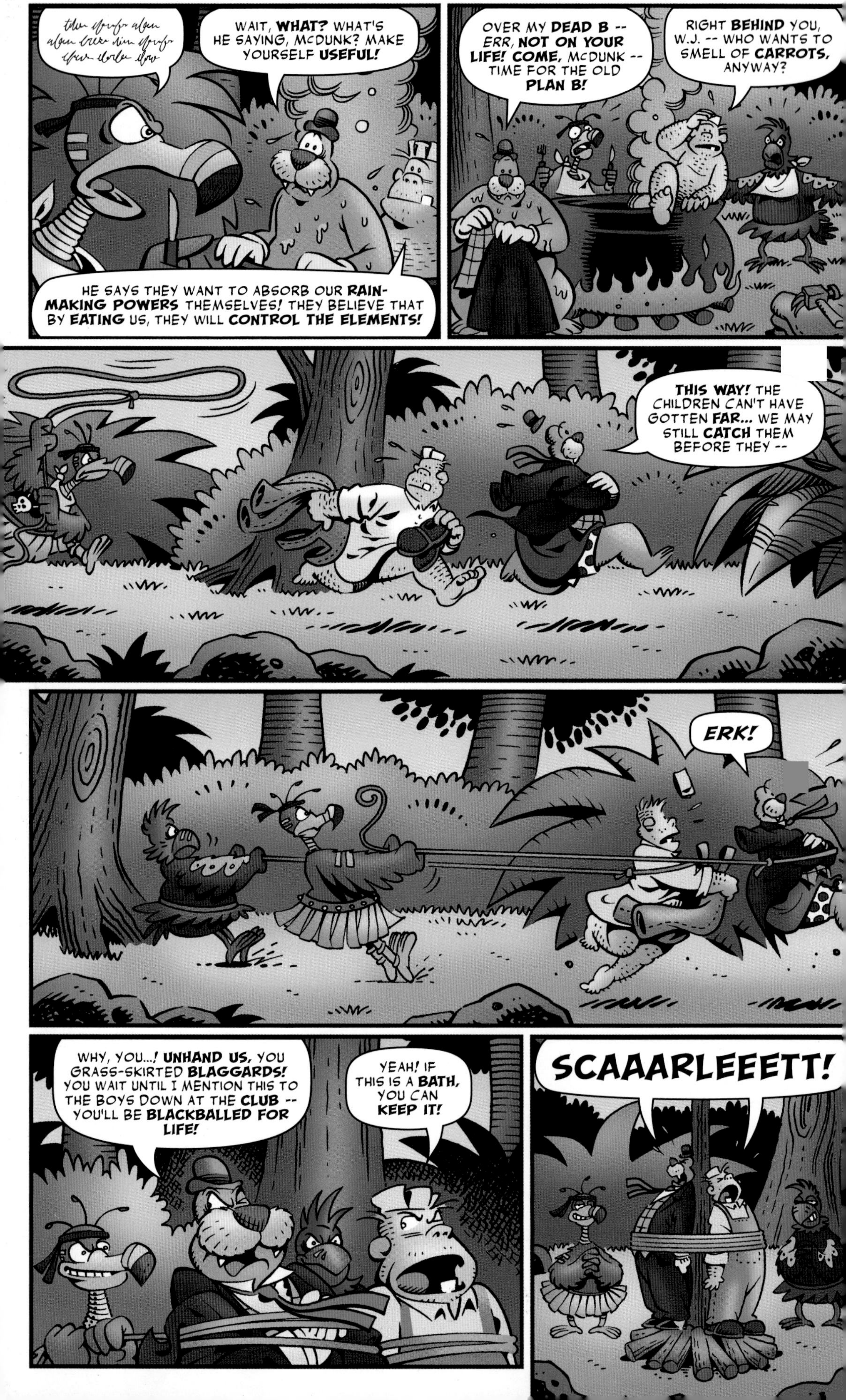
WAIT, WHAT? WHAT'S HE SAYING, McDUNK? MAKE YOURSELF USEFUL!
HE SAYS THEY WANT TO ABSORB OUR RAIN-MAKING POWERS THEMSELVES! THEY BELIEVE THAT BY EATING US, THEY WILL CONTROL THE ELEMENTS!
OVER MY DEAD B -- ERR, NOT ON YOUR LIFE! COME, McDUNK -- TIME FOR THE OLD PLAN B!
RIGHT BEHIND YOU, W.J. -- WHO WANTS TO SMELL OF CARROTS, ANYWAY?
THIS WAY! THE CHILDREN CAN'T HAVE GOTTEN FAR... WE MAY STILL CATCH THEM BEFORE THEY --
ERK!
WHY, YOU...! UNHAND US, YOU GRASS-SKIRTED BLAGGARDS! YOU WAIT UNTIL I MENTION THIS TO THE BOYS DOWN AT THE CLUB -- YOU'LL BE BLACKBALLED FOR LIFE!
YEAH! IF THIS IS A BATH, YOU CAN KEEP IT!
SCAAARLEEETT!

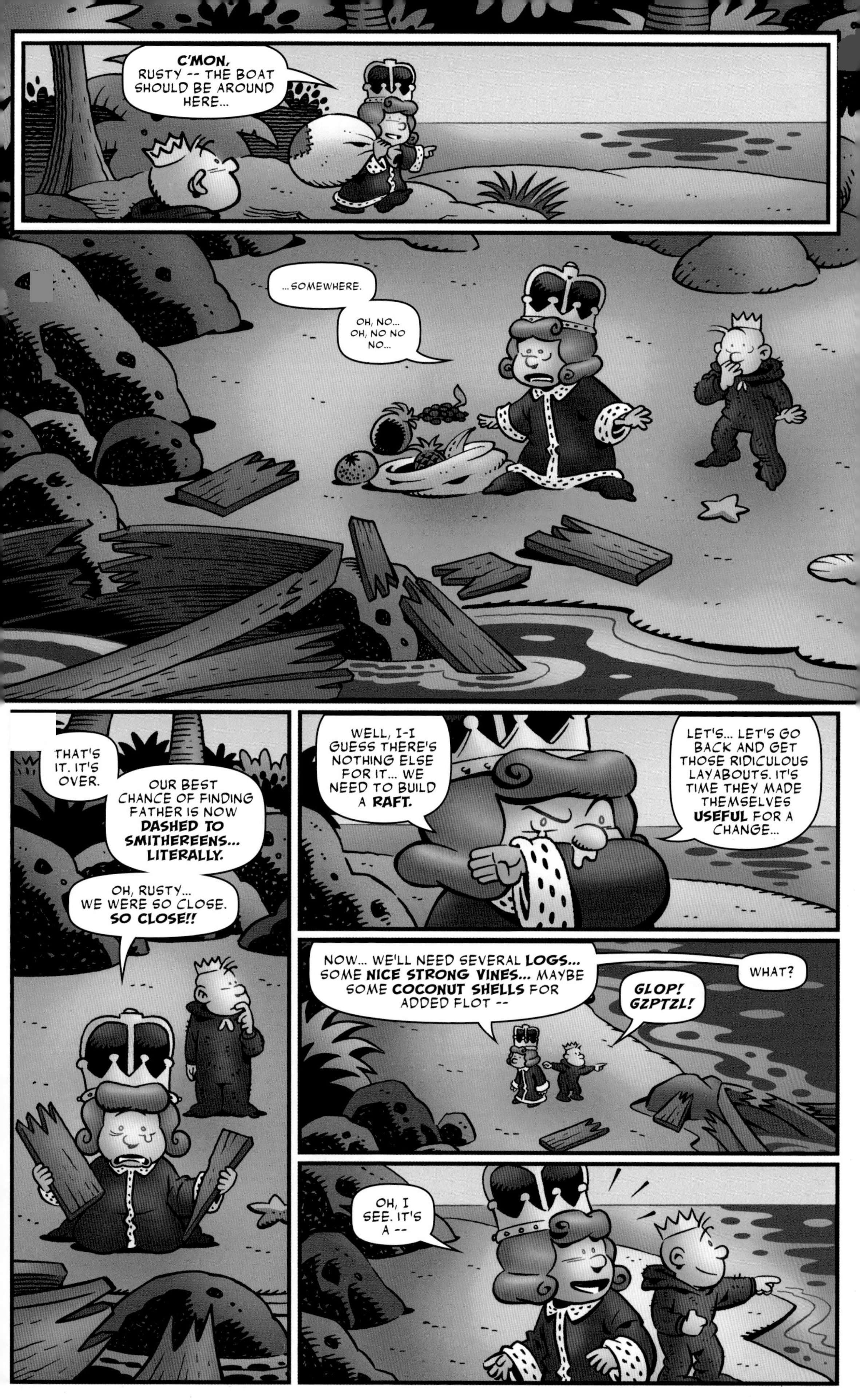
C'MON, RUSTY -- THE BOAT SHOULD BE AROUND HERE...
...SOMEWHERE.
OH, NO... OH, NO NO NO...
THAT'S IT. IT'S OVER.
OUR BEST CHANCE OF FINDING FATHER IS NOW DASHED TO SMITHEREENS... LITERALLY.
OH, RUSTY... WE WERE SO CLOSE. SO CLOSE!!
WELL, I-I GUESS THERE'S NOTHING ELSE FOR IT... WE NEED TO BUILD A RAFT.
LET'S... LET'S GO BACK AND GET THOSE RIDICULOUS LAYABOUTS. IT'S TIME THEY MADE THEMSELVES USEFUL FOR A CHANGE...
NOW... WE'LL NEED SEVERAL LOGS... SOME NICE STRONG VINES... MAYBE SOME COCONUT SHELLS FOR ADDED FLOT --
GLOP! GZPTZL!
WHAT?
OH, I SEE. IT'S A --

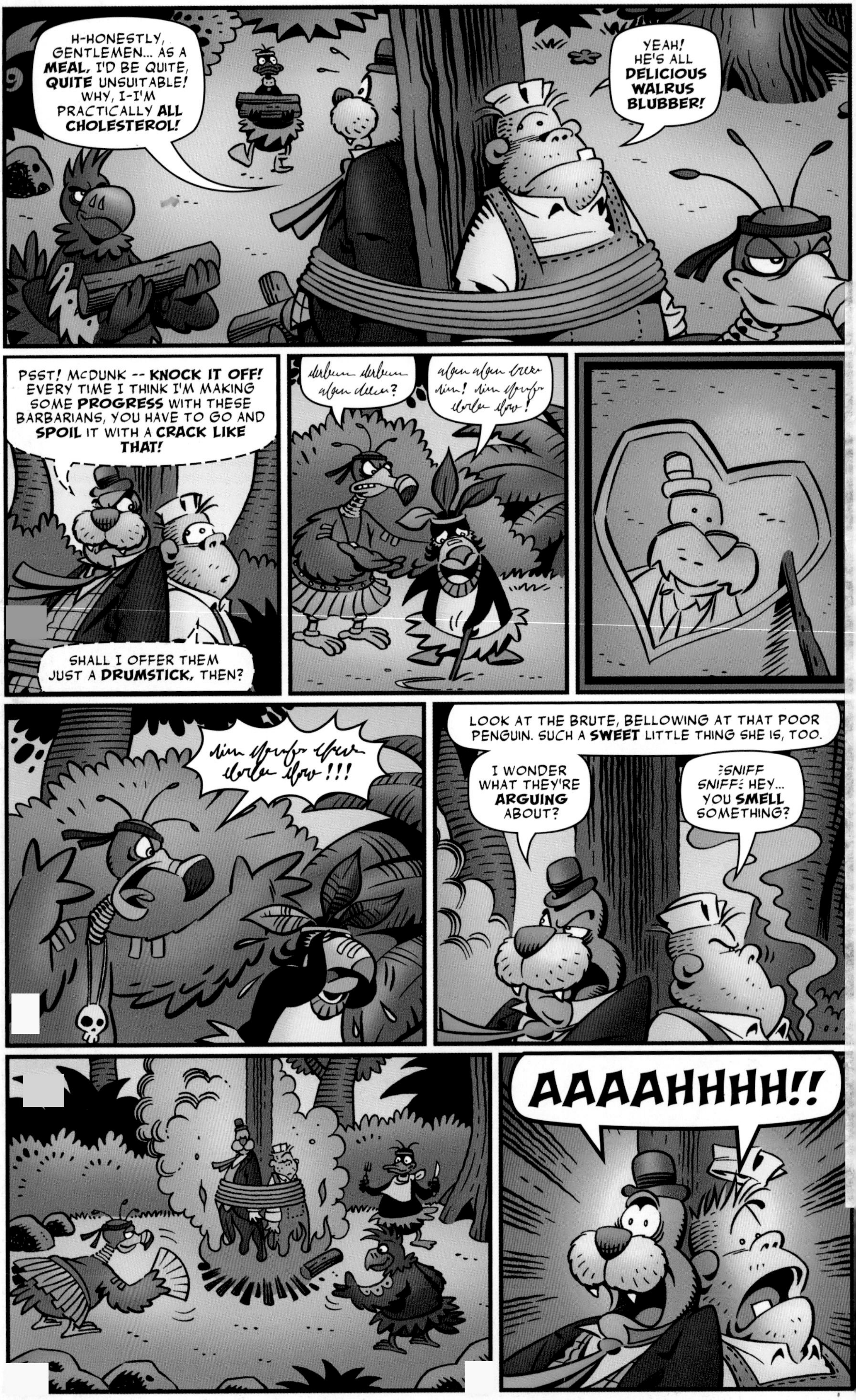
H-HONESTLY, GENTLEMEN... AS A MEAL, I'D BE QUITE, QUITE UNSUITABLE! WHY, I-I'M PRACTICALLY ALL CHOLESTEROL!
YEAH! HE'S ALL DELICIOUS WALRUS BLUBBER!
PSST! McDUNK -- KNOCK IT OFF! EVERY TIME I THINK I'M MAKING SOME PROGRESS WITH THESE BARBARIANS, YOU HAVE TO GO AND SPOIL IT WITH A CRACK LIKE THAT!
SHALL I OFFER THEM JUST A DRUMSTICK, THEN?
LOOK AT THE BRUTE, BELLOWING AT THAT POOR PENGUIN. SUCH A SWEET LITTLE THING SHE IS, TOO.
I WONDER WHAT THEY'RE ARGUING ABOUT?
SNIFF SNIFF HEY... YOU SMELL SOMETHING?
AAAAHHHH!!

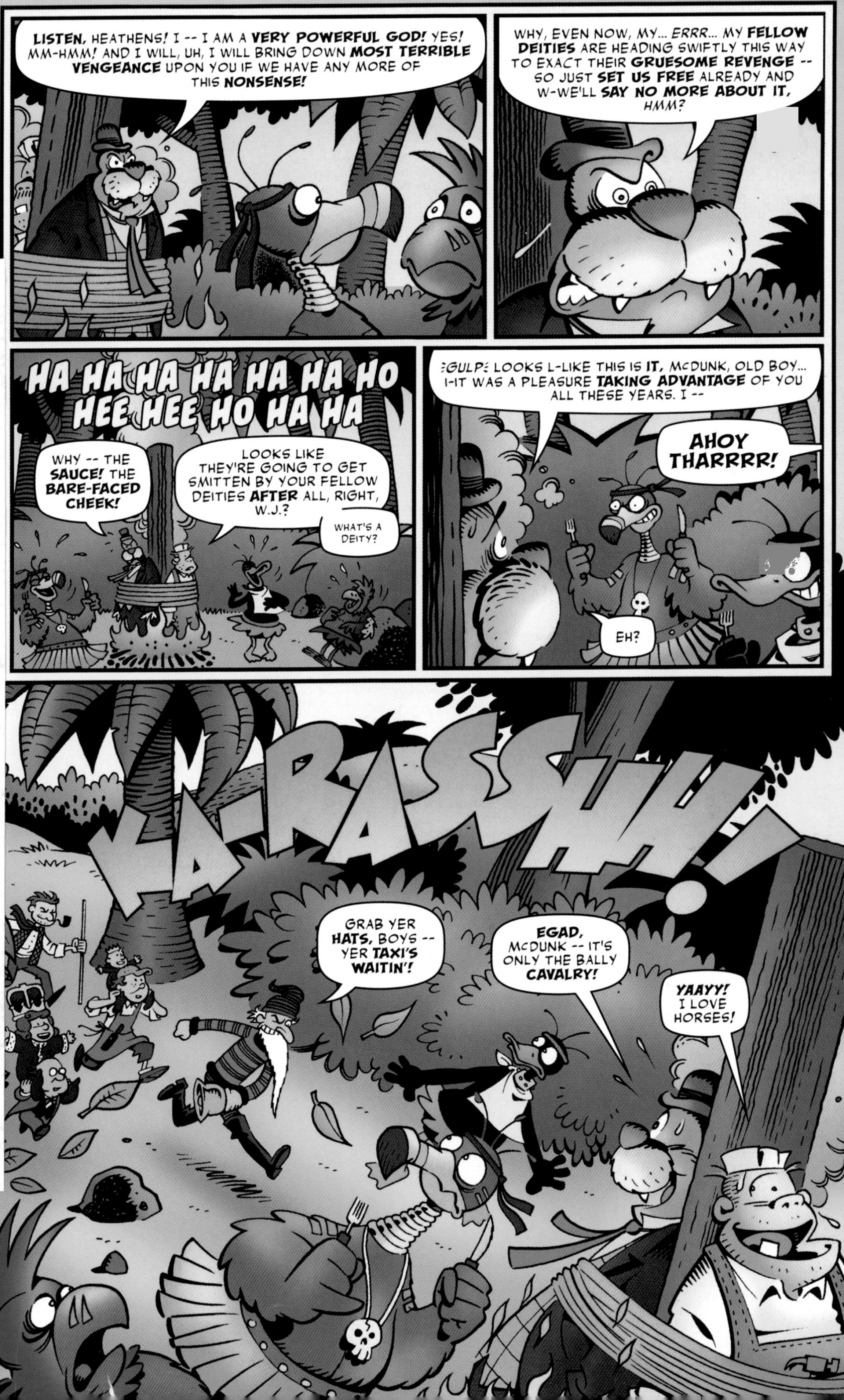
LISTEN, HEATHENS! I -- I AM A VERY POWERFUL GOD! YES! MM-HMM! AND I WILL, UH, I WILL BRING DOWN MOST TERRIBLE VENGEANCE UPON YOU IF WE HAVE ANY MORE OF THIS NONSENSE!
WHY, EVEN NOW, MY... ERRR... MY FELLOW DEITIES ARE HEADING SWIFTLY THIS WAY TO EXACT THEIR GRUESOME REVENGE -- SO JUST SET US FREE ALREADY AND W-WE'LL SAY NO MORE ABOUT IT, HMM?
HA HA HA HA HA HA HO HEE HEE HO HA HA
WHY -- THE SAUCE! THE BARE-FACED CHEEK!
LOOKS LIKE THEY'RE GOING TO GET SMITTEN BY YOUR FELLOW DEITIES AFTER ALL, RIGHT, W.J.?
WHAT'S A DEITY?
GULP LOOKS L-LIKE THIS IS IT, McDUNK, OLD BOY... I-IT WAS A PLEASURE TAKING ADVANTAGE OF YOU ALL THESE YEARS. I --
AHOY THARRRR!
EH?
KA-RASSHH!
GRAB YER HATS, BOYS -- YER TAXI'S WAITIN'!
EGAD, McDUNK -- IT'S ONLY THE BALLY CAVALRY!
YAAYY! I LOVE HORSES!

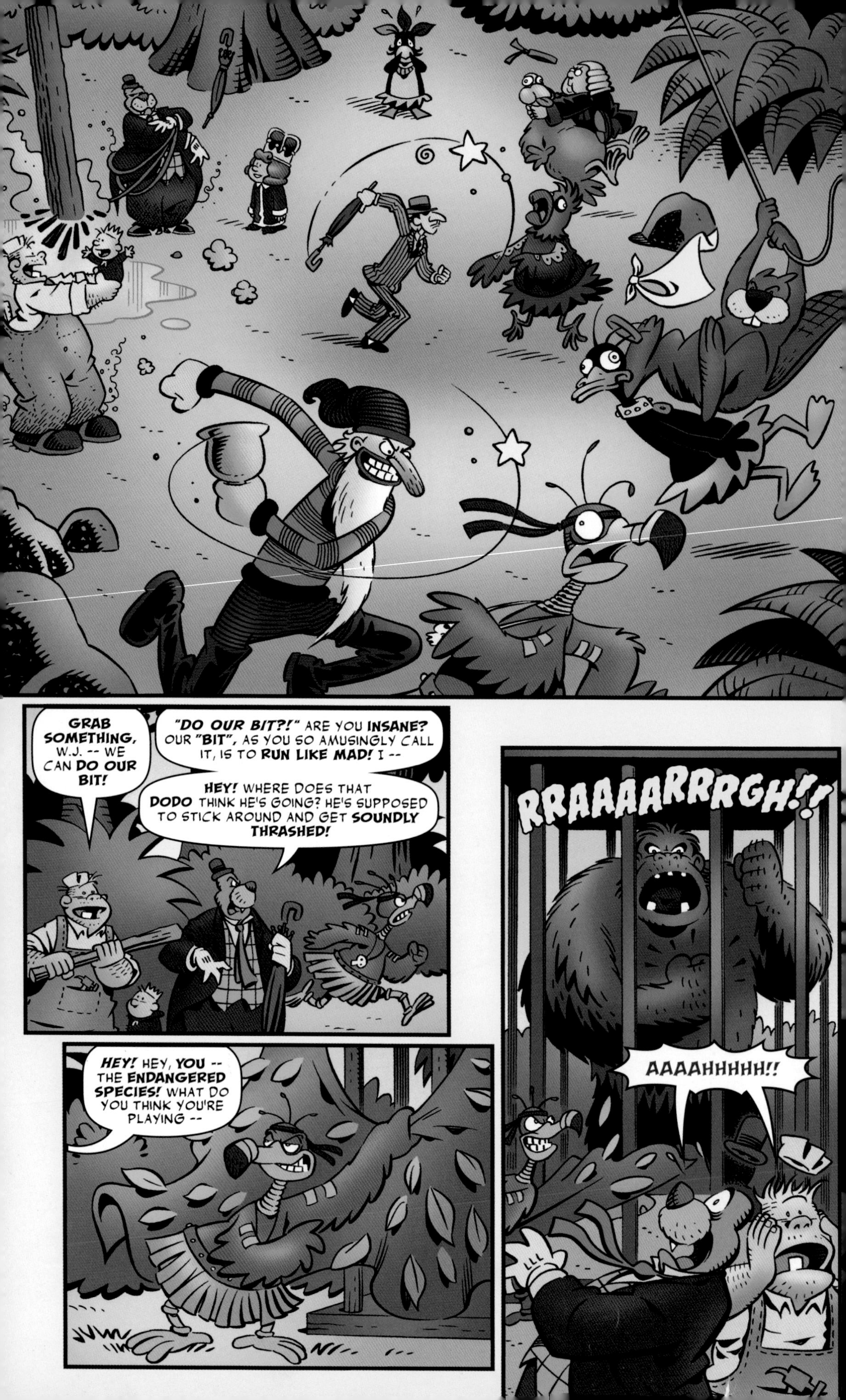

GRAB SOMETHING, W.J. -- WE CAN DO OUR BIT!
"DO OUR BIT?!" ARE YOU INSANE? OUR "BIT", AS YOU SO AMUSINGLY CALL IT, IS TO RUN LIKE MAD! I --
HEY! WHERE DOES THAT DODO THINK HE'S GOING? HE'S SUPPOSED TO STICK AROUND AND GET SOUNDLY THRASHED!
HEY! HEY, YOU -- THE ENDANGERED SPECIES! WHAT DO YOU THINK YOU'RE PLAYING --
RRAAAAARRRGH!!
AAAAHHHHH!!

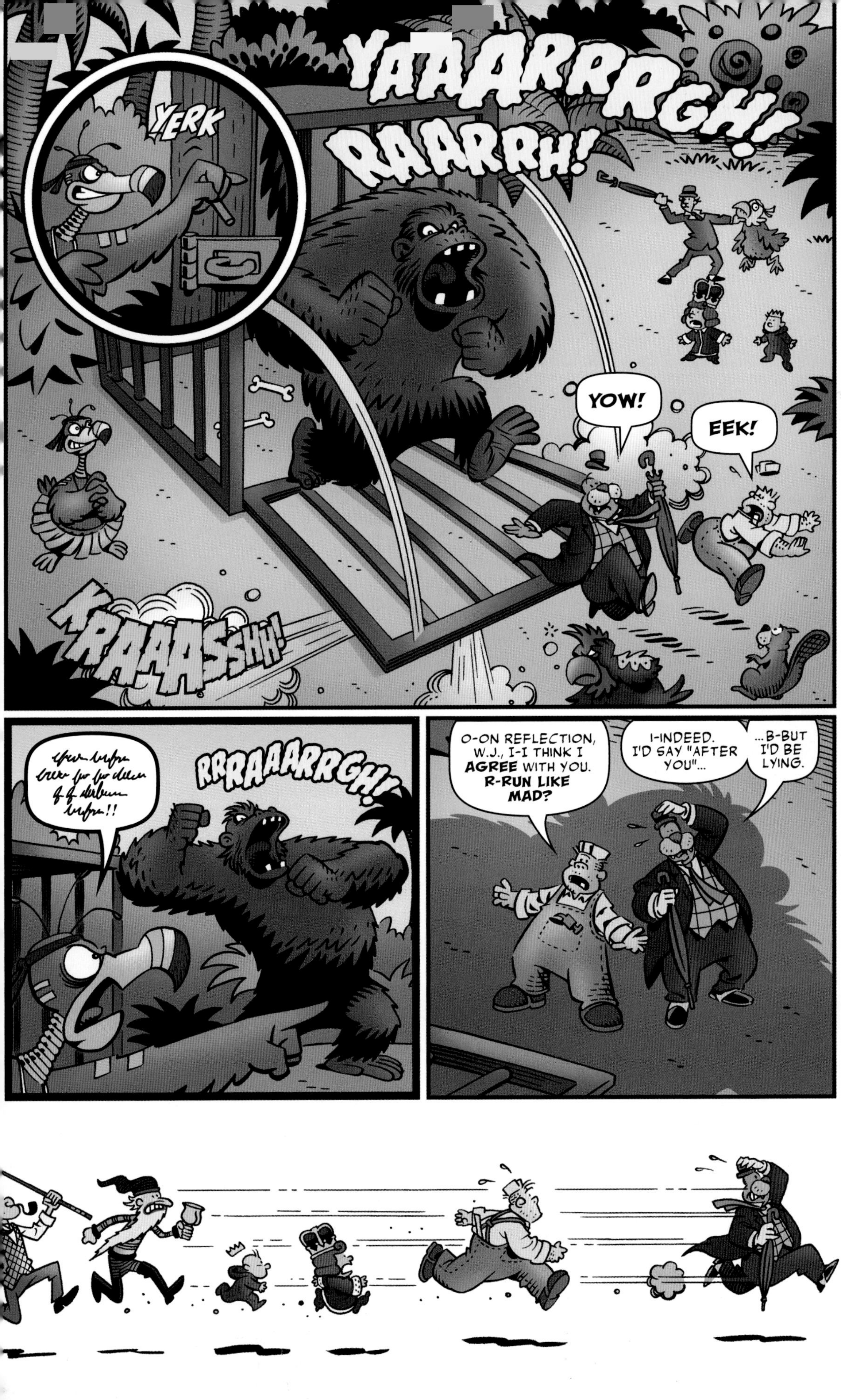
YERK
YAAARRRRGH!
RAARRH!
YOW!
EEK!
KRAAASSHH!
RRRAAARRRGH!
O-ON REFLECTION, W.J., I-I THINK I AGREE WITH YOU. R-RUN LIKE MAD?
I-INDEED. I'D SAY "AFTER YOU"...
...B-BUT I'D BE LYING.

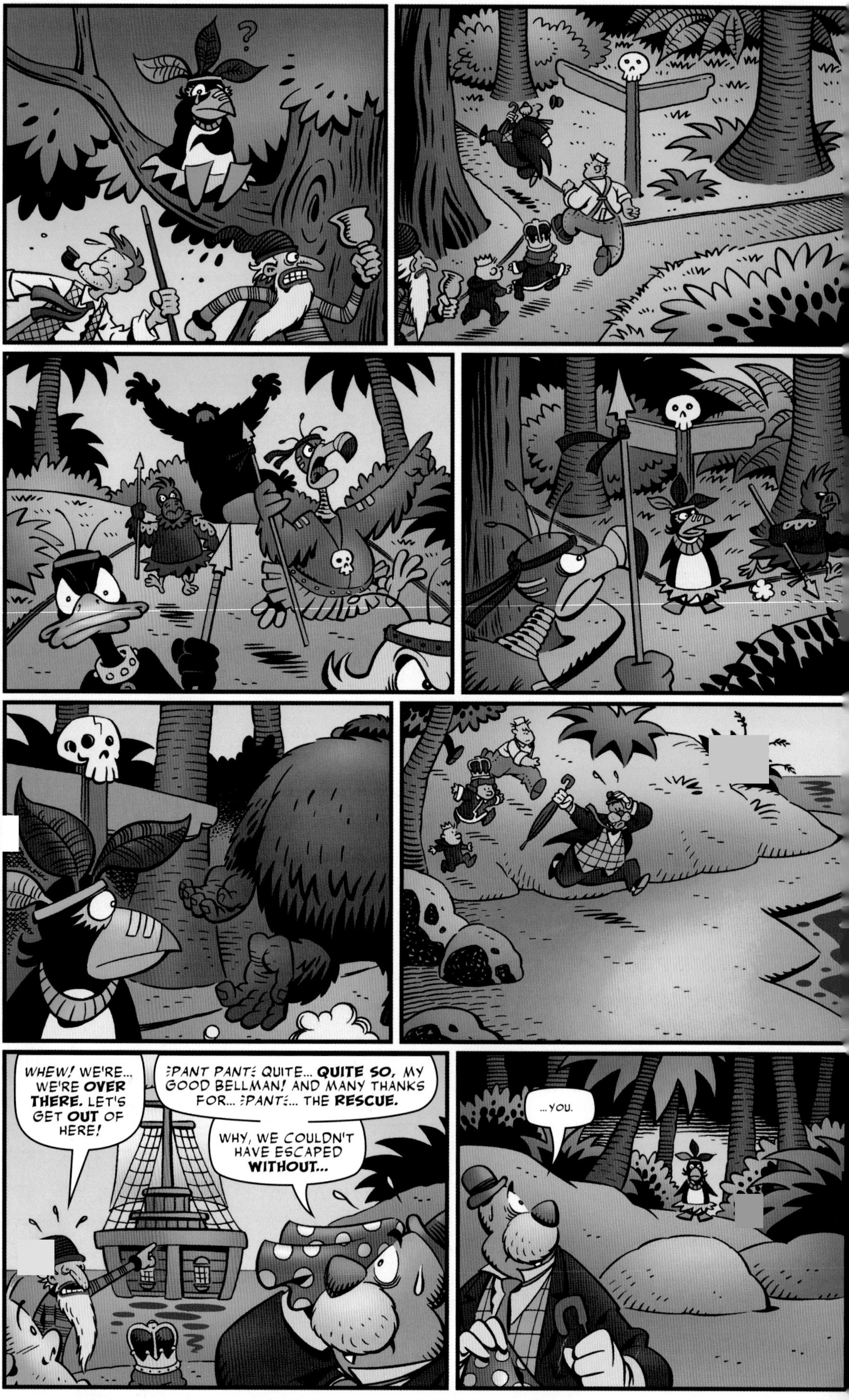
?
WHEW! WE'RE... WE'RE OVER THERE. LET'S GET OUT OF HERE!
=PANT PANT= QUITE... QUITE SO, MY GOOD BELLMAN! AND MANY THANKS FOR... =PANT=... THE RESCUE.
WHY, WE COULDN'T HAVE ESCAPED WITHOUT...
...YOU.

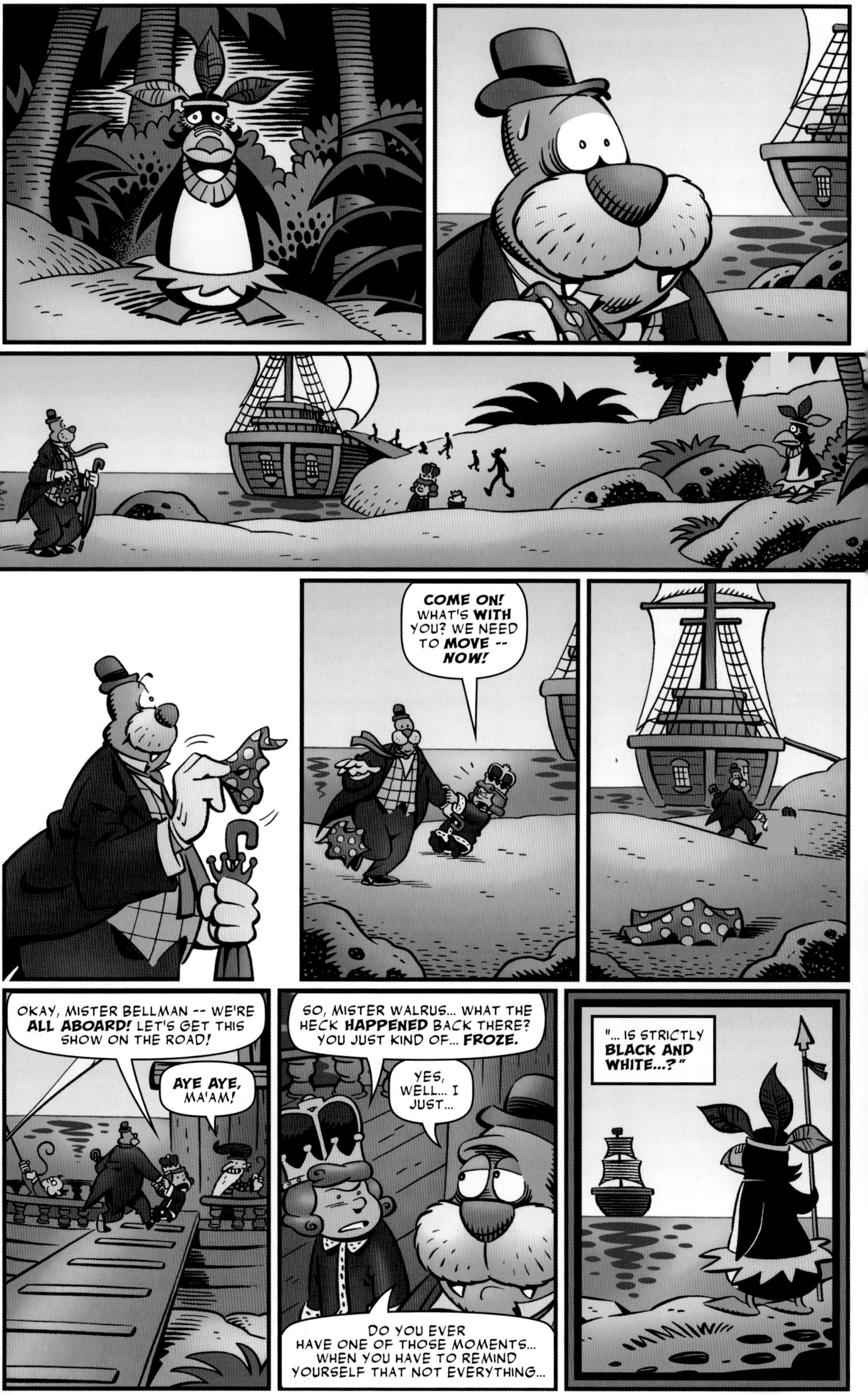
COME ON! WHAT'S WITH YOU? WE NEED TO MOVE -- NOW!
OKAY, MISTER BELLMAN -- WE'RE ALL ABOARD! LET'S GET THIS SHOW ON THE ROAD!
AYE AYE, MA'AM!
SO, MISTER WALRUS... WHAT THE HECK HAPPENED BACK THERE? YOU JUST KIND OF... FROZE.
YES, WELL... I JUST...
DO YOU EVER HAVE ONE OF THOSE MOMENTS... WHEN YOU HAVE TO REMIND YOURSELF THAT NOT EVERYTHING...
"... IS STRICTLY BLACK AND WHITE...?"

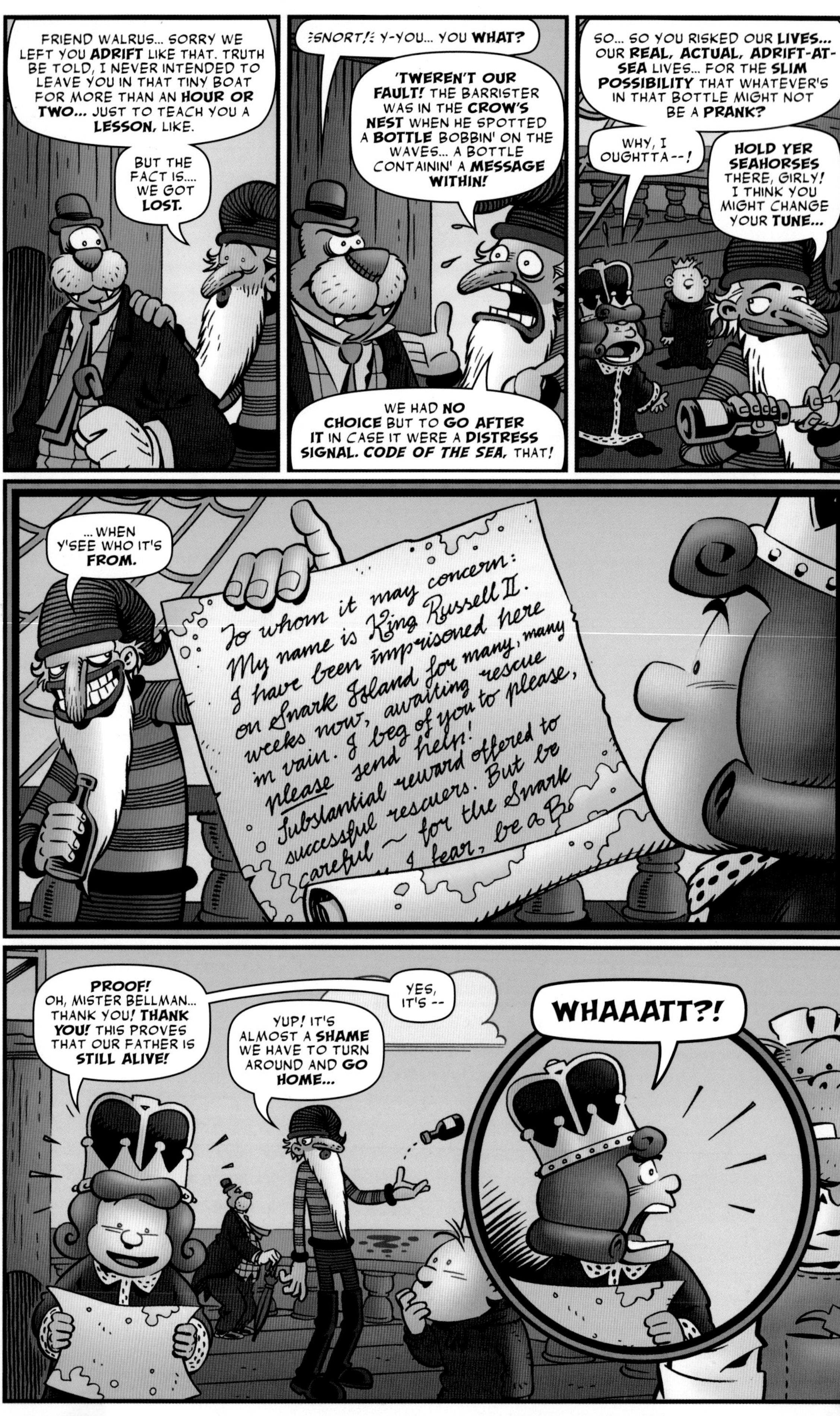

FRIEND WALRUS... SORRY WE LEFT YOU ADRIFT LIKE THAT. TRUTH BE TOLD, I NEVER INTENDED TO LEAVE YOU IN THAT TINY BOAT FOR MORE THAN AN HOUR OR TWO... JUST TO TEACH YOU A LESSON, LIKE.
BUT THE FACT IS.... WE GOT LOST.
:SNORT!: Y-YOU... YOU WHAT?
'TWEREN'T OUR FAULT! THE BARRISTER WAS IN THE CROW'S NEST WHEN HE SPOTTED A BOTTLE BOBBIN' ON THE WAVES... A BOTTLE CONTAININ' A MESSAGE WITHIN!
WE HAD NO CHOICE BUT TO GO AFTER IT IN CASE IT WERE A DISTRESS SIGNAL. CODE OF THE SEA, THAT!
SO... SO YOU RISKED OUR LIVES... OUR REAL, ACTUAL, ADRIFT-AT-SEA LIVES... FOR THE SLIM POSSIBILITY THAT WHATEVER'S IN THAT BOTTLE MIGHT NOT BE A PRANK?
WHY, I OUGHTTA--!
HOLD YER SEAHORSES THERE, GIRLY! I THINK YOU MIGHT CHANGE YOUR TUNE...
...WHEN Y'SEE WHO IT'S FROM.
To whom it may concern: My name is King Russell II. I have been imprisoned here on Snark Island for many, many weeks now, awaiting rescue in vain. I beg of you to please, please send help! Substantial reward offered to successful rescuers. But be careful ~ for the Snark ... I fear, be a B
PROOF! OH, MISTER BELLMAN... THANK YOU! THANK YOU! THIS PROVES THAT OUR FATHER IS STILL ALIVE!
YES, IT'S --
YUP! IT'S ALMOST A SHAME WE HAVE TO TURN AROUND AND GO HOME...
WHAAATT?!

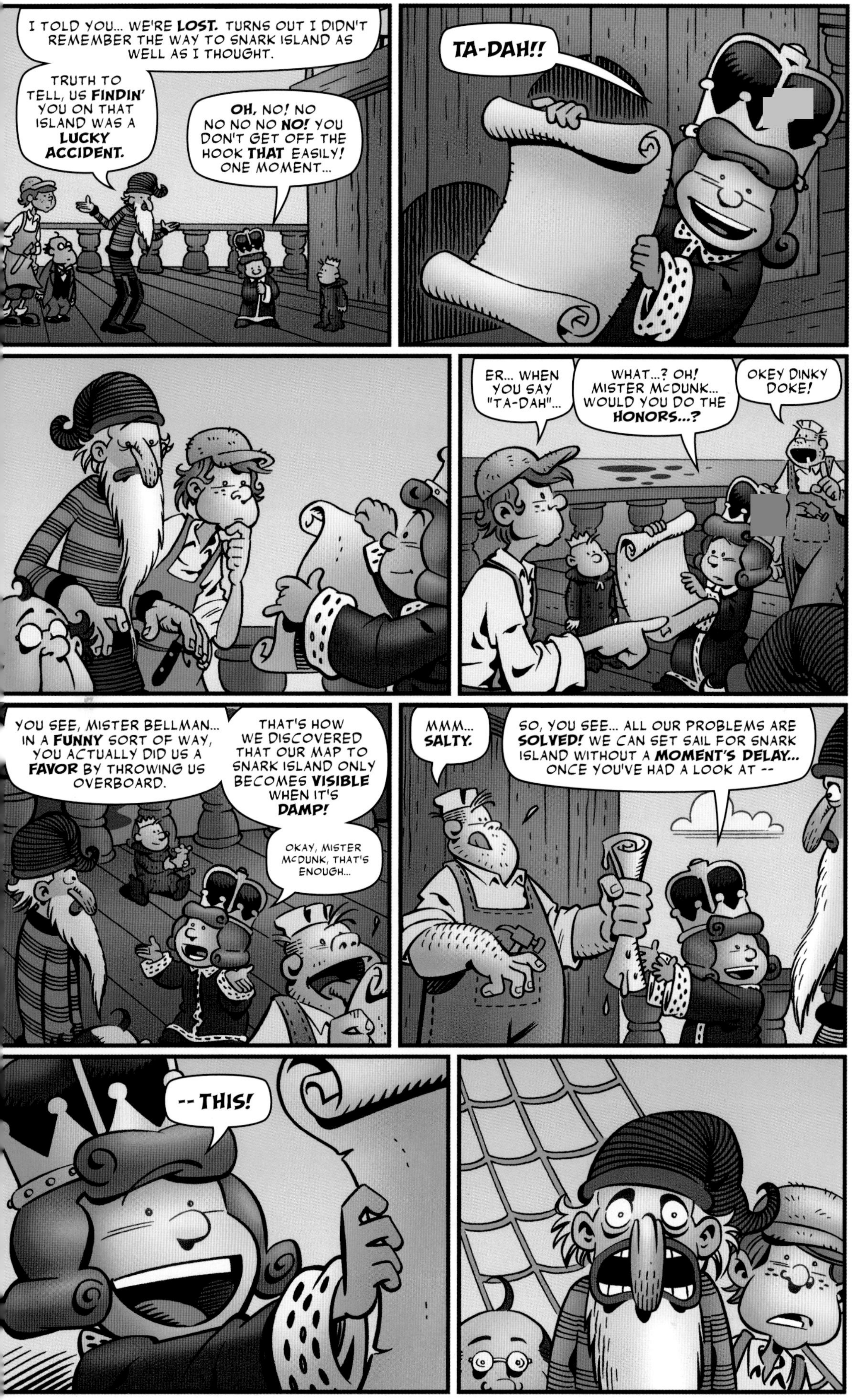
I TOLD YOU... WE'RE LOST. TURNS OUT I DIDN'T REMEMBER THE WAY TO SNARK ISLAND AS WELL AS I THOUGHT.
TRUTH TO TELL, US FINDIN' YOU ON THAT ISLAND WAS A LUCKY ACCIDENT.
OH, NO! NO NO NO NO NO! YOU DON'T GET OFF THE HOOK THAT EASILY! ONE MOMENT...
TA-DAH!!
ER... WHEN YOU SAY "TA-DAH"...
WHAT...? OH! MISTER McDUNK... WOULD YOU DO THE HONORS...?
OKEY DINKY DOKE!
YOU SEE, MISTER BELLMAN... IN A FUNNY SORT OF WAY, YOU ACTUALLY DID US A FAVOR BY THROWING US OVERBOARD.
THAT'S HOW WE DISCOVERED THAT OUR MAP TO SNARK ISLAND ONLY BECOMES VISIBLE WHEN IT'S DAMP!
OKAY, MISTER McDUNK, THAT'S ENOUGH...
MMM... SALTY.
SO, YOU SEE... ALL OUR PROBLEMS ARE SOLVED! WE CAN SET SAIL FOR SNARK ISLAND WITHOUT A MOMENT'S DELAY... ONCE YOU'VE HAD A LOOK AT --
-- THIS!

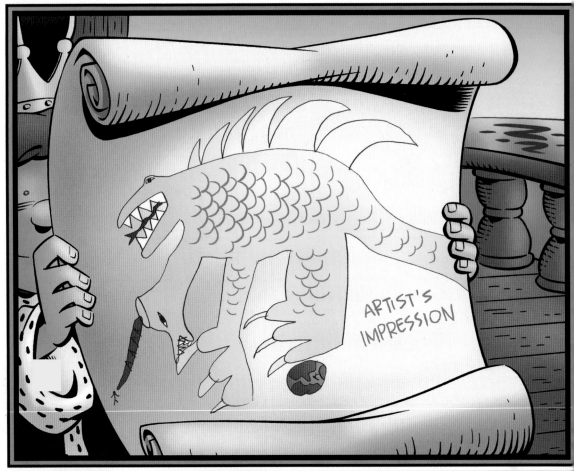

ARTIST'S
IMPRESSION

WHAT?
WHAT ARE
YOU --

AAAHH!

MISTER
McDUNK -- YOU
MUST HAVE LICKED
THE **WRONG**
SIDE!

I'M **ON IT,**
YOUR MAJESTY!
HUM BULUM LUM
LUM LUM...

UM... THANK
YOU?

NOW **GET
MOVING!**
WE'VE NO TIME
TO WASTE!

WELL? **WHAT
ARE YOU
WAITING
FOR?!**

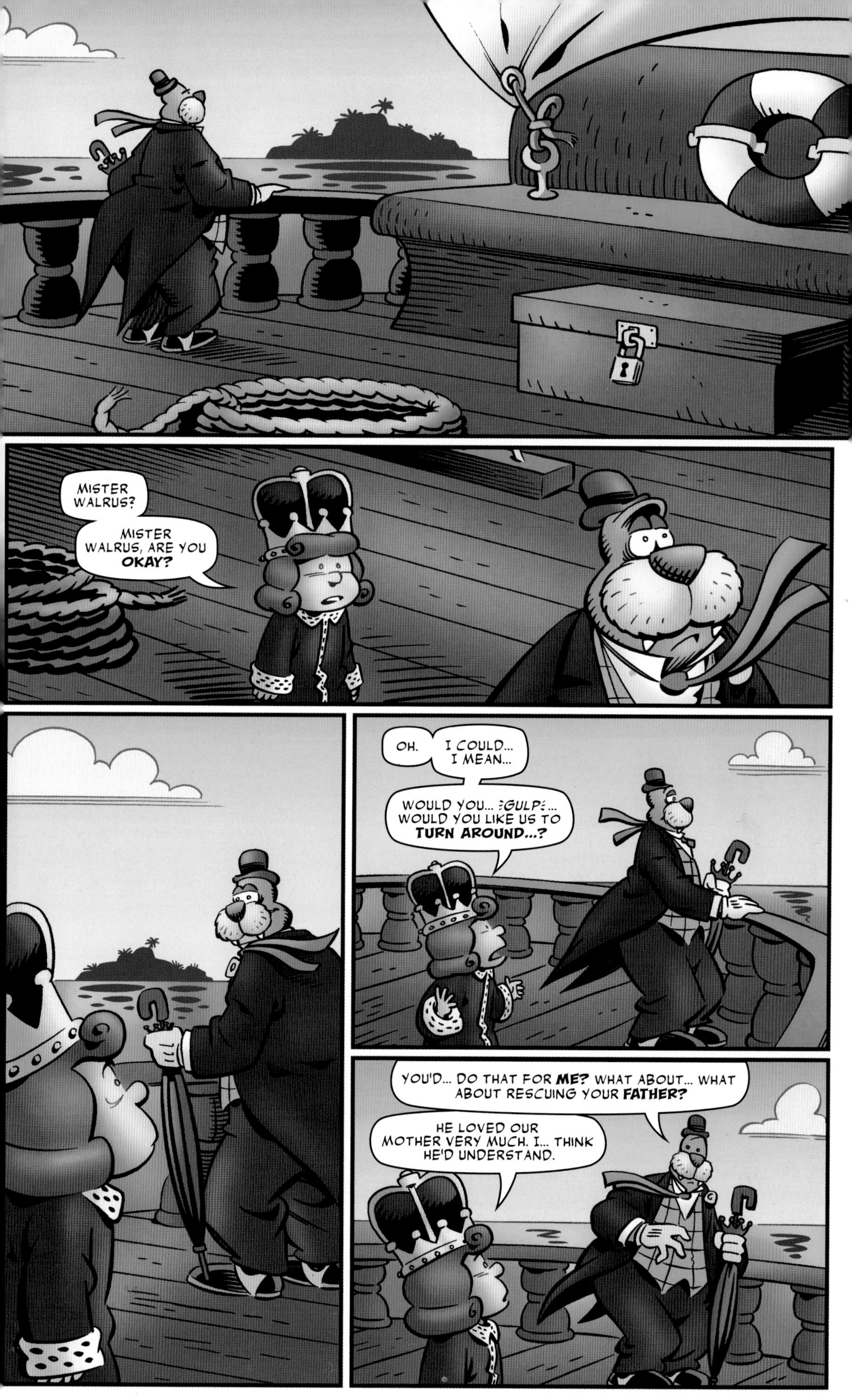

MISTER WALRUS?
MISTER WALRUS, ARE YOU **OKAY?**
OH.
I COULD... I MEAN...
WOULD YOU... *GULP*... WOULD YOU LIKE US TO **TURN AROUND...?**
YOU'D... DO THAT FOR **ME?** WHAT ABOUT... WHAT ABOUT RESCUING YOUR **FATHER?**
HE LOVED OUR MOTHER VERY MUCH. I... THINK HE'D UNDERSTAND.

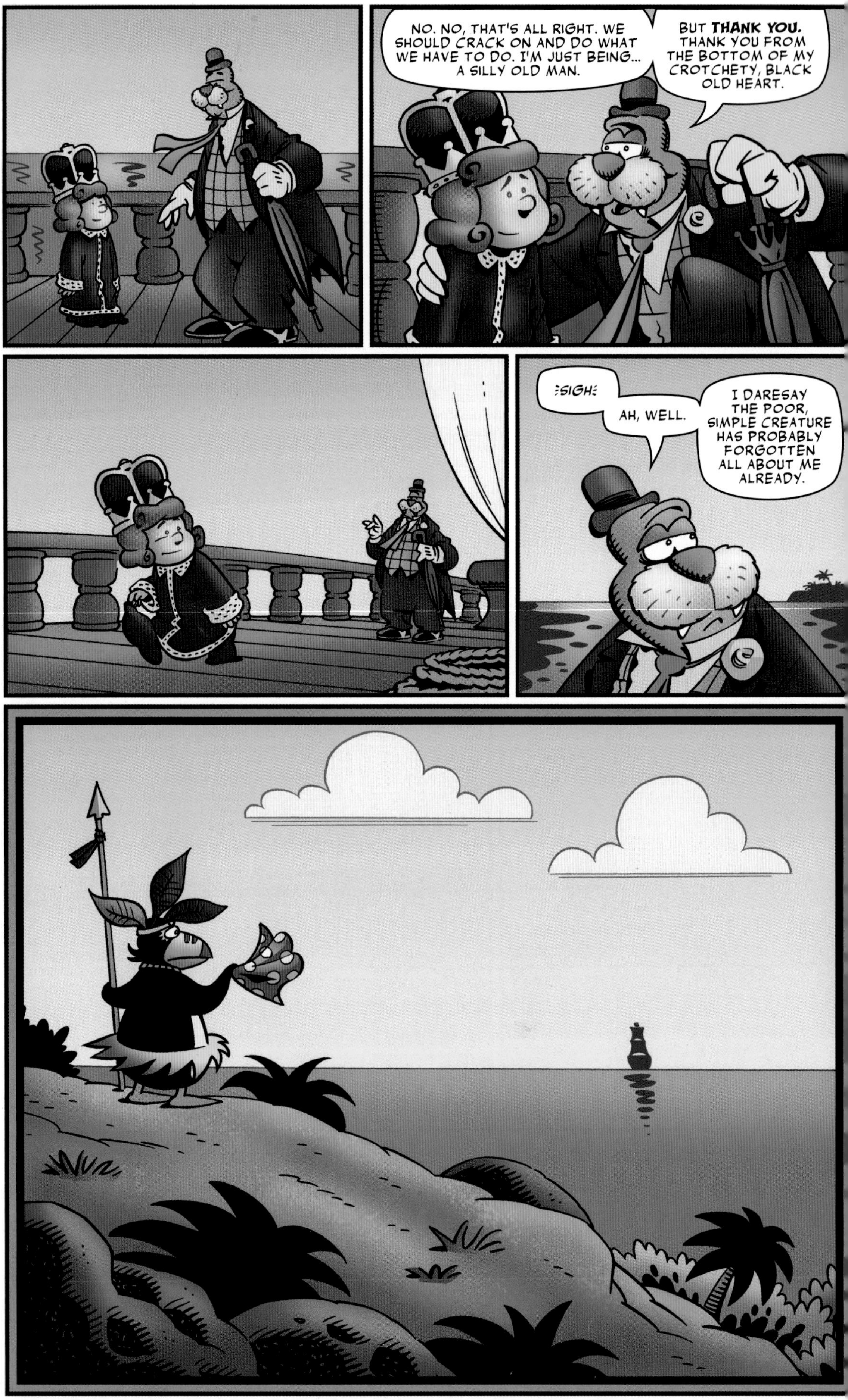
NO. NO, THAT'S ALL RIGHT. WE SHOULD CRACK ON AND DO WHAT WE HAVE TO DO. I'M JUST BEING... A SILLY OLD MAN.
BUT THANK YOU. THANK YOU FROM THE BOTTOM OF MY CROTCHETY, BLACK OLD HEART.
SIGH
AH, WELL.
I DARESAY THE POOR, SIMPLE CREATURE HAS PROBABLY FORGOTTEN ALL ABOUT ME ALREADY.

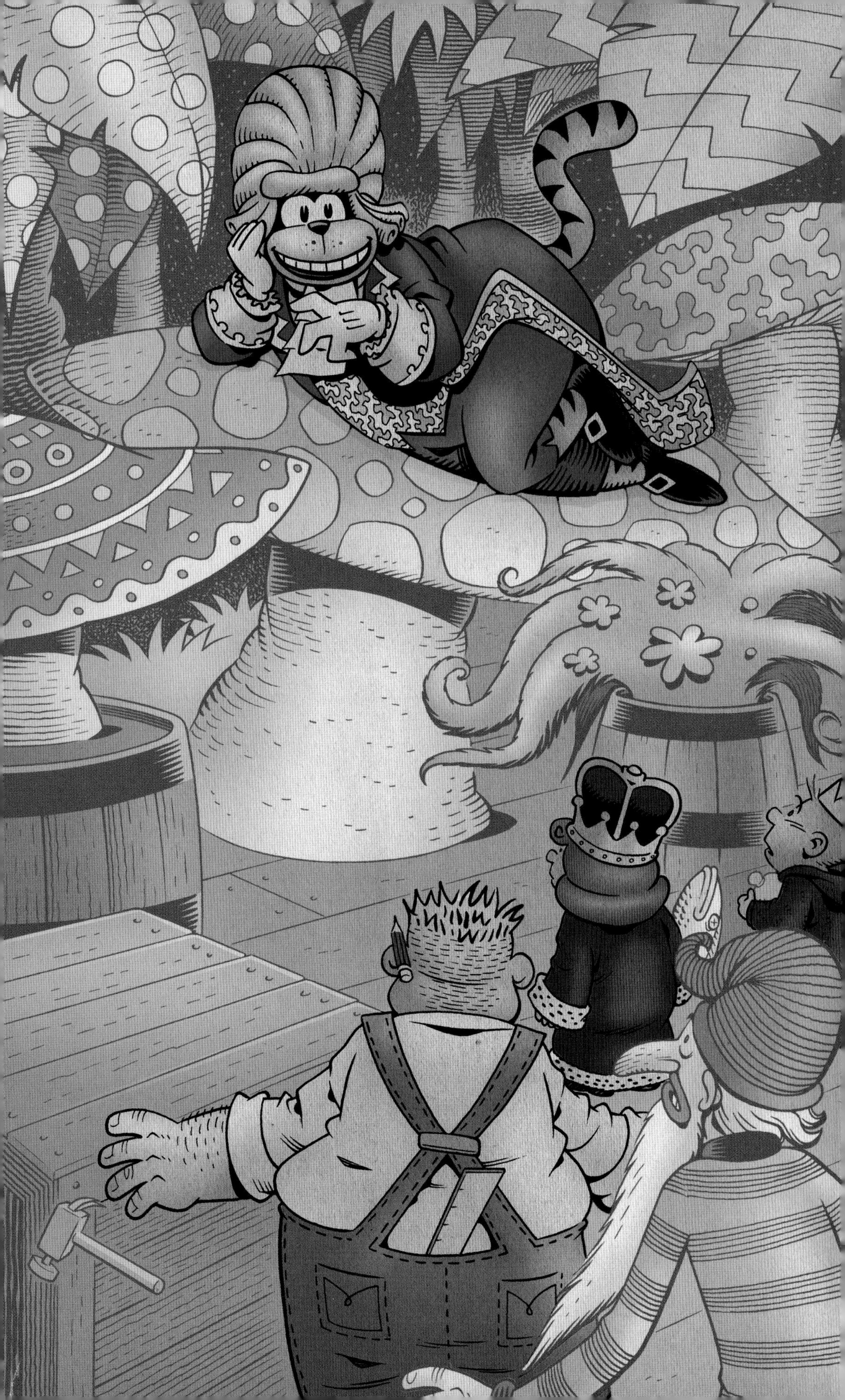

FIT THE EIGHTH

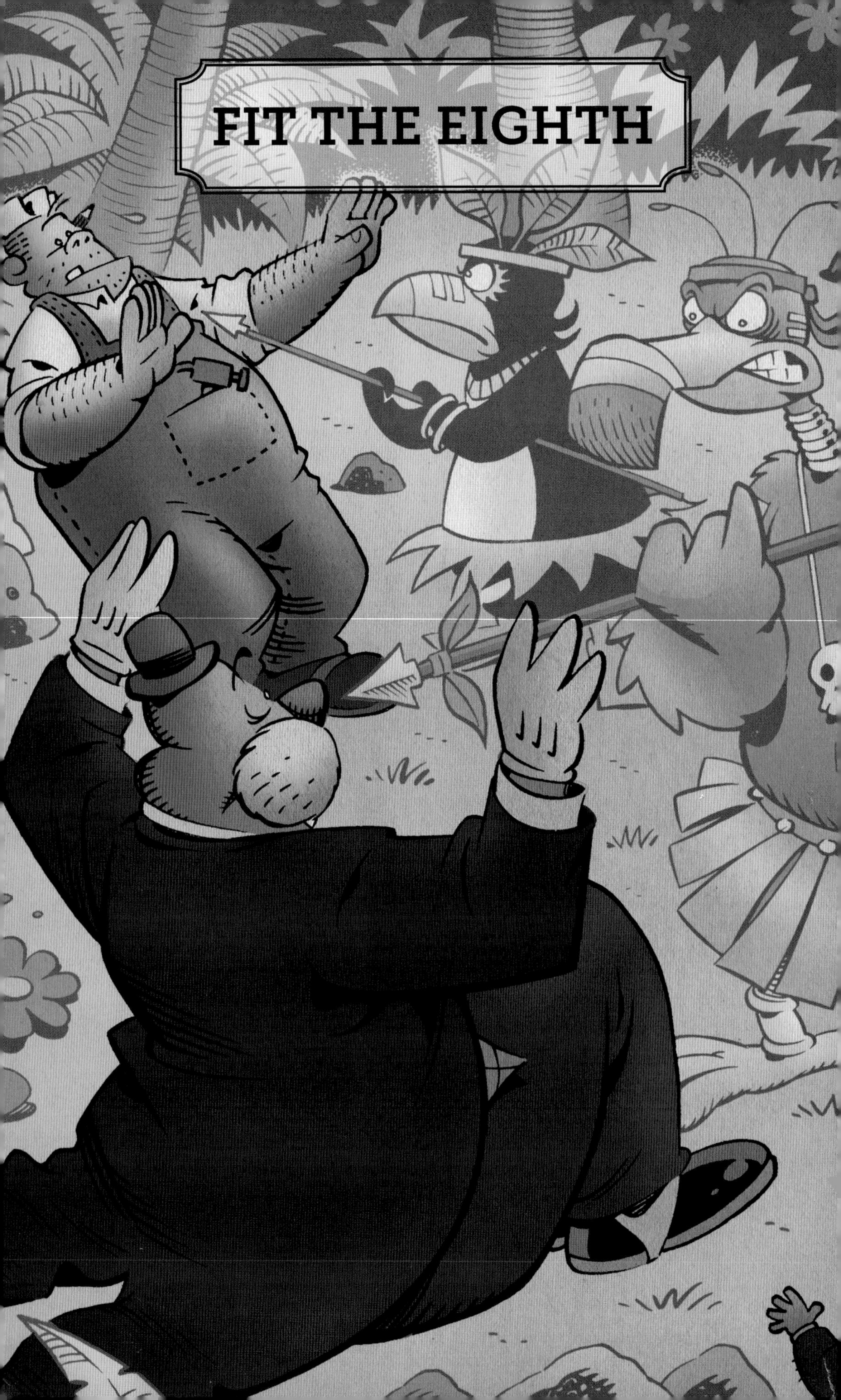

In the sky o'er the water the dark ship glides, and it swoops as it follows its quarry.
And yet, if he finds it, he's in for a fight; the Gryphon may yet find he's sorry...

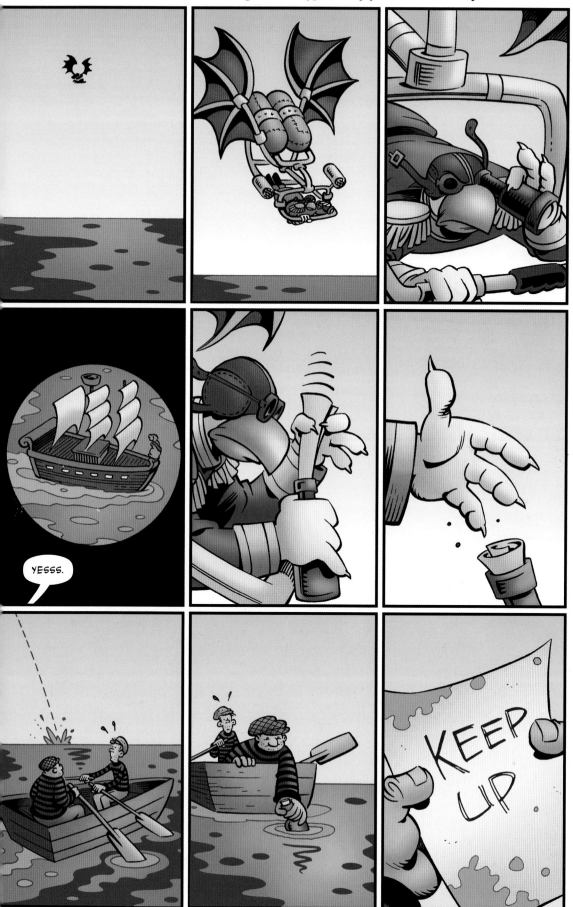

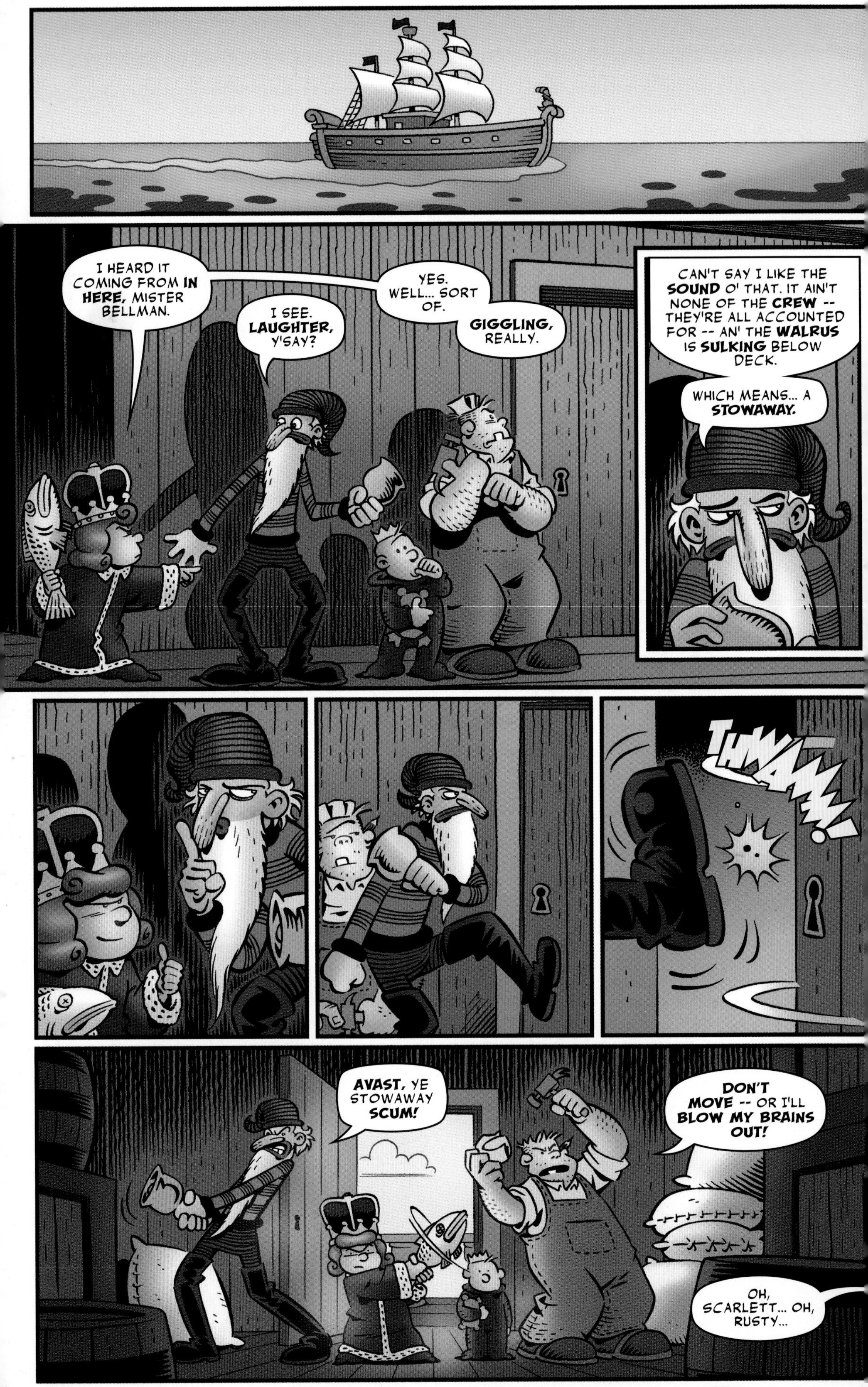
I HEARD IT COMING FROM **IN HERE,** MISTER BELLMAN.
I SEE. **LAUGHTER,** Y'SAY?
YES. WELL... SORT OF.
GIGGLING, REALLY.
CAN'T SAY I LIKE THE **SOUND** O' THAT. IT AIN'T NONE OF THE **CREW** -- THEY'RE ALL ACCOUNTED FOR -- AN' THE **WALRUS** IS **SULKING** BELOW DECK.
WHICH MEANS... A **STOWAWAY.**
THWAM!
AVAST, YE STOWAWAY **SCUM!**
DON'T MOVE -- OR I'LL **BLOW MY BRAINS OUT!**
OH, SCARLETT... OH, RUSTY...

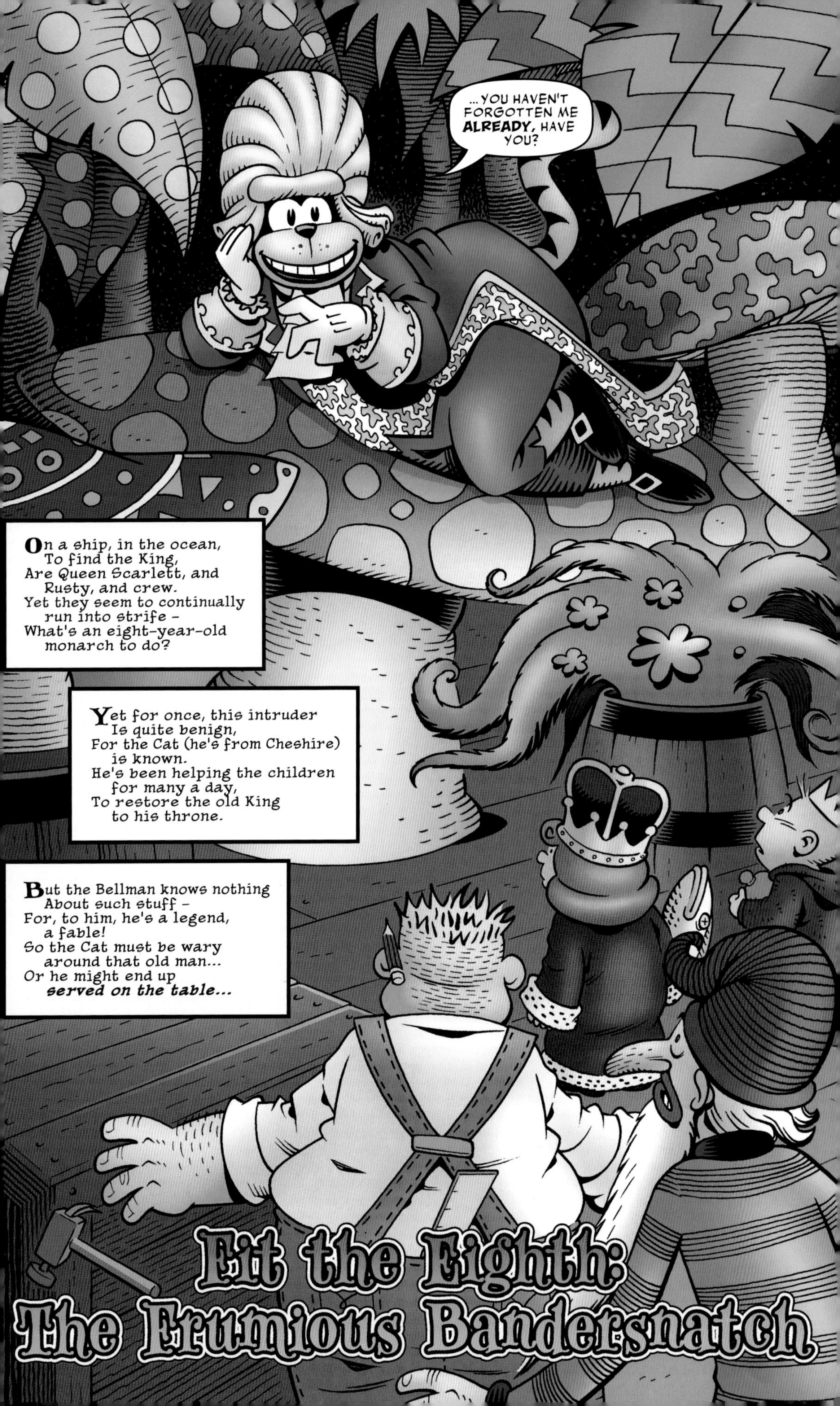
...YOU HAVEN'T FORGOTTEN ME ALREADY, HAVE YOU?
On a ship, in the ocean, To find the King, Are Queen Scarlett, and Rusty, and crew. Yet they seem to continually run into strife - What's an eight-year-old monarch to do?
Yet for once, this intruder Is quite benign, For the Cat (he's from Cheshire) is known. He's been helping the children for many a day, To restore the old King to his throne.
But the Bellman knows nothing About such stuff - For, to him, he's a legend, a fable! So the Cat must be wary around that old man... Or he might end up served on the table...
Fit the Eighth: The Frumious Bandersnatch

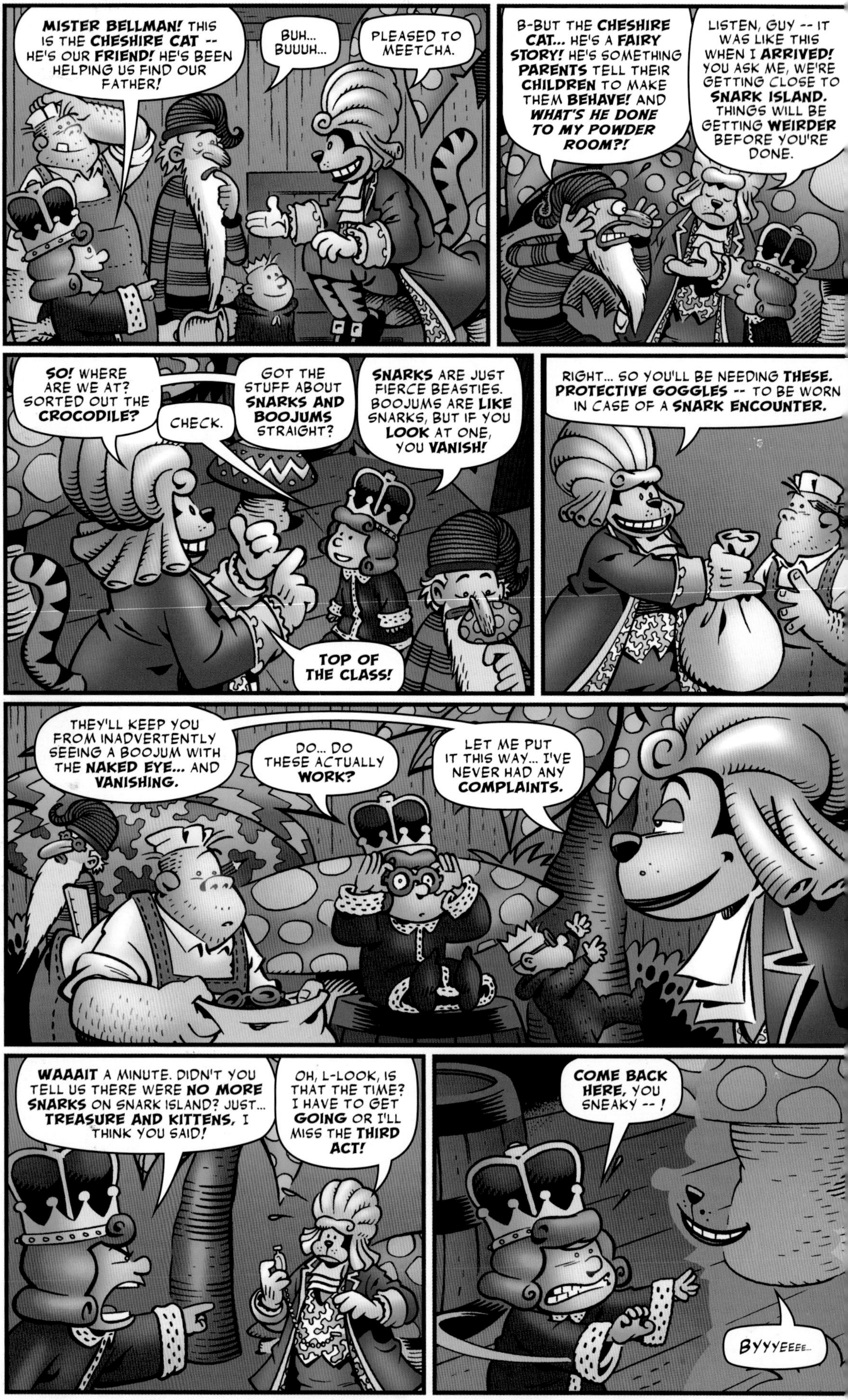

MISTER BELLMAN! THIS IS THE CHESHIRE CAT -- HE'S OUR FRIEND! HE'S BEEN HELPING US FIND OUR FATHER!
BUH... BUUUH...
PLEASED TO MEETCHA.
B-BUT THE CHESHIRE CAT... HE'S A FAIRY STORY! HE'S SOMETHING PARENTS TELL THEIR CHILDREN TO MAKE THEM BEHAVE! AND WHAT'S HE DONE TO MY POWDER ROOM?!
LISTEN, GUY -- IT WAS LIKE THIS WHEN I ARRIVED! YOU ASK ME, WE'RE GETTING CLOSE TO SNARK ISLAND. THINGS WILL BE GETTING WEIRDER BEFORE YOU'RE DONE.
SO! WHERE ARE WE AT? SORTED OUT THE CROCODILE?
CHECK.
GOT THE STUFF ABOUT SNARKS AND BOOJUMS STRAIGHT?
SNARKS ARE JUST FIERCE BEASTIES. BOOJUMS ARE LIKE SNARKS, BUT IF YOU LOOK AT ONE, YOU VANISH!
TOP OF THE CLASS!
RIGHT... SO YOU'LL BE NEEDING THESE. PROTECTIVE GOGGLES -- TO BE WORN IN CASE OF A SNARK ENCOUNTER.
THEY'LL KEEP YOU FROM INADVERTENTLY SEEING A BOOJUM WITH THE NAKED EYE... AND VANISHING.
DO... DO THESE ACTUALLY WORK?
LET ME PUT IT THIS WAY... I'VE NEVER HAD ANY COMPLAINTS.
WAAAIT A MINUTE. DIDN'T YOU TELL US THERE WERE NO MORE SNARKS ON SNARK ISLAND? JUST... TREASURE AND KITTENS, I THINK YOU SAID!
OH, L-LOOK, IS THAT THE TIME? I HAVE TO GET GOING OR I'LL MISS THE THIRD ACT!
COME BACK HERE, YOU SNEAKY -- !
BYYYEEEE...

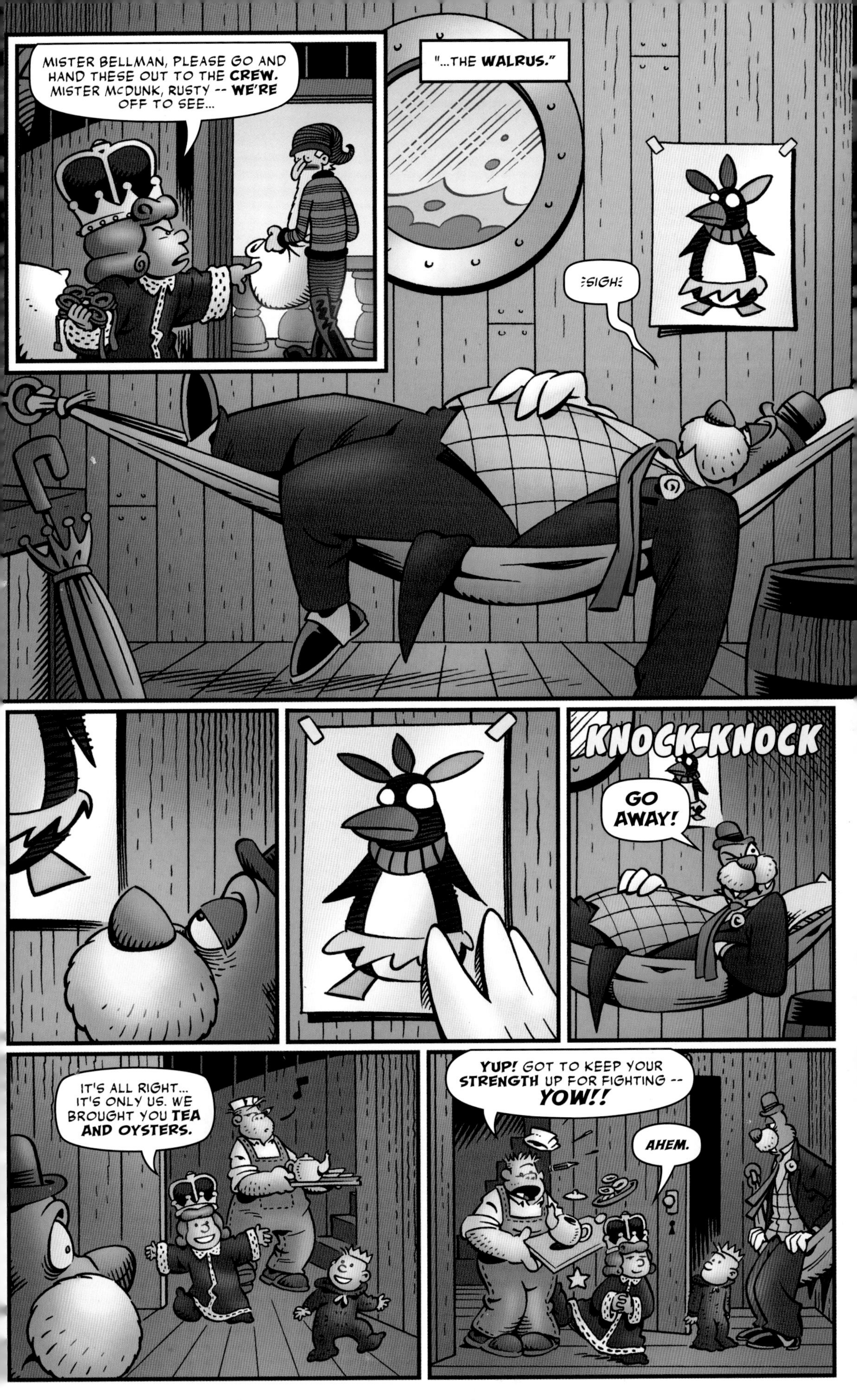
MISTER BELLMAN, PLEASE GO AND HAND THESE OUT TO THE **CREW.** MISTER McDUNK, RUSTY -- **WE'RE** OFF TO SEE...
"...THE **WALRUS.**"
SIGH
KNOCK KNOCK
GO AWAY!
IT'S ALL RIGHT... IT'S ONLY US. WE BROUGHT YOU **TEA AND OYSTERS.**
YUP! GOT TO KEEP YOUR **STRENGTH** UP FOR FIGHTING -- ***YOW!!***
AHEM.

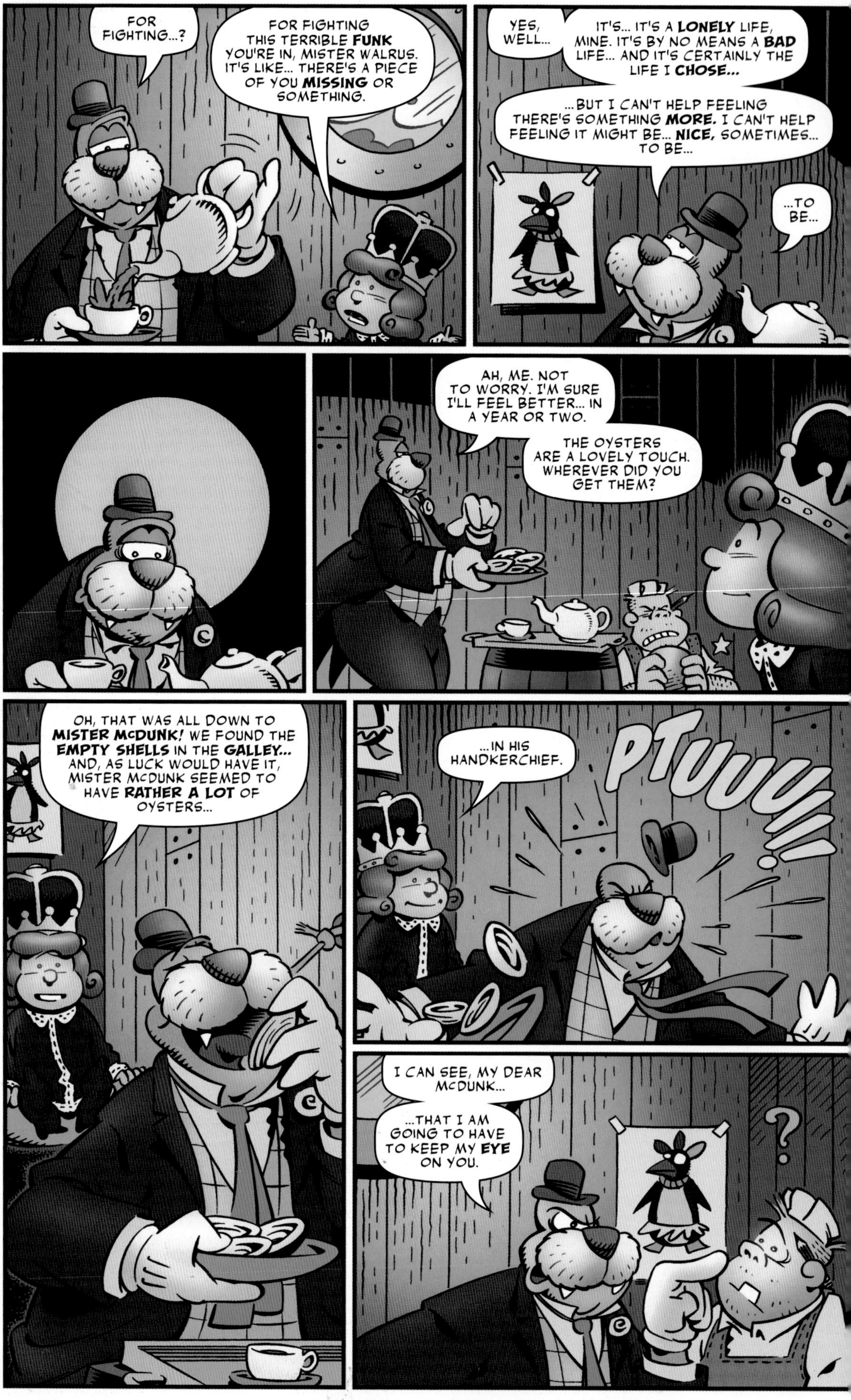
FOR FIGHTING...?
FOR FIGHTING THIS TERRIBLE **FUNK** YOU'RE IN, MISTER WALRUS. IT'S LIKE... THERE'S A PIECE OF YOU **MISSING** OR SOMETHING.
YES, WELL...
IT'S... IT'S A **LONELY** LIFE, MINE. IT'S BY NO MEANS A **BAD** LIFE... AND IT'S CERTAINLY THE LIFE I **CHOSE...**
...BUT I CAN'T HELP FEELING THERE'S SOMETHING **MORE.** I CAN'T HELP FEELING IT MIGHT BE... **NICE,** SOMETIMES... TO BE...
...TO BE...
AH, ME. NOT TO WORRY. I'M SURE I'LL FEEL BETTER... IN A YEAR OR TWO.
THE OYSTERS ARE A LOVELY TOUCH. WHEREVER DID YOU GET THEM?
OH, THAT WAS ALL DOWN TO **MISTER McDUNK!** WE FOUND THE **EMPTY SHELLS** IN THE **GALLEY...** AND, AS LUCK WOULD HAVE IT, MISTER McDUNK SEEMED TO HAVE **RATHER A LOT** OF OYSTERS...
...IN HIS HANDKERCHIEF.
PTUUU!!!
I CAN SEE, MY DEAR McDUNK...
...THAT I AM GOING TO HAVE TO KEEP MY **EYE** ON YOU.
?

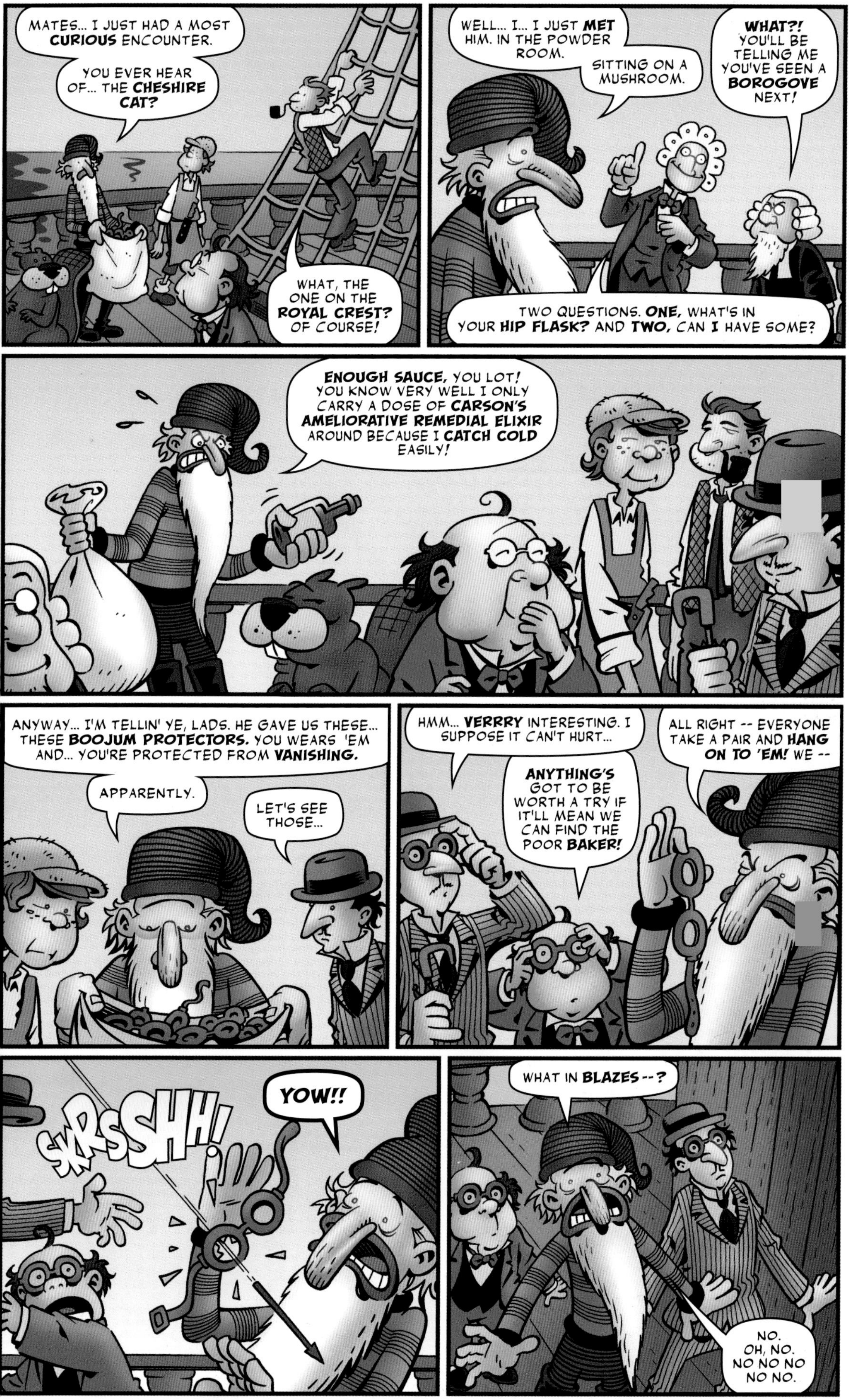

MATES... I JUST HAD A MOST **CURIOUS** ENCOUNTER.
YOU EVER HEAR OF... THE **CHESHIRE CAT?**
WHAT, THE ONE ON THE **ROYAL CREST?** OF COURSE!
WELL... I... I JUST **MET** HIM. IN THE POWDER ROOM.
SITTING ON A MUSHROOM.
WHAT?! YOU'LL BE TELLING ME YOU'VE SEEN A **BOROGOVE** NEXT!
TWO QUESTIONS. **ONE**, WHAT'S IN YOUR **HIP FLASK?** AND **TWO**, CAN **I** HAVE SOME?
ENOUGH SAUCE, YOU LOT! YOU KNOW VERY WELL I ONLY CARRY A DOSE OF **CARSON'S AMELIORATIVE REMEDIAL ELIXIR** AROUND BECAUSE I **CATCH COLD** EASILY!
ANYWAY... I'M TELLIN' YE, LADS. HE GAVE US THESE... THESE **BOOJUM PROTECTORS.** YOU WEARS 'EM AND... YOU'RE PROTECTED FROM **VANISHING.**
APPARENTLY.
LET'S SEE THOSE...
HMM... **VERRRY** INTERESTING. I SUPPOSE IT CAN'T HURT...
ANYTHING'S GOT TO BE WORTH A TRY IF IT'LL MEAN WE CAN FIND THE POOR **BAKER!**
ALL RIGHT -- EVERYONE TAKE A PAIR AND **HANG ON TO 'EM!** WE --
SKRSSHH!
YOW!!
WHAT IN **BLAZES**--?
NO. OH, NO. NO NO NO NO NO.

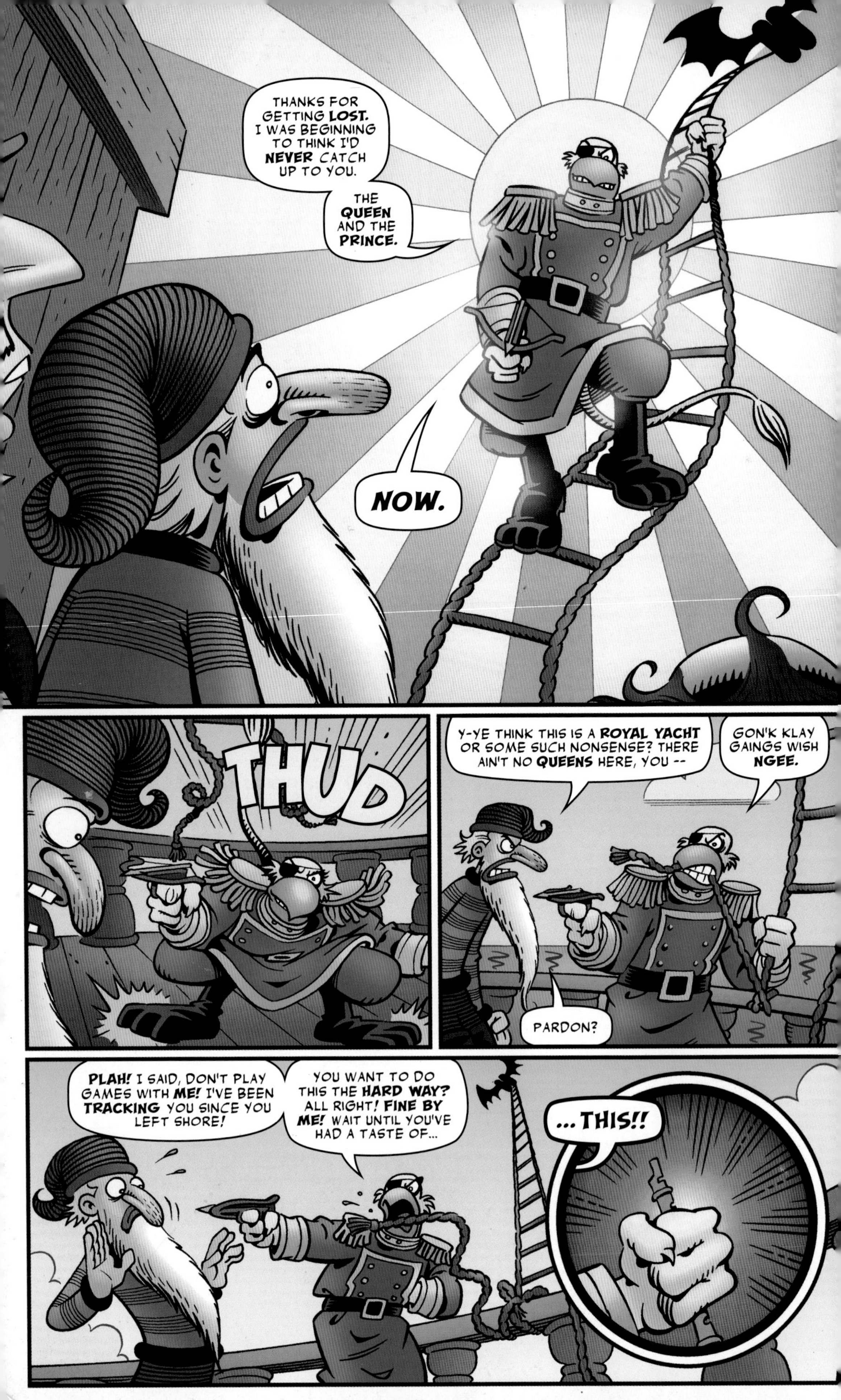
THANKS FOR GETTING **LOST.** I WAS BEGINNING TO THINK I'D **NEVER** CATCH UP TO YOU.
THE **QUEEN** AND THE **PRINCE.**
NOW.
THUD
Y-YE THINK THIS IS A **ROYAL YACHT** OR SOME SUCH NONSENSE? THERE AIN'T NO **QUEENS** HERE, YOU --
GON'K KLAY GAINGS WISH **NGEE.**
PARDON?
PLAH! I SAID, DON'T PLAY GAMES WITH **ME!** I'VE BEEN **TRACKING** YOU SINCE YOU LEFT SHORE!
YOU WANT TO DO THIS THE **HARD WAY?** ALL RIGHT! **FINE BY ME!** WAIT UNTIL YOU'VE HAD A TASTE OF...
...THIS!!

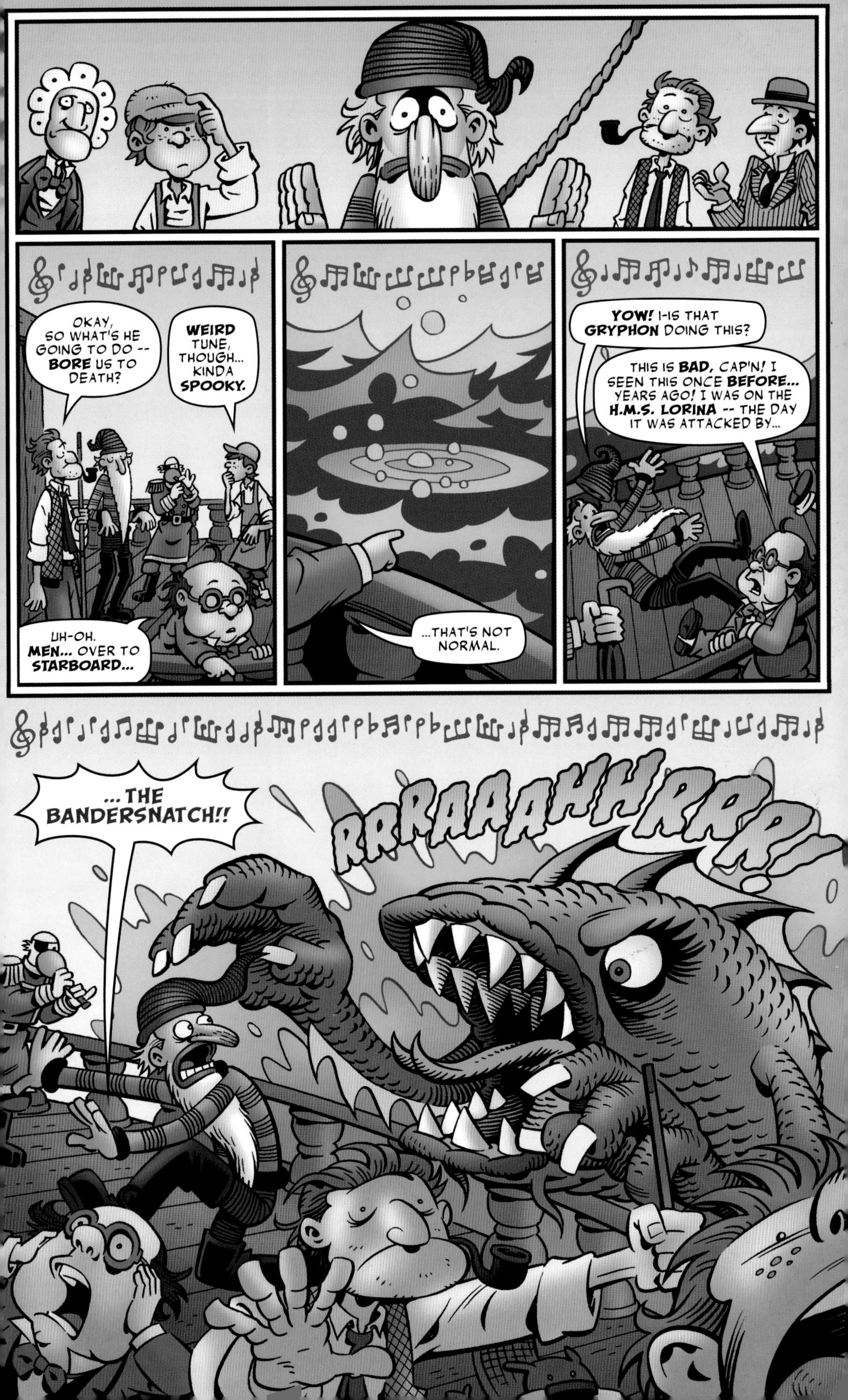
OKAY, SO WHAT'S HE GOING TO DO -- BORE US TO DEATH?
WEIRD TUNE, THOUGH... KINDA SPOOKY.
UH-OH. MEN... OVER TO STARBOARD...
...THAT'S NOT NORMAL.
YOW! I-IS THAT GRYPHON DOING THIS?
THIS IS BAD, CAP'N! I SEEN THIS ONCE BEFORE... YEARS AGO! I WAS ON THE H.M.S. LORINA -- THE DAY IT WAS ATTACKED BY...
...THE BANDERSNATCH!!
RRRAAAAHHRRR!!

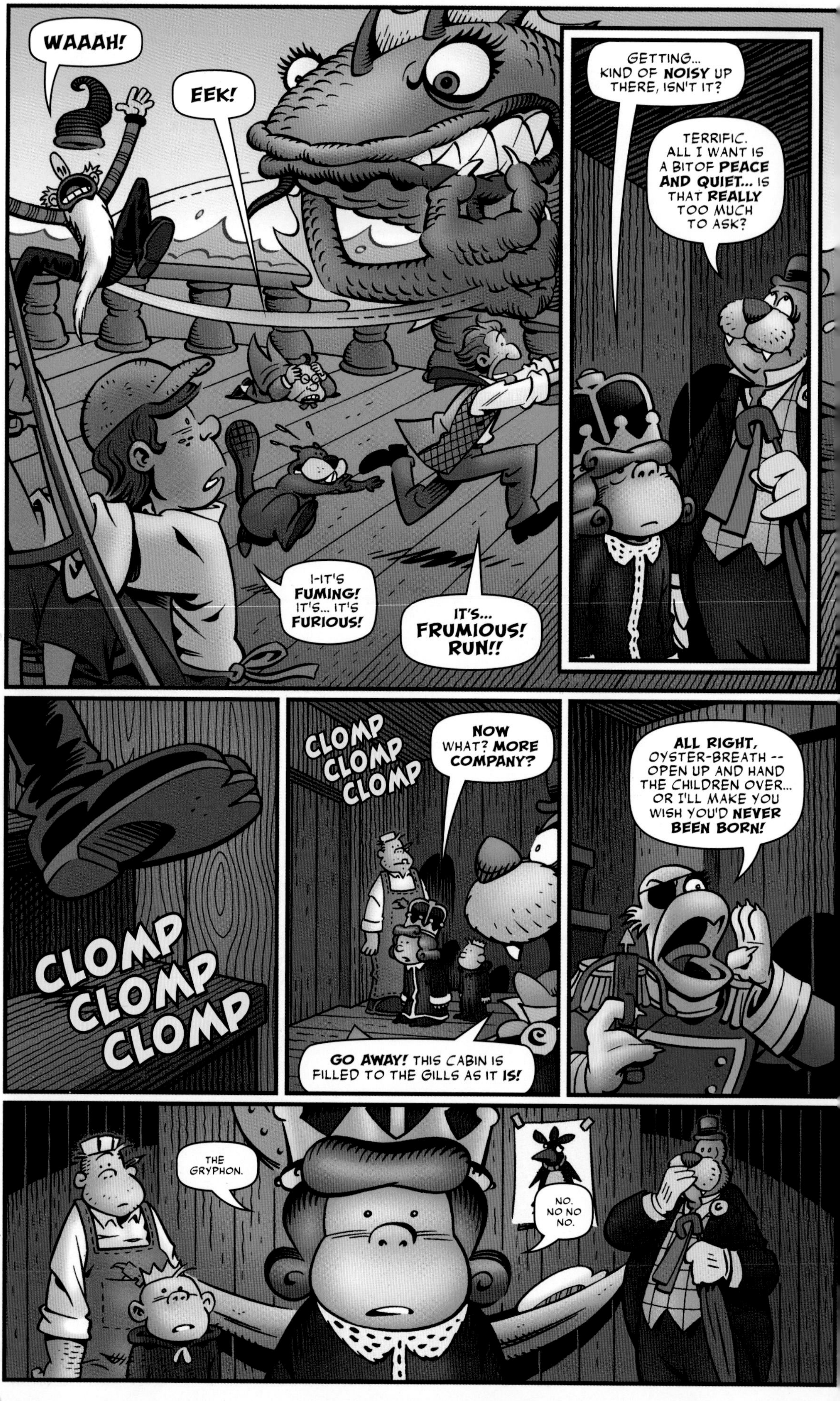
WAAAH!
EEK!
I-IT'S FUMING! IT'S... IT'S FURIOUS!
IT'S... FRUMIOUS! RUN!!
GETTING... KIND OF NOISY UP THERE, ISN'T IT?
TERRIFIC. ALL I WANT IS A BIT OF PEACE AND QUIET... IS THAT REALLY TOO MUCH TO ASK?
CLOMP CLOMP CLOMP
CLOMP CLOMP CLOMP
NOW WHAT? MORE COMPANY?
GO AWAY! THIS CABIN IS FILLED TO THE GILLS AS IT IS!
ALL RIGHT, OYSTER-BREATH -- OPEN UP AND HAND THE CHILDREN OVER... OR I'LL MAKE YOU WISH YOU'D NEVER BEEN BORN!
THE GRYPHON.
NO. NO NO NO.

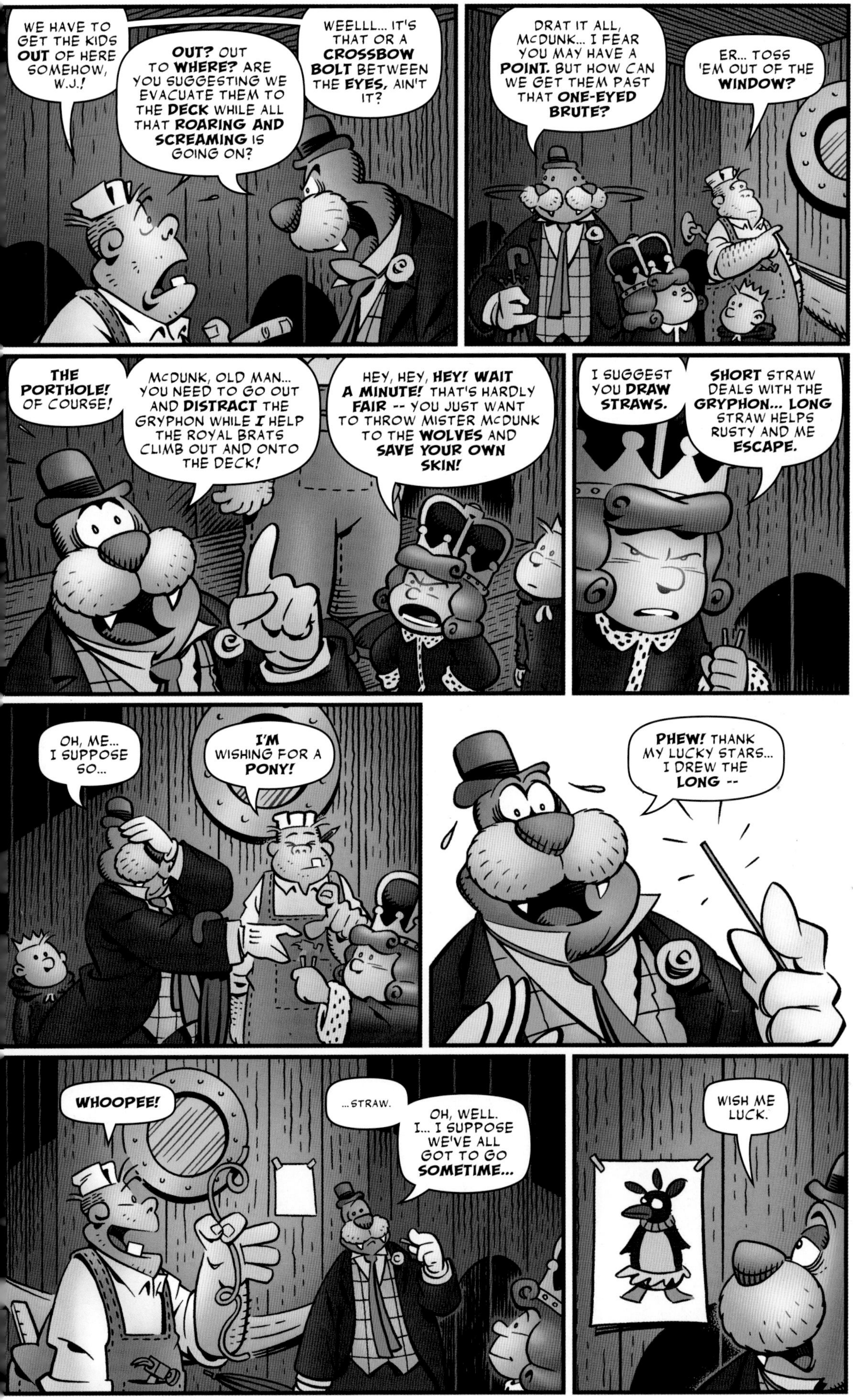
WE HAVE TO GET THE KIDS OUT OF HERE SOMEHOW, W.J.!
OUT? OUT TO WHERE? ARE YOU SUGGESTING WE EVACUATE THEM TO THE DECK WHILE ALL THAT ROARING AND SCREAMING IS GOING ON?
WEELLL... IT'S THAT OR A CROSSBOW BOLT BETWEEN THE EYES, AIN'T IT?
DRAT IT ALL, McDUNK... I FEAR YOU MAY HAVE A POINT. BUT HOW CAN WE GET THEM PAST THAT ONE-EYED BRUTE?
ER... TOSS 'EM OUT OF THE WINDOW?
THE PORTHOLE! OF COURSE!
McDUNK, OLD MAN... YOU NEED TO GO OUT AND DISTRACT THE GRYPHON WHILE I HELP THE ROYAL BRATS CLIMB OUT AND ONTO THE DECK!
HEY, HEY, HEY! WAIT A MINUTE! THAT'S HARDLY FAIR -- YOU JUST WANT TO THROW MISTER McDUNK TO THE WOLVES AND SAVE YOUR OWN SKIN!
I SUGGEST YOU DRAW STRAWS.
SHORT STRAW DEALS WITH THE GRYPHON... LONG STRAW HELPS RUSTY AND ME ESCAPE.
OH, ME... I SUPPOSE SO...
I'M WISHING FOR A PONY!
PHEW! THANK MY LUCKY STARS... I DREW THE LONG --
WHOOPEE!
...STRAW.
OH, WELL. I... I SUPPOSE WE'VE ALL GOT TO GO SOMETIME...
WISH ME LUCK.

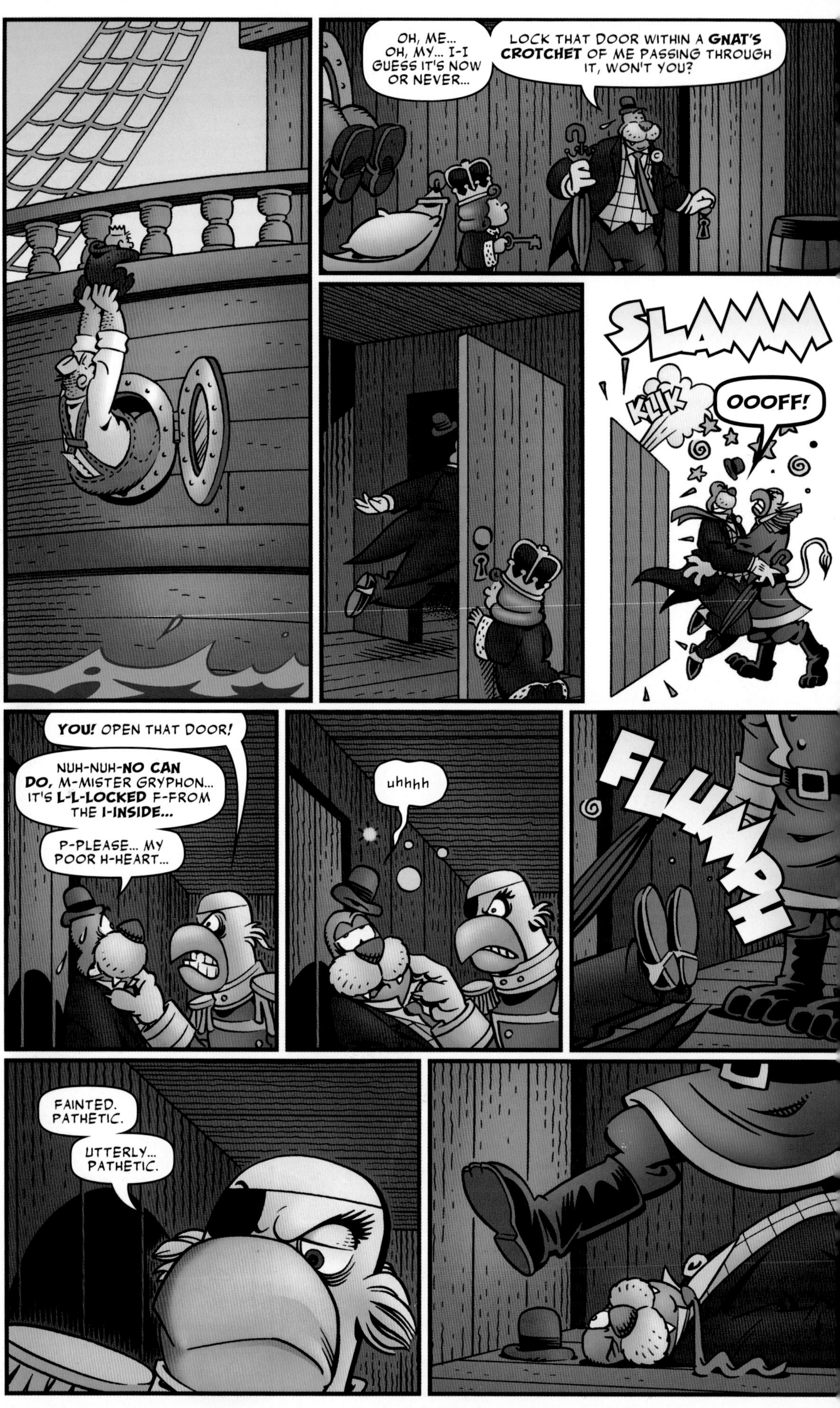
OH, ME... OH, MY... I-I GUESS IT'S NOW OR NEVER...
LOCK THAT DOOR WITHIN A GNAT'S CROTCHET OF ME PASSING THROUGH IT, WON'T YOU?
SLAMM
KLIK
OOOFF!
YOU! OPEN THAT DOOR!
NUH-NUH-NO CAN DO, M-MISTER GRYPHON... IT'S L-L-LOCKED F-FROM THE I-INSIDE...
P-PLEASE... MY POOR H-HEART...
uhhhh
FLUMPH
FAINTED. PATHETIC.
UTTERLY... PATHETIC.

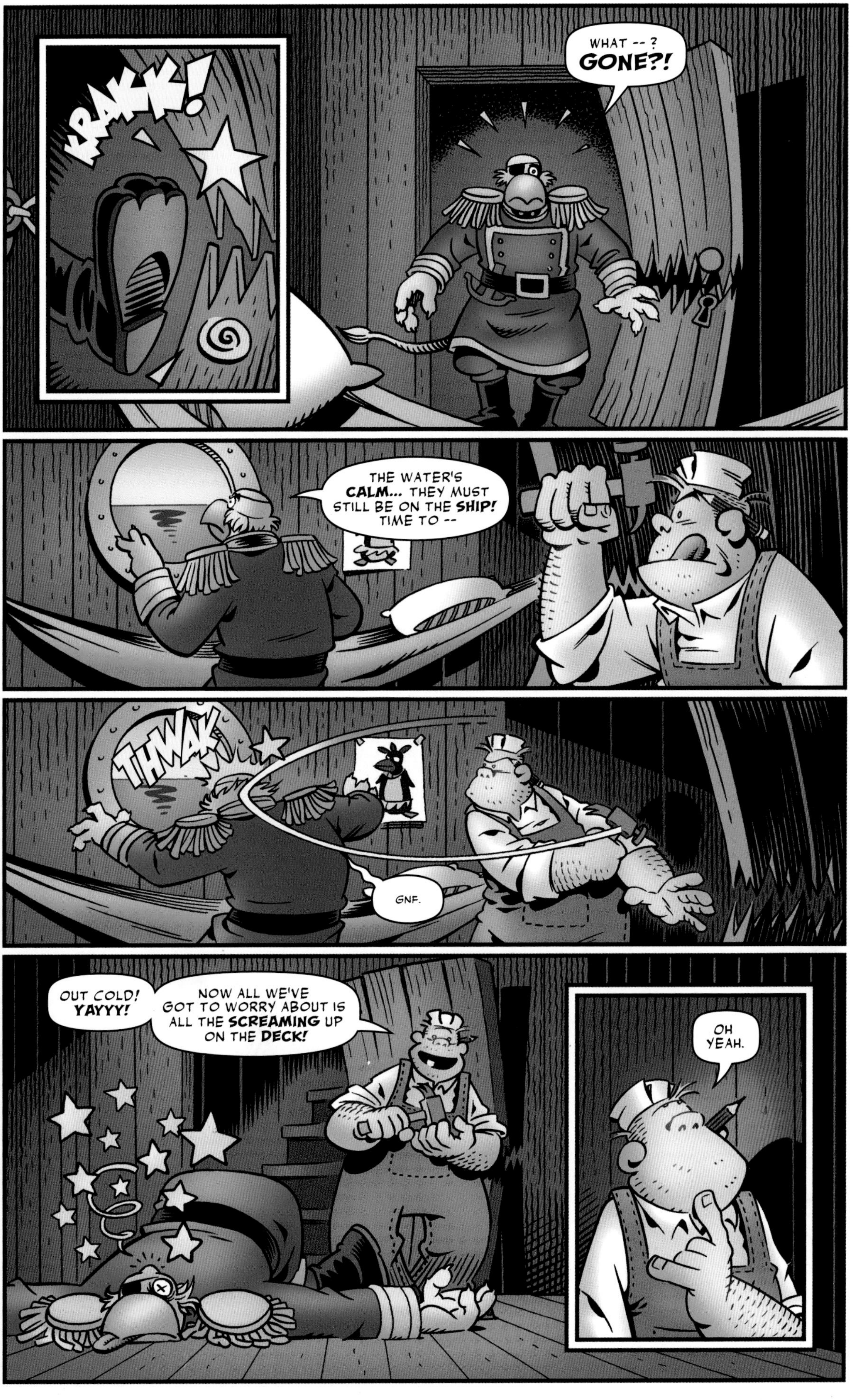
KRAKK!
WHAT -- ? GONE?!
THE WATER'S CALM... THEY MUST STILL BE ON THE SHIP! TIME TO --
THWAK
GNF.
OUT COLD! YAYYY!
NOW ALL WE'VE GOT TO WORRY ABOUT IS ALL THE SCREAMING UP ON THE DECK!
OH YEAH.

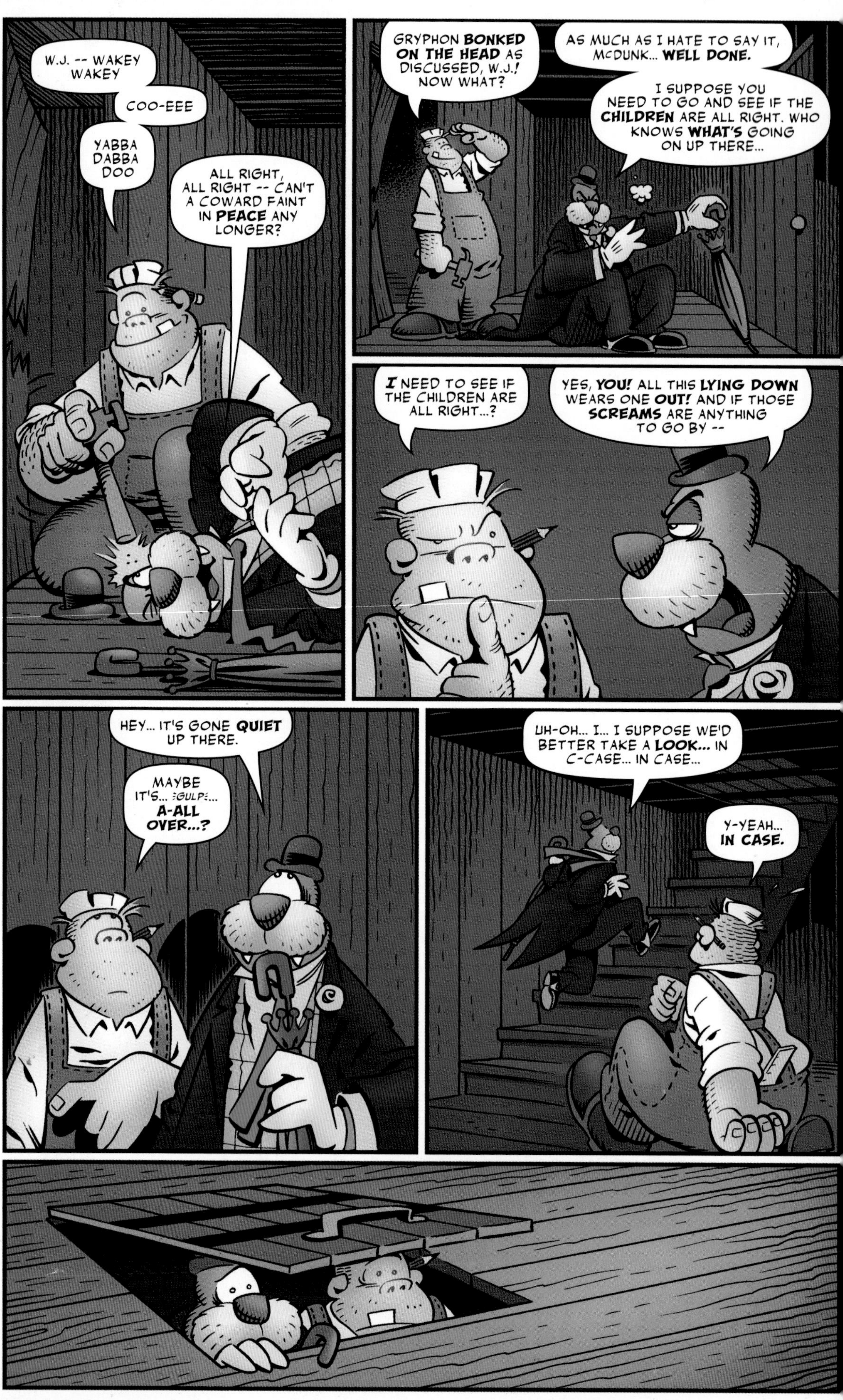
W.J. -- WAKEY WAKEY
COO-EEE
YABBA DABBA DOO
ALL RIGHT, ALL RIGHT -- CAN'T A COWARD FAINT IN **PEACE** ANY LONGER?
GRYPHON **BONKED ON THE HEAD** AS DISCUSSED, W.J.! NOW WHAT?
AS MUCH AS I HATE TO SAY IT, McDUNK... **WELL DONE.**
I SUPPOSE YOU NEED TO GO AND SEE IF THE **CHILDREN** ARE ALL RIGHT. WHO KNOWS **WHAT'S** GOING ON UP THERE...
I NEED TO SEE IF THE CHILDREN ARE ALL RIGHT...?
YES, **YOU!** ALL THIS **LYING DOWN** WEARS ONE **OUT!** AND IF THOSE **SCREAMS** ARE ANYTHING TO GO BY --
HEY... IT'S GONE **QUIET** UP THERE.
MAYBE IT'S... *GULP*... **A-ALL OVER...?**
UH-OH... I... I SUPPOSE WE'D BETTER TAKE A **LOOK...** IN C-CASE... IN CASE...
Y-YEAH... **IN CASE.**

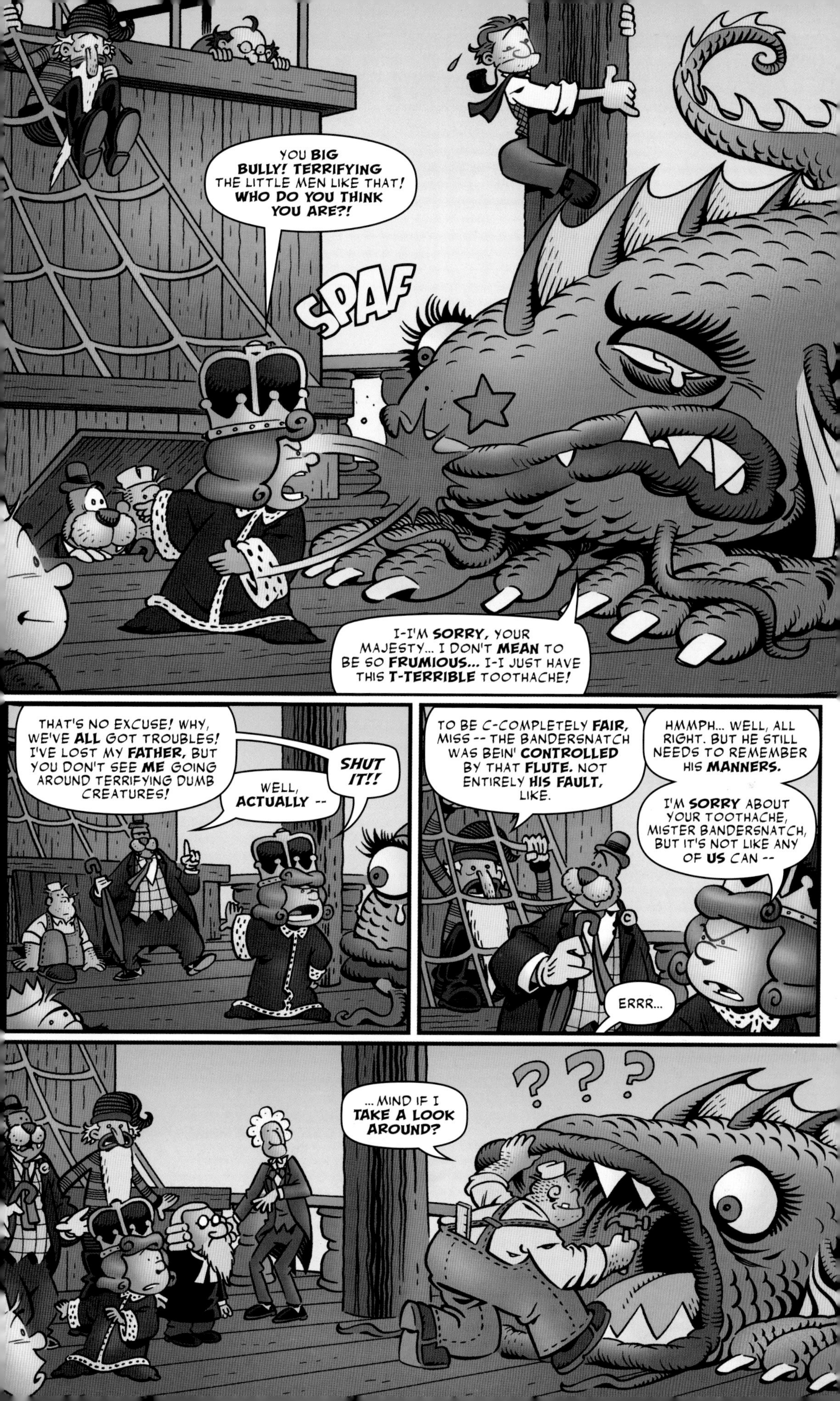
YOU BIG BULLY! TERRIFYING THE LITTLE MEN LIKE THAT! WHO DO YOU THINK YOU ARE?!
SPAF
I-I'M SORRY, YOUR MAJESTY... I DON'T MEAN TO BE SO FRUMIOUS... I-I JUST HAVE THIS T-TERRIBLE TOOTHACHE!
THAT'S NO EXCUSE! WHY, WE'VE ALL GOT TROUBLES! I'VE LOST MY FATHER, BUT YOU DON'T SEE ME GOING AROUND TERRIFYING DUMB CREATURES!
WELL, ACTUALLY --
SHUT IT!!
TO BE C-COMPLETELY FAIR, MISS -- THE BANDERSNATCH WAS BEIN' CONTROLLED BY THAT FLUTE. NOT ENTIRELY HIS FAULT, LIKE.
HMMPH... WELL, ALL RIGHT. BUT HE STILL NEEDS TO REMEMBER HIS MANNERS.
I'M SORRY ABOUT YOUR TOOTHACHE, MISTER BANDERSNATCH, BUT IT'S NOT LIKE ANY OF US CAN --
ERRR...
... MIND IF I TAKE A LOOK AROUND?
? ? ?

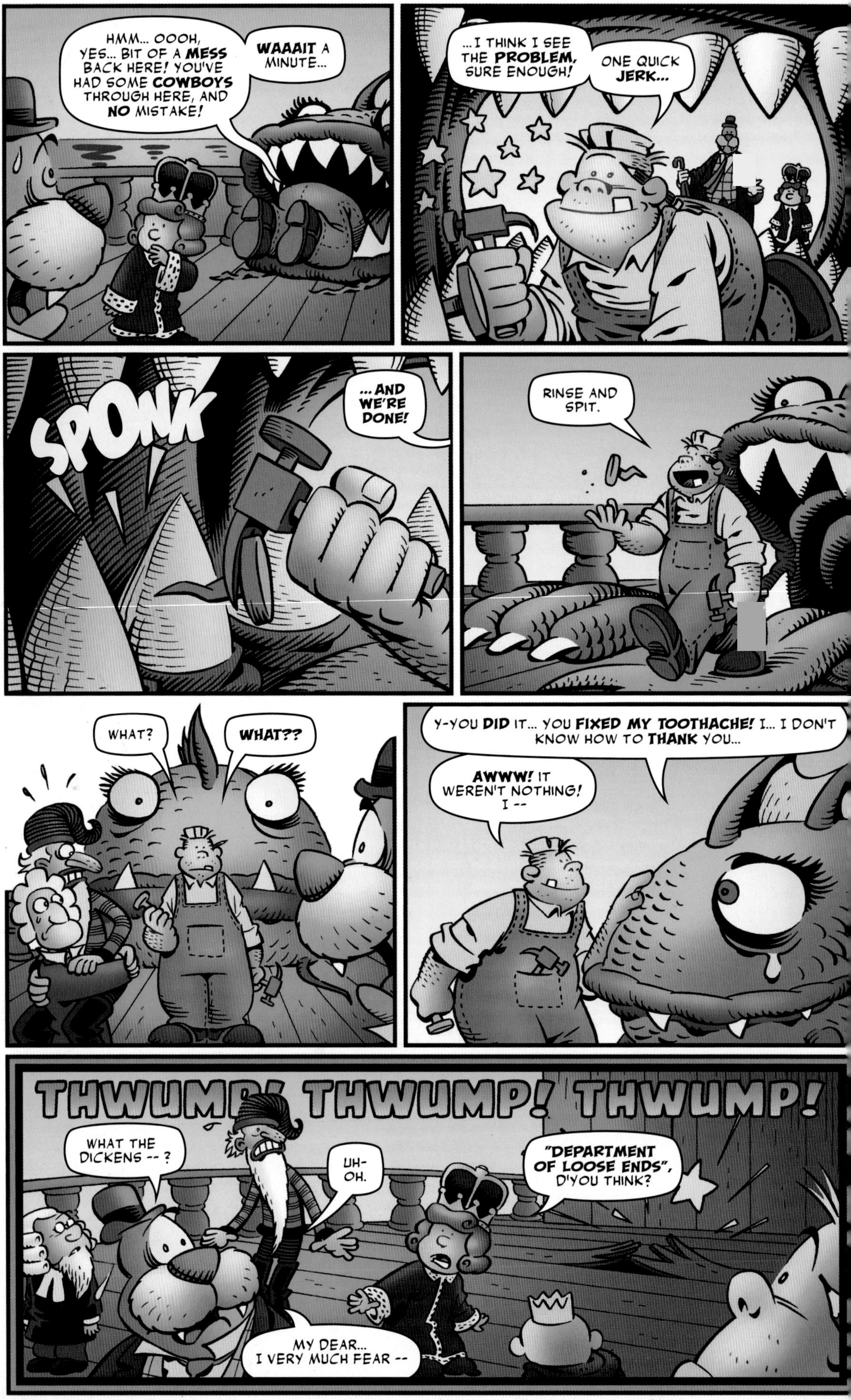
HMM... OOOH, YES... BIT OF A **MESS** BACK HERE! YOU'VE HAD SOME **COWBOYS** THROUGH HERE, AND **NO** MISTAKE!
WAAAIT A MINUTE...
...I THINK I SEE THE **PROBLEM**, SURE ENOUGH!
ONE QUICK **JERK...**
SPONK
...AND WE'RE DONE!
RINSE AND SPIT.
WHAT?
WHAT??
Y-YOU **DID** IT... YOU **FIXED MY TOOTHACHE!** I... I DON'T KNOW HOW TO **THANK** YOU...
AWWW! IT WEREN'T NOTHING! I --
THWUMP! THWUMP! THWUMP!
WHAT THE DICKENS -- ?
UH-OH.
"DEPARTMENT OF LOOSE ENDS", D'YOU THINK?
MY DEAR... I VERY MUCH FEAR --

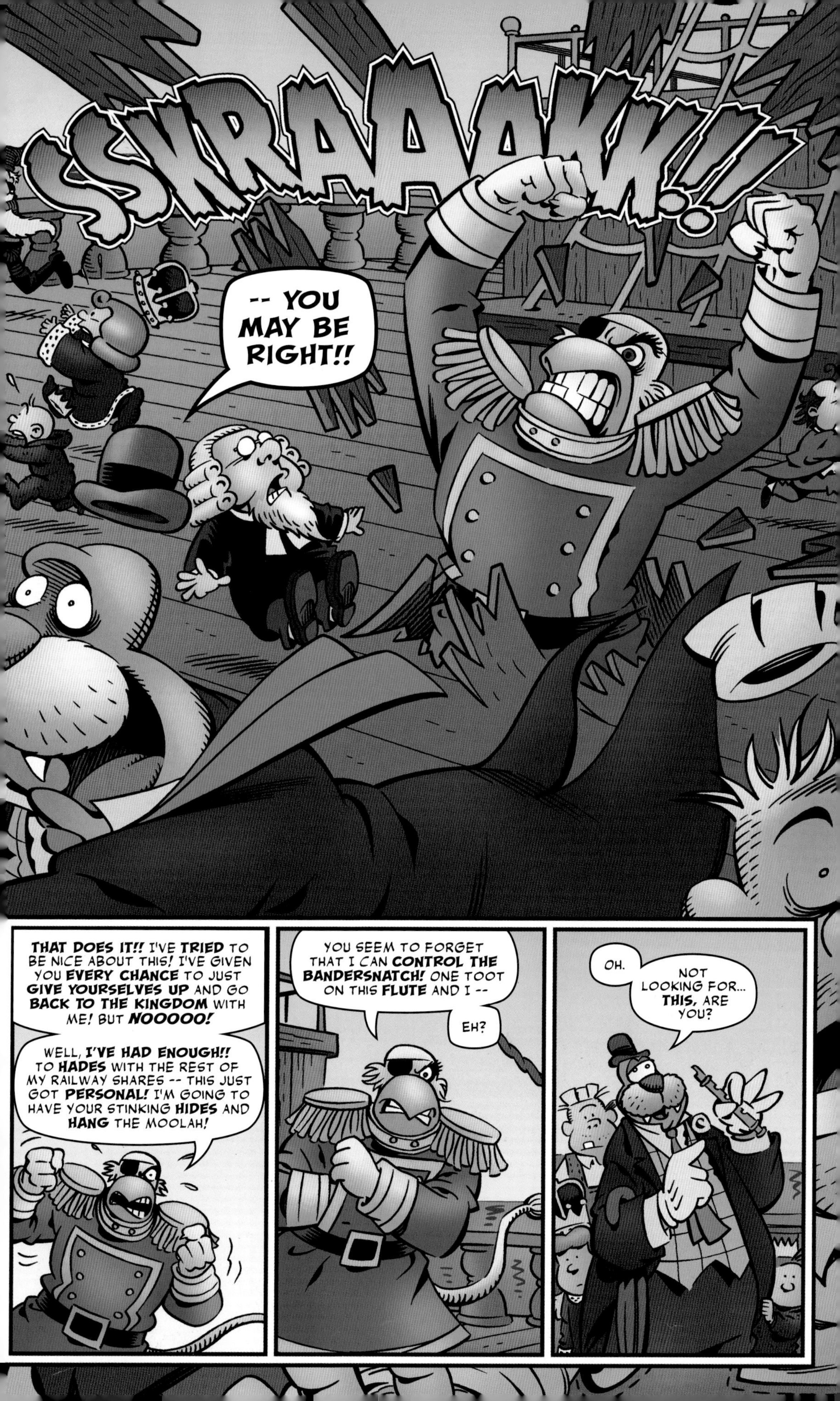

SKRAAKK!!
-- YOU MAY BE RIGHT!!
THAT DOES IT!! I'VE TRIED TO BE NICE ABOUT THIS! I'VE GIVEN YOU EVERY CHANCE TO JUST GIVE YOURSELVES UP AND GO BACK TO THE KINGDOM WITH ME! BUT NOOOOO!
WELL, I'VE HAD ENOUGH!! TO HADES WITH THE REST OF MY RAILWAY SHARES -- THIS JUST GOT PERSONAL! I'M GOING TO HAVE YOUR STINKING HIDES AND HANG THE MOOLAH!
YOU SEEM TO FORGET THAT I CAN CONTROL THE BANDERSNATCH! ONE TOOT ON THIS FLUTE AND I --
EH?
OH.
NOT LOOKING FOR... THIS, ARE YOU?

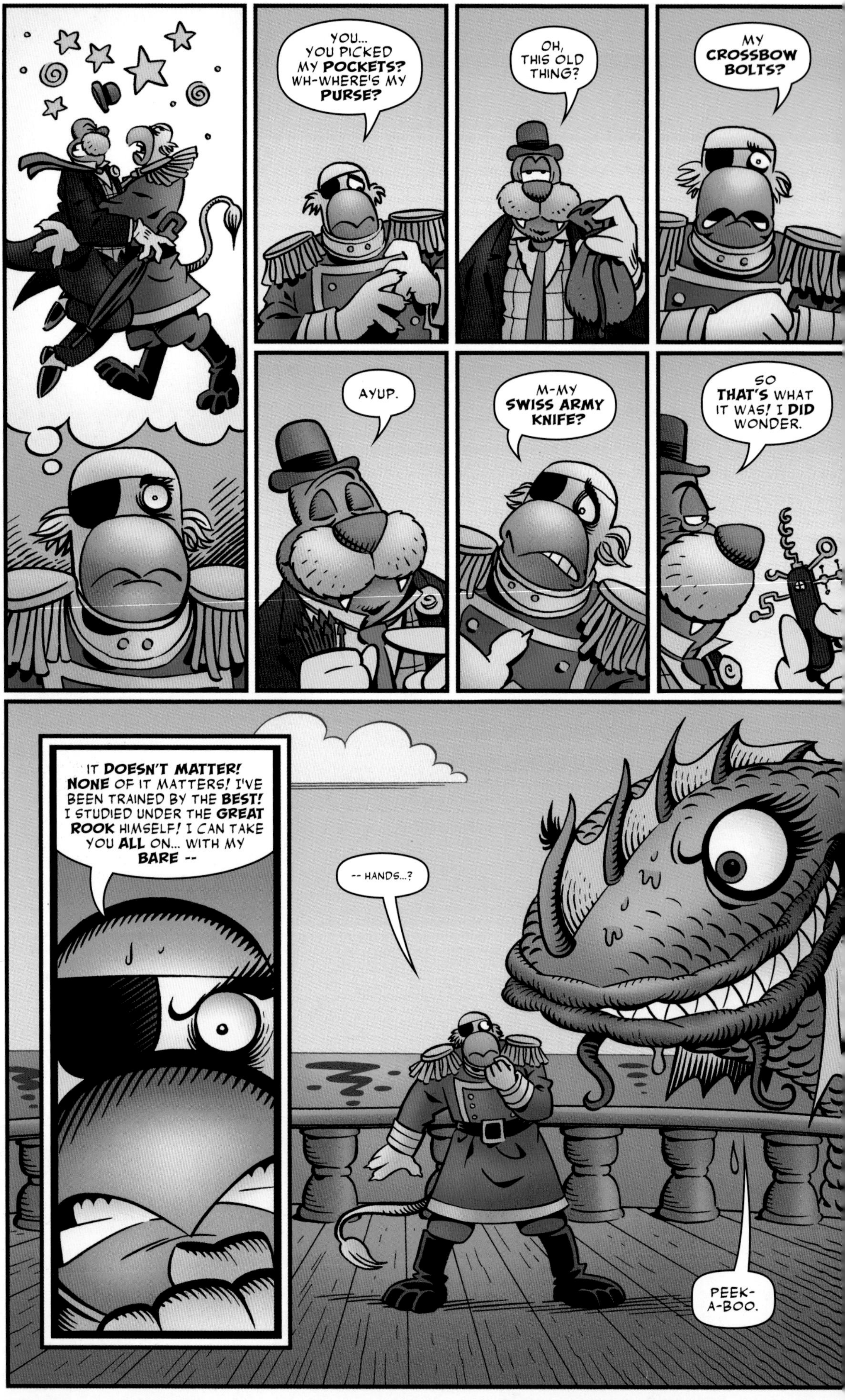
YOU... YOU PICKED MY POCKETS? WH-WHERE'S MY PURSE?
OH, THIS OLD THING?
MY CROSSBOW BOLTS?
AYUP.
M-MY SWISS ARMY KNIFE?
SO THAT'S WHAT IT WAS! I DID WONDER.
IT DOESN'T MATTER! NONE OF IT MATTERS! I'VE BEEN TRAINED BY THE BEST! I STUDIED UNDER THE GREAT ROOK HIMSELF! I CAN TAKE YOU ALL ON... WITH MY BARE --
-- HANDS...?
PEEK-A-BOO.

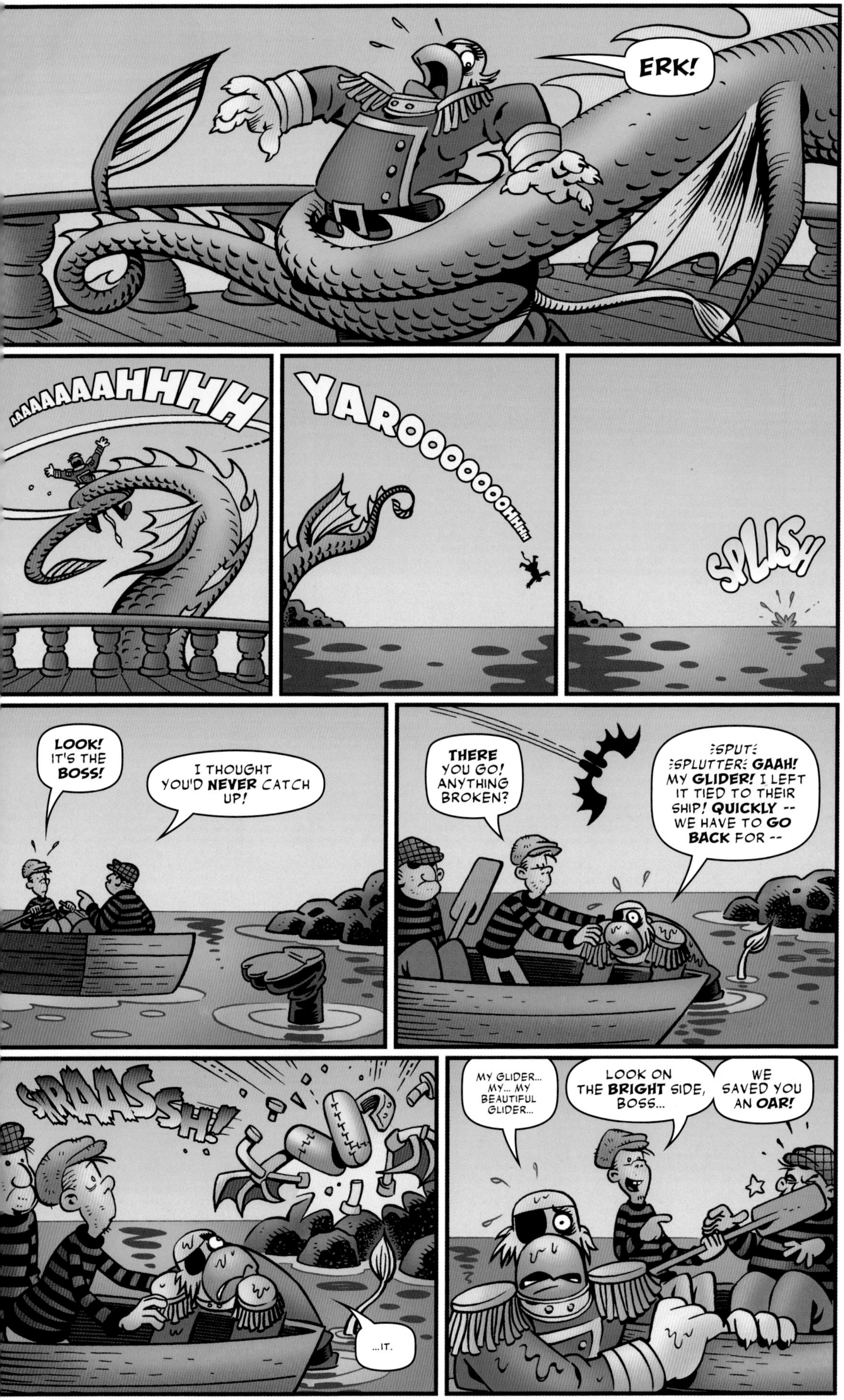
ERK!
AAAAAAAAHHHH
YAROOOOOOOOHHHH
SPLISH
LOOK! IT'S THE BOSS!
I THOUGHT YOU'D NEVER CATCH UP!
THERE YOU GO! ANYTHING BROKEN?
=SPUT= =SPLUTTER= GAAH! MY GLIDER! I LEFT IT TIED TO THEIR SHIP! QUICKLY -- WE HAVE TO GO BACK FOR --
SKRAASSH!
...IT.
MY GLIDER... MY... MY BEAUTIFUL GLIDER...
LOOK ON THE BRIGHT SIDE, BOSS...
WE SAVED YOU AN OAR!

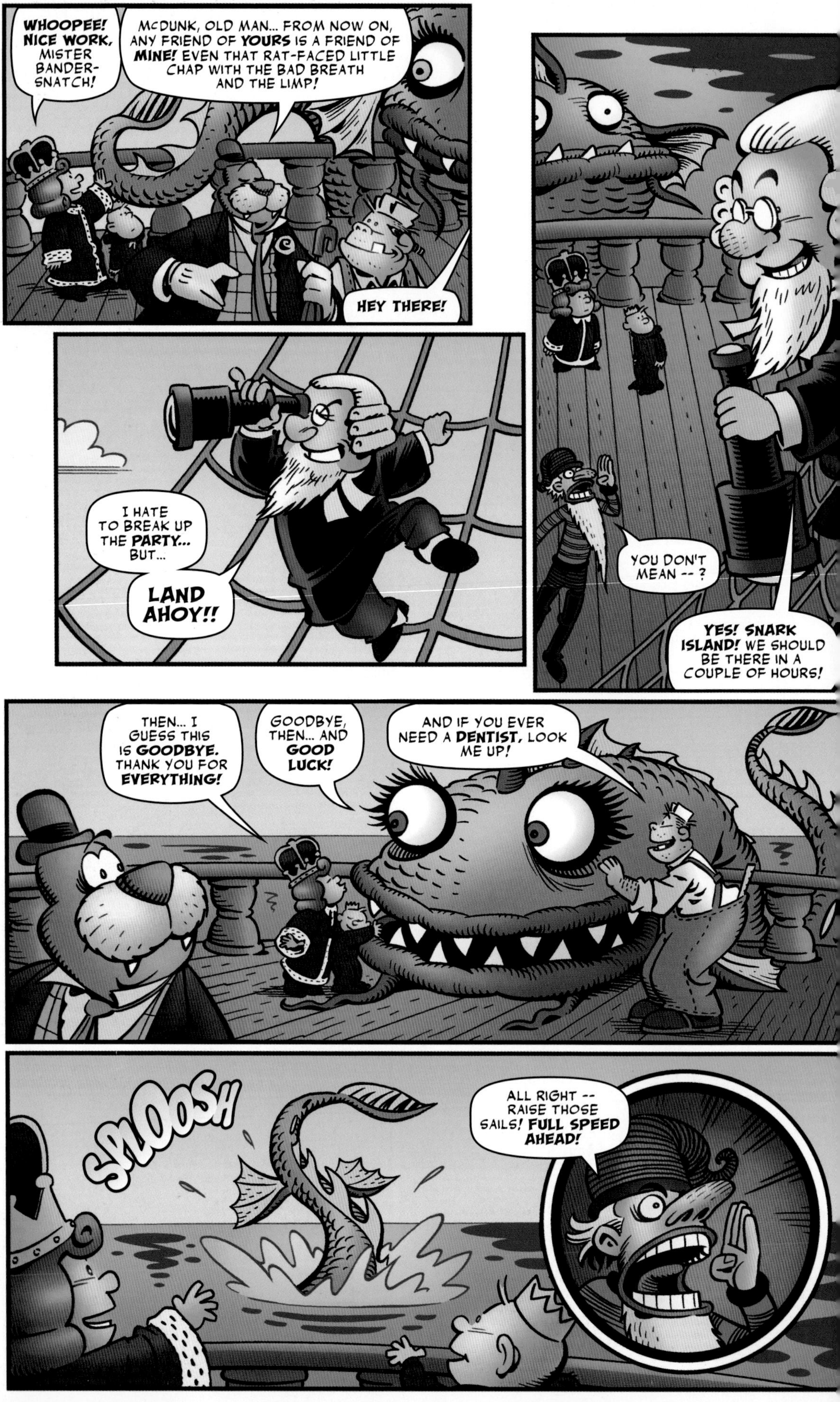
WHOOPEE! NICE WORK, MISTER BANDER-SNATCH!
McDUNK, OLD MAN... FROM NOW ON, ANY FRIEND OF YOURS IS A FRIEND OF MINE! EVEN THAT RAT-FACED LITTLE CHAP WITH THE BAD BREATH AND THE LIMP!
HEY THERE!
I HATE TO BREAK UP THE PARTY... BUT...
LAND AHOY!!
YOU DON'T MEAN -- ?
YES! SNARK ISLAND! WE SHOULD BE THERE IN A COUPLE OF HOURS!
THEN... I GUESS THIS IS GOODBYE. THANK YOU FOR EVERYTHING!
GOODBYE, THEN... AND GOOD LUCK!
AND IF YOU EVER NEED A DENTIST, LOOK ME UP!
SPLOOSH
ALL RIGHT -- RAISE THOSE SAILS! FULL SPEED AHEAD!

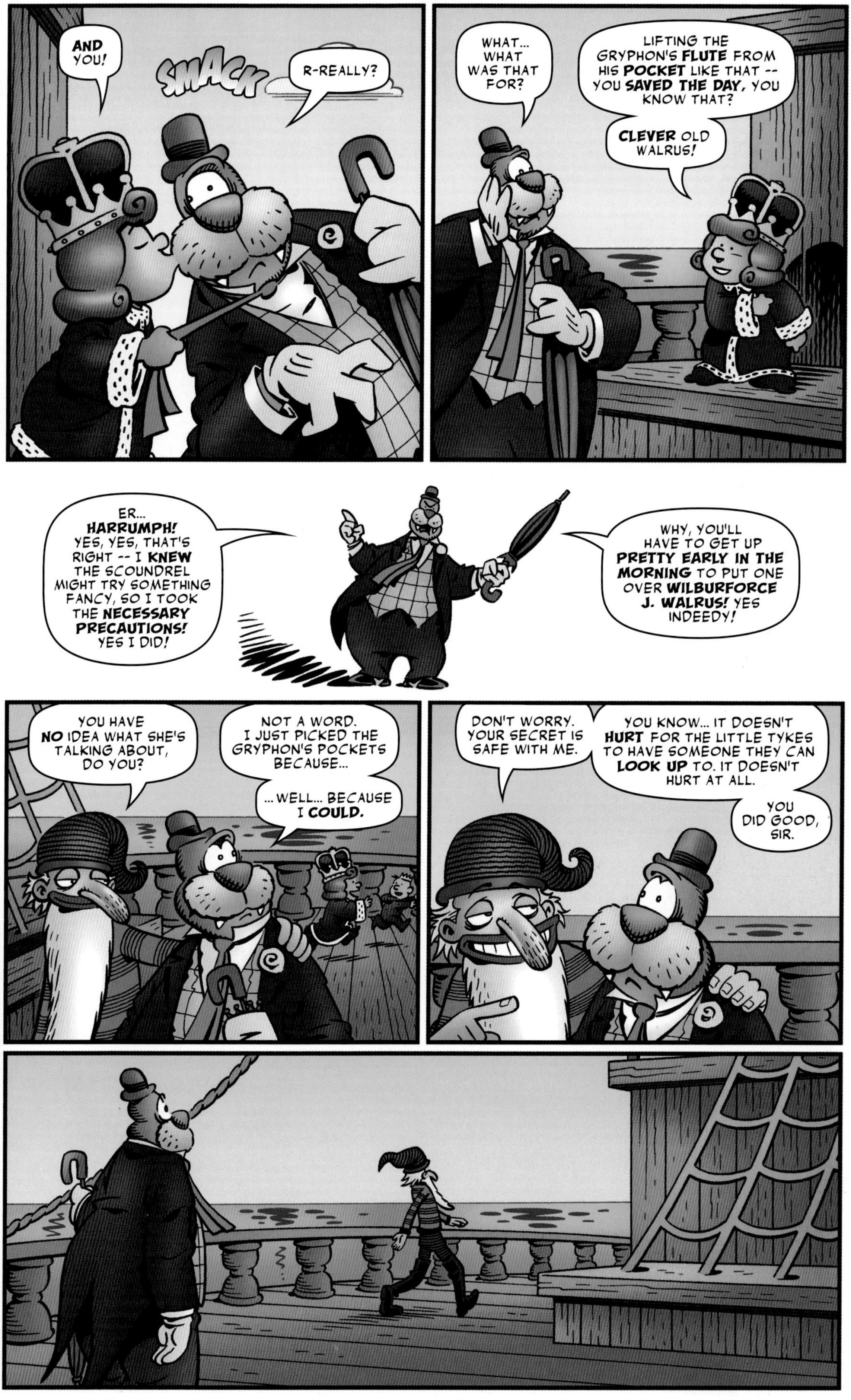
AND YOU!
SMACK
R-REALLY?
WHAT... WHAT WAS THAT FOR?
LIFTING THE GRYPHON'S FLUTE FROM HIS POCKET LIKE THAT -- YOU SAVED THE DAY, YOU KNOW THAT?
CLEVER OLD WALRUS!
ER... HARRUMPH! YES, YES, THAT'S RIGHT -- I KNEW THE SCOUNDREL MIGHT TRY SOMETHING FANCY, SO I TOOK THE NECESSARY PRECAUTIONS! YES I DID!
WHY, YOU'LL HAVE TO GET UP PRETTY EARLY IN THE MORNING TO PUT ONE OVER WILBURFORCE J. WALRUS! YES INDEEDY!
YOU HAVE NO IDEA WHAT SHE'S TALKING ABOUT, DO YOU?
NOT A WORD. I JUST PICKED THE GRYPHON'S POCKETS BECAUSE...
...WELL... BECAUSE I COULD.
DON'T WORRY. YOUR SECRET IS SAFE WITH ME.
YOU KNOW... IT DOESN'T HURT FOR THE LITTLE TYKES TO HAVE SOMEONE THEY CAN LOOK UP TO. IT DOESN'T HURT AT ALL.
YOU DID GOOD, SIR.

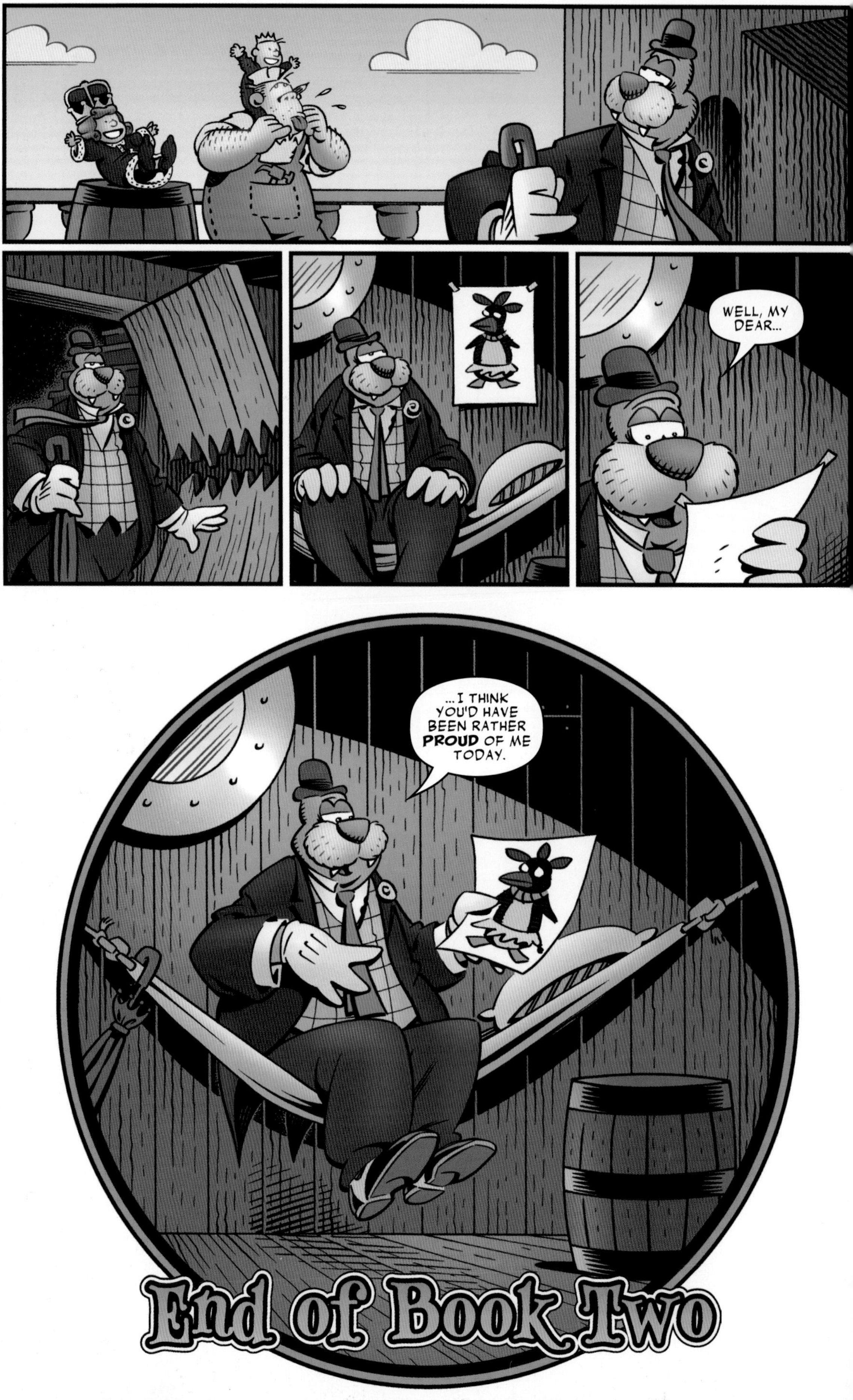

WELL, MY DEAR...
...I THINK YOU'D HAVE BEEN RATHER **PROUD** OF ME TODAY.
End of Book Two

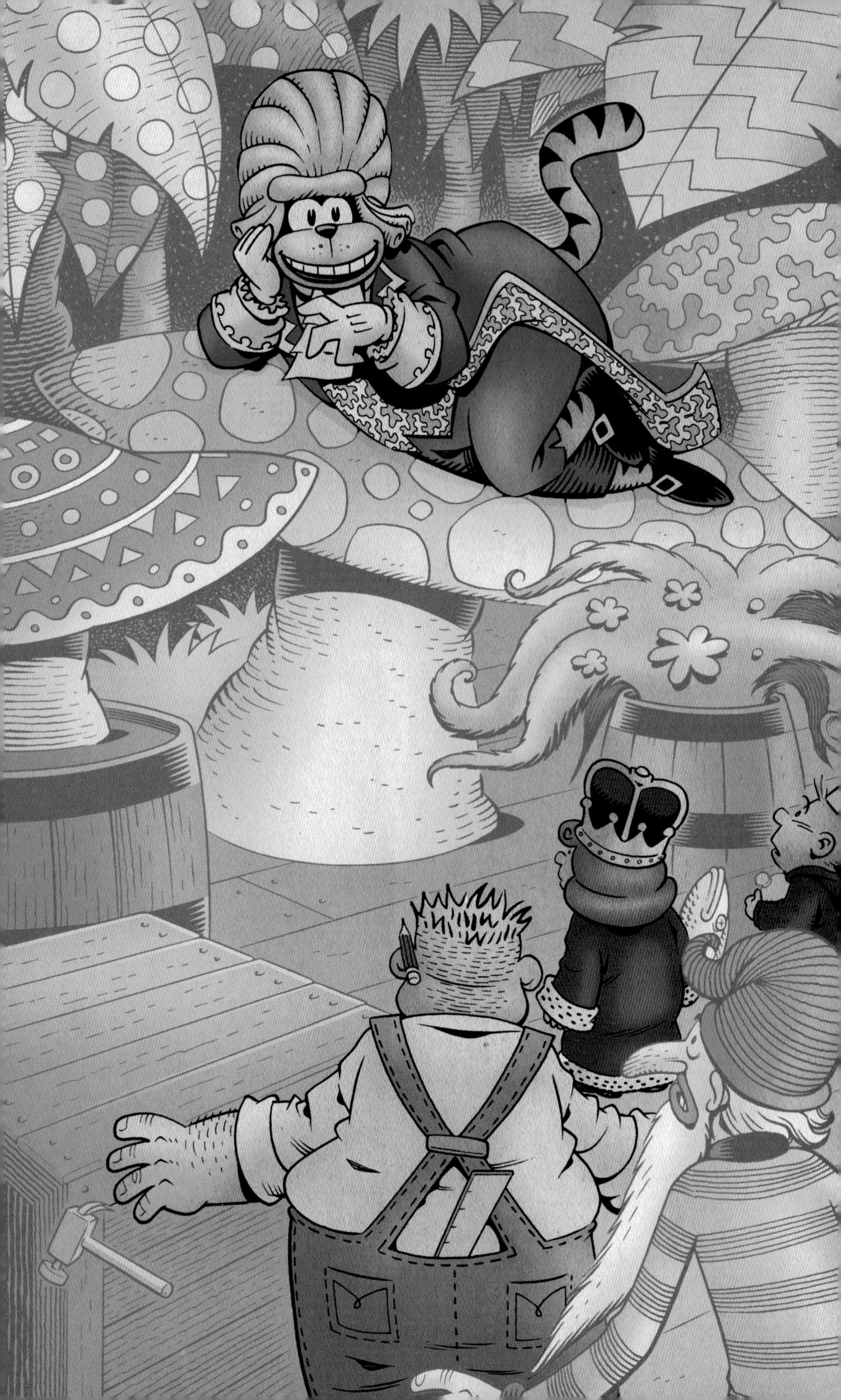

COMING SOON

ROGER LANGRIDGE'S

SNARKED!

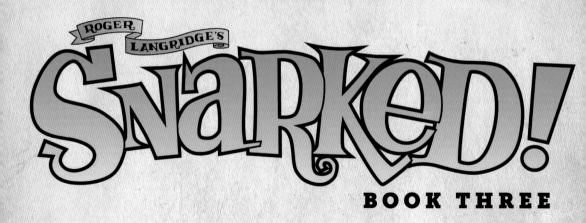

BOOK THREE

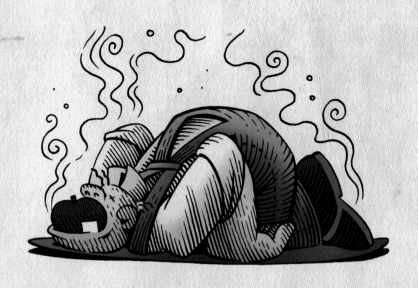

CABBAGES AND KINGS

COVER GALLERY

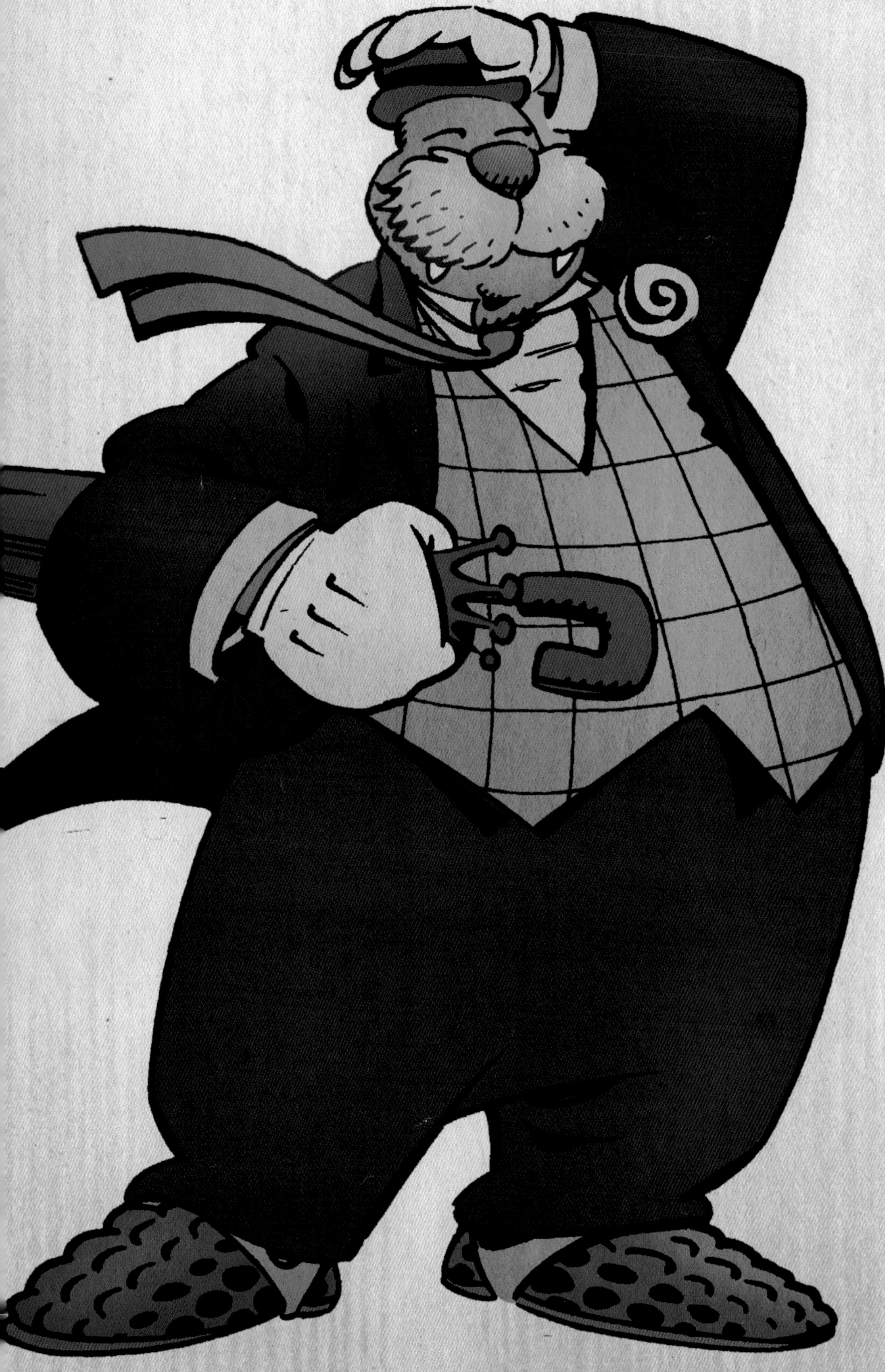

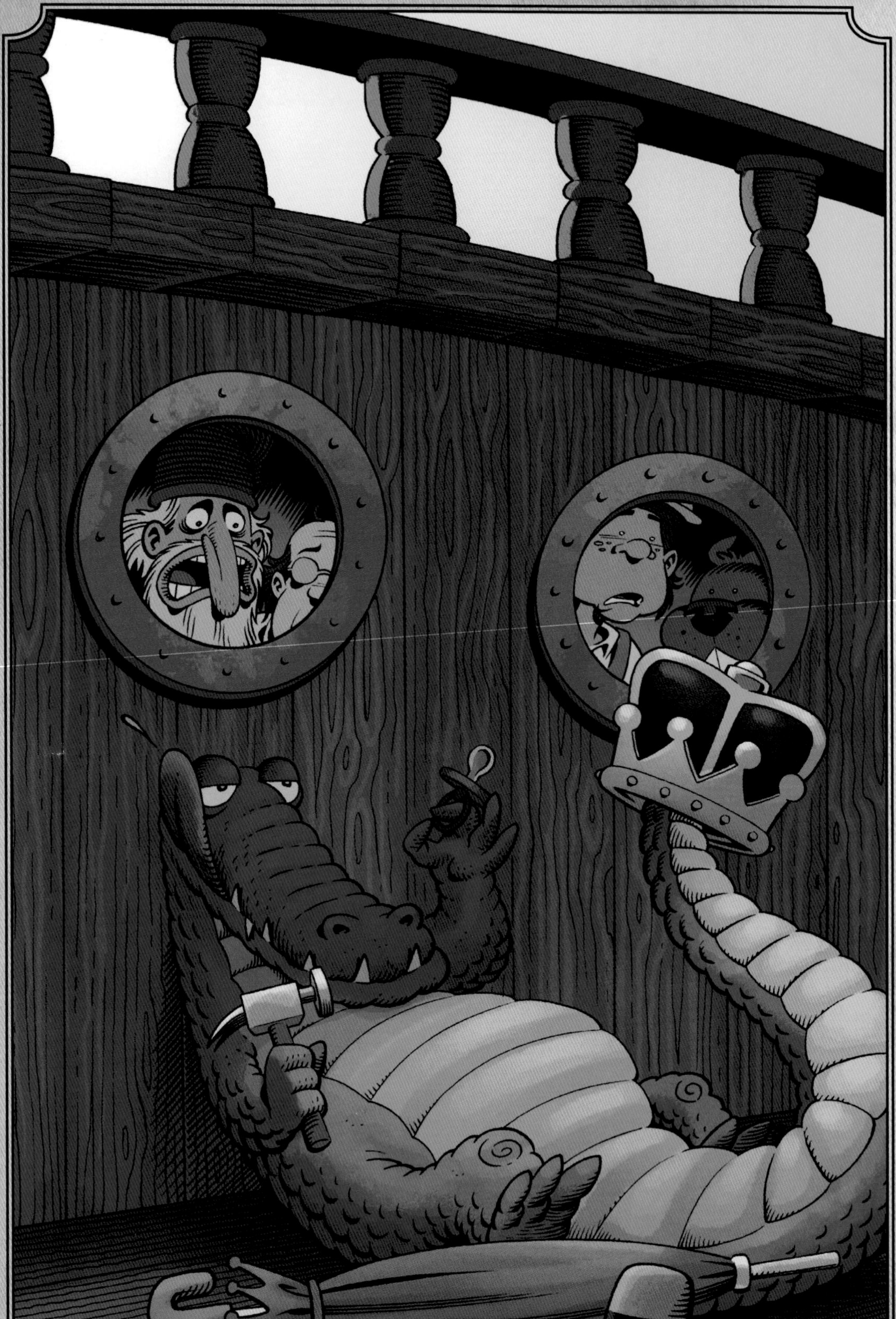

ISSUE FIVE COVER BY **ROGER LANGRIDGE**
WITH COLORS BY **MATTHEW WILSON**

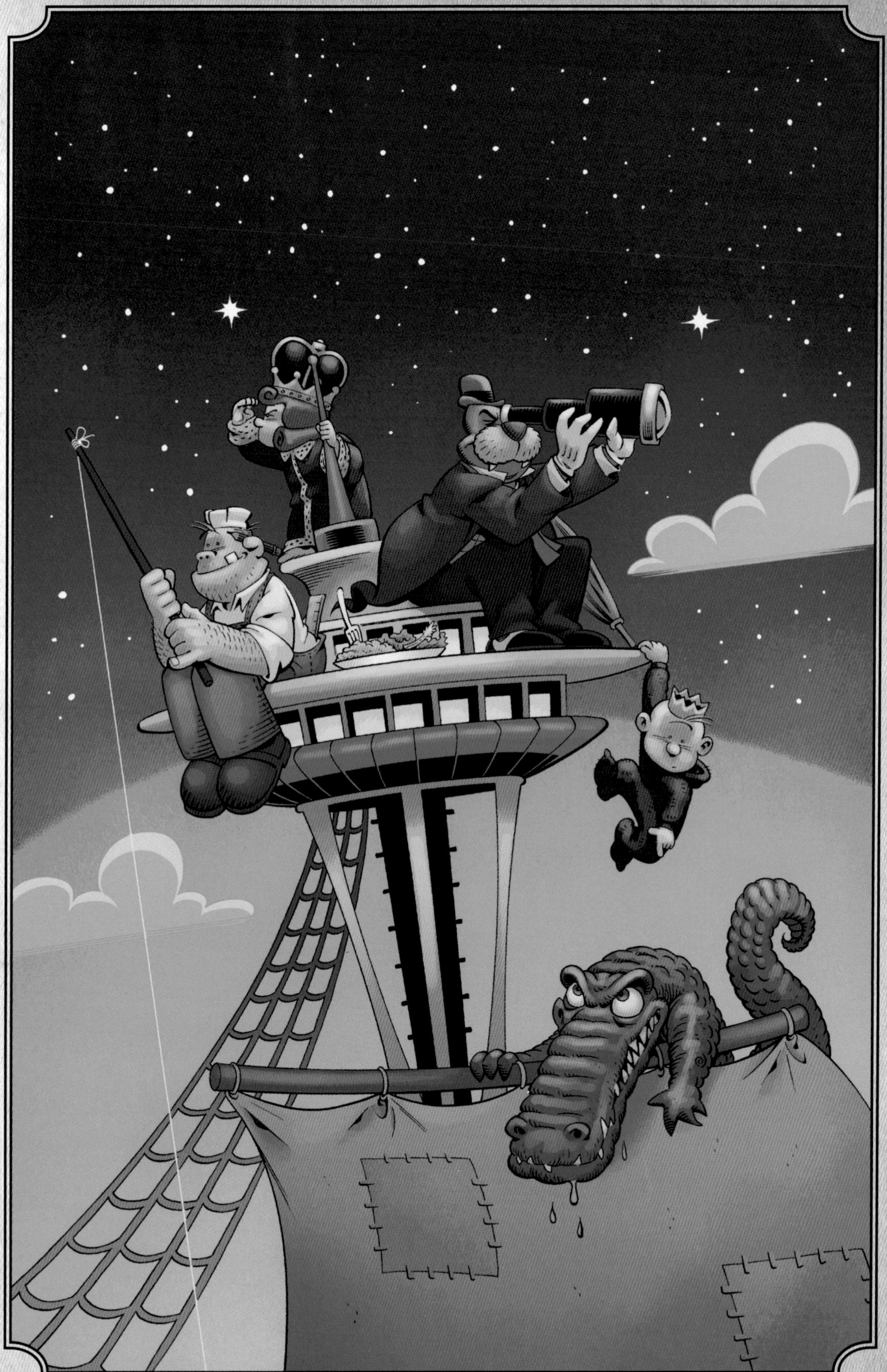

ISSUE FIVE EMERALD CITY COMICON EXCLUSIVE COVER BY **ROGER LANGRIDGE**
WITH COLORS BY **MATTHEW WILSON**

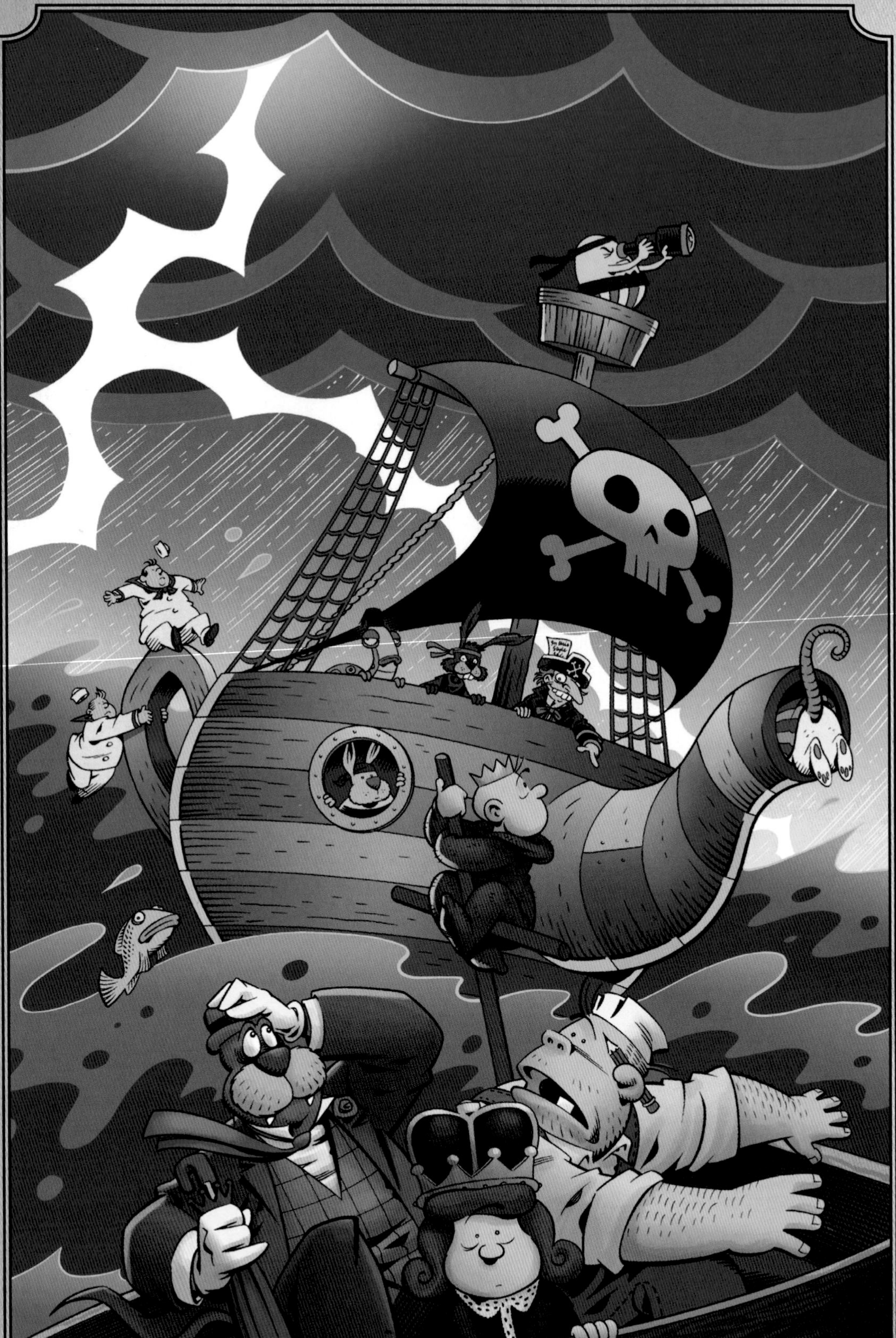

ISSUE SIX COVER BY **ROGER LANGRIDGE**
WITH COLORS BY **MATTHEW WILSON**

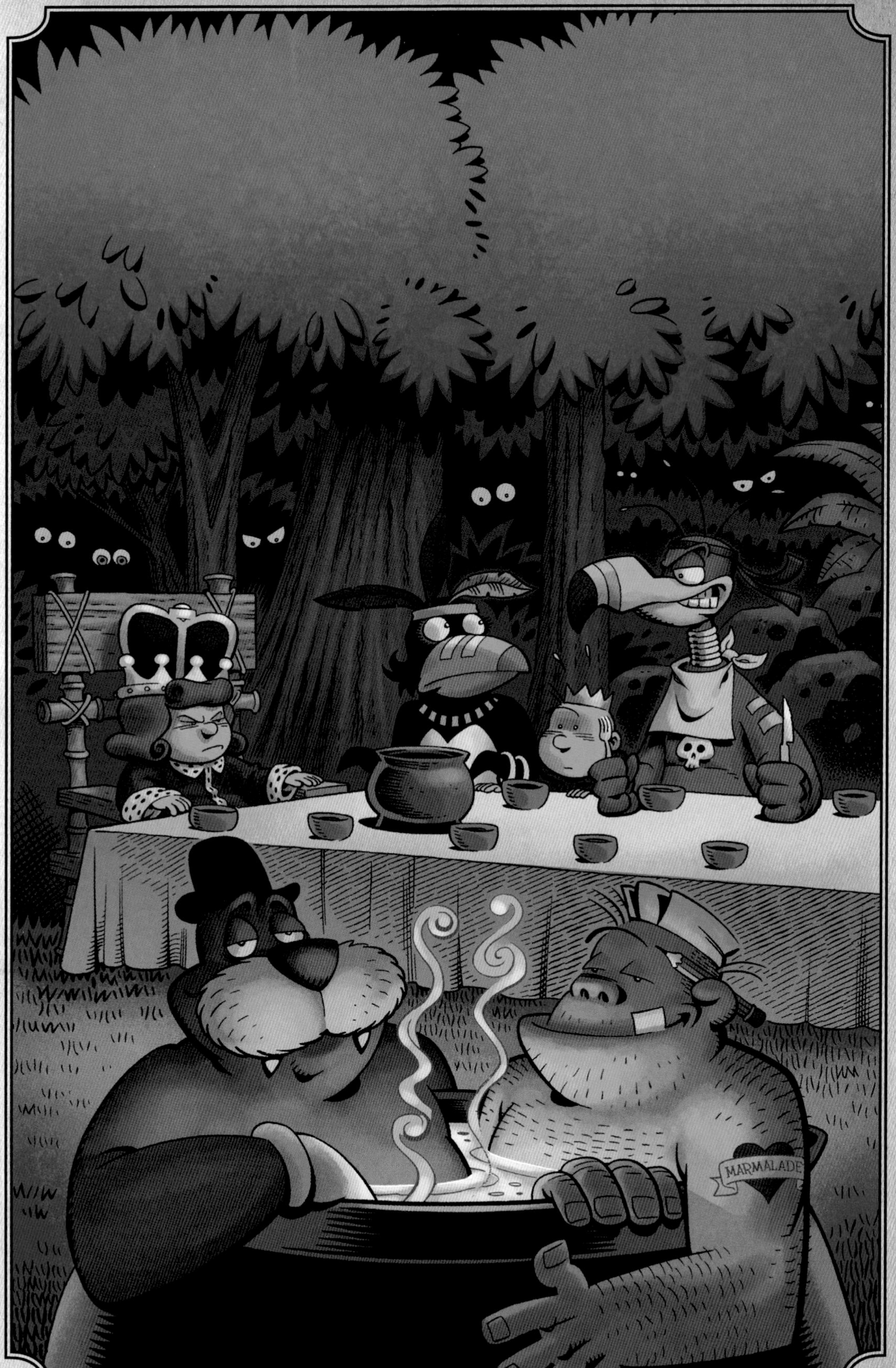
MARMALADE

ISSUE SEVEN COVER BY **ROGER LANGRIDGE**
WITH COLORS BY **MATTHEW WILSON**

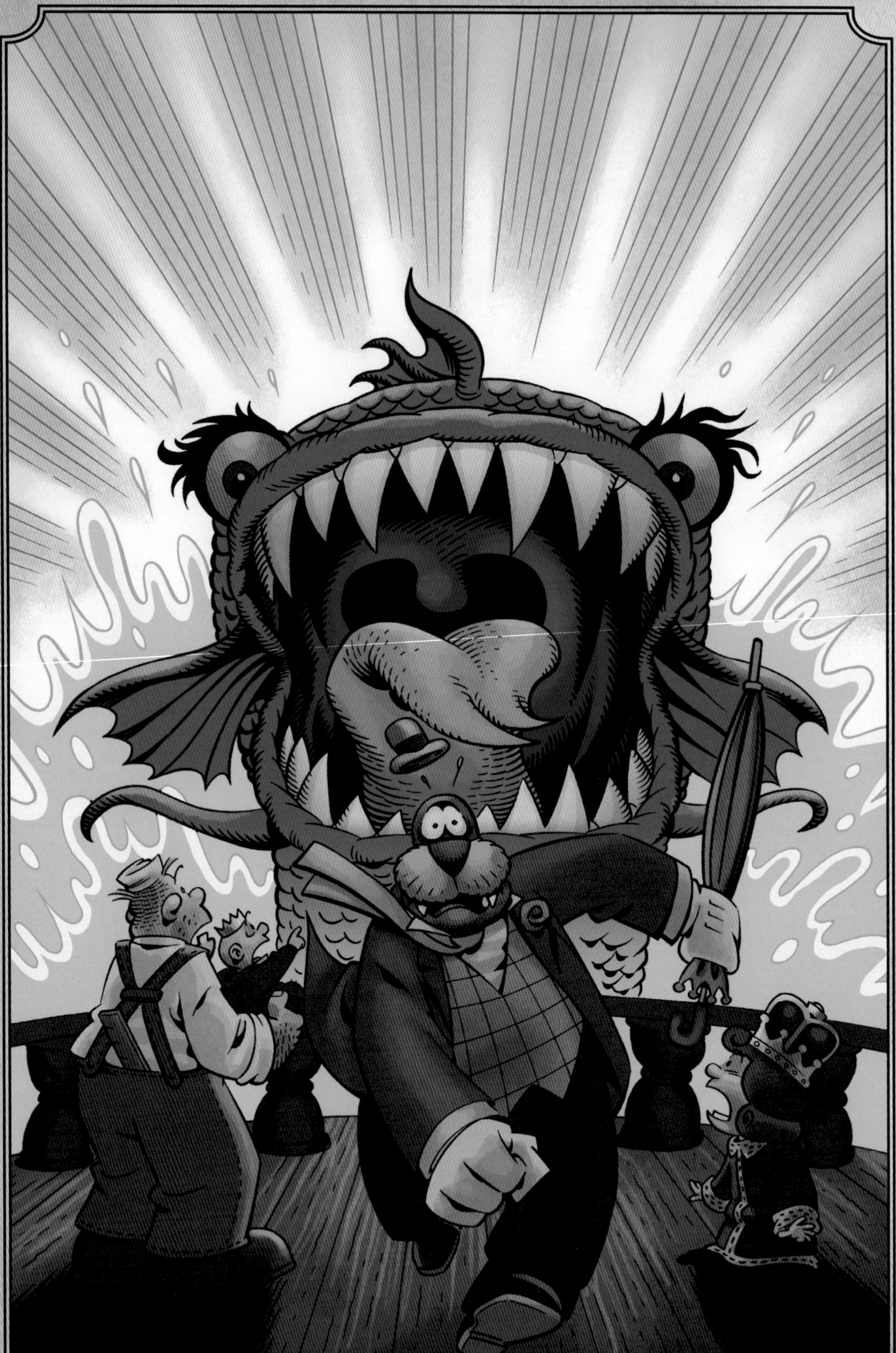

ISSUE EIGHT COVER BY **ROGER LANGRIDGE**
WITH COLORS BY **MATTHEW WILSON**

The HUNTING of the SNARK,

AN AGONY IN EIGHT FITS by Lewis Carroll
Illustrations by Henry Holiday

As Retold with Concision, Forks and Hope by Roger Langridge

Fit the First: THE LANDING

"Just the place for a Snark!" the Bellman cried
As he carefully landed his crew;
"Just the place for a Snark!
Just the place for a Snark!
What I tell you three times is true."

The crew was thus: Banker, Barrister, Butcher,
A maker of Bonnets and Hoods,
A Billiard-Marker, a Baker, a Beaver,
A Boots and a Broker of Goods.

The Butcher could only kill Beavers, he said,
As the Banker accounted his debt;
The Bellman explained, in a tremulous tone,
That the Beaver was loved as a pet.

So a dagger-proof coat
was acquired for the beast,
For whenever the Butcher walked by.
Still the Beaver kept looking the opposite way,
And appeared unaccountably shy.

Fit the Second: THE BELLMAN'S SPEECH

The Bellman had bought a large map of the sea
Without the least vestige of land:
As he stood to deliver a speech to the crew,
They had to admit he looked grand.

"We have sailed many months,
we have sailed many days,
Without the least glimpse of a Snark!
Come listen, my men, while I tell you again
Its five unmistakable marks.

"The first is the taste, which is hollow, but crisp;
The next, that it gets up too late.
The third is its slowness in getting a joke -
A pun makes the thing quite irate.

"The fourth is its fondness for bathing-machines.
Ambition, the fifth. Now I say ~
That a Snark does no harm... unless it's a Boojum."
There, the Baker just fainted away.

Fit the Third:
THE BAKER'S TALE

When the Baker sat up
and was able to speak,
His sad story he offered to tell.
"My dear uncle revealed how to capture a Snark,
The last time I bade him farewell.

"'You may seek it with thimbles -
and seek it with care;
You may hunt it with forks and hope;
You may threaten its life
with a railway-share;
You may charm it with smiles and soap.'

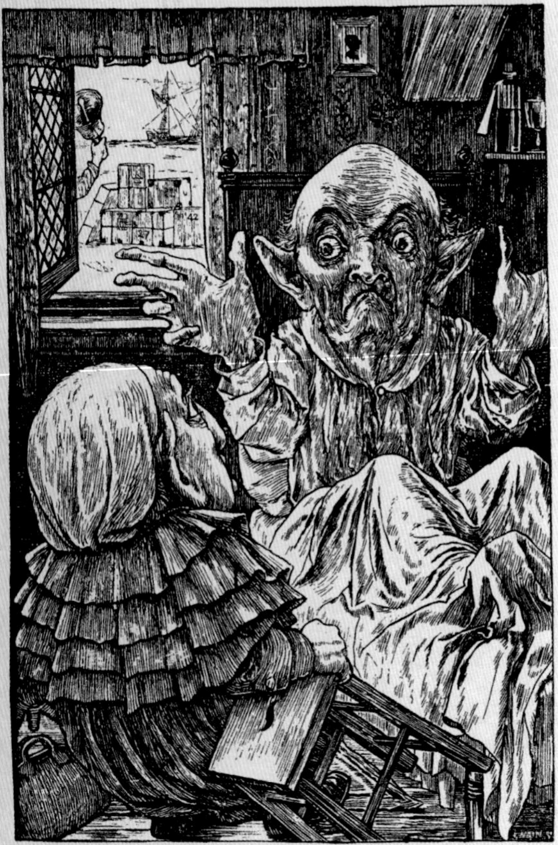

"'But oh,' said my uncle!
'Beware of the day,
If your Snark be a Boojum! For then
You will softly and suddenly vanish away,
And never be met with again!'

"It is this that I dread,"
said the Baker with fear.
"If I meet with a Boojum, I'm sure
I shall softly and suddenly vanish away -
And the notion I cannot endure!"

Fit the Fourth: THE HUNTING

The Bellman looked uffish.
"Why wait until now?
If only you'd spoken before!"
Said the Baker, "I said it in Hebrew and Greek -
Could you honestly ask me for more?"

"Lo! The Snark is at hand!" Bellman cried to the crew.
"You must all arm yourselves with great care."
So the Banker endorsed a blank check
(which he crossed),
And the Baker stood combing his hair.

The Boots and the Broker were sharpening a spade;
The Beaver sat down to make lace.
The Maker of Bonnets arranged little bows;
The Barrister cited his case.

The Billiard-Marker chalked up his nose;
The Butcher dressed sharply all round.
Of the Bellman, he asked that they be introduced
If the creature should ever be found.

Fit the Fifth: THE BEAVER'S LESSON

The Butcher suggested a desolate valley
In which to pursue their prey;
The Beaver, who'd chosen the very same spot,
Claimed he, too, was going that way.

The valley grew dark. They huddled together.
A scream, shrill and high, could be heard.
"'Tis the voice of the Jubjub!" the Bellman cried,
"That strange and desperate bird!"

"It dresses in ages ahead of the fashion;
A bribe it will always eschew.
Its flavour when cooked is exquisite indeed,
Boiled in sawdust, and salted in glue."

The Butcher wept gratefully; as to the Beaver,
These facts made it feel far more clever.
The song of the Jubjub, from that day to this,
Has cemented their friendship forever!

Fit the Sixth:
THE BARRISTER'S DREAM

They sought it with thimbles,
they sought it with care;
They pursued it with forks and hope;
They threatened its life with a railway-share;
They charmed it with smiles and soap.

But the Barrister slept. And he dreamt of a Court
Where the Snark, with a glass in its eye,
Dressed in gown, bands and wig,
was defending a pig
On the charge of deserting its sty.

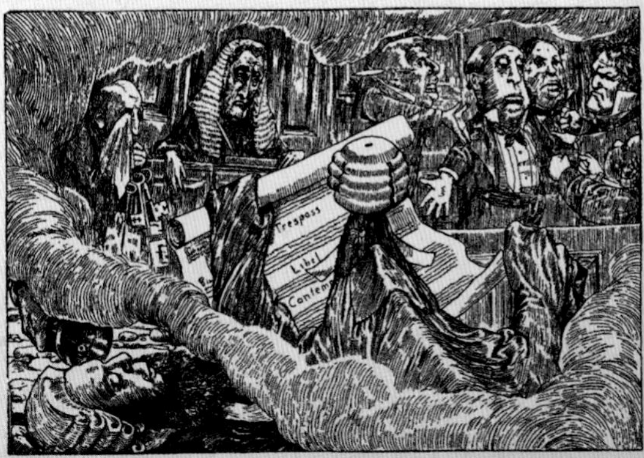
Trespass
Libel

"You must know--" said the Judge:
but the Snark exclaimed "Fudge!"
Summing up the case in its own way.
When it came to the verdict,
the Snark pronounced "GUILTY!"
And the jury all fainted away.

"Transportation for life" was the sentence it gave.
Said the jailer, "The pig's dead a year."
Then the Barrister woke to the sound of a bell
Which the Bellman rang close at his ear.

Fit the Seventh:
THE BANKER'S FATE

The Banker, with courage, rushed madly ahead
Where a Bandersnatch swifty drew nigh
And grabbed at the Banker,
who shrieked in despair,
For he knew it was useless to fly.

He offered large discounts.
He offered a check.
But the creature, at this, gave a roar.
It merely extended its Bandersnatch neck
And grabbed at the Banker once more.

Those frumious jaws went on snapping at him
Till the Banker just fainted and fell.
Then the Bandersnatch fled
as the others appeared,
Led on by that fear-stricken yell.

The Banker, alas, had been stricken quite dumb,
And his face had turned blacker than slate.
Yet so great was his fright
that his vest had turned white.
So they left the man there to his fate.

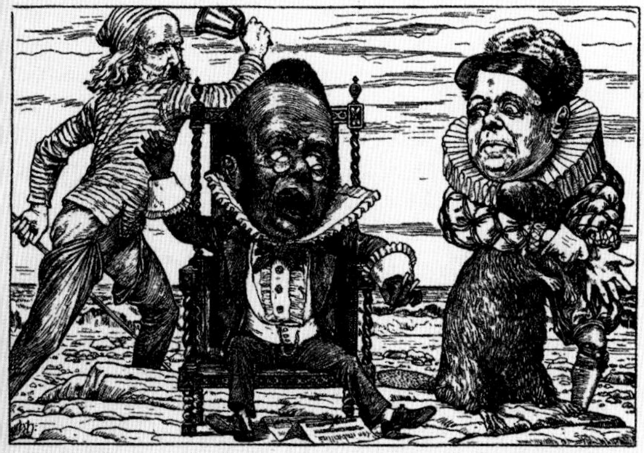

Fit the Eighth: THE VANISHING

The Baker, on top of a neighboring crag,
Waved his hands, cried and waggled his head.
"There is Thingumbob shouting!
He has found us a Snark!"
The Bellman delightedly said.

Then the Baker plunged into a chasm at once.
It seemed almost too good to be true.
"It's a Snark!" their man yelled,
as they cried tears of joy.
Then the ominous words *"It's a Boo--"*

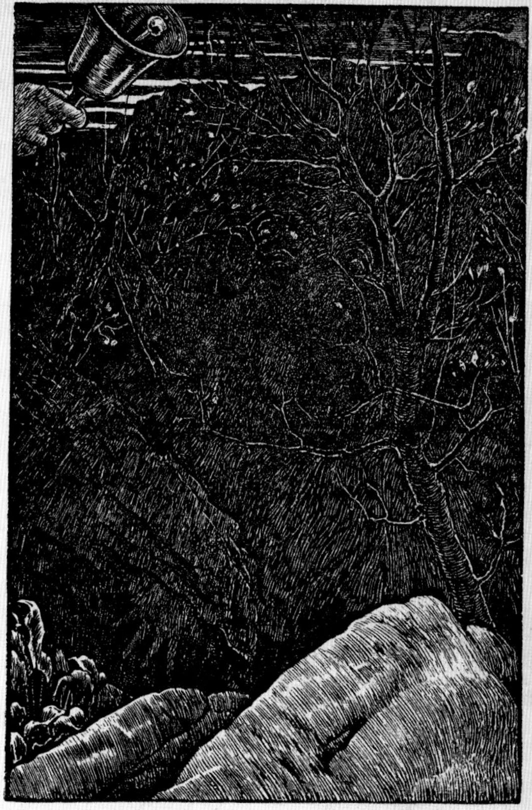

Then silence. Some fancied they heard a faint "-jum!"
But the others heard nary a sound.
After searching till dark they could find not a trace
That the Baker had once touched that ground.

In the midst of the word he was trying to say,
In the midst of his laughter and glee,
He had softly and suddenly vanished away...
For the Snark ***was*** a Boojum, you see.

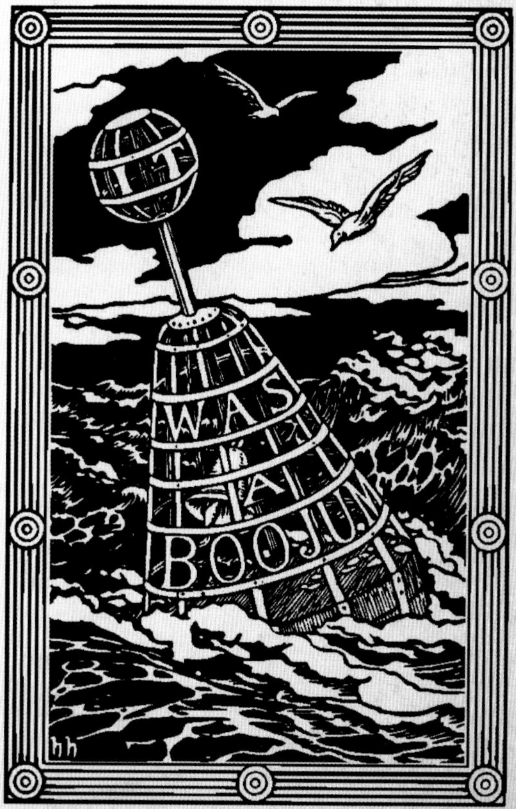
IT
WAS
A
BOOJUM

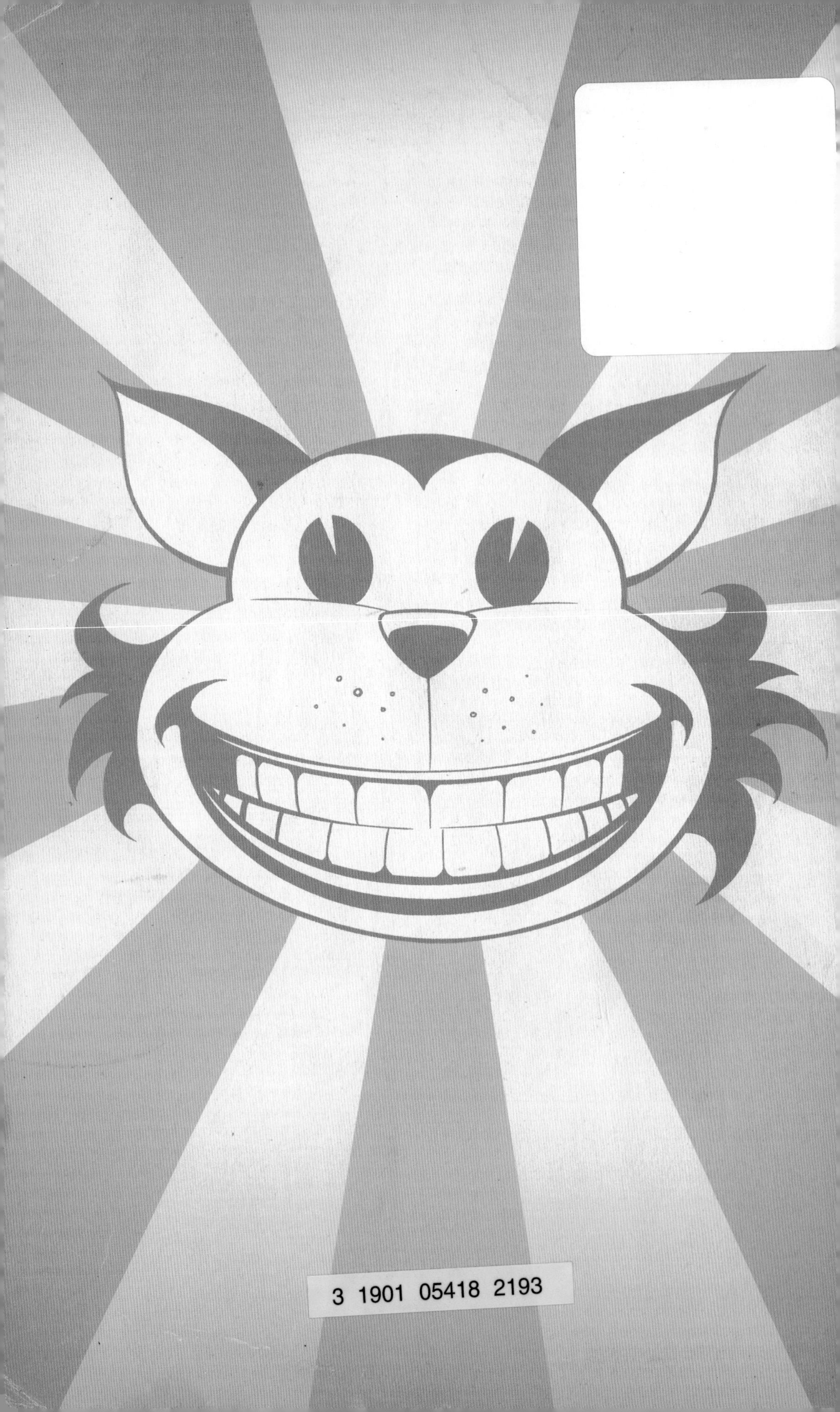